THE UNTAMED SERIES

BOOK 1

UNTAMED

PACT

S.E. JEWELL

THE FORGOTTEN LANDS

SH

AISTRIS

IVIMEA

MIDSTEAD

ARI

ARAMORA

EUGARA EXPANSE

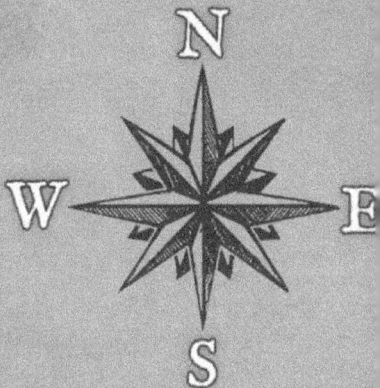

Cover Design by Amber Sanders

For the prey that
dream of predators

UNTAMED PACT

4th of Witril, 414 P.A.

The candlelight flickered across the paper before me, illuminating the words that would seal my fate. It was a piece of paper that Theo and the other generals had spent the last few years crafting to perfection to gain my entry into the royal court. The letter's many lines and fancy dialogue told the story of a wild-raised Fae with information on the growing rebellion that was willing to share it with the crown for citizenship under its rule.

I sighed as I looked over the document again, fidgeting with my hair. Considering what I was tasked to do, my nerves began to flutter about the plan.

"Are you sure you want to do this, Lo?" A low voice lined with worry caused me to turn away from the paper. Light green eyes met my own, "You know it could easily be changed to a lion Fae instead."

I shook my head with a frown in response.

"We both know that getting this kind of information from a unicorn would make them more trusting in the knowledge than from a lower Fae." This was undeniably true, as the dragons often had their heads up their asses too often to look at anyone equally *except* the coveted unicorns. "Not to mention, you're a big deal in the rebellion." I sighed and smiled confidently, betraying the nervousness that churned my stomach. "But don't worry too much, Theo. You taught me everything I know, remember?"

The worry in his eyes receded a fraction, and he gave a tight nod. "I'm not a fan of sending you straight into the dragon's den, but you are right: it is our best option. I wish I trusted someone else to take this task." He ran his hand through his blonde hair, disheveled from an evening of preparing what would come next.

Leading the Ullaven faction of the rebellion had taken its toll on Theo, but he was always confident in his ability to lead. Few saw this worried side of the great southern general, but our relationship was more than just general and soldier. I walked up to him, pulled his hands out of his hair, and leaned into his broad chest for a hug. Despite the towering form that startled at the sudden movement, he quickly wrapped his arms around me like he wasn't sure when he would get to do this again.

I was still struggling to accept that there was no way of knowing when I would next see Theo after this process began.

I took one last inhale of the lemon and rosemary scent before stepping back. Tears threatened to fall, and I knew that Theo would instantly try to get me to change my mind if I let one go, so I patted his chest several times, looking up at him with the best confidence I could muster.

"I've got this T. I have to do this—for Dad." The admission made it harder to fight the tears as Theo smiled in response, squeezing his hand on my shoulder.

"Hart would have been so proud of everything you're doing, Willow."

"Well, maybe not what's coming next." I snorted, tightening my ponytail. My brown hair glinted in the candlelight as I reached over to grab the parchment and rolled it into a scroll that wouldn't be lost as I ran to my intended destination at the border.

"Maybe he will just... look *away* when you complete this part." He smiled coyly before looking up towards the straw ceiling of the attic. "Sorry, Hart."

I couldn't help but chuckle at the idea of him apologizing to my dad, but my adoptive brother always did that when we got into any trouble. He had committed to a promise to protect me before Dad passed on, and as we grew up, we found that our lives would not be without more of that trouble after joining the rebellion.

I tucked the scroll into my satchel and watched as Theo snuffed out the candle with his fingers before leading the way down the ladder to the floor below.

Darkness enveloped the small cottage space, though the faint hint of beef stew lingered. It could be my last home-cooked meal by Amelia, who had gone to bed thinking that her adopted daughter was about to leave on a grand adventure around the Wilds—safe outside the kingdom's borders.

I hated lying to her.

The door creaked open as Theo led me outside, staring at the full moon. Stars flickered around it, and one specifically seemed to shine in our direction as I slightly nodded. My will doubled as I felt the itch of my other half spark with a familiar hint of wildness and anticipation. I glanced once more at Theo, who had a wicked grin on his face as his eyes sparkled with excitement.

"Ready to kill a prince, Willow?"

CHAPTER 1

According to Aulari law, any untamed Fae had to remain in the
form they became imprisoned in when they left the kingdom's boundaries until the region's leader cleared them to return to civilian status.
The paper that was loosely tied around my neck explained how I had de-
fected ten years ago when my mother pulled me out of the kingdom to
live among the untamed in our feral form.

So here I was, being pulled through the streets of Agraxis by guards
as if I were nothing but livestock going to market. I had to roll in some
mud outside of the city to make me look like I was a disgraced member of
Ivimea, desperate for forgiveness for my mother's actions and to be accepted back into 'civilized' society. I would say the act worked well
enough, as the guards who saw me walk up to the city gates grunted in
disgust at the smell as they approached me with swords drawn. A couple
of weeks of running through the forests to get here as soon as possible
from the Wilds without stopping to bathe had made me gag several
times, but it did the trick to get me in with no questions asked.

As I was led through the city, my attention was mainly on the looming castle ahead of me. It was outrageously tall and ornately built, with
stone gargoyles shaped in the forms of dragons roaring down in defense
of the immense fortress. Its bright stone glistened with the remaining

dew from the morning where scores of vines traveled up the structure, reaching at least halfway up the building before it webbed into sparse directions. Though the beauty of the plants and landscaping did its best to alleviate the coldness of the stone, there was still an overwhelming sense of the truth behind its grand walls.

With every step I took, I felt like death was gaining two on me.

Out of all of the leading cities of the kingdom, Agraxis was the least forgiving of the untamed. Most of whom came here seeking refuge only found themselves staring at the wall of a prison cell until they were either sent back to the Wilds or killed on the grounds of aiding the rebellion, whether confirmed or suspected. At least for me, the first sentence would not be so bad—I could return to helping Theo with his plans against the crown. The second option, however. . . I tried to force the thoughts from my mind. It would not come to that.

So long as the letter was written well enough.

As we approached the gates, I heard the squeal of a child near me, pulling me out of my quickly spiraling thoughts. My head whipped to the left, my ears perked, and I was met with a small human child who jumped up and down with their hands outstretched towards me. Her cream-colored hair was pulled into a pair of pigtails that bounced with each jump into the air, and her baby blue eyes sparkled with amazement.

"Mommy, Mommy! Look, it's a real unicorn!" She giggled, reaching out to touch my face, and I couldn't help but respond with a small nicker of an attempt at laughter. As the guards stopped to wait for the castle's gate to open, I leaned down toward the child so she could pat my nose.

Her small hands wandered over my muzzle as she excitedly squealed, rambling something about gingersnap and magic.

"Jodie, honey, please come back here—"

The mother began to walk forward, audibly and physically irritated with the small child, as her gaze wandered over the mess her daughter, Jodie, had gotten into. I could see the irritation quickly melt into fear as she realized the company surrounding me and the sound of the Palace of Ascension's gates being lowered, her eyes marking me as an enemy. I pinned my ears to my head as she stormed closer to us, lifting my head slowly out of the girl's reach in hopes for her to understand that I had no intention of harm and respected the fear-fueled anger that lined the mother's eyes.

The little girl was snatched away into her mother's arms, confusion swirling in Jodie's innocent gaze as she was pulled farther from me. As tears lined her eyes, she cried and kicked and begged to be let go, but the mother kept her tucked close into her chest as she retreated with only swift glances in my direction to make sure I wasn't following. I only bowed my head in as respectful of an apology as I could before my head and hooves were yanked back into the death march into the enemy's heart.

I could still hear the girl's cries of dismay as the gates shut behind me, and it seemed to echo my feelings as the reality of my situation sank in. I could no longer smell the pines or the smells of the natural world around me. I could only smell the damp, musty rot of stone and some cleaning compound that stung my nose with every inhale, the unnatural cold of the stone and surroundings seizing my thoughts. My breathing quickened, and my hooves stumbled over the stones, my sure footing faltering as I could no longer flee to the open expanse of freedom outside these gates.

Though I slowed to regain my footing, the guards didn't stop while I was pulled further into the stone prison called a castle. As we approached the large wooden doors ahead of us, I could only hear the clicking of my hooves and the shuffling of armor echoing off the stone walls. I could feel an overwhelming power thickening the air as we were pulled closer to the carved doors, where I could see crowns and dragons etched all along the dark surface.

It was suffocating.

Two castle guards keeping watch at the doorway gave curt nods to the ones holding me before opening the heavy doors with little more than a grunt of effort. The dark wood opened to a large room tiled with marble flooring and limestone pillars scattered evenly throughout that seemed to reach into the sky. All around the walls were windows of stained glass that were portraits of the previous monarchs of the kingdom decorated in several different abstract mosaics, all looking towards the largest window behind the thrones.

The stained-glass centerpiece was of two Fae dancing, smiling as they looked longingly into each other's eyes. Splashes of the brightest colors in glass surrounded them as if the stars themselves sparkled over the pair. Her white hair was gorgeously sculpted as it swirled around their dance along with his perfectly designed outfit, and I almost felt like I could hear their laughter if I stared at the image long enough. The warmth that filtered through the many colors of the glass seemed to brush my fur gently, bringing the slightest bit of relief in the tension that had settled in my muscles even as I turned my attention to the room's main attraction—the Roamion Royals.

The warmth of the sun shining through the windows barely beat out the temperature drop as I met King Eilbeir's gaze, and I was halted in front of the row of thrones before me. His blue gaze held mine with more intrigue than upset, but the Queen's icy gaze froze me to my very depths. I did not, or could not, bring myself to meet her piercing stare as I bowed my head and leaned down on my front legs before leveling myself once more.

The King and Queen were wearing clothes fitting their titles. The King was dressed in a finely tailored blue suit adorned with many pins and medals to showcase his prowess in the forces, while his fingers were bejeweled with ever more golden trinkets, far beyond what I could ever imagine owning in one lifetime. His crown was a simple ringlet that sat atop his head comfortably, with sapphires and diamonds sprinkled throughout the gold. The Queen's outfit matched her husband's in a light sea green gown that flowed past her feet as if tailored after cascading ocean waves. Even more stunning were the thousands of diamonds embellished in the fabric to mimic sunlight over the waves throughout the Queen's outfit. Her crown followed the same patterns as if to embody golden waves crashing against the beach at a perfect point with a dazzling sapphire.

"An untamed unicorn, hmm?" The Queen hummed from her throne, looking down at me from her seat on high. It took every ounce of willpower not to squirm under the electric purple gaze that seared over every inch of my body. She stared me down a moment longer before her attention settled on my chest, where the scroll hung loosely from a small line of twine. "Princess Sellias, please examine the parchment."

A younger woman's voice rang out, "Yes, mother."

I looked away from the King and Queen to examine the source of the petite voice. The softer tone of the Queen's electric purple eyes was the first aspect I took in, followed by the long black hair flowing around the young woman's shoulders. She wore a shorter teal dress that flowed easily around her slim body, and hands wrapped in long dark blue gloves reached towards my neck. I stiffened as she reached the ring of twine, and for a moment, I could see the slightest flash of pity in her gaze before she began to untie the knot of twine that kept the scroll in its place. Her pretty little silver tiara was right under my nose as she fiddled with the thin rope, and the intrusive thought of grabbing it and tossing it to the floor played out in the safety of my mind.

Even as my imagination toyed with the idea in a thousand different ways, not even one played out in my favor.

She gently removed the twine and parchment and stepped away, turning her attention back to her mother as she began to roll out the paper to read it. Princess Sellias scanned over the contents silently; her eyebrows knit together as she tried to piece together the story before reaching the end and reading it over again. Her violet eyes glanced over her shoulder to me again, scanning over me in a similar unraveling way that her mother had used on me mere minutes before. Though her analyzing gaze made me feel more embarrassed than terrified, my nerves shot through the ceiling of this lavish throne room when her attention returned to Queen Ezyla on her throne.

"This letter states that this is Willow Saugrave, a twenty-six-year-old unicorn Fae who had been forcibly taken outside the kingdom's borders to Ullaven by her mother when she was barely thirteen. She has been living with a small herd of other unicorns in the fields of the Untamed Wilds, and they were deeply involved in the forces and ranks of the Southern Rebellion." The Queen's attention turned to me while Sellias spoke, but this time, I mustered up the confidence to meet her scrutinizing gaze. I poured my feelings of tiredness, wariness, and fear into my stance, hoping she failed to uncover the lie beneath. Her eyes narrowed in either distaste or distrust at the return of her glare, but she continued to listen to her daughter as she finished relaying the scroll contents.

"When she learned the true nature of the herd and the impact of what they were doing to innocents of Aulari and its surrounding provinces, she decided to flee." The Princess glanced up from the paper to meet her mother's steadfast watch. "In return for information on the rebellion's movements and plans, she wishes to become a full citizen of Aulari and return to the kingdom in good standing."

There was silence in the room before my ears swiveled toward the sound of some court members whispering among themselves to my left, but my eyes stayed trained on the royals in front of me. The Queen mulled over her daughter's words for a moment longer before focusing on her husband. He seemed deep in thought as he stared at the space before my hooves, but another voice broke his concentration as it chimed into the conversation from the Queen's side.

"I believe we should give her a chance—with stipulations, of course." The voice belonged to Princess Dityss Roamion, the identical twin sister to Princess Sellias. I only knew her name and her relation to her sister from the small amount of time I had to study the royals before I left Ullaven, but the similarities between the two women were unmistakable. She wore a simple shirt and pants with her black hair tied into a messy bun and crowned with a pair of well-loved reading glasses instead of a tiara. Her impatient yet vibrant lilac gaze was directed at the letter in her sister's hands as if itching to look over the parchment herself.

I likely would have gotten along well with her if we were two people in a different world.

The Queen opened her mouth to answer but was cut off by a deep masculine voice that echoed across the throne room with unwavering confidence. "I believe it best to have her thrown into a prison cell to rot. Being so near the Southern Rebellion's plot for over ten years, and from such a young age, makes me question why she would suddenly wish to return to a 'home' she scarcely can remember."

My head snapped in panic toward the source of the suggestion. I was expecting to meet the king's cold gaze, but I was instead greeted by the brightest hazel eyes ringed by a vibrant blue that swirled with distrust. My full attention turned toward him as one of my ears flicked in surprise, and it took a moment for me to observe the man now standing beside the king.

He stood a couple of inches taller than Theo, but the presence he commanded in a room was far more than what my adoptive brother could muster. His dark brown hair was kept short and clean, presumably to keep it out of his way when he stared down his opponents both in court and on the battlefield. The anger in his eyes darkened his gaze as he met mine, and I could feel that anger as if it were a physical wave as we held our quiet staring contest.

I swore I heard thunder in the distance when his face contorted into a scowl. I realized that the sound wasn't a play of my imagination when I heard the shuffling of fabric and feet of the court around the room.

My rational thoughts screamed at me to turn and run as fast as I could back to Ullaven.

The King seemed to lean more toward the man's suggestion than Princess Dityss's, but Princess Sellias's soft voice filled the deafening silence of the throne room. "Prince Rendros, while I respect your opinion as not only my brother and the general of our forces, I believe such a harsh punishment is unethical in its premise. She was forced into the life without much choice, and it may not have been until recently that she realized the reality of this war." Her voice was clear, but it still had the softest shake underneath the implied strength of her position. "I believe we should attempt Princess Dityss's option first, though the decision is ultimately up to you, King Eilbeir."

All three siblings turned to the king, who seemed to be listening closely to something the queen was whispering to him.

His icy blue gaze turned to me once more as the queen pulled away, a gleam of realization sparking his gaze as he rose from the throne. The court surrounding the room bowed as he began to step down from the dais, his attention focused on looking over me as he approached.

Despite being at least half a foot taller than him as my mare, I felt like I was merely a filly waiting for her father's punishment, and a swift flick of my tail betrayed my rising anxieties.

"Prince Rendros, come here." King Eilbeir commanded, catching the slightest flicker of surprise settle on the prince's handsome features before he came down from the dais to stand at the king's side.

"Yes, Father?"

The king looked over his son for half a moment before turning to me again, "I have listened to my family's opinions, and from your letter, I cannot say I am not intrigued by your situation and the offer you propose." Age had ripened his voice to a deep concentration of authority that I barely kept myself from flinching, "So, with restrictions, I will be allowing your citizenship, as my daughter Princess Dityss suggested."

I could almost fall to my knees right there had King Eilbeir not continued.

"In exchange for the information and your citizenship, you will take a pact with Prince Rendros, in which you will agree to serve alongside him and protect him with your own life. Should you fail these tasks and death claims him, you will die alongside him."

CHAPTER 2

My heart stopped. It must have.

Theo and I had not even considered this being a decision that could have been made – to hold the prince's life in the hands of a commoner? Let alone an *untamed* one?

Prince Rendros stared in shock at his father, seeming to share my thoughts. He opened his mouth to argue, but King Eilbeir held his hand. The anger pointed at me when the prince stared at me earlier, but it only deepened as he looked at his father. I could feel thunder rumble through the castle as his eyes narrowed.

"You will not argue, Rendros. You were the one who suggested that someone so versed in the rebellion shouldn't be allowed free, so the knowledge she may have stored away for us is invaluable if it holds true."

"I can get that information from her in a prison cell." He growled at his father as I felt the fur spike along my spine. "She would break in hours under the right circumstances, and then she could rot down there while we took care of the threats she revealed."

"Yes, perhaps this is true." The king drawled, causing my fear to shift into an auditory response of a nervous snort. The prince angrily snapped his attention towards me, but the king looked disinterested. "Though, I must agree with your sisters and mother as well. She was taken into that life as a child; how could she have decided on anything but the path she was given? If she wishes to rejoin society, she must prove herself."

I could see the flicker of irritation cross his eyes as he turned back to his father, his jaw ticking with a promise to add another complaint to his list, but King Eilbeir once again silenced him with the wave of a hand. "That is my decision. It is final."

The hall shook from a nearby burst of thunder from the storm, but the prince did not argue further.

"Now, Miss Willow," The king reached over to press his palm against my chin, my nostrils flaring with fear and panic at the touch. I could feel a trickle of icy power skitter down my spine like small strikes of lightning searching for some invisible lock beneath my skin.

He was using his magic to try and remove the spell of exile that kept all untamed trapped in their chosen form in which they entered the wilds.

Several more flares of ice-cold magic burst across my spine before his eyes opened with a bright flash of magic that seemed to cascade across the hall of royals and their council. His blue eyes refocused as his gaze moved to mine, "Return to your Fae form, Willow Saugrave."

I did not move as I let my magic wash over my body like a warm blanket that comforted me in familiarity, its warm embrace bringing me back to my familiar Fae form in a flash of silver. My enhanced senses that had become a comfort in the dragon's den dimmed with the transformation, as well as the height that gave me a bit more confidence standing before the tall men who commanded the fates of the continent.

The king and the prince stood over me by a few inches, their eyes examining every inch of this form like I was a sculpture that required studying. I met each of their gazes with as much courage as I could muster in the face of the most powerful beings on the continent, but Prince Rendros held my attention.

As a mare, I was not taken aback by his sheer stature and power that radiated off him. As a Fae, I was astounded by the strength of the male before me. His perfectly form-fitted suit left very little to the imagination regarding his physique, with some sections of stitching seemingly ready to burst at the slightest flex of the muscle beneath. His posture commanded dominance as he stood over me, his hazel eyes lined with blue, seemingly lost in some mixture of thought as he met my stare. We stayed in this staring contest for a few seconds longer before he finally tore his attention away, and I brought mine to meet King Eilbeir's impatient gaze.

He was the older version of his son: a large beard covered his face, though his body was not as defined or toned. Centuries of age suited him well despite the fact, however, as the peppered grey that scattered across his hair was enough to make most women swoon.

It was evident that Prince Rendros received most of his phenotypes from his father, as I could see very little of his mother in his appearance.

I cleared my throat again, feigning that I had not spoken in years. "I appreciate the opportunity, your Highness." I tried to put as much gravel in my voice as possible, though it did not take much. Not speaking for three weeks while running around as a mare helped me pull this part off much easier than expected. "If that is required for me to become a citizen, I will do my best to serve Prince Rendros and honor this pact you graciously offer me."

Out of the corner of my eye, I saw a reaction shoot across the prince's face, but it was gone before I could decipher it.

"Perfect. Then your hand, please." King Eilbeir reached for my hand, which I reluctantly allowed. This was not how the plan was supposed to go, but I was in the same position as the prince—in no place to argue with the king.

His hands were cold with malice as he gripped my hand and leered at me, a dark promise swirling in his eyes. His voice was as sharp as ice as he leaned over to whisper in my ear.

"Place one hand on my son, cause one cut, cause him any suffering...and you will be killed whether he breathes or not." I stood completely still as he pulled away. I could not move my lips or form words to respond, but I could nod slightly in understanding. His hands seemed to warm against my own, seemingly showing his contentment with my assumed answer.

"Prince Rendros." He reached out his other hand to his son, and though he seemed as appalled as I was, he followed his father's command. Once he had both of our hands, he placed the prince's hand on top of mine. It was warmer than the King's, which startled me a bit as I stared at the large hand covering my relatively tiny one. It was such a simple and familiar movement, but something about the sheer difference of our hands had me enthralled.

My gaze unintentionally moved from our hands to the side of Prince Rendros' face, where the rest of the room melted away. Though anger washed off him in waves, it did not damper how attractive he was, even as a muscle in his jaw worked as he stared at his father. The rage-filled aura may have even made him more appealing in the moment. Something about his face and the mixed emotions kept my attention there until he met my prolonged, irritated stare. I blinked a few times, flustered, before quickly snapping my gaze back to King Eilbeir when he spoke.

"As the King of Agraxis and all of Aistris, I call upon the blood of my ancestors to enact a pact between Prince Rendros Eilbeir Roamion and Willow Saugrave." My blood seemed to rise in answer, and I felt goosebumps rise across my arm to the hand below Prince Rendros's. It was as if my very life force was responding to his command, my blood a mere string that he could pluck to his whim with his words. "This pact is being enacted to ensure Prince Rendros's safety and allow Willow to earn her citizenship as one of the tamed. If Prince Rendros is harmed, the pact will be severed, and the unicorn's life shall be forfeit."

A searing pain started on my back, and my hand tensed reflexively. It was as if someone was placing an iron brand heated with the fires of the hells against my bare skin, though I knew no one was behind me. I did my best not to show the pain as I clenched my teeth together and shut my eyes, but I could feel the beginnings of tears well in my eyes as the pain intensified towards the center of my spine. My mare bucked in panic as the invisible brand seemed to sear even into the deepest wells of my core.

I may not have been trapped in a physical prison cell, but there was no longer such a thing as running free.

"If the information provided is true and Willow continues to serve faithfully alongside the prince and the kingdom, then she will eventually be granted true citizenship among our people. I will remove the pact under the gaze of our ancestors, and she will be restored as one of the tamed."

Prince Rendros did not even seem to flinch but just watched his father with a fury I did *not* want to be on the receiving end of. I did not get to glimpse the king's emotions before the pain threatened to buckle my legs and bring me to the ground. The iron sear of the brand mixed with ancient magic that tightened around my lungs and heart as if a thousand sharpened knives were prepared to pierce the vital flesh. Somewhere in the distance, I could hear the king continue speaking, but the pain drowned out whatever the words were.

A few more minutes passed as the overwhelming pain began to ebb, but a dull version of the pain along my spine remained.

The prince quickly pulled his hand away after I assumed his father had finished whatever was left of the hellish speech, but I was slower to remove my hand. I forced my eyes to open to look over the flesh beneath my wrist, expecting to see something that presented a sign of the pact. There was no mark left from the painful ceremony, but I could still feel the weight of the prince's hand on mine.

Thunder rolling outside with a flash of lightning was the only thing that brought my attention back to the voices around me.

"Miss Willow, you will be staying in Prince Rendros' wing of the castle. There are plenty of extra rooms to stay in, so you will not be far from the prince should something occur within our walls." His voice sounded calmer now, as if satisfied I had been magically tied to something I could never get out of. He turned back to the thrones and held his arm out for Queen Ezyla to join him, to which she elegantly floated across the marble to answer his silent summons. Only then was I reminded that we were not alone in the hall full of spectators, and I watched as she approached. She seemed almost joyous at my predicament, but the lightning in her eyes struck me down to the core; she would not welcome me as she walked out.

Princess Sellias and Princess Dityss followed their parents' departure in perfect rhythm with one another. Soon after, the rest of the royal council followed suit until it was just the prince in the room...and me.

He did not say a word as he turned to walk out of the room, stomping away with the thunder echoing his footsteps. I remained still, not immediately following behind him. When he reached the large doorways of the hall, he turned to me with anger illuminating the blue in his eyes as he met my gaze.

"You will follow me and then leave me alone until I call you. Do you understand?"

I dipped my head in understanding, though I let my eyes counter his with what little defiance I could muster through the pain that still hummed in my back. While I was still in shock at the turn of events sealing my fate, I refused to be led around like a prize mare, and I tried to convey that through my narrowed gaze as best as I could as I followed behind him. His eyes only glazed over me briefly before he snorted and walked ahead again.

Though I expected to go up the ornate stairs leading to the higher reaches of the castle, we stayed on the same floor as the throne room. It took about ten minutes to reach the doors to his wing, marked by a placard on the side of the door that read *Crown Prince Rendros Roamion's Wing*. The idea of having an entire wing of a castle was almost impossible to comprehend, and my brain only spun further when he threw open the doors.

They opened into an entry room the size of Amelia's house in Ullaven, with clothing strewn about and a small kitchen on the left. In the middle of the room was an oversized couch that seemed to be able to seat at least twenty people, and a pool table was nestled into the space on the right side of it. I had to blink to remind myself where I was—this was more like something I had seen in a wild bachelor's house in Ullaven.

Dark hardwood floors stretched across the entire space, only closed in by polished stones that created panel-like stripes along the wall. All sorts of paintings lined the spaces in the walls, most depicting various intricately realistic landscapes.

"Who is *that*?"

The voice broke me from my stunned trance as I reached for the sword usually kept on my side in defensive surprise. However, the weapon was buried just outside of the city gates, and the movement served as a dangerous reminder that I was defenseless.

Three men were settled around a taller table at the corner of the room, each of their piercing gazes sizing me up and down.

More predators.

"This is nobody." Prince Rendros growled in response, stalking past them into a connected hallway that led deeper into the chamber. I followed him with a few steps in his direction before I turned my attention to the three men again. One was a golden blonde with bright green eyes, who seemed most interested in what the prince had dragged in. Another had light brown hair, honey eyes that sparkled with amusement, and a crooked smile, more interested in the prince's response than me. The last was likely the most interesting, with short black hair fashioned similarly to the prince and black eyes sparkling with silver dots. His expression was twisted slightly into concern; his eyes focused on Prince Rendros.

I stopped in the entryway to the hall, giving a small wave and a smile.

"This is Willow Saugrave. It is lovely to meet you." My voice had recovered nearly entirely from the scratchy version that plagued me in the throne room, and the one sentence gave me the confidence I had lost since first entering the palace's stone walls.

The black-haired man seemed most surprised by my sudden introduction, blinking once as he looked back at me. The other two seemed interested in continuing the conversation when a strong hand wrapped around my wrist and dragged me into the hallway.

"You were not permitted to speak to them." His voice was low and irritated, and I could see the tick in his jaw as he pulled me down the empty hallway.

"I do not need permission to speak, your Highness. The pact did not cover my ability to communicate with others." As we stopped before a door about halfway down the hall, I stuck my tongue out. The door was nothing special against the stone, but I could see the dust on the handle as I examined it.

"This is your room—you will stay in it until you're called. Do you understand?" His grip tightened on my arm, bringing my attention back to him. His face was set in a slight snarl; irritation settled deep into the handsome features, but I could see that not all of it was pointed toward me. I could see a bit of distance hiding behind the frustrated front that he displayed.

"What if I need to use the washroom or need something to eat?" I lightly challenged, meeting his eyes with a hardened glare.

"It has everything you need, and you will be fed regularly." He said with a tone of finality, letting go of my arm to twist the dusty handle and open the door into the room. "We will be discussing your information in the morning. You are dismissed."

I opened my mouth to retort when he spun away from me and further down the hall, approaching a large wooden door not unlike mine and disappearing into the room behind it with a loud slam. I could have sworn it had splintered, and a part of my curiosity wanted to inspect it, but my attention was quickly taken by the sound of whispering from the other side of the hall. The three men were standing in the archway we had passed a minute ago—lost in conversation—before they realized my attention had turned to them and disappeared.

I didn't know who they were, but at least I had other company beyond Prince Thundercloud.

While the curiosity to learn more about the three men in the prince's wing was strong, the exhaustion that had settled into my bones was more substantial, so I walked into the room instead of heading back into the front room. The room was covered in dust and fabric-covered furniture, but it had large windows that looked out over a small garden that seemed to be in the same decay that the room had been. I walked closer to the window as the rain pattered down the glass and looked farther into what used to be a beautiful garden that was now rotted and covered in vines and weeds—it was a shame to see it left in such disarray. A door that led outside was to my left, and though I was glad I could get some outside time when I desired it, I knew it was nothing more than a gilded cage.

I sighed and turned away from the garden to the dust-covered room. This was better than what I had ever stayed in, even in this state, but I would at least spend my prison time cleaning it up and making it a nice place to stay. I did not know how long I would be here, but I could at least make it feel a bit more like a home. My mind wandered as I continued to look at the space, imagining what it could be until I stretched and caught a whiff of myself.

I had spent *far* too much time without a bath.

I looked around the large room and its doors until I found myself in a private bath. It was just as dusty yet elegant as the room it was attached to, with a large marble basin for a tub and light green walls, adding much-needed color to a primarily colorless space.

My attention on the room quickly dwindled when I walked over to the tub to turn the handles on the faucet to start the bath I desperately needed. As it began to fill and steam rose in the room, I turned to an old mirror and removed my shirt to wipe away the dust and steam that clouded it. However, as the large mirror began to clear, I was stunned to see the female who looked back at me.

I was a mess was the short version.

The extended version was that my light brown hair had tangled into knots I was not ready to run a brush through, I was covered head to toe in dirt, and the only semi-clean spot of me was where my shirt was before I removed it. My eyes were the only bright part of my usually clean exterior, and the gold that lined my pupils had expanded into the blue from exhaustion. I would have to spend at least an hour in the bath to grind all the dirt off, and even then, I'd need another hour tomorrow to get the rest of it.

Hopefully.

I turned to look at my back to see if dirt or sweat had collected there, but where I had expected to see grime, I only saw a blurry mess of black. My usually empty back was now covered in what looked like ink, and I wiped down the mirror several more times with the gathering steam and my shirt to make sure I was not hallucinating.

What I initially thought was just a large blotch of ink on my entire upper back was what seemed to be a tattoo of sorts, with swirls of black, purple, blue, gold, and silver. Within the swirls and intricate markings was the form of a giant black dragon flying across my shoulder blades, with white lightning-like markings spreading across its form. The eyes were the matching hazel of the prince, with blue surrounding the green and brown colorings. Below the eerily familiar dragon was a greyscale rendition of my mare—from the interrupted stripe that runs down my face to the white socks that decorated my pasterns.

As steam continued to rise from the nearly full basin behind me, I kneeled beside the marble to stare into the water and look over my face again. My mind began to reel at all the thoughts that threatened to pull me into a spiral, but I couldn't get the image of the permanent etching in my back.

How was I going to kill the prince when I had the glaring reminder that if he died, I would die too?

CHAPTER 3

Sleep evaded me nearly all night. Being in a new place was torture enough, but tying that in with the fact that I was in a glorified prison cell and the itching from the cursed ink on my back, being comfortable was nearly impossible.

Just as the sun began to break the horizon, I gave up trying to get more sleep and wandered to the window overlooking the pathetic garden.

The rain had let up from the evening before, though a drizzle glazed over the wilting plants outside. The low light from the fire lamps around the room to the dim beginnings of sunlight warming the world created a mirror in the window's reflection.

Though most of the dirt was gone, I still felt like I was looking at a different version of myself. My hair had become a rat's nest of tangles and knots from the fitful sleep, and the bags that decorated my eyes only further emphasized how little sleep I had. The clothes I wore into the borders of Agraxis still decorated my petite frame and were still layered with dirt that I could not get off, even after three or four rounds of washing them the night before.

I would have kept looking over myself and done a better overview of my physical status had it not been for a knock at my door—gentle but with enough force to show they would not leave if I did not answer.

I quickly ran my fingers through my hair to brush it before I walked over to the door and opened it only enough to be able to peek my head out. Where I was expecting to meet the angry hazel eyes of the prince, I was surprised to see a soft purple looking at me instead.

"Good morning, Miss Willow." Princess Sellias smiled warmly. Her black hair had been braided back, and she was wearing a loose-fitting dress that did not hide the significance of her curves. Curiosity and a kind brightness sparkled in her violet eyes as she scanned my face.

"Princess Sellias." My only movement was to incline my head in greeting, not to open the door further.

"Have a bit of a rough night?" she asked, looking me over from head to toe through the space in the door. I could feel her gaze focus on the dirt spots still left on my clothing when she waved her hand in dismissal, shaking her head. "I'm sorry, I mean no harm. That comment was out of line." She sighed, bringing her gaze back up to meet mine. "I want to offer some help in navigating this new home of yours—especially dealing with my hot head of a brother. May I come in?"

I was surprised by the genuine kindness in her voice, but my instincts kept me hesitant as I peeked a little further out of my door. The hallway was quiet at the beginning of the day, with no one other than the princess wandering the walkway. The princess followed my looks around the hall before our eyes met again, and she put on the dazzling smile of royalty in the form of comfort. I did not return the smile as I narrowed my eyes toward her, trying to discern any sort of prank or ill-intention, but nothing seemed out of sorts.

I sighed as I stepped back to open the door enough for her to walk in.

She took the gesture with a polite nod and walked into the dust-covered room, looking around at its state. Her hands went on her hips as she nodded a few more times as if debating something.

"Is there something I can help you with, Princess Sellias?" I asked hesitantly, with a voice cleared of any grogginess from the night before. When her reply was her finger running over one of the dusty wood furniture pieces, I added, "I didn't expect any guests."

"I wanted to give you a proper hello now that I don't have to stick to formalities and help you get settled." She turned toward me, her eyes sparkling with a curiosity and excitement I hadn't expected. "Starting with your clothes, since you could not bring any others, I figured I could bring you some of my sister and I's old outfits we don't use anymore."

I finally noticed the trunk she had wheeled into the room as she dropped it on the floor with a *thud*.

"It isn't much, mainly some of Dityss' reading clothes and workout gear." She began as she opened the trunk, and I took a step beside her to investigate it. It had been filled to the brim with all kinds of clothes ranging from bright to dull colors, but even the dullest were far nicer than anything I had. "Since you'll be doing a lot of war work and such with Ren, I figured that might be better than my fancy dresses and comfort wear."

Confusion settled on my features as she began organizing the contents of the trunk on the bed, where the dust had been brushed and patted out of the sheets when I had tried to fall asleep last night. "Why are you helping me by giving me all these clothes? I'm here as a prisoner of sorts, not a guest."

Her attention did not stray from the clothing as she separated it into piles of loungewear, formal wear, and fitness wear. "Because despite the rules of the reasoning for the pact, you *are* here for an unknown amount of time as a unique guest of the crown." She glanced from the clothing momentarily to look at me, "Maybe for selfish reasons, too. I love Dityss, and I couldn't ask for a better twin. However, our conversations lately have been looping over the same topics, and I'd like to get to know someone who has seen more of the world than we could dream of."

My eyebrows knitted together as she turned back to the clothes, "You haven't traveled?"

"Contrary to popular belief that we constantly travel, no." She half-heartedly laughed, her unpacking slowing as she pulled a lavish black and gold dress from the trunk and held it to the firelight of a nearby lamp. "My mother and father are constantly away, either enjoying their older years as king and queen or visiting the other cities of Aistris for political engagements. But my brother is the only one of the children that gets to travel." She folded the dress into the formal wear pile. "Though I don't know if I envy his travels, considering it is mainly to lead or partake in war. But I wish I could see the lands that he does in a calmer circumstance."

I could not help but run a finger over a black-furred jacket she folded into the winter wear section she had started, the mixture of leather and fur expertly crafted. "It doesn't make sense that you two can't leave. If everyone else in the house can, why not you and Princess Dityss?"

Her laugh filled the room like the gentle sound of a windchime, "Please, no need for formalities. Dityss will be here in a bit, and she might throw a fit if you keep addressing her so formally." She smiled at me as her eyes sparked with amusement. "Just call me Selli."

I could not help but turn my head to the side, trying not to sniff the woman before me to detect her true intentions. My gut told me she was being truthful, but I found it hard to believe that the Roamion Princesses welcomed me so quickly.

"As for why we can't leave, Ren and my father continue to say it's for security purposes because of the current state of the rebel wars. Which I disagree with, considering Ren is the Crown Prince, which means losing him would be more of a detriment to the kingdom than if we were to lose Diti or I." She continued when I did not respond, taking out a final pair of workout clothes and setting them on the bed. They were a pair of black leggings with a white gradient from the bottom, alongside a matching teal shirt that read *"Let the inner YOU shine!"* alongside a series of stars beside the text. "So, we stay home and watch from our wing as they leave."

I reached for the cheesy tank top alongside the leggings, examining the silky yet breathable texture as I met her gaze again. "That's unfair, to say the least. Not even being able to go with them to visit the other regions diplomatically? That alienates you from being a better heir should something happen to the prince."

Even if that *something* happened to be me.

"You're telling me!" Selli let out a huff and a small giggle, closing the trunk before moving to a nearby sitting chair and removing the dusty cover that protected the furniture underneath. She did her best not to inhale the particles but ended up coughing a few times before she finally deemed it safe to sit on the cushion. "But I have yet to be able to convince any of them to let me go beyond Agraxis, even though my dragon is pissed at not being able to leave the confines."

"So why stay within them? Take off on an adventure one of the times they have gone on a trip. What are they going to do, *ground* you?" I snorted, a small smile beginning to form on my face.

Her laugh echoed in the old room, and once again, the princess caught me off guard. Her laughter and her joy were infectious, causing the slight smile on my face to grow.

"This is why I needed someone outside the castle to talk to. You think of such outrageous ideas that they might work!" Her smile made her eyes gleam, but a noise at the door made her attention turn from me to the entrance to the hallway. "Come in!"

Before I could object, Princess Dityss entered the room with her hands full of different bottles and brushes. "You could have at least helped me get the door open instead of laughing like a hyena, Sellias." She grumbled, kicking the door shut and approaching the bed as if she owned the space. "If you are trying to welcome the unicorn without Ren finding out, you could at least try to keep your voice down. Or did you forget that he is only right down the hall?" Her purple eyes were sharper than Selli's as she narrowed them to her sister, but they still held nothing ill towards my presence as she walked to where I was by the bed to drop the mixture of supplies on the fabric. "I went to the storage room today and found extra cleaning and bathing supplies for you. I assumed Ren had left this room a mess, and I don't like living or working in unkempt spaces, so I figured these would be sufficient help." Dityss shrugged, walking past the bed to settle on a wooden desk chair I had uncovered last night when trying to scrub out my clothes.

"Thank you, your highn—Dityss." I quickly corrected myself, watching as Dityss fiddled with a quill she had stored in her hair. Both Sellias and Dityss acted as if I were a familiar friend instead of a prisoner, but I was beginning to feel overwhelmed by the kindness each of them presented toward me. In what world was anyone *this* kind, especially when they were royals of an enemy faction?

My eyes must have betrayed my disbelief as Dityss responded, "Selli has always had a heart of gold, and when the pact was finalized, she felt bad for your predicament. So, she begged me for hours last night to help get things together for you to feel more comfortable." She shrugged lightly, looking towards her sister, who sighed briefly.

"It's too true. I'm a terrible worry-wart and knew Ren wouldn't have made you feel like you were anything but a prisoner." Selli looked around the room, focusing on the garden outside the windows. "It is worse than I thought it would be, however. He's kept every room in his wing clean, but this one. Of course, it's the one he puts you in."

"He did want her thrown into the prison instead, so this was probably the closest he could get to it in the space he was given to keep her." Dityss chimed in as she twirled the quill in her fingers, curiosity flickering in her gaze as she looked over me. "So, out of all the places you could have sought refuge, why choose Agraxis? You would have known that the other regions under our rule are kinder to those who seek citizenship, especially if you returned to your kin in Midstead."

I could not answer truthfully, so I thought about it momentarily. It was a reasonable question; if I were on any other mission, it would have made more sense to go somewhere I would not be in mortal peril. But here I was in the thick of it all and likely in the worst situation possible.

"I'm not a fan of dry heat, so the Eugara Expanse was instantly ruled out. And I didn't feel like scaling huge mountains in a terrain I didn't know, *especially* as a mare, to make it to the Sinos Cordillera." I shrugged, my fingers absentmindedly running over the fabric of my shirt. "As for Midstead, I figured I wouldn't make it past Agraxis to even make it within any reasonable distance to my ancestral home. So Agraxis it was, and I banked on the fact that the king would want the information more than my life. I guess I was only partially correct on that, though."

The sisters exchanged a glance of an emotion I couldn't quite place, though it might as well have just been pity. Being seen as a charity case or someone to feel sympathy for turned my stomach, so I stood from my seat on the bed and walked toward the bathing chamber. "I'm going to change, and when I get back, we can talk about my adventures outside the castle."

"How did the pact manifest?" Selli suddenly asked.

"As a stain on my back," I responded, looking over my shoulder as I stopped in the archway to the bath. "Why?"

Again, there was that glance between sisters as if they were talking over the silence that filled the room. They looked seemingly lost in thought as they watched each other, Selli slightly rubbing her wrist as my irritation bubbled. Another minute passed of silence before I returned to the bath, "I don't need the pity party nor to be forgotten I'm in the room. If you continue to do that, you can take your leave."

I could feel both looking at me quickly in surprise as Dityss spoke. "We apologize—as siblings who have spent years speaking to each other silently, we sometimes forget that others are in the room." Her apology was genuine, and she finished with a soft sigh, "As for the pity, it's hard not to sympathize with your situation."

"All three of us are stuck in our versions of gilded cages, remember?" Selli whispered softly, causing me to bite my lip with a soft pang of guilt. She had just told me about their soft imprisonment, but I had already forgotten.

"As for the pact's manifestation, we were curious about how it had branded itself on you," Dityss continued, "Sometimes it appears as a vast image of ink, while other times it appears as a ring of ink on a finger or a wrist. The size is usually relative to the stakes of the pact taken, and considering that your hands and wrists bear no symbol of it, I was curious about just how large it ended up being."

"Oh." Was all I could muster in response, and I subconsciously reached over my shoulder to scratch at my back. The itching had eased since Selli arrived, but it was beginning to bother me again as attention was drawn to it.

"Can we see it?" Selli asked, sitting up in her chair with interest. I stopped itching and made eye contact with the princesses as Dityss came and stood beside her sister. "If you don't mind, that is. You can turn away and lift your shirt or take it off. Whatever is more comfortable for you." She quickly added in, her face reddening a bit as she clarified.

I had never had a problem removing my shirt in front of others since my workouts usually consisted of only using a wrap around my breasts, so I set the fresh clothes that Sellias had brought on a cabinet. "I guess so, but don't touch it—it's sore." I pulled the dirty shirt from my torso before I used it as a makeshift wrap to cover my bare breasts, keeping my eyes pointed on the floor leading into the bath.

I stiffened as the two princesses rushed to investigate my bare back in a matter of seconds. They were murmuring something to themselves, and my skin prickled in goosebumps as I felt a delicate finger graze over the top of the ink.

"This is extraordinary." Dityss exhaled, "I have never seen a pact brand quite like this."

"It painted all of Ren's features down to the smallest scar," Selli added, not speaking louder than an awed whisper, "I'm assuming it has each of your details as well?"

A low growl ripped across the quiet hush that had fallen over the room, causing all three of us to step away from each other in panicked surprise. Selli seemed the most spooked as she nervously ran her hands down her braid, and Dityss was calmly watching the doorway as if she knew what was coming.

"Care to explain why you are deciding to visit and touch my prisoner?"

Rendros Roamion was leaning against the frame, his hazel eyes simmering with quiet anger as our gazes met.

CHAPTER 4

Rendros was pissed.

I could not help but take the chance to fully take in the man in the doorway, from his sharp jawline to his intimidating posture. His hazel eyes were pinpointed on me, the blue that rimmed the exterior crashing against the darker colors as his gaze traveled down my nearly bare chest.

"You have no clue how dangerous she could be, and I'm the only one protected by that stretch of ink branded into her back." He growled as he pulled his eyes away from me to glare at his sisters, pushing off of the doorframe to stomp toward us. Any confidence I had speaking with the princess cowered in his presence, but I refused to step away when he stopped in front of us.

His fancy attire from the night before had been swapped for a simple T-shirt and sweatpants, freshly damp from what seemed like a morning workout. His arms were crossed over each other across his chest as he stood over both Sellias and Dityss, and it took a lot to tear my attention away from the strain of the shirt over his biceps.

"You don't know what a female needs to feel at home, Ren." Selli challenged her brother, crossing her arms in defiance as if trying to look like her brother did in the moment. "You could have at least given her one of your cleaner spare rooms and sent some clothes this morning. Not a dusty abandoned room where she might as well be thrown into the dungeons like you wanted."

"She is a criminal, Sellias. Not a houseguest." He bared his teeth toward her, and I swore I was running out of breathable air.

"I think it would be best for you to stop saying she is a criminal, Ren. Unless you *want* your soldiers and the people of our kingdom to question your sanity over the choice to pact yourself to one." Dityss stepped into the space between Selli and the prince, "So either go take your anger out on the field or get your shit together. We all knew she had no other clothes than what she arrived in, and we both knew that Sellias would not accept someone living in the castle stuck in those rags."

As she spoke, Rendros's attention turned to the taller Roamion sister, breaking the tension in the room long enough for me to inhale a few good breaths of air.

"Selli's bleeding heart is going to get her killed one day, and you just let it lead her towards that fate." He growled as I watched Selli's defiant stare fracture out of the corner of my eye, her eyes falling to the ground.

"A bleeding heart isn't a bad thing, Your *Highass*." I cut in, causing all three siblings to snap their attention back to me. Sellias' eyes began to sparkle with hints of amusement, counteracting the dark presence that began to fill the room as hazel eyes sparking with lightning met mine.

"She's not wrong, Ren," Dityss rebuked, her anger beginning to push back the presence surrounding the prince, maybe even starting to overcome it with the additional support. "That was a low blow, and you are well aware of that. Apologize."

Rendros did not take his attention from me, but I could see his body visibly relax as he sighed, "Sorry, Selli."

The princess did not respond to the apology but held her head higher again as he shifted on his feet.

"Regardless, that still doesn't answer why you had her shirt off and were examining her pact mark," He grumbled, his eyes fixed on my chest as if they could see straight through the skin to the lines of ink stretched across my back. "You both know what a pact does and the mark it leaves. If you were so curious, you could have asked me."

"We know of the mark but have never seen a pact with such meaning and rules before," Selli answered, absent-mindedly rubbing her left wrist, where there was a colorfully inked band of flowers and vines. "Besides, we *also* know that each version of a pact appears differently on its host. We could ask you at any time, but since we were stopping by anyways..."

I failed to notice it before, but as I glanced between them, I could see similarly inked bands on each sibling's left wrist. Dityss's band was a string of words on her left wrist in a language I could not understand, tied together in a never-ending loop. The one on Rendros's was a chain of purple lightning and stars spread across his wrist in sharp turns and edges, each speckle of a star seemingly glowing as he turned his wrist.

Each band was unique, tying in parts of themselves and their personalities in a single ink band. Were they pacts, too?

"Read about them, yes. But seeing one like this in person? It's a once-in-a-century kind of thing." Dityss continued where her sister left off, beginning to shift her weight as she tried to look around her brother. They were close in height, with maybe only an inch or two in the prince's favor. "Is yours also on your back? How did yours manifest?"

"Yes, and now is not the time to ask about it." The prince growled, shifting his stance to keep Dityss from reaching for his shirt or attempting to see his back. Though I could still see the irritation as he set his jaw when Dityss narrowed her eyes at him, most of the anger that he had entered the room with had dissipated.

Selli stomped her foot on the ground, the noise quickly returning my attention to her. Her chin was held high with defiance again, and her violet eyes sparkled with the confidence it brought. "That's so unfair! You just said you'd show us if we asked, yet you're being more stubborn than Willow was!"

I exhaled, raising a hand to slowly run it down my face as if it would hide me from the turn in the conversation.

"She's wild-raised, Selli. She's probably used to constantly flaunting her skin around bonfires and other Fae." He snorted, drawing instant ire into my gaze as I narrowed my eyes toward him.

"I don't know what stories you have read about life in the Untamed Wilds, but I can assure you we are *not* some feral, hormone-crazed beasts that dance around fires and chant blessings for fertility." I snarled back, and I could feel Selli bristle beside me in irritation at her brother's remark. Dityss looked like she was lost in thought, trying to recall information.

A huff on my right followed quickly by stomping feet as Sellias stalked toward the exit, opening the door with a swift movement fueled by anger. "I'll come back tomorrow to help you clean up everything to be a *proper* room, Willow. Maybe by then, my brother will have learned some actual manners."

Dityss turned to follow her twin, but she stopped beside Rendros to put a hand on his shoulder. He turned his eyes to hers, and just as Sellias and Dityss had done earlier, they seemed to be locked in silent conversation that no one else could hear.

A part of me was glad that I did not have siblings who fought me or bothered me like Sellias and Dityss seemed to, but another part yearned to have that closeness the Roamion siblings had. Theo had been a great adoptive brother with our own share of arguments and annoyances, but it felt...*different* than what the three Fae in front of me had.

The conversation seemed to end as Dityss walked out with a slight wave, leaving the door open as she left with Selli.

The only two in this castle who could protect me from the swelling anger of the prince had left me alone with him, leaving the reality of that fact standing at me with a spark of anger in his hazel eyes.

Before I could react, I was pressed against the wall with a large hand pressing around my throat, and the prince's face was mere inches from mine. My eyes widened in sudden panic and surprise; I dropped my shirt to the ground to put my hands up to try to push back against his arms to help alleviate the pressure on my throat. For a few seconds, I was able to relieve some of the pressure before he pressed harder, causing me to choke out a cough.

Though I knew the initial anger he had entered the room with had not entirely dissolved, I was not expecting it to come back tenfold and end with me trapped against the wall.

"This pact only protects *me* from you," He growled as he lifted me on the wall, my fingers desperately trying to pull his hand away. Though his grip was not enough to kill me, it was enough to demonstrate that I was no match against the prince in a fight. His free hand grabbed my chin, returning my attention to his face, "It does not protect *you* from me."

I could feel my mare scream in fear and panic as the predator Fae brought his nails pressed against my neck, sharp points forming and pushing against the soft skin. I wanted to cry out for help, to do anything to help save me from the pain that was coming, but I refused to be weak prey that cowered instantly at the jaws of a predator.

"If you so much as *pinch* them, I will know and flay you alive. I do not care if you have given me the information you say you have." He growled as I held his gaze with as much defiance as I could muster.

"I have no intention of harming either of them," I whispered past the hand gripped around my throat, "Out of any person I met inside of this castle, they have been the *only* ones that have treated me as another Fae. I might be untamed, but I am not a beast."

"Yet every untamed I have ever met has only greeted me with a blade and an intent to kill." He snarled back, the low tone of his voice vibrating in the space between us. "You expect me to believe you won't do the same?"

The tension between our gazes was like a tangible thread—as if I could reach up and pluck it like a harp string. He was walking a line that teetered the truth of my arrival here in the castle, and if I inhaled too quickly, he could catch onto the truth.

"I can't expect you to see me as anything more than an enemy," I took in a slow, deep breath, closing my eyes for just a moment to try and press back the tide of irritation. "But I'd like to be seen as more than a feral beast."

His eyes darted back and forth between each of mine, searching for any deception or lie that may lie behind them, but I kept my gaze firm yet gentle. His jaw ticked in frustration as he pulled his hands back from my throat and face, causing me to nearly fall to my knees from the sudden rebalance of weight on my feet.

As I rubbed my throat where he had kept me pinned against the wall, I watched him step back with a hand running down his face until it stopped to cover his mouth. His gaze was turned toward the ceiling, but I could see his chest rising and falling in labored and pained breaths that nearly mimicked my own.

"Are you all—"

"I don't know what brought you here or why my father spared you the prison cell. I don't know why he decided this pact was the best path." He brought his gaze down from the ceiling as something like sorrow flickered through the blue rim of his iris for only a second before he continued, "I have fought hundreds, maybe thousands, of the untamed through the years this rebel war has raged. Not one has ever treated me as anything more than a savage killer of their people. It is...*difficult* to believe you are different."

My breathing became quiet as I watched him shake his head before looking back at me through a hooded gaze.

"I am the general and the prince of your enemy, and I am protected from your blade if you wish to use it by the tether of your own life. Yet my sisters are not, and if what I fear is true, you could turn your sword to them instead. So, I will remind you once again—if you harm my sisters in any capacity, then you forfeit your life to me. Do you understand, Wildie?"

I watched him look over me again before he grabbed the teal shirt I had set aside on the cabinet before he arrived and tossed it toward me. I grabbed it just as it reached me, holding it up to my breasts as a new makeshift cover while returning a slight nod of gratitude. "I understand, Prince Rendros. Hopefully, one day, you may see that all the untamed aren't as bloodthirsty as you fear."

A rumble of thunder echoed far above the castle in response, but the rain didn't pour down the windows as he turned to the doorway that was the exit of my room. "Get dressed in something they brought you, then join me in the atrium further down the hallway. It's time for you to start talking."

CHAPTER 5

The atrium was ginormous—the size of at least half of Ullaven—and littered on all sides with maps, plans, and scribblings from a war room.

Though it was five times the size, it reminded me of Theo's bunker.

Instead of dirt covering every surface, there were ancient stone walls with large glass windows and substantial rolling doors open to the outside, where I could see an open field stretching for miles. Several tables lined the walls, each with piles of paper and in-depth maps dotted with scribbled notes. In the center of the room was a mix of several different rugs and oversized pillows, with only a few pieces of paper across it and more empty bottles littering the plush centerpiece.

If I could get a closer look at one of these tables of plans and see what they were doing...

"Wildie." Prince Rendros' voice echoed through the room, prompting me to turn my attention to where he was standing near the exit to the green fields. He was leaning against a table with only a few papers on it alongside three males, all looking unamused by my scan of the surroundings. Little about his outfit had changed from our incident that morning—besides a change into dress slacks—but the all too soon recollection of it had my hand unconsciously drifting up to my throat.

Before I followed the prince to the atrium, I looked at myself in the mirror, expecting to see red marks where his hand had been minutes before, but nothing was there. My skin was as clear as day—as if it had never happened. There was no lingering pain from where his grip had pressed against my neck, and if I did not know better, I would have thought he had healed the wounds with his magic.

However, I knew that was impossible from the little training sessions and history lessons Theo gave me.

"To understand how the other shifters work, it's best to understand each of their respective powers," Theo explained as I sat on the couch in his mother's living room, lazily thumbing through a book I had traded for in town. I was not interested in learning history or its meanings, but Theo told me it was necessary.

So, I would listen, but I was more interested in the book in my hands.

"Lo, you have to pay attention." He growled, walking over and plucking the book from my hands. I protested as I desperately reached for the novel, but he opened it to somewhere in the middle and grimaced at the scene I was currently reading. "By the Gods, Lo. This isn't even realistic!"

My face darkened to a deep red as I crossed my arms over my chest. "Good way to spoil it, T. But please, droll about the different shifters instead of letting me enjoy an escape into something interesting."

He tossed the book aside as if it were nothing more than a piece of trash to disregard.

"Each species group in a house can perform a specific magic. Everyone can use the basics, like creating fire, warming water, drying themselves off with the wind, assisting in cleaning their homes, things like that." He demonstrated by bringing a piece of fire to his hand and

wreathing it around his fingers. "However, those born from the original lines of their lineage can sometimes access more."

"In the Midstead Lineage of the unicorns and hooved shifters, it often manifests in some measure of divination magic. Things like seeing the future, detecting certain kinds of magic, or reading minds. It's probably the most screwed up of the list, but at least it's only found in the purebloods. The Eugara Lineage encompasses all feline-type shifters, but the lions of the original lineage hold the most power. Those purebloods can conjure things out of thin air, summon elemental minions or creatures, and be able to teleport to a location they have been before." *He snorted, and the flame that danced on his fingers disappeared before taking a deep breath to continue.*

"The Sinos Lineage of the canine-type shifters is said to have descended directly from the god Sinos, known best for his healing abilities. They are solely known for their ability to heal those from near-death, no matter how severe, and those in the pureblood pack of wolves are rumored to do even more than that. They keep the extent of what they can do pretty under wraps, though." *His hand ran down his face as he stared at the age-stained carpet on the floor, lost in recollection.*

"As for the Agraxis Lineage, they are the only one I truly fear beyond the Midsteads. Dragons can control nature and the world around us to be whatever they want. It was Akis, the first King of Aistris, who wielded the terrain to create the continent. His children were rumored to be able to control the storms and the oceans, but luckily, the terrain-shifting gene seems to have been used up on him. That major turn in our history is why our years are counted as 'Before Akis' and 'After Akis.'"

I took a moment to absorb all the information, leaning back onto the couch and staring at the ceiling as my thoughts swirled. "Can the lineages merge? Would an ocean-controlling dragon mix with a mind-reading unicorn and create a child with both abilities?"

Theo leaned back in his chair, let out the largest exhale I had ever heard from him, and ran his hands through his long blonde hair. "Thank the Gods, no. I've heard of it being tried but never being successful. Mainly, any offspring between species has only one shift over the other, and their magic follows that piece of the gene pool." He gave a nervous chuckle, "We'd be fucked if magics could intermingle like that."

"Wildie."

I was pulled out of my thoughts by the deep rumble of a growl that was Prince Rendros, now standing directly in front of me with his hazel eyes sparking with irritation.

"Sorry, Your Highass. Got distracted by the fields of tasty-looking dandelions right outside those doors." I lowered myself in a mock bow with a fake smile before looking past him to the three males gathered around the table. "Do I finally get an introduction to your boyfriends?"

The room went quiet as my words echoed against the stone walls. The blonde of the group let out a snort as he tried to conceal his chuckle. There were a couple more seconds of silence before all three were howling in laughter.

"Holy shit, dude!" The brown one barked, "I can't believe you got pacted to a hottie with a sense of humor!"

The third one with black hair reigned in his laughter the fastest, his dark eyes sparking with joy. However, the laughter quickly fizzled out as

Rendros snapped his attention back to them with a silent threat hanging in the air.

All three males stood entirely still—as if they had been turned into stone.

"Since you introduced yourself yesterday, there is no need to go back over your introduction," the prince said with obvious irritation, motioning me to the table where the males were standing. "This is my war council."

"Rygur Dozemm, at your service." The tallest of the group started off the line of greetings, his short black hair cut just like the prince's barely falling past the middle of his forehead as he gave a slight bow. Silver flecks sparked in his dark brown eyes and sparkled in contrast to his ebony skin, their unique beauty briefly entrancing me as they scanned over my entire form. "I help keep Ren in line when he gets too cocky with a plan and goes all 'world-savior' on us."

The blonde, whose long hair tinged a fiery orange in some layers that looked like fire against his tawny skin, was next to introduce himself. His eyes were a deep green that failed to hold me in the same trance as Rygur's had but still watched me with an all-too-intense stare that made the hair on my arms stand in discomfort. "Peter Harrison. The hottest of the group and the only one who knows how to read a map to strategize where to put forces properly, so you and I will be working together a lot to prepare for future campaigns against the untamed forces."

I let out a flustered snort but gave a slight nod in recognition—he had not done anything beyond a swift introduction. However, something about the way he looked at me sent a chill down my spine.

The last came to stand beside the prince, whose warm russet skin contrasted beautifully with the light brown tussle of his hair that was pulled back into a bun to reveal warm honey-gold eyes. His fangs glistened as he gave the widest grin of them all, "Jaeden Carver, gorgeous." He leaned over, grabbed my hand, and kissed my fingers delicately as I felt the heat rise in my cheeks at the smooth action. "Since I don't want to hurt the precious prince's pride, I'll say that my fighting skills are only second to his. However, if you need the best lay in the castle..."

My cheeks were as red as an apple when Rendros suddenly pushed Jaeden away, irritation coming off him in waves as the entire group devolved into senseless bickering. In only a few steps, the prince and his second rejoined the other two at the table, and for just a moment, I saw a group of friends. Though it was apparent that Rendros was upset about something Jaeden had said, there was a hint of teasing laughter behind the upset tone he used in the argument. In front of me was nothing more than a group of males bickering about their rank as the strongest or the most desirable, in a teasing fashion I had seen so many groups in the Untamed Wilds participate in. No prince nor general was here, no fussing about ranks or fighting techniques.

I could not help the small smile that formed on my lips as I took a step toward them, despite knowing that they were my enemies, not a group of males to relate to.

My motion pulled them out of their argument, closely monitoring my footsteps as I gave a soft bow just beyond the table. "It's lovely to meet all of you."

The blonde, Peter, scoffed as he crossed his arms over his chest. "There's no need for formalities here, mare." Another not-so-charming smile spread across his face as he leaned forward with a wink. "We might work for the future king of Aistris and the general of the Imperial army, but we don't suck up to him and his title. Bring back your feisty mare attitude, and you'll fit right in." His smile widened, but I turned my attention to the unmarked map of the continent that Rendros was flattening out on the table instead of meeting his green gaze any longer.

"I want you to write down all the camps that you know of with an 'X,'" he ordered, pointing to the Untamed Wilds on the southern side of the continent with an inked quill. My heart twinged at the sight of the territory on the map, and I delicately stroked my fingers over the parchment. I stopped when I saw the printed mark for Ullaven—a small drawing of some cottages—as memories and worries began to plague my thoughts.

Would I ever return there? Would people I know survive the consequences of this mission?

"Then write down their numbers and what weapons they have. As well as the types of shifters that form their ranks." The general prince continued, though I could feel his attention turn back to me when my hand did not move to grab the quill.

"Woah, woah, Ren," Rygur interrupted, pulling the map slightly towards him on the other side of the table. "I know you want out of this pact as soon as possible, but the girl just got here yesterday. She hasn't been out of her mare form for who knows how long, and this is where she grew up." He pointed to the wilds to continue, "What you're asking her to do is like a random stranger asking you to show them your sisters' exact schedules."

Rendros's jaw ticked at the comparison, but his attention stayed on me as if searching for the similarities.

"She needs time to adjust to this...*predicament* just as much as you do. Let Pete or Jae take her outside to run through the fields or eat some dandelions." My face flushed at the reminder of my joking comment, obviously taken somewhat seriously. "Then, ask her a couple of questions. But you must take it slow if you want this to work out in our favor."

I finally turned to meet the prince's searching stare, clearing my head to stand up straighter, even though it did little to level the height difference. My ponytail fell from over my shoulder, the strands of hair swiping across the top of my back as I lifted my head to look at him. Though I did not want to admit it, I needed the air. Seeing that map and what I was being asked to do distracted my thoughts from the task at hand, and I could not continue the mission if I became an anxious mess.

There was more silence before Rendros's eyes met mine with a growl, "Fine. However, if you even *think* of running away, Pete and Jae have permission to hunt you down like prey."

My heart fluttered with relief and excitement to be outside, but I kept my face calm as an idea popped into my head.

"Fine." I smirked back, "But only if they can catch me."

Then, with a flash of silver light, I galloped into the open fields beyond the atrium.

CHAPTER 6

The wind whipped through my mane as my hooves met grass and dirt, pulling me farther into a silent siren song of freedom. It felt like it had been years since I could run like this—so wild and carefree—as if the world was nothing more than a landscape for me to explore.

The sound of my hoofbeats against the earth was a melody to my heart.

Despite my sudden departure from the prince's atrium and what the prince and his council had probably assumed was an attempt to flee, I had just wanted to *run*. I wanted to find myself in the sunlight—to feel any sense of ordinary in a world where it felt like normal did not belong to me. It was a silly notion when I was barely permitted to go beyond the atrium, but grazing and sunbathing was not what I wanted.

As a consequence of my decision, colorful flashes of light poured out of the stone atrium when I was barely a quarter down the small hill, answering any question about their reaction. I would be chased down like a prey animal in a hunt.

Which was expected, but it added to the thrill. A quiet trot in the sun would have to wait for another day.

I turned my head momentarily as I sped through a stream to see a large dark brown wolf barreling towards me alongside a blonde and red-furred lion, keeping a swift pace with the wolf beside him. Their honey-gold and emerald eyes were trained on me as if I were their next meal, sending a shiver of excitement and nerves down my spine.

Since I had a reasonable distance between myself and my pursuers and adrenaline flooding my system, a flash of silver surrounded me briefly as I caught myself running on two legs again. My momentum nose-dived with the sudden transformation, but I cupped my hands to my lips to yell, "Gotta be faster than that, boys!"

My voice cracked with the taunt, thanks to my lack of use in the last few weeks, but I did not allow myself to linger on the embarrassment too long as I let my mare take control once more. A few heavy strides would get me back to my initial pace, especially when I heard the bark and roars that answered not too far behind.

However, I was unprepared for the dark shadow suddenly blocking the sun.

I barely turned my head to the sky to see the giant silhouette of a winged beast flying parallel to my running path through the field, causing my heart to nearly double its already hastened pace.

I brought my attention back to the ground as I nearly tripped over a large stone, trying desperately to pick up speed and avoid the death that awaited me at the beast's giant claws.

Thunder shook somewhere nearby, and my suspicions of *who* the beast was were quickly confirmed.

My ears pinned as I jumped out of the way of claws the size of my mare, attempting to pluck me from the comforts of solid ground. I turned my direction towards the forest creeping closer to the east. I could still see the castle as a distant outline, so I knew I could return if I were to become lost. A strike of lightning somewhere to my left joined a roar of frustration above me, and I decided.

I plunged into the forest at a full gallop and felt the skim of branches against my skin as I jumped around and over obstacles in my way. I could feel my lungs heaving with each thrum of my hooves against the ground, and though I had not felt this free in ages, I knew I would have to stop somewhere in this forest to return to the stone walls of my gilded cage.

Deep down, I knew there was no escape from the path that fate had set me on. I could not keep running forever and find my way back to Ullaven, for even if I could outrun the lion and the wolf on my trail, I could never outrun the dragon that searched the skies.

Not to mention the disappointment on Theo's face if I returned without results.

As I approached a creek, I slowed to a trot, looked around my surroundings, and listened with swiveling ears for potential threats. I could still hear the flapping of giant wings above the tree canopy when another pair joined them, my pride swelling when I listened to the irritated growls that seemed to communicate that they had not yet found me.

I took a deep breath as I leaned over to sip from the creek, my tail flicking back and forth in a silent, soothing motion to help ease any rising anxieties. I did not doubt that the wolf or the lion would pounce and take me down without a second thought, but I tried my best to be ready for anything.

After drinking some water, I looked at myself in the creek to look over my form, pleased to see that my scrub down last night was good enough that my light brown coat shone under the rays of sunlight that trickled through the trees. The white socks and interrupted stripe on my face were as soft and clean as fresh linen, the bright streaks complimented by the lighter cream dapples covering most of my body. My brown and silver hair was a little windswept but otherwise clean and loose in the gentle breeze that swept through the forest.

However, the one thing I did not recognize as I looked at myself in the creek was the long trails of black ink that spread across my back.

The pact mark did not disappear even when I shifted.

Instead, it had reformed to look like black wings that trailed down my spine and over the top of my back, lined with several swirls and intricate additions to the wing-like structure. I could imagine myself as a pegasus, a variant of the unicorn ancestry that my father had always told me stories about. They were courageous, and they always had an eye for adventure, keeping to the skies as they plotted the initial confines of the world.

As I strutted in front of the water, I snorted in entertainment at the idea, my ears tilted toward my reflection.

"So, the pretty pony stops to admire herself in her reflection." Low laughter rumbled through the forest, drawing my attention to the source of the sound. Peter stepped out of the tree line, his green eyes lit with humor. "You know, you *really* set off Ren. He may just kill you when we get back."

I rolled my eyes and snorted, pulling my attention from the creek to meet Peter's stare. They had not received any information from me yet, and I could recognize the prince's stubborn pride enough to know that he would not kill me without at least getting *some* knowledge.

Pete's laughter continued as he stepped closer to me. The ordinarily natural movement made me uneasy as I focused on some fresh grass below me. Though he had done nothing to warrant the nervousness that grew with every inch closer he came, I kept my distance.

"Holy shit." Another voice joined in the conversation, and I saw Jae leaning against a tree just out of my peripheral vision. He was breathing heavily, his attention darting between me and Peter. "How in the hells do you even manage to run like that? That was a solid sprint for at *least* fifteen minutes." He heaved as I nickered in a sort of laughter.

"Maybe you should take more time to work on your legs than just your arms, Jae," Pete teased, earning an eye-roll from Jae. He did not stop taking deep breaths as he sat on a rock and put his head between his knees.

Pete's attention returned to me, causing whatever comfort that had entered the space when Jaeden arrived to nearly instantly dissipate. He looked over me with such a slow pull of his gaze that I might have believed he had never seen a unicorn Fae before. I pinned my ears back and turned away with a snort of warning, but I could hear his feet crunch the grass right behind me as I watched his arm reach out toward my haunch.

My breathing hitched, panic overtook my senses, and a flash of silver illuminated the creek side.

"Don't you know it is not kind to touch someone without asking?" My voice cracked slightly with anger as I swiftly created space between us, my muscles stiff as I pulled my hand to my chest. "I could have easily kicked you into the hells if I didn't have better control over myself. Never do that again."

"My apologies, Willow," Pete murmured, his hand returning to his side like it had never been outstretched in the first place. "I have never been that close to a unicorn Fae as their mare, and my curiosity seems to have got the better of me."

Anger still rose in my chest, followed by tight irritation in my stomach. When I finally reached a small boulder closer to the tree line, I stopped, trying to rationalize my breathing and thoughts. People thought it was the untamed that were feral, boundary-less beasts, but I had never been so close to being touched by someone uninvited in the Wilds.

"Mr. Handsy never learned the polite manner of a personal bubble." Jaeden chimed in, having recovered enough from his sprint to walk over to wrap an arm around Pete. The lion Fae shot daggers back at the wolf, who answered with a charming smile. "Don't let him ruin such a good time we just had with that run. Ren will do plenty of that when we return." He finished with a wink in my direction, earning an eye-roll from me as well.

Had these males never been in close working proximity with a female before?

I turned my attention to the skies above us, listening for any sounds of the prince above, still searching above the canopy. It had gone quiet, meaning Rendros had entered the forest to search for me on foot or returned to the atrium to hang me from the castle walls. Neither option was charming, but I could breathe more manageably now that I had a good run and could get my blood pumping.

I would have to thank Rygur later for his comforting words and suggestions to the prince.

"I suppose I won't be able to get away from you two again?" I flashed the two a playful smirk as I pulled my panic back together into a small bubble to store away. The lion and wolf Fae reorganized themselves in a position prime to strike if I tried anything, but I raised my hands in surrender with a snort. "Don't get your panties in a twist. I just wanted to get a good run in before I'm put under house arrest again."

"Thank the gods," Jae whispered, leaning over his knees again as a soft chuckle left his lips. "I'd do it, but I may need to rest for a whole day afterward."

"Aren't you supposed to be the big bad wolf, Jaeden?" I teased, crossing my arms over my chest. "Not a little puppy who can't last without naps? Hmm…" I raised a hand to my face, tapping my finger against my jawline as I looked to the sky again. "Maybe your title of who can please a lover the most should be changed."

"Hey—now hang on a second!" Jae shot straight up, stomping over to me like a toddler who had just been told he was not the strongest on the playground. "I may not be able to run forever, but my stamina in the bedroom has no issues!"

"If only you had been here a couple of weeks earlier, Willow." Pete chimed in, seemingly easing back down from his stunned silence at seeing a unicorn up close. "I watched a girl leave his room within thirty minutes of entering it, maybe even twenty! The dissatisfaction that came off her was nearly palpable." Jaeden whipped his head towards Pete, and in a matter of seconds, there was a flash of green and gray light; the wolf was on top of the lion.

It was entertaining to see the two fight in the small clearing of the forest. Peter stayed underneath the larger Jaeden, but he did not seem to be having any problem with the weight on him. He sunk his teeth into

Jae's neck fur rather far, but I had learned from watching Theo clash with others that no real damage would be done in such fights. So, I sat on the rocks by the creek and began to brush my hair with my fingers as I watched them roll around the clearing.

I had only seen a lion Fae on one other occasion with Theo. He had the thickest golden mane I ever knew possible on a shifter until then, but I was not too surprised by how he would constantly fuss about his hair in either form. The same went with the rest of the fur that gilded the muscle mass of the feline that was Theo—if it were not for the scars that lined his arms and haunches, I would have thought he was someone's pet.

Some of the same went with Pete, as similar golden fur began to darken with dirt as they rolled closer to the creek bed, but the red and orange that tinged the gold added more depth to his coat. It fell over him like wildfire, with peppered golden fields of wheat-colored hair centered around the mane that seemed to be the center point of the warm colors. It moved with him as he thrashed his head around to finally get momentum to push Jaeden underneath him. His deep green eyes reflected the forest around us. He let out a teasing growl, their amusement apparent in their wrestling match.

Laying underneath the golden mass was a deep brown wolf who only bared his teeth in response, mimicking snapping his teeth. He did not have as much color and looked more like a shadow underneath the sun that stood above him, but that did not matter too much when you had a form like he did. His fur was thick from the fall weather that had started just a couple of weeks ago, but the muscles underneath were not hidden as he pushed himself up and Peter off. His hackles rose in play as he challenged Peter to jump at him again, though his dark brown eyes danced in amusement contrary to the stance.

Suddenly, a roar echoed in the distance, bringing the sparring match to an immediate end as their heads instantly swiveled toward the sound. Both stood still as their ears flicked back and forth before Jaeden let out a long howl in what seemed to be a response. Silence echoed in the forest for a few seconds afterward, causing goosebumps to run up my arms as I stopped messing with my ponytail.

A flash of grey light lit up the clearing as Jae transformed back, dusting dirt off his jacket. "That was Ren. He wants us back at the atrium." Peter shook his head and neck in a stress-relieving motion, choosing to stay as his lion instead of transforming back.

"And your response?" I asked as I stood from my perch to stretch out my arms and legs in preparation for the shift.

"That we were on our way." He shrugged as gray light washed over the clearing, returning the predator to his alternative form. His honeyed eyes watched me expectantly as Peter began to trot back through the forest, leaving us behind.

I rolled my neck before letting the warmth of silver light envelope me, returning to the comfort of being on four legs. Jaeden looked at me warily as he tried to read if I would run again, but I lowered myself to the ground in a mock bow.

Lead the way.

Jae snorted with irritation as he rolled his head forward and began to trot back toward the palace. Despite leaving a few moments before us, it felt as if I could still feel the piercing green gaze that belonged to Peter, causing my unease to return ever so slightly.

On the way back, we mostly stayed within the confines of the forest, and I took the opportunity to bask in the scenery around me. Pine scents filled my nose as I took a deep breath, and the warmth of the noon sun on my back was pleasant against the chilly winds that occasionally danced through the surrounding trees.

My thoughts wandered as I focused on the crunch of the grass under my hooves while watching Jaeden pad ahead of me. He seemed on high alert, though I could not quite understand why as we approached through the forest and the palace grew more prominent in the distance. All I could hear was the birds chirping around us and our breathing, but nothing would be hiding in the trees, even in such a dense forest like this. We were within a mile of the castle by now; if anyone or anything decided to attack, they were signing their lives off as the next barbecue platter.

The prince's face popped into my mind, and I sighed internally. I imagined his handsome face contorting into its usual scowl and thunderclouds surrounding him, my death next on his to-do list. I tried to shake the image of him from my mind as we drew closer to the open gate of the atrium, but it stayed as if to continuously remind me of the decision I made to piss him off. I stared him down in my mind, holding my ground before the imaginary general prince.

Was I seriously having a staring contest in my imagination? Gods, I was already starting to go crazy.

So, I stuck my tongue out at him instead, blowing a raspberry. It was my imagination, so I could have all the ballsy moments I wanted against the royal Highass as I wanted. I had not expected Rendros's stunned expression at my silly taunt. I blinked in surprise at the near recognition the fictional prince gave me before I closed my eyes as hard as possible.

It's just my imagination running wild, as it usually does. I tried to reassure myself.

But as we approached the open gates of the atrium, I caught the same stare I saw in my imagination looking right back at me from the actual prince.

CHAPTER 7

Whatever sense of surprise the prince had on his face vanished behind stormy eyes in seconds as we all shifted back to our Fae forms. I stood between Jae and Pete while the prince stood beside Rygur.

"Did you have fun on your escapade?" Rendros growled. The sound of his voice and the thunder that followed firmly cemented that any look of bewilderment on his face was my imagination.

"I did." I responded with a mocking curtsy and a curt wink, "It is a shame you couldn't keep up."

Rygur cleared his throat at the taunt, the room otherwise silent.

"I'm glad to hear such, as that won't be permitted again." He took a few steps closer as I steeled myself to hold his stare and my ground. "You will be going on your morning and afternoon outings accompanied by Rygur," He smirked as he leaned closer, "Or myself."

I sneered back at him with a wicked smile, "It would be my pleasure, your Highass."

I was not thrilled about spending more one-on-one time with the prince—especially considering how well that went this morning—but I was pleasantly surprised not to be under complete castle arrest.

His hazel eyes scanned over me a second longer before he turned back to Peter and Jaeden on either side of me. "You two spent far too much time playing her game and saw her more like a toy than a rebel sympathizer withholding important information from us. So, while you still did your job to bring her back, neither of you will be permitted to watch over her alone again."

I had to hold back the sigh of relief I did not know I was holding as Jaeden moved to the table and leaned against it with a shrug.

"A shame—we haven't had a prey chase like that in years. Maybe one day we can play that game again when his *Highass*—" I stifled a laugh at how he drawled over my preferred name for the prince "—finally understands that he doesn't have to play royal all the time."

"It is honorable that he takes his work so seriously," Peter argued, his attention sitting on me for a few seconds before he looked at Jaeden. "It isn't a war that can be won between parties."

I cleared my throat as tension sparked between the two males, eager to avoid what would likely turn into a not-so-friendly fight. "So, you wanted to know where some of the camps are?" I moved away from the group of males to the table Jaeden was leaning on, flattening out the empty map still sitting on the table.

Despite the mind-clearing chase and my battle to restructure my thoughts before I returned to the parchment, I could not help the memories that still flashed in my mind as my attention caught on Ullaven. Even on such a simple map, I could see the fields where my father and I played and remember the streets where Theo and I chased each other through the farmer's market every weekend.

It had been nearly a month since I had left, but it felt closer to almost six.

A hand softly landed on my shoulder as Rygur moved to stand next to me, pulling my attention from the deepening tunnel of memories. Where Peter had caused me a near-panic attack with a similar movement, Rygur's expression was full of genuine kindness and understanding as he gave me a soft smile of reassurance.

"I know that Ren asked for a lot, but just a few would help start to get this going and get him off your back," he encouraged. "I imagine how difficult it must be."

"You don't know the half of it," I whispered.

I mentally checked where every camp was situated on the map, reaching for the quill left on the side of the table. Theo had suspected I would be asked about this, so he gave me a few camp locations I could give up without much trouble. He promised they would be evacuated and moved to safety before the Imperial army made its move, but it did little to stop the shiver of wariness from running down my spine.

"I know a lot are scattered," I answered truthfully. I had no intentions of lying, at least blatantly, as the gravity of what this pact did was not something I fully understood. Would Ren be able to tell I was lying if I decided to obscure all of them?

My hand moved into the forests between Ullaven and the border with Aulari as my wrist flicked to write a clear X. "This is one of the wolves' main camps." I whispered as an image of helping a small pack of pups learn their first stalking skills passed over my mind. I tried to stop the memory as another hand pressed on my other shoulder, not even having to look to recognize the honey and stone scent.

Jaeden.

"They are the main defense at the border with Aulari and the Cordillera. Their noses are invaluable to help spot approaching forces, though they occasionally leave gaps between patrols." My voice began to break as my heart started to race. "They don't think you'll go over the border and lose half of yourselves to take them out, considering it's a pretty significant camp of at least five hundred. From what I heard, you rarely send more than a hundred soldiers at a time across the border, so they are rather confident in their choices." I took another step away when I heard the sounds of the memory of that stalking lesson, their yips and whines of excitement becoming deafening.

And about two hundred mothers and pups were stationed with them.

Four sets of unfamiliar eyes watched me as I felt tears gather. My gaze quickly focused on the hazel eyes, which watched me with cold interest. "May I please have a moment? I'll be right back. I... I need a moment."

He looked me over with an expression I could not entirely read before giving a slight nod and conversing with the males surrounding the table about their next steps. Peter was scribbling in a notebook, but I could not focus on its contents as I swiftly walked out of the room.

I kept my composure as my walk turned into a slight jog down the hall to my room, but I crumbled against the door as soon as it clicked shut behind me.

I knew this mission was going to be complicated. I knew I would have to give up essential and life-altering information to get them to trust me. I knew that Theo would take care of the puppies and the families that now haunted my mind and get all of them to safety.

Though I did not know that I would be forced into a pact with the prince and that—out of fear of Theo, Amelia, and the little young ones out there—I would have to share more truth than I initially thought. The tears I held back began running down my cheeks as my imagination brought up the resulting scenario as if watching it play out on a stage before me.

A group of imperial guards, mainly of wolf Fae, had been dispatched between the patrols. Some walked in their Fae form, others in their wolves, for the most tactical advantage.

Jaeden led them through the camp, which had mainly been turned into smolders by a preliminary group of scouts that had gained the pack's trust. Bodies, both imperial and rebel, were strewn across the soot-covered grass.

The wolf Fae stopped before the burnt form of a mother huddled over a small child in her arms, screaming so much that her voice had become entirely horse. I could see the shame that flashed over Jaeden's face as he looked away, walking farther to assess the damage.

Theo kept his promise, ensuring almost all the pack had been evacuated. But the loyal, the ones who refused to believe that I would make it and survive the original meeting with the Roamions, those who insisted on protecting the borders, had stayed.

And they paid the price.

My fingers dug into my chest as I bit back a sob, my other hand burying itself in my hair and raking across my scalp.

I always thought my vivid imagination was a gift, especially when I was little. I could make anything up, and it felt *so* real. But as I sat against the door in an unfamiliar place, lost in the thoughts of the unimaginable, I wished I could experience it normally like everyone else. If only I could shut my eyes physically, it would make my mind's eye shut off, too.

If only I were that lucky.

The scene became a constant loop in my imagination as I became numb to the tears and emotions racking through the replaying moment. When I was in Ullaven and would have a fit of overly detailed dreams or nightmares, Theo would leave calming tea at the door to help me recover from however long an episode would take. However, I was no longer there, and there would be no tea or time to sit and recover.

I needed to get up and do *something*, so I looked around the room for something to distract me.

The room was a mess, except for the bed I slept in last night and the sitting chairs Selli and Dityss had cleaned off this morning. Everything else was still covered in blankets to help keep the dust off the furniture, and the hardwood was littered with footprints from visitors this morning. The furniture that had been uncovered looked like it had been here for ages, or at least since the last inhabitant had lived here.

I pulled myself up and off the floor, still holding my arms tightly around my chest as I approached the western wall, where several pieces of large furniture were pressed against the wall. I ran my hand over the blanket of one of the longer pieces, my hand leaving a clean layer of white through the thick layer of dust. Underneath it was a gorgeously ornate dark wood chest that did not look like it had been off the woodcarver's bench for over a minute. I would never have imagined using something so lovely in my lifetime, but here it was in the room that was mine for the foreseeable future.

Along the chest lid were carvings that danced across the wood like a living piece of work. A unicorn ran alongside two dragons through an extensive plain, joy etched into their faces. Though there was no color on the carving, it was not necessary. It was to tell a story of another time when dragons and unicorns lived carefree; the dust covering the room was telling enough of what the royals thought of that concept. My fingers ran over the unicorn as I gave a half-hearted smile.

What a world we've turned into now.

I stood from the wooden chest to look at the taller object alongside it and pulled back the blanket to examine it. The story from the chest continued on its doors, but this continued its telling. The three creatures were still present, with the doors separating them, yet more characters were added to the story. On the left door, the unicorn stood alongside a wolf in the field from the chest. The right door had the two dragons, but instead of being in the field, they stood on the stones of the pathway that led into a large castle. It was a crafted tale of farewells, but from the looks on their faces etched in the wood, I could not see any sadness in it. The only negative emotion I could tell was added after the original craftsman finished their masterpiece, where long claw marks dragged down the unicorn, wolf, and the rest of the plains.

I laid my hand on the claw marks, thinking of how much anguish its owner must have felt when they created this addition. They were much larger than I was, as my hand did not do the size of the destruction justice. It was almost like I could hear the cries of agony that caused this damage to be done. I quickly removed my hand to avoid my imagination, turning it into something to endure even longer.

I shook my head as I turned back towards the door. The sun had moved barely into the beginnings of twilight, which meant I was not gone too long, but I was surprised that no one had come to break down my door for more answers. Though I knew it would only be a matter of time, I cleaned myself up in the bathroom before I unlocked my door and walked back toward the atrium.

The males were still surrounding the table, discussing the beginnings of a plan to deal with that camp I had revealed. My imagination tried to resurface, but I cleared it away with a small smile and a gentle head dip.

"I'm sorry about that outburst, your Highness," I spoke with as clear of a voice as I could muster, too focused on not breaking down again that I missed the chance to call the prince my favored title.

Jaeden, Peter, and Rygur quickly snapped their attention to me and shut their mouths, but the prince was the only one to speak.

"Just call me Ren, please."

The informality caught me off guard as I stood beside the table, looking over the new notes and marks that had been added since I had been gone. They had already started some rather detailed notes on the little I had given them, but I was more intrigued by the prince hunched over those plans. His eyes were pinpointed on a particular spot on the map—as if trying to analyze a note—before he took a deep breath and looked at me.

I had seen anger and so many distressed or upset emotions in those eyes, but the hazel eyes that looked towards me now seemed to crack open a window behind that stone wall.

"All right, Ren."

CHAPTER 8

I spent the next few hours sitting in the atrium with the males as they settled around the table. I was not pressured to give them any more information, but neither was I asked to leave the room, so I hung around to chime in occasionally. Most of the time, I gave snarky comments or said something to purposely irritate Peter, who was trying desperately to get more information on what they could expect and the camp's weak points.

"Willow, it is imperative that I understand where the best place to enter the camp is from. 'Up my ass' is not an answer." Peter growled, but I shrugged from my place in a wooden chair I had pulled up alongside the table a while ago. "So why don't you give me a better answer so we can all go about our business for the rest of the day?"

If they planned to attack sooner rather than later, I could not guarantee that the wolves would be evacuated. I barely knew the camp beyond the things I had shared anyway. Theo had shown me around a couple of times—I even tried to pay attention to the war lessons there—but I was more interested in the carefree play of the pups around me.

"It's a camp surrounded by palisades that only has one way in and one way out, as I've already told you," I grumbled, "If I knew of a backdoor, I would have something more interesting to say." This was true for the most part, as speaking in riddles to see if they were smart enough to get the answer was one of my favorite games to play. Especially here, I could hear the cogs turning in their minds and the high-fives shared between Rygur and Peter when they figured one out.

Peter groaned and ran a hand across his face, holding his jaw and rubbing it as he studied me. In response, I stuck my tongue out, which only made him groan again and throw his notebook on the table.

"I give up. I'm hungry, so I'm going to find some food." Peter stood with a huff, waving his hand in farewell as he moved through the atrium to the hallway. His steps were heavy with frustration, but his well-maintained form moved as smoothly as a lion stalking the savannah, similar to how Theo crept around the house.

"Pete has the right idea." Jaeden stretched from where he had sat on a nearby couch, starting to doze off when he suddenly spoke and stood. He looked like he could use a long nap in the sun, but the sun had long disappeared beyond the mountains in the distance, relinquishing only the last rays of daylight to thin around the palace. "I'll be heading out after dinner, so don't wait for me at Dryaden's." He added in farewell as he marched down the hall after Pete.

Then it was just me, the prince, and Rygur.

Rygur was still mumbling about some plan, taking a few extra notes here and there, seeming utterly disinterested in the world around him except for the scattered parchment on the table. Rendros had moved over to the large exits of the atrium a while ago, watching the sunset as if he were not planning to attack innocents.

It was the first time I saw Rendros seemingly lost in thought, giving me a moment to look at him—not as a prince, my prison and captor, or someone I was tasked to kill.

He was tall and presumably had a regular workout routine, showcased by how his muscles filled out his clothes pleasantly. His arms and upper body were his most prominent focus, considering the snug fit of his shirt. It was not an awful sight. If I were in any other situation, I would want to find out how intense his workout routines were from the evidence under the fabric.

His face was just as good-looking as his body, if not more so. His expression was calm and thoughtful, contemplating something causing a rather distracting discussion in his brain. I could see his eyes flicker back and forth over something in the distance, but I was more interested in examining those hazel eyes. I had seen a lot of unique looks in my life, but nothing was quite like that hazel as the brown clashed with green and blue in a gorgeous mixture of color. Such color seemed to be hypnotizing considering the rigid way he held himself physically—a bright pop of softness in a steel wall. Not to mention when the storms would mix with those gorgeous colors and create a beautiful landscape in those deep pools...

"Is something interesting, Wildie?"

Rendros' voice pulled me out of my stupor, shaking my head rapidly in response. "Just inspecting how you hold so much bullheadedness in that frame of yours. Did it come from your father?" I hid my embarrassment with a coy smile as his brows knitted in irritation from my deflection.

"I am nothing like either of my parents." His hands gripped his forearms tighter in his pose at the comment, causing a small surge of confidence to wash over me. I moved to the other side of the doorway to lean on the stone, looking out to the forest from the castle's side.

"Surely not—you only fight their battles for them and listen to daddy's commands to shack up with an ex-rebel magically." I shrugged, watching the outside world succumb to night. With no storm clouds in sight, it was a gorgeous view as the stars cascaded across the early night sky—one that took your breath away.

"I am a prince and the general of the Imperial Forces." He growled, his gaze not leaving me as I moved to lean on the opposite side of the archway. "If I had told him no, he would have killed you on the spot instead of taking your information at all."

The thought had crossed my mind, but I tried to suppress it whenever it surfaced. "I imagine it would have been easier on you that way." My eyes moved from the landscape to his gaze. A muscle tightened in his jaw as he slowly looked me up and down before he turned back to the landscape in front of us.

"Yes, in most ways." He said while the green and blue of his eyes mingled together as some soft emotion passed along them. "Not in others."

"Because I can give you good information on the rebel movements in the south?"

He was silent for a second longer before pressing off the wall and moving closer to me. His presence was imposing and powerful but almost gentle now as he approached. My breathing hitched as I looked up at him, our eyes meeting as he seemingly tried to search through the depths of mine. He almost seemed to want to say something else but shook his head and turned to the plains outside.

"Yeah, because of that." He murmured, running his hand through his hair that barely fell over the top of his fingers. His face was shadowed by the darkening evening, but I could see him glance back at me as he moved into the field. "Stay in your room or the wing tonight, Wildie. Rygur will be here a little longer to help close everything up before he goes out with Peter for the night."

"Wow, you're leaving me alone in the castle with more than several opportunities to escape? You're turning very trusting on me, your

Highass." I could not help but smile, surprised by the look I got from the prince, which was a mixture of a pointed look and quiet amusement.

"The castle has guards, the atrium will be locked, and as far as I know, unicorns do not grow wings." I caught his lips turning up in the moonlight, suddenly causing my heart to forget how to beat in an easy rhythm. "So, I *trust* my knowledge in your inability to escape."

I went to rebuke the insult, to say something about how he does not know how smart I am, but the space around the entrance of the atrium was engulfed in a flash of blue. Where Ren had been standing was the immense shadow of a night black dragon with scars that traveled down through his scales like white bolts of light in a sea of darkness. I could not help but be in awe of the beast before me, those hazel eyes burning brighter as they looked up at the stars.

"Have fun, Ren," I responded instead, catching myself off guard with the softness of my usually sharp tongue. I was unsure why I wished my mortal enemy a good flight, but his wings spread far beyond the door's opening as he launched himself into the air with a mighty *woosh* of downward force. A warm, tingling feeling spread across my back as I watched him fly off, the massive dragon outline becoming nothing but a speck in the distance before disappearing amongst the stars.

"He's not that bad of a guy. A hard ass for sure, but he's a softie deep under there." Rygur's voice, soft but still settled with an assurance of strength, sounded behind me, but my eyes did not leave the darkened skyline. The silence in the successive few beats was only interrupted by large doors being pulled shut, squealing against age-old hinges, and ending with a giant *thud*. The sound echoed throughout the room, only escaping when it reached the open doors I leaned against and pulled me out of my trance.

Rygur came to stand alongside me to look up into the night, tracing the path where Rendros had disappeared into the sky. He had several pieces of parchment tucked under his arm with a book and a quill, and his stance had become relatively relaxed despite standing next to a prisoner of the crown.

"Not afraid of me bolting before you shut the door?" I pulled my lips into a teasing smirk, and the rumble of easy laughter from Rygur made my smirk turn into a full smile. "I can lose you in the forest like I did this morning, especially with Jae gone and Pete distracted with food..."

"I think if you were going to, you would have run off already." He smiled back at me, the silver flecks in his eyes sparkling in the firelight. "But do you want to know why I don't think you will?" My curiosity peaked, so I raised an eyebrow and crossed my arms over my chest, fully turning to him.

"One, you've never lived this well before, even with the caveat that you are a prisoner. Two, you know that however far you run, the Imperial Forces will hunt you down to kill you, and the forests only go on for so long before the open fields of Aulari expose you." His gaze scoured down every inch of me while he spoke as if assessing who I was and what I was thinking. I could not help but pull my arms a little closer to my chest to try to fight the feeling of being stripped mentally naked under that knowing stare. "Three, I think you know that pact you made is much more than just ink on your back and a promise to keep the prince safe. And you're afraid of what that means."

I had not voiced my fear about the pact or what I felt was more than just a promise to keep someone safe, but the way Rygur laid it out in the open made me avert my gaze to the floor. I could sense the confidence that he guessed right spill from him as I shook my head, the memory of the prince's departure resurfacing.

"You and all the males think I'm just a little mare afraid of the predators surrounding her." I brought my eyes to him to hold the stare firmly, pouring my conviction into my words. "I may not have claws or teeth built for tearing flesh apart. I may not have your brute strength or power either."

I smiled again, running my tongue over my teeth in threat and promise. The display showed the sharpened canines I spent every night for the last ten years sharpening, ensuring they were enough to tear through flesh. Surprise and something else ran through his eyes as he watched, his gaze lingering on my teeth. Magic surged behind me as I felt my eyes light with its strength, empowering me in that moment.

"But that does not mean I have suffocated in my circumstances. I merely adapted to them."

I held Rygur's stare for a few breaths longer before I stalked out of the room, listening to my steady and confident footsteps echo as I entered the hallway and exited the atrium.

CHAPTER 9

My room was pleasantly warm as I settled in for the night. I dressed in some warm sleepwear Sellias had left this morning, which was not what I usually wore, but the fluffy cotton and soft fabric were irresistible.

It was a two-piece set comprised of a long-sleeved button-up shirt and loose pants that were majorly black, but the buttons and hems were trimmed gold. I could only imagine how expensive it was as I examined myself in the mirror, pleased with how it fell amongst my curves and was comfortable against my sensitive skin. I felt...*pretty,* even in what would be considered comfort clothing. My smile reflected in the mirror as I let my hair fall around my face and halfway down my back in my favored style, framing my face with a nice contrast against the darkness of the outfit.

Peter had knocked on my door about an hour earlier to let me know he was heading out with Rygur into town, alongside a reminder that I was to stay within my quarters for the evening. I had been reading a book that I had found packed in between some of the clothes Selli left for me and waved him off with little interest beyond recognition that I had heard him. I was not a child needing a constant reminder of the rules, especially when the surrounding stone walls did the job well enough.

A usual free-roaming mare stuck within unbreakable walls could never forget how trapped she was, so I tried to drown myself in the book's pages.

It was some book about a human and a Fae chained to one another by their mate bond, which the Fae fought against wildly, refusing to believe that a human was their fated love. I made it through about a hundred pages before I was irritated with their stupid arguments surrounding misunderstanding. I needed a break lest I throw the book into a drawer, never to be finished.

I propped a loose thread between the pages in place of a bookmark, leaving the frustrating pages to examine the wall of windows overlooking the now-dark garden. It was full of decaying plants that spiraled up the stone walls like skeletal structures, desperate to find a way out of their seamless cage, and husks of what must have been bountiful rose bushes were now left to nothing but thorny tendrils. There was not a drop of color in the dilapidated space, with only the simple light of the moon illuminating the tragic reality of this poor garden.

I decided to open the door to go outside to look closer at the garden, looking over each of the wilted plants as my lips pressed together in a thin line. I had never been the best with plants, but I had helped Amelia with her garden several times over the years, so I had some hope I could do better than whatever the world had done to this garden.

I crouched beside a small patch of what was once a flower bed beside the window of my room, lifting a sad stalk that had fallen across the stones when it lost its strength to stay upright. It had no weight in my hand as I carefully examined it, afraid that a too-heavy exhalation would turn it into dust.

"You kind of remind me of myself, little guy," I murmured to the withered plant, bringing my other hand to cover the plant as I began to reach for the links and reigns of my magic, "Let's see if I can help you."

Whenever I took the journey into myself to reach my magic in its purest form, it was like entering an expansive library where there were only a few books I could get to. I would walk down the aisles of books, some rows blocked off by impassable rope while others were open to browsing, granting me the ability to use the magic listed in the book's pages. Each bookcase was built in gorgeous dark wood that had seen the chips and weather of age and use, but the slight imperfections seemed intentional, with the light and comfort of the space bouncing off the crevices, making them appear almost living.

The library was usually quiet beyond the crackling of the firelight whenever I visited; however, the usual silence was missing. There was a gentle *thrum* pulsing through the room in a steady heartbeat rhythm, but it also swayed as if it were a mother gently calling her babe to come home. It was an unusual event I had never experienced before; the steady beat caused my hair to stand on end as I cautiously followed it to a marble hall at the end of the bookshelves.

This library had only four halls I never visited or cared about after discovering I could not enter them, but this encounter was the first time I had ever been drawn to one. They were usually permanently shut off from access; one night of no sleep had led me to spend hours trying to figure out what might be hiding behind each door, listening and sniffing around the cracks before leaving an imaginary plaque above each door for what I thought hid behind them. I was standing at the entrance to the Nature Wing, its typically sealed iron door left barely ajar, and a whisper of the mother's song alongside the scent of fresh rain and cedar trailed from behind it.

It made sense that this wing called to me since I was trying to heal a plant, but I was not supposed to *see* into it, let alone open the door. Nature magic had been given to the dragons thousands of years ago, and no one else could call upon it. Everyone could reach small amounts of fire, water, earth, and air magic to help with everyday tasks. But nature magic... This was not something I was supposed to be able to access.

I reached out to the iron door, the cool metal welcome against my warm palms. If I had only taken a magic molecule to help bring this plant back, surely no one would have noticed that a non-dragon had used some, right?

The door opened with a creak that announced its lack of use before I entered the unknown.

I had expected to see more shelves of books interspersed with plants and maybe vines lining the floors with artificial sunlight beaming through the roof, but the room was not an expansion of my library. It was an expansive yet empty room, with only a piano, violin, and cello decorating it. Maybe once books had been here, as there were large shelves embedded in the walls, but they had long since been emptied. There was a wall of windows that instead allowed the dim lighting of the moon to filter silver strands of light through the jigsaw glass that created several shapes of random order, all seemingly pointing to the collection of instruments in the center of the room.

My steps echoed in the emptiness of the space as I wandered over and ran my finger across the dust-lined shelves. There was no trace of magic under my fingers as I did so, but the steady hum of the room told me it was here, causing my attention to turn back to the glistening silver instruments in the middle.

I had not played an instrument in over ten years—the last time my father was still alive. I could remember the days pouring over sheet music and singing with the instruments as I played tunes for him.

Most were joyful.

The last time I picked up one was not.

Each instrument had a pull to it, not only from magic but also from the emotion that seemed to live in each inanimate object. The piano sang to me in a melancholy tune, a pensive play across the keys that threatened to pull my heart in two. The cello played only in lower registers and with a sharp tempo as if creating a barrier that promised harm to those who got too close. Neither instrument felt like the song calling me from the library, as both were too harsh and sharp for the emotion that seemed to brush against my soul.

I turned to the last instrument, my heart slowing and my breath hitching as I listened.

The violin played a song I had not heard since I was a filly. The female voice was a muffled melody above the gorgeous upswings in tempo and notes, drawing me closer to it. It was joy and songs of a better time, a peaceful time before I became a pawn in a vicious game.

It was calling me to play it, and I did not intend to ignore its hypnotic call.

My hand reached for the violin, the thrums of magic cascading over my body and soul as a beautiful tune of fantasy and joy danced up my arm. As I picked up the bow, I felt like I was standing in my living room for the first time, ready to play for my father and show him what I learned. To show him I still remembered the lullaby he had sung to me every night since my mother left.

I pulled the bow lightly across the strings, and a gorgeous drone of a higher note in perfect tune replied. My senses opened as I took a deep breath while the revitalizing magic washed over me. Old habits and muscle memory took over as I moved my fingers over the strings and the bow back and forth, the old tune coming out as beautifully as I had ever practiced. It was a song about love and its never-ending beauty, even when fate worked against it. It danced elegantly between slow paces when everything seemed like it was falling apart and high bravado tones when everything was most beautiful.

I could feel the tears falling down my face as I played, but I did not stop.

I *could not* stop.

Phantom instruments picked up the tune behind me to echo and caress the song into a deeper submergence of emotion. My voice joined in with beautiful intonation as I began to sing the song's ending, where fate had sent the mates apart but left them with one final gift of their love forever of a little girl who was their pride and joy, blessed under a willow tree.

The song ended with one final low note from the cello, and I placed the violin back in its stand, prying my fingers from the neck. I did not want to let this feeling go, that joy, that unrequited memory of a time long since passed. Flowers danced along my fingers in a soft farewell from the instrument, my eyes following the floating petals to look at the long wall of jigsaw glass windows. I was covered in flowers and foliage, a crown of dandelions sitting atop my head, and a dress of willow cascading past my torso and hips. The gold in my eyes shimmered like liquid, a bright color returning to the blue I had not seen since my father got ill all those years ago. Tears stained my cheeks as I looked at myself in the window, a ghostly silhouette forming behind me, its warmness and familiarity bringing more tears to my eyes.

"Father?" My words caught in a choked whisper as I turned around, but the man standing behind me was not the male who had raised me.

Prince Rendros was staring at me with admiration and surprise, extending his hand gently toward me as if I were a startled doe.

I stepped back straight into the piano, its lip biting into my lower back. My breathing came in rushed inhales as my lungs struggled to find enough air in the space. Did I leave my room on accident, imagining I had reached into my magic to distract me from doing something I was not supposed to do? Had I somehow come across a room I was not supposed to find?

"I-I'm sorry, I—" I stumbled across my own words. His advance stopped as his head turned to the side while he looked me up and down, his eyes softening as they discovered the tear stains on my cheeks.

"What are you doing here?" His voice was as clear as if I was standing before him, and I must have been. I must have left my room in a trance or done something stupid to end up here, and I knew I needed to go.

"Please forgive me for intruding your Highness. I don't know how I got here; I thought I was... I don't know. I'll return to my quarters." I quickly rushed out, wiping off all the foliage that had grown in place of a dress. I ran with my eyes closed as I bumped into all sorts of things on my way out, fueled by pure fear and blind memory to find my way back to my quarters.

I was in the garden outside my room when I opened my eyes. I was kneeling before the flowerbed, a light dusting of mist brushing over my skin, something that could have only lingered if I had never moved from the spot. I glanced at my chest and my arms in surprise and confusion, but my attention was glued to my hands.

They were still holding the small flower, now a gorgeous lily.

CHAPTER 10

The next few days passed with the same routine as the first did, if not a bit more extensive and demanding of details about the camps and the Southern Rebellion's numbers. Rendros had allowed Rygur to handle my outdoor exercise, any interest with me only for the information I could provide. The only time I saw him was when he stood at the table in the center of the atrium, pointing at different camps I had provided information for and asking for more elements I had skirted around in prior conversations.

It was becoming an aggressive barrage of interrogations from them since I had shown Rygur my teeth, and my confidence in the daring act was shaken with every prying question.

For today, however, I was ceremoniously graced with the day to myself when the prince and his groupies had to go off to a meeting with the Imperial Captain in the north. I had not been able to clean or get a whole night's sleep since that night in the instrument room, making today the perfect time to do just that.

Or so I thought until I was interrupted midday by a knock at the door.

I was wearing a simple pair of leggings and a solid color tank top that I had found in my new wardrobe with my hair tied back in a ponytail. There were better ways to greet visitors, but being in a royal palace as a prisoner, I did not have the comfort of telling whoever it was on the other side of the door to wait.

"Coming!" I called out to the visitors as I put a broom beside the doorframe, barely opening the door before the Roamion twins nearly trampled me.

"Willow! Oh, my stars, I'm so sorry it took us so long to stop by! We intended to come to help you clean the day after we last spoke, but then Ren had that fit when you ran off. Mother called us for some royal duties and—" Selli's words tumbled out of her mouth faster than I could comprehend them while Dityss squeezed her sister's shoulder and pushed past her into the room. Her long black hair was braided behind her shoulders, shaking this way and that as she continued to ramble about meetings and other distractions.

"Several things popped up for all of us, and we could not spare the time to visit." The older twin interrupted her sister, her reading glasses nestled comfortably on the bridge of her nose with her silky black hair tied back into a loose bun.

Sellias's bright purple eyes were apologetic as she looked at me after the interruption before I gave her a tired smile and invited her in after Dityss.

I quietly watched them start to examine the room, fingers running over dust-covered surfaces I had not gotten to yet and their shudders in response to the thick layers of dirt and time that cascaded over them. A part of me felt ashamed that the room was still in such a state, but I quickly reminded myself that I had been a workhorse of information for the prince and his war council with little time to do much else.

"Prince Rendros had a fit when I ran off that day?" I asked, moving from the doorway to an armchair I had finished cleaning moments before. It was awkward to try and start a casual conversation with royalty, but the silence was worse.

Selli spun around to me dumbfounded; her jaw slacked open. "Oh *yes*, I'm surprised you didn't hear about it! He was so angry we could hear his screams and roars from our wings! We quickly rushed down there to find out what he was raving about. By the time we made it into his atrium, he was about ready to strangle Rygur, who was desperately trying to calm him down, poor male. He kept screaming about how foolish you were, running into the forests like that—"

Dityss interrupted her sister's ramblings with a raise of her hand, her violet eyes silently reminding her Sellias to take a breath. How she conveyed that with nothing more than a look was fascinating, my mind racing with how close the twin princesses were.

"Diti was quick to pull Ren off Rygur, but where she expected a fight, there was very little resistance to pull him off. He listened to Diti for a while but seemed so...*out* of it." Selli unconsciously rubbed the markings on her wrist as her eyes scanned the floor, "He is usually so confident and skilled in handling a situation gone awry, especially when Jae, Pete, and Rygur are there to back him up. But the look in his eyes... I had never seen him so genuinely afraid of something."

The response I saw from him that day was not fear or worry, but my curiosity reminded me of how Jae had constantly watched our surroundings when we returned to the castle. He had watched the forest as if it might wake up and swallow him whole, where I had found nothing wrong with it beyond being a thickly forested wood.

"Why have such a response to a forest? Does something live in there?" I asked as I moved to a side table beside the armchair and removed a dusty old blanket. Dust particles scattered across the air as I resumed cleaning the space to look as if my curiosity was not through the roof. Dityss and Selli began doing the same, taking some cleaning supplies out of a basket and running rags down some of the surfaces I had uncovered.

"As far as we know, no," Dityss responded as she cleaned off the trunk and wardrobe set, her hands slowly moving over the intricate markings. "Those woods are part of Mytha's orchards—a plethora of trees that constantly seem to be in season—where we often host many of our balls and gatherings with neighboring provinces." I began to fold the fabric of the side table I had just uncovered, letting my imagination bring me back to the forest. The grass had been a bright and healthy green, but the trees were...odd. Unhealthy. They still stood as if they were living with bushes of leaves amongst their branches. However, nearly all of their color was drained to dull greys and browns.

"I am sure you noticed that the trees there are decaying or somehow ill." Dityss continued, running a finger over the claw marks on the wardrobe as she examined it. "The best herbalists, botanists, and arborists have been brought in from all over Aistris, but they cannot find what is happening to that section of the orchard. We worry that if they are unsuccessful in finding a cause, it may soon spread to the healthy and flourishing trees. The mysterious illness has already taken several acres of the once beautiful flora from where it used to connect to our brother's atrium."

I could imagine how spectacular of a sight that must have been: hundreds of rows of healthy trees sprouting flowers and fruits in a contrast of beautiful color against the simple rolling fields that run out from the atrium. Sunlight beaming rays of warmth and comfort as the wind gently blew leaves from the branches, bringing the sweet smell of spring.

A peaceful place of eternity.

"That's tragic," I sighed as I ran my hands over a newly folded dust cover before placing it in a pile with the other ones that had already been removed from the furniture. "I bet it was beautiful while it stood."

"It was." Selli sighed, bringing a wet rag down the windows that opened into the depressing garden I had spent several hours in over the last few days. I had been unable to resurrect any other plants in my attempts to do so without magic, but the lily stood firm amongst its dying brethren—a bright pop of purple and white against a sea of muted greys. It was a single symbol of growth from my efforts, but I doubted I could stop the rest of the garden from trudging toward its tragic fate.

I had refused to enter the bright marble halls of my imaginary library again, afraid the temptation of what hid behind the Nature Wing's door would overwhelm me.

Silence blanketed the room for a few minutes as each of us continued to clean, the room quickly regaining its color as cleanliness brought the room from a forgotten space to a lived-in one. The beautiful dark wood furniture pieces matched in a gorgeous set throughout the entire room, though only the wardrobe and trunk had any intricate etchings of a story long forgotten. The pale green walls tied the dark wood furniture into a tale of spring indoors, creating a comfortable balance between light and dark coloring. The light that shimmered through the garden windows allowed the space to brighten further, and the room felt like...home.

My admiration of the room was paused as I watched Selli turn to Dityss, her hands tightly clasped together as she gave the most irresistible pout face that I had ever seen—which was impressive, considering I had been around puppies asking for sweets their mothers had said no to.

"Must you always turn to such diabolical methods?" Dityss chuckled, giving in to the silent plea. She wiped off the last of the dust from the desk beside the garden before taking a seat in its simple dark oak chair, her eyes sparkling with amusement. "You may ask."

Selli quickly threw down her rag as if it were on fire, moving toward me in some strange mix of a skip and a run. Her eyes were bright with excitement and anticipation by whatever she wanted to ask me, but I was unsure whether that was a good or bad sign.

"You *have* to join us for the Fall Feasts!" She proclaimed excitedly, her voice so bright that I nearly forgot that she was a princess of the highest royal family in Aistris. "I know it's the last minute, and we *were* going to invite you earlier, but I didn't want to send you a letter to invite you. It's taking place in the gardens tonight, and you won't have to attend like you're a prisoner so that you can enjoy yourself!"

"The Fall Feasts?" I murmured, half to myself as I tried to remember what sort of holiday or event would be happening this time of year. It was mid-Witril, which meant… "Wait, you mean the Wild Feasts?"

"I imagine the untamed still celebrate the event traditionally. However, we no longer call it nor celebrate it as the old ways do. It would cause an uproar in royal courts should something untoward happen to anyone, so we changed it to something more civil to allow the celebration to continue within Aistris." Dityss clarified, "So you will not have to worry about becoming someone's dinner tonight."

My eyes shifted between the twins as hesitation seized my chest at the idea of a 'civil' celebration. Though the lack of fear would be nice, it felt wrong not to celebrate as the Wild Goddess had intended. "I don't know. I've never celebrated the feasts without shifting," I admitted, "How do you celebrate Winulla if you don't partake in the gift she gave us?"

Selli seemed confused by the question, tilting her head to the side as she turned to Dityss, her braid bouncing over her shoulder. It was apparent she was unaware that there was another way to celebrate the feasts, the question plain on her face. Dityss let out a gentle sigh, but her voice was filled with a warm explanation of the celebration's history.

"Before Akis' Ascension, when most of the world was still wild, Winulla, Goddess of the Wilds and of Fall, was the most powerful deity thanks to her follower's dedication. She was—and still is—worshipped every year on the 22nd of Witril," Dityss explained, pulling a spark of power from her hand, creating a magical shadow puppet to tell the story on the ceiling, her magic bouncing around and creating several little figures and small pieces of scenery. "All members of a pack or a township would come together to partake in large feasts that celebrate the successful harvest of that year's crop and to dance under the blessing of their Wild mother."

"Then it's not different from how we celebrate now." Sellias interrupted, watching the figures dance around bonfires and feasting upon delicious plates of assorted meals. Dityss did not stop her retelling to answer Selli's question as the image on the ceiling began to flare in various colors from the positions of the magic-made figures.

"After the feasts concluded and the sun fell over the horizon, each of the Fae would let their wild sides free. Transforming into lions, wolves, dragons, unicorns, and everything in between." Each beast began appearing on the projection, and though they looked tamed, each predator's posture was stiff and sharply angled, their shadowed snouts pulling back to show their teeth. "The instinct of predator and prey would be willingly given back to Winulla, and chaos would reign for a single night of the year as the feral feast began."

The unicorns and other prey beasts of the projected images ran into the nearby forests, where the predators quickly pursued them before turning into a burst of magic mist as Dityss recalled her magic. "Most prey would survive since Winulla granted enough control to the Fae's mind to understand that this was a blessing and a celebratory game. But some predators would give too much to their beasts and would tragically take the lives of those who could not depict play from reality."

My gaze drifted to my hands, revisiting the exhilarating memories of unstoppable freedom as my mare ran through the most untamed parts of the Ullaven forests.

Even though I had forgotten that tonight was the night of the purest freedom, my mare was pacing impatiently as if awaiting the shift in which she got to run free.

"That is barbaric." Selli finally said, her voice quiet as her eyes fixed on me. "You went through these things?"

"Every year, exactly as Dityss told it." I smiled a bit, remembering the time Theo had let his lion take so much of his mind that the pride Theo often kept in check left him trapped at the bottom of a small canyon with a broken ankle. "Though it wasn't always so brutal. If someone did end up being the reason for a loss of life, they were usually exiled."

I left out the part that those who were the causes of multiple deaths were often hanged publicly for their crimes for fear that my people would be called barbaric again.

Sellias barely paid attention to my addition to the conversation beyond a slight nod, excitement returning to her gaze. "Well, like Dityss said, we just celebrate the fun parts with dancing and feasts. Feral shifting like that isn't allowed on the night of the Fall Feasts." Sellias said with some semblance of pride, though it made my heart ache at the idea of being unable to shift tonight. "So, you'll come?"

I had no plan on doing anything tonight besides reading the book that I was now getting close to finishing. Even if I had been reminded it was the Wild Feasts and there was no ball happening tonight, it was unlikely I would be in search of company anyway. "I'll be out of place; this sounds more like a royal extravaganza than something I would participate in, so I'm afraid I'll have to pass this time."

"Nonsense! You'll be our royal guest!" Sellias pleaded, grabbing my hands and pulling them toward her chest. "We can leave right away to our wing, where the tailor is already waiting! I can get you all dressed up, and with the masks, no one will even know who you are." The smile on her face was genuine; the irresistible pleading puppy eyes now turned on me. "Please?"

I kept my eyes level with Selli's. I was never a fan of large crowds or fancy parties, but there was something about how Sellias looked at me with excitement in her eyes or how Dityss seemed at peace with the situation. Maybe it was because I knew that the males were all gone for the day anyway that I decided.

"You *do* use unfair methods, Selli." I gave a slight smile, "But call me Lo, all right? If we forget that we are prisoners and royalty tonight, I'd like to at least attend as friends."

Her smile and joy at my acceptance could have blinded me, and I realized I was unsure what I had gotten myself into.

CHAPTER 11

I never questioned what it was like to be a princess, nor did I have any interest in it. All the young females had screamed and squealed about it when we were young kids, but I was always more interested in practicing my instruments or helping in the garden. It was never a dream of mine to be an actual princess, so I was never all that interested in the gilded amenities that came with such a title.

Even as I stood in a princess's dressing room with a flock of females examining each nook and cranny of my figure, I would have much preferred to be in the garden's dirt.

I was situated on the middle of a marble pedestal in the center of what was *only* their dressing room as a group of three females fussed over my body with lines of measuring types and color swatches. As soon as I arrived in the room, I was stripped of my leggings and tank top and placed on the pedestal like a dress-up doll awaiting her outfit change. The three females continued to speak nonsense about color theory or skin contrast.

The two princesses stood just beyond the maid's space, Sellias watching every movement and color comparison with calculating eyes. Dityss seemed less than interested as she seemed to be marking something in her current read, though she occasionally glanced over the pages to see the progress.

What I would give to change places with the studious princess.

"I think she would look lovely in something form-fitting but let it fall off the shoulders." Selli thought aloud, her finger tapping on her chin, "Maybe make it dark blue... with a sequin top with flowing sleeves and a sweep train over her back. Don't forget a leg slit, too. All of that running she does has done wonders for their sleek beauty, so they should be shown off." She nodded as her hands went up to form a square over her eyes, humming as she looked over my stiff form in calculating interest.

As I watched Selli look over the different colors of fabric that were held against my skin, I realized she had a natural eye for fashion. Her attention was well-placed, and her ideas were beautifully put together. If I had not known any better, I would have thought she was the head designer of a boutique. I had no eye for clothing detail and would have happily worn my workout gear to the ball if I was allowed to, but knowing Sellias, I might have made her faint from the admission.

The main seamstress's—a human woman likely in her forties—voice interrupted my thoughts as she asked the princess if they had any ideas for my hair or jewelry to compliment the dress, droning out the debate when it lasted longer than a simple 'yes' or 'no' answer.

I allowed my eyes to wander along the expanse of the living chamber. While I thought my room was pristine and expensive now that it had been cleaned up and taken care of, there was no comparison with this one. There were floor-to-ceiling windows all around that were separated by large shelves of dresses, shoes, and other beauty garments, with the floor made of a gorgeous granite that had gold striking through the veins of grey and silver. Each handle and mirror were lined with genuine gold and gems, their colors and sparkling beauty only enhanced by the sunlight that poured in from the large windows—a fitting room perfectly detailed and made for a royal princess.

Most females I grew up with would kill to be in my spot, but I felt utterly displaced.

"What do you think of this fabric, my lady?" One of the Fae maids had brought out a gorgeous mirage blue fabric that seemed to redirect the room's brightness into a cool reprieve from it, like finding a shady spot underneath an oak on a hot day. I was enamored with the way it moved in the autumn breeze as the chill circled the room from an open window, hidden reflective sparkles of silver catching in the light from the movement.

"It's perfect." Selli's voice pulled me out of my trance as my gaze returned to her, a wry smile on her face as the maid nodded.

The human and Fae group of seamstresses gathered their supplies before disappearing into a side door connected to the dressing room between a couple of the closets. I could hear them pushing aside different tools and supplies when the door opened again as the human woman dipped her head respectfully. "We will have it ready in a little over an hour alongside her mask, Your Highness. Please excuse us."

Dityss gave a dip of her head in thanks before the woman gently shut the door behind her, but Sellias was too busy beaming at me with far too much excitement.

"Oh, Lo, you are just going to be breathtaking!" She squealed, walking towards a couple of mannequins dressed in two phenomenal outfits, pulling up the long train of the orange dress littered with flowers and fall leaves. "I might have outdone myself with yours, but you may very well take the breath of every male there tonight instead of me." She pouted, though her eyes sparked with mischief when she side-eyed me.

"I don't think that will be a problem, Selli. That dress, in combination with your stunning looks, will likely be the death of the males you say no to." I returned with a teasing smile, the flattery causing Selli's face to brighten as red as a pepper. A soft giggle escaped my lips as my gaze lingered on the door where the sewists had gone through to work, a soft sigh finishing the laughter. "I don't know how I'll be able to pay you or properly thank you for all of this."

"That will not be needed," Dityss commented, a soft smile on her face, though it seemed to be tinged with sadness. Before I could ask or investigate why, the shadow disappeared as it formed into a more genuine, teasing smile. "As long as you enjoy your time and maybe dance with a few males, that will be enough for us."

"I think I might be able to do that."

"Good. For now, I will be leaving you both to play dress up while I take care of some research before I am also forced to join the festivities. Good luck, Willow." Dityss dipped her head in farewell to both of us before exiting the room.

Selli gave her sister a small wave and a grin on her face as she walked over to me with a black robe with gold trim in her hands. "As for you, you will sit in that chair over there and let me make you beautiful."

I took the robe and covered myself, sinking into the warmth of the fabric as I walked over to a desk surrounded by firelight and headed by a mirror while Selli turned the seat toward me.

"This is a very nice, albeit fancy, setup, Selli," I commented as I sat down, the chair swiveling to face more toward the mirror. The lack of sleep had left some bags under my eyes, but the light that burned in them had been the brightest since I left Ullaven. My hair cascaded down my back in small waves as Selli began to comb through the strands, humming softly.

"Thank you. Sometimes, I wish this was all I had to do." Her voice carried an undertone of regret when she spoke, her nails running through my scalp as she pulled more strands out to brush through. "To run a little boutique, sell my dresses, and make people feel special. It would be a dream."

"Then why don't you? If you're stuck in the kingdom all of the time anyways, why not build a little boutique to run when you don't have to dance at balls or entertain visiting royalty?" I asked, trying to meet her eyes in the mirror, but she kept her focus on my hair as she parted it.

"It would mean I'd have to mingle with commoners, which is strictly forbidden." She sighed with a bite at the end of her sentence. "If my mother would allow it, I would do it in a heartbeat."

I watched her pull my hair into separate strands, then grab a small piece of metal that had been fashioned into a rod of sorts with another metal piece attached to it to create a kind of clip. The metal warmed under her palm, and I felt the gentle heat radiate toward my scalp as she rolled some of my hair in the gadget.

"That doesn't seem like a bad thing—to talk and be around your subjects. Why would your mother forbid such a thing?" I snorted, once again perplexed by the reasonings of a queen who would keep her daughters like prisoners. "I would love to speak to someone in power in a comfortable setting where I felt like I was talking to another person instead of royalty."

"She says it is unnecessary because I'm not the Crown Princess." Her voice quieted as she gently pulled back on the metal, allowing a perfectly formed curl to bounce in its absence. A marvel of invention, one that I was inclined to believe Selli had built herself. "I must stay as a pillar of beauty and strength of the royal family, even though I'm third in line." Her voice quieted to the point that I almost missed what she said. "A bonus spare."

My eyes widened in pain for the female before me, my eyes stinging as I reigned in the tears that threatened to fall for her. I turned to face her as she finished the next curl, her movements stopping to meet my gaze finally. "That's complete shit, Selli. You are *not* a spare." My hands balled into fists as I turned back around in my chair, continuing to hold her wide-eyed stare in the reflection. "You are a Fae with a heart of pure gold who should be allowed to do whatever the hell you want and follow your dreams. Not think of yourself as just an *extra* against your siblings." Silver began to line her eyes as she took in my words, a sigh escaping my lips as I told her, "Don't ever call yourself a spare again, Selli. Please."

Sellias pulled her gaze back down to my hair, continuing with the meticulous repetition of curling my long hair in layers as she wiped her eyes with her free hand. She cleared her throat, a tentative smile returning to her face. "Are you looking forward at least a little bit to experiencing the ball tonight?"

"I'm not used to something so fancy, but I would be lying if I said I wasn't a little excited. Maybe I'll meet some handsome male that will sweep me off my feet." I smiled playfully as I lifted my arms to sarcastically fan my face, watching the joy return to her purple eyes. "Though I don't think we'd make it very far, considering I've got a rather close contract of sorts with the prince."

"Who knows, maybe you'll find someone within the castle, and you won't have to worry about that." She teased, sticking her tongue out as she began to finish the last few curls. "We have quite a few handsome males here, the best looking of them you see daily." She finished up the previous curl and fluffed my hair together seamlessly; my look elevated far beyond anything I had thought it could be, even though all she did was my hair. The light brown mixed seamlessly with the tips of the cream, creating a soft look that perfectly framed my face, the curls loose enough that they did not get stuck on each other as they moved with my head.

"They are all good-looking, but I don't think any are quite my type. Though I wouldn't mind getting to know them better." Rendros' face flashed in my memory as I began to think of my type, but I quickly rushed to shake the image out of my head. He was usually my type, with short hair and an air of power around him; however, he was my enemy— a general who had killed who knows how many innocents under the lie that they were dangerous rebels. "Jaeden and Rygur, I like to be around. Peter is decent looking, but I think he reminds me too much of my brother, so it is an instant turn-off."

Shit.

"Your brother?" Selli questioned, innocent curiosity lining her words. "I thought you were a single child?"

"Adoptive brother. His mother raised him around me when we were brought over the borders, and we became close." I quickly explained, trying not to tie my words into too big of a knot. "His name is Theo."

"That sounds like it was difficult, but I'm glad you had someone. I couldn't imagine being raised alone." She smiled, spinning the chair around to face her so she could begin fussing with flower dust under my eyes to cover the bags. "What is he like?"

I searched her eyes for any sense of trap or of looking at me to find a lie in my letter and my intentions, but nothing screamed danger—she seemed to genuinely want to know more about me rather than find faults in my already crumbling plans.

"He looks like Pete without the orange flecks and undertones." I hummed in thought as she reached into a drawer to grab a simple necklace, the focal point being a vast diamond, before placing it around my throat. "But he's kinder and is always helping the little ones who don't have someone to help them. His mother, Amelia, has taken in several orphans, helping raise them to succeed and thrive in a world they know nothing about." I was sharing far too much, but talking to Selli about them felt good, as if healing a sore wound in my heart. I had not been able to talk about him or reminisce about our time together since the males cared little about my past or my family.

"He does sound lovely." She smiled, finishing up the final brush of petal dust before turning me back to the mirror. "I think he would be rather proud of how well you clean up for royal parties."

I could recognize that the female looking back at me in the mirror was *me*, but the dusting of flower petals and hair had made me look more refined—less wild. The pale yellow dust brought out the gold rings in my eyes, while the diamond necklace brought out the blue, making them the focal point of my entire look. Pale pink lined my lips, making them look healthy and full instead of dry and cracked like I was used to.

"Selli, this is..." My breath had been taken from my lungs as I looked at myself, completely dumbfounded by the reflection. "I've never been this dressed up before, but I doubt that anyone else could have made me look this beautiful. I'm even surprised that this is even possible with only petal dust and that metal contraption of yours."

"You are gorgeous all on your own, Lo, but sometimes you need a little push to remind yourself you are." The princess smiled just as the door opened between the dress closets, and the lead seamstress walked out with a heap of folded blue fabric.

"It's done, your Highness. Shall we get your party dressed?"

CHAPTER 12

$\mathbf{A}$ beautiful twilight blanketed the lush apple trees that surrounded the field that held the ball while music enveloped the forest's sounds as violins sang and cellos echoed their melody. It was like walking into a fairy tale: at least a couple hundred Fae dancing and mingling in the open space with masks covering their faces to pay tribute to their wild halves, their dresses each at least a thousand gold pieces each as their colors sparkled in the moonlight.

The mask felt like its own cage fitted on my face that my mare absolutely hated, and something profound in my chest recoiled at the concept. Though they thought it was a way to follow laws while still celebrating the original tradition, it also felt...disrespectful to the goddess who had granted us our shifts.

Before I had been fitted for my dress, I was asked by one of the costume designers who handled the creation of most of the royal visitor's masks to show them my shift. It was odd to be asked of such a thing randomly, but—with Sellias's encouragement—I had done so, standing patiently as the designer took notes of my face. They had even run their hands across my muzzle to make sure they were getting the curve and depth right, which felt all too intimate for what it was.

When my dress was finished, the mask maker returned with his completed piece as well, placing it in my hands after I finished getting the final finishes and trims done on my outfit for the night. It was such a perfect recreation of my mare, from the light gradients of cream and brown to the shape and feel of its weight, that it was almost uncanny to hold the craft. The broken stripe that ran down the center of my shift's face was also detailed to perfection so that when I looked at myself in the mirror after putting it on, I nearly forgot that I had not shifted.

"Confidence, Lo. You've got this." Selli whispered to me at the entrance to the ball, waiting for our turn to be announced to the guests and welcomed into the ball. I could not see the smile I knew she had under the magnificent mask she wore—it was the slim yet powerful face of a black dragon, shimmering gold under the carved scales with curved horns that went past her head and curled perfectly behind her pointed ears. The gold and black brought out the brightness in her purple eyes as she turned to the servant who had just finished the announcement of some important figure before us.

"Princess Sellias Evnos Roamion."

The attendant announced her name with a loud call of pride and grace to the crowd while she took her first steps into the spotlight of the fading sun. She was nothing less than radiant in her sleeveless gown, the sunset orange highlighted by its namesake as she bowed her respects to the crowd. It had been beautifully tailored into a sweeping V-neck and corset adorned in floral tulle while her tiara sparkled in the sunlight that filtered through the orchard. Her black hair had been let loose to flow behind her in long curls dusted with glitter as she held the stage with a confidence I could only dream of.

Her attention turned back to us as she held out a hand toward her sister, who had been standing beside her before she walked into the spotlight.

"Princess Dityss Irylth Roamion."

Dityss had told me before we left that she had never been a fan of formal celebrations, so she often brought a book to keep herself occupied over what she called unintelligent gatherings. She refused to wear any dress, instead choosing to wear a well-tailored suit. It was such a deep purple, nearly black, with silver buttons that trailed down the front of her tailcoat. The tails of her coat were longer than most, almost dragging against the ground, with golden dragons embroidered on each angled piece of fabric that resembled the emblem of the Roamion family. Her black dragon mask had gold scales that only surrounded the eyes, and she stunned everyone into a bow as she took Sellias' arm in her own, leading her sister down the center of the event to the King's table in the back. The long floral train of Selli's dress was the last thing that passed through the crowd before I was up, the announcer looking expectantly at me for my name.

I had hoped that Sellias or Dityss would have mentioned my name or announced me themselves, but the expectant look of the announcer gave me my answer. "Um..." My voice caught in my throat as my anxiety threatened to send me in the other direction, but the long line of guests growing impatient behind me made escape impossible.

"Willow Saugrave." I finally choked out, my nerves getting the best of me as a pair of guests behind me began to whisper. I never did well in crowds, my chest tightening as the announcer turned back to the ballroom.

"Lady Willow Saugrave."

All eyes turned to me, and I felt like the world had gone silent except for the musicians introducing a quiet tune on the piano. A flute slowly began to echo the piano's melody, allowing me a moment to take a deep breath as the orchestra joined in a lovely chorus. Wind instruments flirted back and forth with the strings, and the percussion quietly brought up the backbone of the song with the brass section. It filled my soul and my confidence as I closed my eyes, allowing the music to guide me into the light.

The sequins and jewels of my corset sparkled like small stars across a sea of night as the blue beckoned in the final rays of sunlight and absorbed it to brighten itself against its beams. The light and airy fabric cascaded against my limbs in soft waves of sheer silk when I curtsied to the crowd, the long sleeves falling past the ankle to thigh slit in the dress. I straightened up as I finished greeting the crowd, feeling the curls create an ivory frame of my mask as they settled. Firelight began to appear in the sky above the dance floor as the sun disappeared behind the mountains, the new light sources illuminating the sleek white horn and the silver speckles embroidered into the mask. All eyes were on me as the conversation started to flow alongside the music again, the attention surreal.

I smiled sheepishly behind the mask as I tried to move my way out of the spotlight and the prying eyes of attention.

"You clean up well, Willow." A familiar voice sounded behind me, turning on my heel to be met with a golden lion mask that looked as if it was tinged with fire. Peter's smile quirked up, and a low growl in his chest rumbled in amusement at the surprise on his face.

He was wearing a deep emerald tuxedo that was fitted to his rigid physique, the buttons on the collar and his cuffs reflecting the firelight to create a deep orange and gold sparkle. His blonde hair was pulled into a tight bun behind the mask, with a loose strand falling over the front of the lion-shaped disguise. Most females would likely fall to their knees at the sight, but there was a darkness swirling behind the bright green of his eyes that pushed me away.

"It seems even pigs know how to clean up sometimes." I snorted, brushing off the discomfort as part of the anxiety that crawled under my skin from the eyes still lingering on my back.

"May I have this dance?" Pete asked, extending a hand towards me as an invitation. The hushed conversations of nearby party quests turned to whispered scoffs when I did not immediately accept the offer, causing my stomach to flip and twist. I despised being the center of attention, and receiving negative attention only made that feeling sour further, so I took the hand quickly.

Peter grabbed onto my hand as his other hand slid to my waist, taking the lead to the grassy dance floor with moves that glided across the soft green blades.

Glide might have been too generous, as I did not have time to take dancing lessons for fancy balls like this one. My feet tripped over one another like they were lead stones, occasionally stepping on my partner's feet as Peter continued to lead the routine unbothered.

The fact that Pete did not seem to care about my abysmal dancing skills was a blessing from the gods if I had ever seen one.

"I don't think you are supposed to be here." He commented, his green eyes meeting mine as I tried to keep my attention up on him instead of the mess that was my footing. "But I think a pair of sisters may have had a change of plans for that, though, didn't they?"

"I thought *you* weren't supposed to be here. Didn't you four have some circle jerk to get to tonight?" I teased, then cursed under my breath as I stumbled yet again. "Such a shame to miss it to attend this."

"Well, we did have a *war meeting*," He emphasized with a click of his tongue, "That only ran a couple of hours to be sure we were completed in plenty of time for this ball since it would be rude for the Crown Prince not to attend." Peter's hand lifted mine as he twirled me around in the spot, his eyes focused on the slit in my dress as it opened a broader window to my legs. "Which I can thank Winulla for later." The comment was hushed, but goosebumps ran along my arms —and not the good ones.

"I guess you guys were trying to keep me out of the fun then," I forced myself to smile, struggling to look around his broad shoulders for someone I could run to safety for. "Too bad I have friends in higher places, which, speaking of, look like they are calling for me to join them."

Something glimmered in his eyes, my mare anxiously pressing against my conscience in warning.

I gave a polite smile as I moved to pull away, but he was more assertive as he pulled my waist closer to his and my other hand to his chest. I sucked in a deep breath as he pulled his mask closer to mine, the smell of putrid alcohol thick on his breath as he whispered into my ear, "I think we should pick up our little game of cat and mouse that we started when you arrived."

My internal alarm bells were ringing so loud that all I could hear was their warning tones echoing off the chambers of my mind. All I had to do was shift in a flash of light, sprint into the orchard, forget about this ball —

"I believe the lady dismissed herself, Peter." A deep rumble of a growl sounded behind me, and Peter slowly let go of my hand and my waist. I was quick to move as far back as possible, though it was only a foot or two before I hit what felt like a stone wall, my eyes wide as I stared at the lion shifter in front of me. Peter's green eyes were cold and icy as he stared at the savior standing behind me before he fell in an embellished bow.

"We were just playing a little game, your Highness." I could not see the smile behind the lion mask, but I could feel its sneer as his gaze raked down my dress like phantom claws tearing through my flesh. "But I can see she has other suitors who wish to dance with her, so I shall leave you be. Farewell, Lady Willow." My name coming out of his mouth was like claws raking down a chalkboard to my ears, though I was happy to see him slip into the crowd and out of sight.

I turned to the man behind me with a deep breath of relief gathering in my lungs.

Well, until I exhaled it all as soon as I saw who it was.

The prince was wearing a solid black suit with a light blue dress shirt under the overcoat, perfectly buttoned up to cover his chest where the tailors did not attempt to hide the marvel underneath—not to the fault of its craftsman. The fabric curved perfectly around every muscle and flexed with his arms as he lifted my chin ever so gently to meet his eyes behind a black dragon mask with long silver gradient horns that turned up far beyond his head.

The hazel and blue gaze that looked over me was filled with so many mixed emotions, though not even one I recognized.

"Your Highness." I barely breathed; all confidence I entered the clearing with dissipated after the encounter with Peter.

"Are you all right?" Ren asked calmly, his attention not leaving my face even when I knew panic ran wild behind my eyes.

"Yes, I am." I quickly nodded, flicking my gaze downwards to try to calm my rising panic and to hide from the genuine worry that I saw in his eyes—for fear that if I held it much longer, I might forget who I was talking to. "Thank you...for saving me from whatever that was. Was that Peter?"

"It was." He responded with a sigh, his other hand gently moving a stray strand of hair that had fallen in front of my face behind my ear, a finger dancing delicately over the pointed cartilage with the action. My cheeks warmed and were likely turning a deep shade of red as I kept my gaze centered on the ground while he spoke. "He has decent control over his lion, but it usually beats out his common sense during this holiday."

A small giggle escaped my lips as the tension began to fall off my shoulders, a strange feeling of comfort and safety coming from the male standing in front of me. He was supposed to be enemy number one, yet as I met those hazel eyes of his again, I only saw the kindness of a gentleman.

Then he extended his hand out to me in an invitation to dance.

I should have been reserved to ask for a break after what had happened with Peter. I should have prayed to the gods for the strength to decline and walk away, for a reminder that this male was supposed to be my *target*, not my dance partner.

There was a list that was too long of what I should *not* do in this situation.

I took his hand anyway.

I had no clue what I was doing, but how I was led across the open field of dancers made me feel like I had been dancing for years. His firm grip on my lower back kept me from tripping, and I could keep pace with how he danced around the guests we passed by. The orchestra was playing a faster song that focused mainly on the strings, with French horns sounding off in echo, and the trills of flutes and piccolos cut through the strings intermittently. It was such a beautiful tune, losing myself in the prince's eyes and the music as he twirled me through each major crescendo.

Music was a trance that always lured me in with its solid movements and beautiful chords, the weight of the world lifting from my shoulders when I focused on the breathing melody of the violins. A genuine smile came onto my face as I was spun and led through the other patrons of the dance floor, my breathing and my heart the lightest it had been since I had arrived at the Palace of Ascension.

"Did Sellias design your dress?" His voice pulled me out of my thoughts and my musical trance, my eyes meeting his as they drifted down my torso to glance at the open neckline to my breasts, where something primal darted across the blue and hazel mix.

It was not fear that rose in response to the hungry gaze.

"She did, and I told her she needed to open a boutique for the masses," I answered truthfully, his attention returning to my face when I spoke. "She has far too much skill to rot in a castle day in and day out."

"She does, but whatever our mother proclaims for them might as well be written law." He sighed while pulling me closer to avoid running into another couple that had moved a little too close to our space. His mask was within inches of mine, my breath hitching when my gaze tumbled to where his lips were behind it.

His hand tightened on my lower back, daring me to close the distance.

How badly I wanted to take that dare surprised me, but I was confused by his sudden interest. He had made it clear he wanted as much distance as possible between the two of us by his lack of attention or care since I had arrived, yet now...

"I don't understand that. Why can you go wherever you want, but Sellias and Dityss have to stay in the castle?" I quickly continued the conversation, careful not to fall prey to the sudden interest.

Ren's chest fell with a heavy sigh before he explained, "Our mother wants to keep them safe for the kingdom's sake and her own heart. I don't think she would survive if something happened to either of them."

Confusion crossed my face, my eyebrows bunching in thought. "But not if something happened to you? That's unfair."

A deep rumble of laughter blossomed from his mouth, causing me to blink several times in surprise at the deep yet warm sound. "I constantly throw myself in harm's way. I do not blame her for writing me off as something to worry about when she has plenty else."

"I think you're deflecting your real feelings." I protested, making it his turn for his hazel eyes to grow wide with surprise. His eyes looked just like they did in my imagination the day I returned from my 'escape attempt,' making it seem like his mask was not even there. "You should see yourself as something to be worried about and not feel so nonchalantly about your death."

I was supposed to kill the man before me, but instead, I was giving him a pep talk about his perspective of his self-worth.

I was doing a *great* job as a first-time assassin.

His eyes softened at the sentiment, "A fantasy, Wildie. I know my place and where I am headed, likely sooner rather than later."

He stepped back to bow to me, getting ready to leave me for his next dance partner, in which there was no shortage of females fanning themselves around us for his attention. Something soured in my belly as the idea of him leaving me so soon after what was such a different kind of conversation between the two of us, where I finally got to see a bit of the true male hiding behind that general prince mask of his that he wore every day.

He began to turn into a blonde female with the mask of a champagne-colored dragon, and that feeling in my gut twisted further.

Before I knew what I was doing, I grabbed his arm and pulled him back to me, his mask reflecting the colors of the firelight as the blue ring around his hazel eyes brightened at the sudden action.

"Do you want to join me in celebrating the true reason for the feasts?" I asked, my heart beating as fast and as hard as a gallop as I searched his face for an answer.

His hazel eyes sparked in recognition of what I meant, but he did not say no.

CHAPTER 13

"**Y**ou do know that if we are caught doing this, you could end up in the dungeons? Permanently?" Rendros' voice sounded amused as we weaved through the orchard and away from the sounds and guests of the Fall Feast ball until they were barely a mumbled pulse in the distance. I was still holding onto his arm as I pulled him farther into an overgrown section of the orchard, my mare pacing for the freedom she knew was coming.

I finally came to a stop in an open space of the orchard where a tree likely had once been, releasing his arm before pulling off the mask as I finally took in a deep breath of air without the crafted cage. "I'm well aware of the consequences. However, I have a rather good scapegoat with me should that happen." The relief of being away from the party and feeling fresh air on my face allowed a broad, genuine smile to spread on my face.

"Rygur wasn't lying," Ren's voice lowered as he removed his mask, dropping it to the ground by his feet. His gaze hovered on my grin for a moment before meeting mine, and I could see the primal sheen of a predator cross his gaze as he stepped closer. "Did you really file them in an attempt for a different kind of protection against predators?"

"Ever since I was thirteen," I answered breathlessly as I saw his canines protrude from his gumline, nearly touching his lower gums in unmistakably perfect predator prowess. Whether the length of those teeth was because of his impending shift or his bloodline, I could not tell, but my face heated either way when he took another step closer, his hand reaching for mine.

"It's quite the feat for a predator to find prey that had prepared themselves for an attack." He murmured as his hand gently wrapped around my wrist, my feet losing ground as I stepped back before my spine hit the rough wall of bark. The predator in his eyes was there and *alive* when he moved my arm above my head, pressing the exposed skin into the tree.

I had no chance of fighting off or escaping from the position I had been pinned in, yet where fear should have responded, only heat and desire pooled in my core.

If he was going to devour me here and now, I was ready to let him.

"Ren," I whispered as I watched his gaze travel from my face down to my neck, the blue in his eyes almost illuminating as he moved his face forward. His nose pressed against the side of my neck while his teeth grazed the sensitive skin that pulsed with every beat of my frantic heart, pulling a soft groan from my throat with the teasingly slow movements.

Winulla's influence on our compass of feral composure had to be the reason for the sudden shift in his attention, the sudden desire that burned in his eyes. It must have affected me, too, considering both my conscience and my mare were silent as death lingered like a breeze against my skin, and all I wanted at this moment was...him. To feel his hands travel to delicate places, to take me just as brutally as predator catching their prey—

"That day in the throne room, I wanted nothing but to do this." He whispered against my neck, interrupting my thoughts as he pushed rough kisses into the curve of my throat. "But you were confident and a danger to my willpower, so I fought for you to go into the dungeons. I thought that if I could do that and keep you in those iron and stone cages, it would also cage that feeling." He growled in pent-up frustration, my throat letting out a breathy plea for more as he continued. "But my sisters, with their damned ideas, swaying the king and queen to decide to link us in a pact, where I would be *forced* to see those blue eyes and say no. When I had to treat you like the beautiful female you are. To give you a room in my wing for Kanos' sake, a flame kept close to a moth." His hazel eyes crashed into mine with primal hunger as he drank in my scent, "Then you played that damn violin, and my magic was so quick to rise right alongside yours, adding fuel to an ever-growing flame—greeting you like an old friend." His eyes moved to my lips, which were parted in baited anticipation.

Ren's free hand pulled up to them and gently pressed against my lower lip as if about to close the distance when I saw conflict shoot across his gaze as he fought an invisible battle behind his eyes.

One that I would sadly lose.

His grip loosened on my forearm as he took a step back with a hand running through his hair, the other fiddling with his belt as he tried to hide his arousal behind the dark fabric. "I have tried to take a step back. I *must* keep my distance, or I might do something we'll both regret. Or start something we cannot finish. If Jae, Pete, and Ry could handle getting the information from you, I could focus on the actual point of your stay. Get you out of here sooner before I lose control."

I wanted to say something, but there was very little breath in my lungs for me to do anything beyond breathe. Ren's gaze inspected every inch of the dress hanging off my frame, the wind playing a sinister game for the prince as it pushed the slit of my gown wider as soon as hazel eyes became pointed at the space just above my thigh. I could hear the curse under his breath as he turned away, taking my heart with it.

"Then you showed up tonight in that *fucking* dress, and Peter got to you first. He felt your curves, saw your breasts, salivated over you like some sex-starved beast." Tension rose with his shoulders, thunder rumbling somewhere in the distance alongside the movement as he recalled the events, "And you were so *scared*. I wanted to tear him apart right there."

Though I was pretty sure I was looking at the prince like *I* was the sex-starved beast, my eyebrows rose at the comment. "You knew I was scared?"

His eyes came back to center on me, acknowledging my question with a slight nod. "I think the pact allows me to sense your emotions when they are heightened, like some kind of transferable bond." He answered, and though he was trying to act civilized, I knew he could feel the emotions that had consumed me in the last few minutes.

Desire. Lust. Hunger.

The knowledge of that spread a wicked smile on my face, the height of the evening beginning to unravel whatever tamed control I had left.

"What do you think you are doing?" The commanding voice of the general prince returned, its low and unforgiving tone sending shivers down every inch of my body.

"I told you I wanted to show you what it was like to experience the true nature of Winulla's night, did I not?" I bit a canine into my lip, his nostrils flaring as I watched the final bit of his control over himself begin to slip. "Let's see if your tamed beast can keep up with an untamed one."

I did not wait for his response as I finally gave into the impatient shift that had become like an insufferable itch, a silver light illuminating the small clearing as I shifted. I stayed a moment longer as I walked past the gathering storm that was Rendros—predator instincts breaking through the creaks in his normally civilized nature—to stomp on the mask that was the image and intent of a tamed cage before galloping into the depths of the orchard and toward the lake I knew awaited on its north-western side.

I found the lake a few days ago with Rygur on a walk around the territory, and the location has become a frequent spot for us to walk and enjoy the sunlight. I had gone frequently enough that I knew it was only a short sprint from the location of the ball, allowing the game of predator and prey Ren and I were playing to happen on even ground. Where he could see and fit without the restrictions of a fruit tree canopy and where I could run free with no worry of watching my footing.

My hooves thrummed against the earth in perfect rhythm as I sped through a darker section of the orchard, my mare taking over all semblance of control as I allowed her to gallop in full strides like I was being stalked and hunted. In some manner, I suppose I was—I was being chased by a predator that could kill me with barely a thought or a twitch of muscle—but some inner voice was telling me he would not hurt me.

I finally emerged from the forest, moonlight washing over me like a warm embrace as I made it to the lakeside, stopping to take a few deep breaths while I still had a head start. It was eerily quiet—as if the world itself silenced to listen to Ren and I's game that played with the very strings of Vomuna's realm of life and death. No crickets were chirping, no hum or buzz of bugs to fill the comforting chorus of night.

Complete, utter silence.

Dityss's voice reminded me of our conversation that morning as it echoed in my head, *"Nothing lives in the decaying orchards."*

My attention turned to the southern end of the tree line, where the darkened trees looked like a mist of shadow in the moonlight. It was as silent as still as the lakeside and the healthy section of the orchard, and though I felt like I was far enough away not to worry about the supposedly cursed wood, something felt wrong.

Very wrong.

I did not drink from the lake—fearful of what may be lurking beneath the surface—as I walked alongside its waters, scanning the sky and waiting for that black shadow to appear from amongst the stars and for the game to start anew. As the minutes passed, my hope for relief from the unsettling silence began to dwindle as there was nothing but the stars and the moon illuminating the dark expanse.

My fur stood on end as my mare joined the surrounding silence, afraid a single sound would mean death.

Primal fear quickly overtook my carnal desire for the confusing yet attractive prince and the game we were supposed to be playing, my pace becoming a brisk trot toward the healthy fruit trees where I had left the prince behind, aiming to head back to the palace and the safety harbored. I wanted to be back in my room, away from the empty sky, away from the *forest-*

A twig snapped in the tree line, causing every muscle in my body to tense in response, my head snapping toward the origin of the sound.

There was no movement, no sign of what had snapped the twig—only the return of the blood-chilling silence.

Ren?

The game had ended when his shadow never graced the sky. There was only pure terror flooding my veins as I scanned the forest for the source of the sound, waiting to see the brown hair and hazel eyes of a prince who got lost in the forest. Maybe, for some reason, he had not shifted, had hesitated, and decided to follow me on two feet.

Some part of me prayed that the pact could do more than send my terror down the imaginary string that linked us both, that I could call to him, and he would tell me where he was—

Wildie, run! NOW!

A familiar commanding voice bellowed in my mind, moving my feet into quick motion from the sudden sound and adrenaline burning in my veins. Some god must have been listening to my prayer and allowed me the word of warning to free me from the prey freeze that had seized all my muscles just in time to notice the mass of golden fur that sprinted from my left.

Though I was given a blessing by way of warning, nothing could have stopped the beast from its sprint. I pushed against the dirt as hard as my legs would let me, catching only a glimpse of wild emerald eyes as I glanced back to my pursuer. There was nothing human or Fae beneath the exterior of the lion's eyes—only a mindless predator.

If I could gain traction, I could outrun him. I had done it before. I could do it again.

But I did not have the blessing of every god—the fear becoming fact as I felt claws and teeth tear deep scores into the muscled flesh of my backside.

I screamed in both terror and agonizing pain as I tried to buck the beast from its grapple, but his claws and teeth sank deeper. There were only my cries in the suffocating silence that had taken over the lakeside and the orchard.

There would be no savior coming for me.

My mare was in a complete and irreversible panic, trying desperately to get free by thrashing and bucking, but no matter what she did, his claws only sunk deeper. I *had* to get him off me because if I continued to let him hold and tear as he was, I was going to lose tendons. Muscles.

I would never run again if that happened—and that scared me more than death.

I pulled all the strength I could from all four of my legs to throw myself onto the ground and on top of the lion, hoping the weight would knock him off balance and cause him to break free of the grapple in favor of saving himself. My body twisted as I pushed myself over as far as I could land on top of the green-eyed lion, the wounds tearing farther as he twisted below me, but one by one, the hooks lost their position in my flesh.

Run.

My muscles screamed in protest as I pulled myself from the ground, taking off down the lakeside with my focus being to put whatever magic and willpower I could towards trying to stifle the significant bleeding that poured out of the deep wounds. I was lucky that I had been able to pull free before any more muscle was destroyed or a tendon snapped, but he had hit an artery, the blood running down my legs in alarming amounts that continued to drain with every stride. Darkness had begun to surround the edges of my vision as more blood stained my light fur, but I would not stop running. I refused to die as prey to a predator on the night of the Wild Feasts.

His paws beat the ground behind me in the chase, each slowing second allowing him to gain on me as my wounded leg began to fail me. I knew there would be no more distance to gain. Claws and teeth would hit my body again, and I would not be able to get away from it.

Tears began to burn at the edges of my eyes as I desperately pushed forward, both terror and realization of my failures hitting me all at once. If I had just completed what I had been tasked to do, if I had not agreed to that *stupid* pact, if the prince was *dead*, I would have been home by now, helping Amelia with her garden. Looking forward to the better world Theo promised me and every single one of the hopeful souls living in the Untamed Wilds. I was supposed to be an assassin, a herald for a better world for the untamed, but instead, I was going to be murdered by the general prince's war planner.

I could feel his breath closing in on my hocks, the finale to this hopeless endeavor mere seconds behind me—

An enraged roar split the silence as rain suddenly pelted onto the open meadow and lightning burst from the sudden overcast sky, sound finally returning to my ears as beautiful as any symphony. There was someone there, *he* was there—

The beating of paws was interrupted by the *slam* of a much larger creature hitting the ground, bone-crunching with the landing, the force causing the ground to shake, and what little balance I had left to falter.

My back leg gave out with the loss of balance, and I fell to the ground, limp. My eyelids were heavy as I tried to recognize the gigantic blob of black and silver that had landed on the golden lion. More roars joined in the wild melody of thunder, but I could not lift my head to look anywhere else than the dragon in front of me.

The last thing I saw was its head turn toward me; then everything went black.

CHAPTER 14

There was a cool breeze that brushed over me with the scent of fresh rain on it as it drifted across the plains. I could not sense any incoming storm beyond the smell of it in the wind, but I might have slept through it when I had fallen asleep last night.

When I was a young filly, my father had taught me that storms were lullabies weaved by the storm god Kanos for the nature goddess Etia to help her sleep when insomnia kept her wide awake for weeks at a time. When I had asked him why she could not sleep without the storms that Kanos gave her, he had told me that god had crafted them to help distract her mind from the reality they lived in. Etia's insomnia had been a result of nightmares that plagued the darkness behind her eyes stemming from the way mortals had treated her creation, with the only thing able to overcome the visions and phantom pains being the sound of rolling thunder and gentle rain.

I took a deep breath of the comforting smell as it passed, wanting to soak in every detail as if I would never smell it again.

My eyes wandered over the green fields of never-ending bliss, holding my knees close to my chest. Not a single cloud dotted the skies as the sun's rays beamed liquid gold onto the open expanse, its warmth bathing me as it settled comfortably over my shoulders. It was a perfect dream of comfort and bliss, but I knew it was nothing more than a glimpse into the realms beyond Aistris—somewhere in between life and death.

The only thing I could remember was that something terrible happened. One moment, I had been running under a moonlit sky with joy and excitement, and the next, I had seen a massive beast running toward me, and then I woke up here in sunlit fields. I knew I had been wounded, but something about it had been *wrong*.

My finger absent-mindedly ran over my thigh as if it knew the answer.

Another breeze scattered blades of grass across the field, carrying the sweetest smell of wildflowers with it instead of rain. The new scent wrapped around me in comfort with its sweet lullabies of roses and daisies, but even its scent was muted compared to the freshness of the sky's showers.

"Once upon a time, you fought tooth and nail to survive to avoid this field—running the other way to find the darkened forests of your home even when they were plagued with death and horrors none should endure." A female voice came from behind me, full of a stern kind of gentleness that was ageless at the same time.

I did not respond immediately as I avoided looking at her, shaking my head while pulling my knees closer to my chest. "That was a different time, a very long time ago."

"Tell me, wild one. What has changed the unbreakable spirit that runs through you?" The woman placed a warm and gentle hand on my shoulder, "I know that it has not been broken, but something about it has changed."

"Isn't seeing me here enough proof that it has broken? That it doesn't exist anymore?" A low growl rumbled from my throat, "What changed was my circumstances. What *changed* was that I could no longer complete my task—I failed my brother and all the people fighting in the Untamed Wilds. I would welcome death sooner than greet them with an invisible chain binding me to their enemy."

How *could* I return to Theo or see him again after everything that had happened since my departure? It had not taken me a full day in the capital kingdom for everything to fall apart—for a plan we spent months devising to fall apart in a whisper of dust as if it had never existed in the first place. I knew Theo would not be angry, but he would be disappointed, and that silent disappointment would haunt me for the rest of my days. The rebellion's fate lay in this plan, and so many resources were put into it to ensure it would work. Though I had been playing along like nothing had changed—hoping Theo would think I was getting close for a clean kill—he did not know I could not take out the prince anymore without dying myself.

I had even failed *that*.

I was now sitting on the fields that led to the afterlife, talking to some ghostly or godly woman because I had been playing a dangerous game with the prince instead of trying to kill him. I was going to die because of my stupidity rather than at *least* dying for the good of the rebellion.

Selfish, foolish girl.

"You do not believe that the lion would hate you for your circumstances, yet you have such low worth of yourself that you believe it is better for him if you die now." The female chimed, "You truly are a pathetic waste of life."

"Excuse me?" I started, blinking my eyes rapidly in disbelief that she had just called me openly what I was silently calling myself.

"It is true if that is what you think of yourself. You most definitely should not return to life to live it, even in the circumstances that you are in. You should stay here and drift into the ether as a poor soul who wishes for pity."

"You are doing great at encouraging me to keep living." I scoffed, burying my head between my knees.

"Because you clearly are better off to the rebellion dead than alive, as you have said." She hummed momentarily as if debating something before a phantom hand lifted my head from its place between my knees. My heart screamed to fight it, to accept my fate as a useless soul, but my muscles did not heed my heart's pleas as my head lifted from the shadowed space where my mind had fallen.

I was standing behind a large row of rain-soaked windows with an outside view, looking inside a room decorated with fancy furniture and green walls that sang stories of spring, which seemed to hum audibly from where I was in between. However, the room itself was quiet, with only a dim firelight hovering in the middle of the space by the ceiling, casting long shadows across each piece of furniture and familiar figures that filled the room.

The desk closest to the window was occupied by the hunched figure of a younger woman, scribbling something over pieces of parchment while fiddling with a black bunch of hair that had fallen out of a bun in a mess of strands and tangles. Her glasses were haphazardly thrown onto the other side of the table as she wrote in increasing frustration over something on the paper, though I could not make out exactly its cause. The creases on her forehead were only further indicators of her focus, alongside a string of curse words that left her mouth when she finished writing on one piece of parchment and moved on to the next.

Dityss.

My eyes wandered next to the figure dressed in orange that had been muddied along the train, who looked nothing like the woman I had seen earlier that day. Her tiara had been ditched somewhere, and the once beautiful powders and ink that had lined her face were left in streaks and smudges across her porcelain skin. She was sitting against the entrance to the connecting washroom, the ordinarily bright purple of her eyes dull and glazed over as she stared at the floor. What little of her face I could see was lined with guilt and worry, my hand instinctively moving up to the window as if I could comfort her.

Her attention suddenly turned to the window, sending a phantom shiver down my spine as I watched her eyes look directly at where I was standing, though there was no shine of recognition in them. Tears welled in her eyes as her gaze fell to the ground at my feet, where the lily I had revived had begun to wilt under the storm that echoed overhead.

Sellias.

The last figure was sitting in an old armchair beside the bed, hazel eyes fighting a torrent of emotions.

Rendros.

As if saying his name was the command of some spell, I was whisked from outside in the pouring rain into the room, standing beside the crown prince.

His posture was the heaviest of the three siblings. His overcoat from the feast had been left behind somewhere, and his undershirt was stained with blood and dirt. The same stains also clung to his slacks, though they were also torn and sliced as if he had been attacked. However, his clothes and appearance were no match for the haggard expression on his face and the soulless look in his eyes as he stared at the bed ahead of him. I knew what lay there, but I was not ready to accept that this man had so much emotion on his face for the woman he barely knew lying on the mattress. It broke my heart to know that two women in the room were distraught over my condition, but it destroyed it to see the hard-a prince in the same—if not worse—state.

Then he began humming the tune I had played the night he found me on that imaginary stage, his hum cracking with emotion.

"What is he doing?" I whispered to the female presence that had brought me to this scene, a tear running down my cheek though I still did not look at her. "Why?"

"Death does not have to be the answer for the greater good, wild one. For centuries, it has tried to be the answer—screamed to be used to push forward another part of the war—and it has won time and time again." Her voice echoed in the room as I finally turned to the bed, Re humming continuing as I stared at the form tucked under the sheets. I look at my own body devoid of color, my chest barely rising and falling under the fabric.

They must have used some elixir to get me back into my Fae form to assess better and move me while also removing the formal attire I had on in trade for bandages and wraps. The attack's memory replayed again in my head when I saw the state of my physical form, but the state of my flesh was worse than what I could remember. My ribs were jutting out as if I was starved, my eyes sat low in the deep sockets of my skull, and my hair had turned silver at the tips instead of the light cream that was usually there.

"There are other ways to take victory in war, wild one. It may be difficult and cause more death in the process, but the result will be long-lasting." My eyes absentmindedly drifted back to Ren, who laid his head against the bed when he had finished humming. "Peaceful."

"Things will change if a prominent figure dies, and they see how strong the rebellion truly is." My words tasted different in my mouth.

Sour, almost.

"Or will they fight back with stronger forces that will wipe everyone but them off of the map?" The female questioned gently, my imagination instantly bringing back the image of the mother holding her dead pup. "I have seen many wars, and I have seen many deaths because of similar revenge ideals. What haunts you will not be the last if that is the route that is chosen."

I weighed the words in my head as my imagination blurred reality.

Ren stood on top of a hill overlooking smoldering fields, but no bodies littered the expanse. Blood did not stain the grass, and there did not seem to be a single life lost on this field. There was a great deal of destruction, with stones littering the fields and remains of houses and banners scattered around the scene.

He spoke to someone he was standing next to with a smile, no sign of the stiff general I had come to know.

"Do you still believe it better to die as a failure? Or to live with the knowledge that things can change?" the voice asked, breaking me out of my trance.

My gaze turned back to my body while I reached out to Ren's hair, gently brushing a couple of phantom fingers through the short softness of it. His back stiffened in response, his head whipping back to my physical form as if he knew that it was somehow me standing behind him.

"I think it's time I look at this war with a new perspective, goddess," I replied, returning my other hand to where my physical form lay in a soft stasis. I felt my spirit begin to melt from the space between life and death back into the near corpse; the smell of fresh rain surrounded me again as my vision tunneled into a settled darkness.

"Wildie?" A rough voice was the first thing I heard, my lips curving upward with what little strength I had.

"Your Highass."

CHAPTER 15

Everything in my body felt like it was full of lead, and I felt like I was being dragged to the bottom of the sea, my chest struggling to rise and fall in full breath. Lifting my head—or any part of my body—was out of the question, as every time I tried to move, my vision would spin. It was a miserable readmission into existence, though the three Roamion siblings were trying to give me words of encouragement that I could move again soon.

"You need to take it easy, Willow. Whatever poison Peter's claws were doused in was extreme, and though it did not kill you, it sapped every ounce of life out of you." Dityss moved to sit on my bed, her hands lifting one of my sickly arms to take a closer look at the way my muscles did not twitch in response.

"How—" A cough racked my chest as I tried to speak, "How long will it be until I can...run again? Move?" The answer I knew was coming terrified me, but I tried to swallow my fear like it was an oversized pill.

Dityss' hesitance to respond was all the answer I needed, though she answered the question after a few more seconds of silence.

"There is no clear answer to that. I have been going over all of the poison research we have in the castle, and not a single one matches your symptoms. The only thing I know is that it likely will not be a fast recovery." Her voice was filled with regret, and the way she gently laid my hand back on my chest, I could feel the weight of her guilt for not having a better answer.

In the little time I had known Dityss, I could tell how much pride she held in her unrivaled knowledge and the time she spent reading to learn more. It was something she had grown to love rather than dancing and mingling with other wealthy royals, and I had to commend her for that.

Her hand squeezed mine before she pulled back, our eyes locking in a quiet examination of each other. Despite the regret that plagued her, those dark purple eyes still held onto steel determination. She did not have to say anything else for me to know she would keep researching until she found the cause and the fastest cure. The only thing I could do was give a reassuring smile that I trusted her ability, to which she responded with a curt nod before moving back to the desk and re-sorting the scattered papers of a distressed archivist into neat stacks of renewed determination.

I could see Selli standing in the doorway of my private bathing chambers out of the corner of my eye, but she did not step toward me. The light and the joy that had once danced in her eyes seemed to be ripped from the light purple seas, and I could see silver lining them when she realized my attention had turned to her. She took a hesitant step forward while shaking her head, the black strands of her hair tangled and slick from rain, flipping back and forth over her face with the motion.

I did not understand why she kept her distance until I saw the dried blood that tinged her once vibrant dress, seemingly draining all light from the bright color.

"Selli—"

Tears ran down the princess's cheeks, following stained paths from previous tears shed, her eyes drowned in a mixture of emotion. Joy, sorrow, anger, and guilt washed through them in crashing waves. Her delicate hand reached up to cover her mouth, and she finally walked over and stood at the side of my bed. I wanted to reach out to her, to show her I was all right, but my muscles refused to answer.

"Selli, I'm okay—"

"You almost *died*, Willow!" Her voice was a force of nature when she raised it, her emotions enhancing the pain in her voice. Whatever I was trying to say died in my throat; the words were swallowed completely. Anger had won out the storm of pain in those lilac eyes as she continued, "You let yourself fall to that stupid, *stupid*, untamed instinct and nearly got yourself killed!" She took a step closer, and somewhere to my left, I heard the distinct sound of a chair being pushed against the hardwood as someone stood. "Not to mention that you dragged *Ren* into it, and now he's, he's…" Her tears overflowed as she choked back another sob, and both Ren and Dityss walked over to pull her into a soft hug. Her sobbing grew louder in the embrace, and the other two siblings looked at each other while swapping faces of quiet sadness.

This was a view I had seen several times over in my time in the rebellion forces, my heart doubling over in guilt for thinking that it would have been simple to kill the prince and expect something like this would not happen here—that no one would mourn his death and the foolish hope that no one would retaliate for the attack on the crown in devastating numbers.

Not to mention that now something withered in *my* chest at the mere notion of his death.

I tore my attention away from the siblings and back to my sorry form. This would take months, maybe years, to recover if a cure could not be found. I bit back a grunt as I forced my arms to plant at my sides and pushed my palms into the bed to try to sit myself up, even as my muscles screamed in agony at the mere idea. My eyes squeezed shut in effort and frustration. I did not leave those bliss-filled plains of painless existence to sit here and wait for something to come along to fix me, nor would laying here help the people I had left behind or the ones I had found now. I had to move and fight, even if that meant fighting my body to make it happen.

I could hear the door latch with a small click, but I did not look up to see who had left; I was too focused on trying to get myself to move. I had hurt Sellias with my foolishness, and her siblings likely escorted her out when they realized I would not sit still, putting myself under more strain. Maybe they thought I would retaliate against the young princess, shout something back at her, or try to do something to justify my actions. But as I finally felt my back hit the cold wood of my headboard and threw my head into the back of it in complete exhaustion, I knew she was right. I had done something that risked and potentially even harmed her brother, doing something I knew was very illegal in the capital.

I also knew, however, that I would not have been able to put off the shift either. The celebration of Winulla was something I had partaken in for as long as I could remember, and it was the one night of the year that I knew my mare would do whatever was necessary to stretch her legs.

"She doesn't mean all of that. She's had a... rough night." The deep voice that reminded me of thunder echoed in the now silent room, the bed dipping with a slight groan from the additional weight as he took a seat beside me. "Just give her some time, and she will come back around."

I shook my head, feeling my hair fall over my face and my shoulders in a mess. I opened my eyes slowly to stare down at my hands and my chest, my bandaged breasts highlighted by the firelight in the room as the blanket slipped from my attempts to sit up. I could feel his stare as I watched the blanket fall, but I did not go to fix it. Instead, I picked up my head to look towards the prince who was sitting beside me.

"I promise those look better when I'm not a shell of a corpse. I'm at least a decent C cup on a good day, but not these…I don't know." I let out a breathy laugh, trying to bring some semblance of happiness into what had become a suffocating room of despair. "Smaller things."

"I think they are beautiful, regardless."

"You may have a warped sense of size then, Your Highass. I hope that doesn't speak for other things in the bedroom." I snorted with a cocked smile before sighing and shaking my head as I looked him over. He did not seem to be injured, thank the gods, and there was a shot of amusement in his eyes despite the haunted glaze that overshadowed them.

"I can promise you that my sense of *size* is not warped," An award-winning grin spread across his face, and I felt like I was going to pass out again as all the breath left my lungs. "If you hadn't made our game so difficult earlier, you might have had a chance to see that yourself."

"You thought *that* was difficult?" I let out a small giggle, watching the blue in his eyes brighten at the action. "I thought I was making it easier for you by going out in the open where you could see me instead of guessing where I was in the trees."

"I suppose that would have been easier for me, except I had no clue you knew where the lake was. I expected you to run towards the castle."

I blinked, "Rygur didn't tell you that he took me to the lake a couple of days ago?"

His answer was a slight shrug, then a shake of his head. "I only told Rygur to report your outings if you did something out of line I needed to step in for. But you were well-behaved, and he never had a reason to tell me about your precise locations."

The room went silent, the next part of the conversation looming like a wolf ready to pounce on a rabbit. I cleared my throat and glanced down where his hands were bunched in his lap, stuck in white-knuckled fists.

"How did you find me? If Rygur didn't tell you that I knew where the lake was…"

"After you ran off, I was so distracted I did not hear anything around me." His eyes fell to the ground beside the bed before shutting them tightly. "I was flying towards the castle when Dityss intercepted m stopping me within a couple of hundred feet of the fields by my quarters. I had started to yell at her for stopping my 'hunt' when she told me that Sellias saw Peter sneaking away from the party before shifting and taking off into a full sprint for the lakeside. I didn't understand what t concern was at first until I realized that you weren't in the fields by the castle. That you must have run to the lake instead." He took a deep breath, "Then I felt your fear when you said my name. Asking i something *was* me, but I knew I was too far for you to see me."

Wildie, run! NOW!

I did not say a word as his warning echoed in my head, my heart twisting in panic as I remembered that moment all too clearly.

"I flew so fast I wasn't even sure I was breathing. I knew you had your teeth, but that doesn't amount to any predator that can bring you down in their shifted form, and I didn't know what else you had been trained or taught with the rebels. I could feel the agony and panic from the pact to the point that I *knew* you were being torn apart. I knew you were in pain, afraid, and it felt like your life was being leeched right out of your very being and my own." He growled, and with whatever strength I had left, I pulled myself forward to lean on his shoulder in solidarity as I remembered those last fleeting moments at the lakeside. I did not bend as gracefully as I wanted to and instead fell on his shoulder like a ragdoll. "When I got close enough to smell your blood, and I could see Peter was about to pounce again, everything went red for me. I knew that my sisters were somewhere behind me, and I slammed myself into that bastard with every ounce of force I could." His attention did not leave the floor for the next few minutes, his entire body tense as he lost himself in that memory.

There was something he was not telling me, but now was not the time to push about it.

It seemed a silent eternity passed before he finally turned back to me, carefully moving his arms around my chest and pulling me closer, running one of his hands through my rat's nest of hair. Despite his strength and the way his chest could nearly envelop me on its own, I had never felt a touch this soft and so careful. He was afraid of hurting me, and down whatever connection that damn pact made to my emotions, I made sure that he understood how comforted I felt in that moment.

How *safe* I felt in his arms.

"I'm okay now, Ren," I whispered, leaning back to look at him. "I'm alive, and I'm going to get better." I did not know why I needed to comfort him, but it felt as natural as breathing.

It must have felt similar to him as he held onto me a little tighter as he met my gaze. "Peter has been taken care of, so you don't have to be afraid of him." His voice was firm, but that darkness from before had returned.

"Did you...?"

"No. He was put into the dungeons for what he did and will interrogated thoroughly for information leading to the attack and the poison that laced his claws."

A part of me was relieved to know he was in the dungeon, another part of me wished he was dead and on the ground somewhere. Dungeons could be broken out of, plans could be resorted and replanned, and new attackers could be hired.

"Ren?"

"Yes, Wildie?"

"When I can walk and not fall around like a limp fish," I said, tilting my head as far as I could to meet his gaze. "I want you to train me to fight back properly, both shifted and Fae."

He blinked—the only tell he had that he was surprised by the question. His eyes darted over my face in careful thought, but a slight smirk picked up on the left side of his mouth. "Wildie, I can teach you all you need to know about sword work and defense moves as Fae shifted...I don't think I could help you there. My dragon doesn't particularly like to go easy, so it might be better if you were to train with Jaeden for that."

"Absolutely not." I swallowed, putting on a face that still played with some amusement from earlier. It had to be Ren, for the sake of getting closer to him to help change his mind on the rebellion, and I was *not* trusting anyone else in his council right now.

Peter was one of his closest friends. What was there to argue that Jaeden or Rygur would not do the same thing given the chance?

"I once willingly asked to go in a game with that dragon as a defenseless unicorn, and he accepted without a second thought. I trust him to have more control regarding training exercises, considering you won't be distracted with other ideas." I teased with a soft chuckle before all semblance of trying to be playful withered with a sharp cough from my chest.

He hummed with thought, considering the proposal for a second and seemingly trying to have an internal conversation with himself as he laid me back down in the bed and pulled the covers over my shoulders. His attention turned to the window, looking out into the small garden, unintentionally allowing me to see the glimmer of conflict in his hazel eyes.

"Ask me again when you can walk and shift again." He murmured, standing from the bedside and walking towards my door, all semblance of a playful conversation gone once again.

Had I laid on the allure too thick or tried to be too forceful in wanting his attention? My chest deflated as I sank into the bed, staring straight at the ceiling. There were a few more moments of silence before I heard the click of my door shut as he left, an exasperated sigh leaving my lips as I looked toward where he last stood.

I had never felt so alone more than I did that night.

CHAPTER 16

I was going insane.

It had only been three days since the incident at the lakeside, yet Ren had not come back to visit. Only Dityss and some wolf Fae healers seemed interested in stopping by my room, looking over me like a specimen in a jar needing extensive monitoring.

The constant checkups did not bother me as much as Ren's lack of appearance. That night—from the heated interaction before the attack to the comforting words in my bed—it felt like something clicked between us. I could not get his rigid jawline or that heart-stopping smile out of my head, which made his disappearance even more infuriating. Today I was determined to use that anger to walk my ass out of this room to confront him about it.

I was grateful to be surrounded by healers who dedicated their time to ensuring I was getting plenty to eat and helping my natural healing processes speed along. I could already sit up on my own, and though the scars on my thigh would never entirely disappear, they had lessened significantly. I was keeping down food and doing daily arm workouts to bring the strength back into my muscles, but I had not been able to put my feet on the ground yet.

Before I could rally my strength to throw my legs off the side of my bed and start to stand, I heard the door creak open as Dityss made her usual visiting rounds. I left the blankets I had kicked off of myself at the foot of the bed. I leveled a look at the princess as she walked around the bed with papers in her hand.

"Can I start standing today?" I asked dryly, opening and closing my fists in frustration that I even had to ask.

"Not unless you want to write off all the work done to get you to this point. The next part of your healing will be your legs, now that most of your upper body strength has returned." She answered with a bored expression, taking her usual seat beside the bed and pulling out her pen. "How do you feel?"

"Like I want to *walk* and not be coddled like an infant," I growled, my teeth grinding in irritation. The irritation in Ren's lack of presence, my inability to walk, and my mare's returned restlessness had bubbled over to a point where I needed to get it out somehow. "Where's Sellias?"

"She still does not want to visit. Give her time." Dityss answered, her eyes leaving her notes to give me a hard stare as a reminder not to ask again. "Range of upper body movement?"

"Fully restored. Where's the healers?"

Her attention turned back to her papers, clicking her tongue with the impatience that resounded in my voice. "They are taking the day off. Healer Melania and her pupils will return tomorrow. I will not call any of them sooner. They have depleted most of their stores in removing the poison and healing your atrophy and need time to commune and rest."

Dityss had me on that one. I had intended to rush and insist they return today to begin working on my legs, but they needed to be healthy to continue their work. I was not so heartless to drain them of their life force to heal what would take a whole day of uninterrupted focus, and I owed Melania and her companions plenty already.

"Have you come any closer to what it could have been?" I asked calmly, trying to reign in the ripples of impatience that ran through my system. "I have never heard of a poison that could do this level of damage."

"I've narrowed it down to two herbs that may have been the base, but they would have had to have been mixed with something to bring about this effect." She murmured, pulling out some pieces of paper from the bottom of the stack with lines of scrawled notes, drawings of leaves, and diagrams. I pulled myself across the bed to sit closer to the princess as she placed the pieces of paper on the bed, spreading them out next to each other.

"The poison that coursed through your body when we first found you was a yellow and green mixture. Upon first inspection of the injury, I could see it leaking from the initial contact point both out of the wound with your blood while also seeping further into the muscle. There were no initial signs that your body would begin degrading at such a rapid rate, and I incorrectly assumed that it was a general poison that your system would fight with little to no difficulty. Within the short flight back to the castle where Sellias carried you ahead of me, I noticed your fur begin to dull as your body went limp in her claws. You had been semi-conscious and able to keep your head up as you flailed in panic up until that point—all in a matter of fifteen minutes at most."

Dityss moved another paper to the forefront, a detailed time frame of how fast I went downhill from the moment they found me. I had already asked what had happened after I blacked out, but hearing it again made my stomach twist uncomfortably.

"When we reached the entrance to Ren's atrium, you still had not shifted back. You were a unicorn that had lost all luster and all signs of life, your muscles and fat seemingly degrading into nothing. I knew the best way we could care for the mysterious illness was first to have you in Fae form and then transported into a bed for observation as well as to supply fluids, so I called Healer Melania, who brought some Eaprite to force your shift. Then Sellias and I carried you to your room and began to set up a system to keep blood circulating to try to force the poison out through the wound in a controlled environment. At that point, all of it had absorbed into the wounds and even into your fur, leaving nothing but a stain that the poison was even there. You were continuing to waste away to bones, and though I did not voice it to Sellias, Healer Melania and I were worried there was nothing that could be done. Nearly two hours passed of watching helplessly before Ren finally arrived. You had become barely a husk of a corpse, and no matter what magic Melania and I could muster, nothing was changing." Dityss held her head low, a strand of hair falling from the black bun wound tightly to her head as she read the notes. "Ren was instantly at your side, holding your hand, whispering something I could not hear, and I was afraid that his words would have whisked you away to Vomuna's Realms. But instead, whatever he said did *something* because the color returned to your body." Her attention returned to me, trying to analyze my face and the sorrowful expression I knew was there. "You do not recall what he said?"

"Not a word," I whispered, absentmindedly lifting my hand to push a bit of hair that had fallen in front of my face behind my ear. His words were one of the few things I could not remember, no matter how hard I tried to.

"He will not tell me either, even though I have insisted that whatever he did might have been the reason you narrowly avoided death. It *must* have been some spell or something he had learned or read about, but he will not even tell me what section of the library he found it in." She growled half-heartedly, looking back to the papers and bringing the two pieces with images of plants back to the front. "Regardless of what he did, I still need to find out what caused this sort of damage in the first place so that we can fight against it properly should another attack occur. I sorted through hundreds of poisonous plants and concoctions but could only come across these two that had anything to do with the physical drain we witnessed." She handed me the first research paper depicting a vibrant green vine, "That is Hanging Tongue, a vine that grows exclusively in the Druinn Marshes. It is illegal to plant or bring into any province of the kingdom, no matter the form, as it has been recorded as a magical plant originally designed with the intent of extreme bodily harm or worse. In the few studies I could find, researchers had gone into the marsh to find any magical plants that could be used to aid those without Odos's blessing to heal their wounded. Many researchers traveled through the bog's solid walkways, where Hanging Tongue grew the thickest, making most of those researchers found as colorless corpses."

"So, Hanging Tongue is a sort of plant that drains vitality, therefore color, from a victim?"

"Essentially. Though it never had the power to suck muscle mass from its victim like the poison you endured. I have started a line of research to determine if there is a combination of ingredients or if boiling down the vine will create a more substantial event. That research is on hold, however, as I have not been able to get my hands on the plant, and I am worried about the effects of its properties."

"And the fact that it is illegal." I raised an eyebrow as Dityss took the paper back from me to replace it with another, her eyes sparking with a mischievous glint that I had not seen from the princess.

"Just because something is illegal does not mean it is impossible to obtain. I would think an ex-rebel would understand such a trick well." Her voice was full of playful danger, a light laugh breaking free from my lips at the idea of the female sitting before me. I had thought she was a princess who was a rule-following lady who would do nothing against the crown, the unblemished image of perfection to those who looked up to her.

How wonderfully and curiously wrong I was.

"Regardless, Hanging Tongue is not the only potential culprit." Dityss continued, the playful look leaving her eyes as she pointed at the paper in my hands. It had a beautifully drawn purple and white lily-looking flower, but the notes were considerably less than what she had on the vine. "The only reliable knowledge I have on this flower is its name and a single account of its effects, though I have been unable to get the full story since its teller refuses to tell it to me. It is called Vomuna's Lily, a mysterious piece of flora that has a plethora of rumors about its origin. A single specimen is on display but is heavily guarded under lock and key with several trained guardsmen on watch around the clock." Her eyes could burn holes in the paper with how hard she stared at it, so I placed it down on the bed before it could burn me.

"Why won't the person who knows the information about its effects tell you more?" I asked as my eyes drifted to the healthy lily in the garden just outside my room. It stood tall in the early afternoon sunlight alongside some smaller flowers that had begun to bloom around it in the flowerbed. "Couldn't you just pay them to get what you need?"

"Usually, I could, and in any regular situation, I would have already. However, the one who owns the only known specimen is the same as the one who knows the story, and we share an unfavorable history. He does not particularly trust me with the information."

I mock a pout, bringing my voice to a whiny sing-song tone, "Awe, pretty little Princess Dityss can't get what she wants?"

The stare that she returned was full of malice at the taunt, but a tiny smile lifted her lips.

"Oh, I can, and I will, on everything I intend to obtain. Yet I am not overly egotistical to say that I could do this without help, and that is where you come in." The smile grew, mine falling in response. "After tomorrow, of course, when Melania can finish your healing process, you can walk again. Then you will be making a little trip into town for both of us to help find out what poison nearly killed you."

"I get no say in what the first thing I walk to is?"

"Consider it payment for my persuasive abilities going to great lengths to ensure Healer Melania and her studies are supercharged tomorrow, and you get back on your feet quickly." Her grin was nearly cat-like as she knew she had the winning hand, but she added, "Besides, I think where I am asking you to go will have what you are looking for as well."

I did not understand how she possibly knew what I was looking for, but I could not argue against the dragoness that had been working non-stop to save my life. "Fine then, I'll get this information about Vomuna's Lily from your informant. Where will I be heading?"

"You'll visit Argus Dryaden, the owner of The Golden Garden."

It was hard to fall asleep knowing that tomorrow I was going to walk again, my mind only whirring in the excitement that I could go out into Agraxis and do a little sightseeing by myself. I had been excited to learn that The Golden Garden was a well-known pub, meaning I would be able to get my first drink since I left Ullaven with some quiet time to myself to reflect on what had happened in the last few weeks. I would even get to talk to someone *new,* even if it was only for interrogation purposes about a flower that could have very well been used to kill me.

Another part of me was frustrated that I had to go to the pub instead of straight to wherever Ren had been hiding to chastise him for leaving me in complete silence.

Unless...I could find a way to do that before I left for town in the morning.

There was another place I had seen Ren before, and it required no physical walking at all.

My imagination brought up the magical library I perused whenever I wanted to use any magical abilities, rushing quickly past all the aisles of shelves to the usually restricted hallway where the 'Nature Wing' door was standing shut. My excitement deflated at the sight, believing that the door had been locked away from my prying eyes once more, but I pushed past my worry to grab onto the handle.

It opened without much effort, allowing a breath I did not realize I had been holding to escape my lungs in a quick rush of air.

The room looked just like it had when I had last seen it, with the instruments being the space's centerpiece, but a few small things were added to the shelves of the surrounding bookcases. The moonlight from the windows peeking into the imaginary room seemed to land on a sparkling item in the middle of the trinkets, pulling my attention.

It was a collection of senseless items: a random tooth, a dandelion, a sword, some other unnecessary knick-knacks, and a pile of dark fabric. The fabric was glittering in the mind-generated moonlight, my curiosity leading me to pick up the soft layers until the whole expanse of it cascaded into the light.

The dress had been torn down its entire side from the chest to the end of the train, but I could recognize the midnight blue and the silver sequins that created a mesmerizing shine in the moonlight. I did not understand why it was here when it should have been burned in case the poison tainted it, but I could not help my relief to see that such a gorgeous piece of clothing that had highlighted one of the most exciting— yet horrifying—nights of my life still existed.

For an evening, it had given me the illusion that I could live a fool's dream with a happily ever after.

"I didn't realize you were so sentimental," I whispered half to myself, though the smell of fresh rain and cedar that had filled my senses told me that the reason for this visit had joined me.

"I felt you would be upset if I got rid of your first royal present." Ren's voice filled the space, though I did not turn to greet him as I began to gently fold the tattered pieces of fabric to place them back on the shelf. I could see him out of the corner of my eye to my left, leaning against the shelving in effortless comfort. "What are you doing in here?"

"I came here looking for you," I responded coolly, putting the dress back in its place before I turned to look at him, joining in his casual demeanor against the bookshelf with my arms crossed. "Since someone doesn't know how to visit an injured prisoner after saving her life."

His eyes were clear as he assessed the situation. "I know how to visit. I just have had better things to attend to."

I could feel anger rise like a wave ready to crash into the sand, narrowing my eyes to attempt to keep the rage at bay. "Why yes, of course, his Highass has better things to do. How many rebels did you kill in the last three days? Or did you finally run out of camps, and that's why you decided it important enough to meet me here?" The words poured out of my lips as quickly as the venom that had nearly killed me, but he seemed unbothered by the sting in the words.

"The whole reason you're here is to give me rebel information so I can take care of it. I don't owe you information in return." His voice was lined with irritation as he watched my every movement like a hawk. "I came here to see if you plan to use any of my magic again without asking."

I wanted to scream, to tackle him to the ground and remind him of the events of the night of the attack, both before and after. To slam my lips into his and to see that carnal hunger that had plagued his eyes that night and to show him its echo in mine, but I knew that would not help me navigate whatever the hell was happening.

"If I did, I would be over there playing the violin and donning that absolutely stunning outfit of nature that *your* magic blessed me with that night." I grinned, standing my ground. "I don't think that's what I'm doing, right?"

His growl echoed through the room, marking one point to me.

"Then why *are* you here, Wildie?" Those hazel eyes of his burned into the depths of my blue, making me shiver under the strength that commanded him.

"I'm here to have a conversation with Prince Rendros Roamion, the man whom I'm invisibly chained to because he hasn't visited me after I was gravely injured." I snorted, not breaking the staring competition. "You left off our very *close* conversation on a cliffhanger, and I'm here to get your answer since you refuse to give it to me yourself."

His jaw ticked as he listened until his face softened ever so slightly as he thought. Though the change in expression was not in sympathy—it was an opportunity to fuck with me.

"You haven't started walking, though, have you? Otherwise, I imagine you would have stormed out of your room straight to mine instead of this place. Though in that possibility, we might have danced into something much more physical." He smiled that wall-destroying smile of his, my teeth clenching hard together as I tried to hold his stare without wavering. He could feel my emotions, but I could not feel his, making every inch of his change of pace in the argument wildly unfair. How I had ever seen him as anything different than the serpent he was short-circuited my brain's ability to think past the soft expression and genuine smile that had been on his face that night, the way his body pressed against mine—

His pupils dilated while his devilish grin widened, clearly seeing through my lament.

Shit.

"Or I ran out of the castle to sleep somewhere you wouldn't come looking for me so I could come here to tease you from a safe distance." I winked as I watched his smug demeanor crack at the idea that I was not in the castle, that smugness almost entirely dropping as a corner of my lip lifted.

"You didn't." He whispered, his eyes pinning me as he pushed off the wall, stalking towards me with a predator's intent.

When his hand reached out, I was quick to turn the situation in my favor.

I grabbed the sword from the trinket pile before I jumped backward, landing in the filtered moonlight that bathed the room from the windows with a swift twirl of the blade. It was a perfect weight that seemed happily balanced in my grip, its sharp edges bouncing the moonlight in several beams across the room. As I twirled it again to feel the comfort of a weapon in my hand again, one of the shafts of light bounced into Ren's face, highlighting the blue in his eyes as it clashed with the hazel like a storm.

"You want to find out, Highass?" I purred, allowing my magic to disperse around me in several strands to arrange my hair into a ponytail. "Agree to train me."

A growl ripped from his chest before he disappeared into thin air.

My chest rumbled with a growling response, but my senses took over as I let them take control, his scent still lingering in the space, an indication that he had not left it. There was silence for a heartbeat before there was a shift in light to my left, and my feet turned me in a swift spin to deflect claws with steel. Ren brought his other clawed hand down on the blade after the first, pushing with all the muscles I had been marveling at since I first met him, nearly against the bookshelf-lined wall that we had just been leaning against.

I let myself fall to a knee under the force, his hands quickly taking the opportunity to release the blade and reach for me. With my bent leg, I kicked hard against the bookshelves to push myself on the slick tile under his outstretched arms and out of the way, my hair falling on my shoulders when I shot back up to my feet, bouncing between each planted step as I reveled in the ability to move.

"So, the unicorn does know how to fight, or at least knows how to avoid being hit." His voice was deep with calculated interest, his eyes watching every movement of mine with exact precision. "We will see how long you last."

Within seconds, he had refocused, throwing himself across the room toward where I was standing, his brown hair slicking back in the movement. When he was only a few feet away, I jumped into the air to let him pass under me, letting momentum and magic bring me to a soft landing behind him where I could get the tip of my blade to the apex of his shoulders. A victory-taunting line had begun to rise in my throat when the sword clattered to the ground suddenly before I was spun and shoved against the window with an audible *crack* in the glass.

He pinned me to the window with my hands held high above my head, leaving the rest of my body exposed and defenseless. I wriggled and pushed against the restraint, but only more of his weight was pressed against me in response to keep me still, and I knew there was nothing else I could do.

The look he had given me the night of the feasts returned, his eyes roaming agonizingly slowly over each of my curves like he was a hunter examining the best place to make the deadliest bite. My breathing was heavy as I tried to catch it from the mock fight, though the heat that pooled in my stomach and stiffened my breasts from the predatory glare he had locked onto me threatened my ability to keep calm emotions.

"I let you play your pretty dance, Wildie. You surprised me with some of your moves, but you are still as untrained as a babe." He murmured, bringing his other hand up to run a finger down the curve of my neck to my sternum. "Despite how much work you will need, I am not opposed to training you. So long as you follow my rules and understand the risks." His voice had dropped to barely a whisper, its tone and his touch sending bolts of lightning down every nerve.

"And what are those rules, prince?" I asked breathily, my eyes locked onto his face as he lifted his gaze to focus on my lips. His tongue slowly slid over his lower lip as he watched me squirm under his grip again before he brought his gaze to mine again, allowing me to glimpse the slight break of desire that swam behind his eyes.

"Rule one, you listen to every single word I say. If I say go, you go. If I say jump, you jump." A storm gathered in the hazel, diamonds of its color brightening when lightning struck. "Two, you will not train with anyone else. You train only with me and follow only my regimen, and if I catch you training with anyone else, I will kill them and punish you. Three," He was barely audible as a predatory growl underlined his words, "You will refer to me as master when we train."

The rules were extreme—and something I had never heard about before from any of the trainers Leo had talked to—but I already knew my answer. The way 'master' rolled off his tongue and coiled around us like a waiting snare was different, having to smother my desire to whimper at the command.

"And the risks?" I could not keep my voice from trembling and my legs from shuffling against each other, but neither action was from fear.

"I will not go easy on you. In no combat scenario will anyone treat you with the same fairness, and my training will simulate reality. When we fight in our shifted forms, the same will apply, and the risks will be greater. You are the prey to my predator, and I love playing with my meals." The grin that spread across his face was feral and full of tense intent. "I will not kill you, but injuries might be inflicted for a lesson. Do you accept?"

I knew this was a bad idea and that I should listen to my brain that was screaming at me to say no and to run as far as I possibly could, but I was already tied to the man in front of me by the pact on my back. There was no running for me anymore; all I could do was make the best of the situation I had laid out ahead of me.

"Yes, master."

"Good girl, Wildie."

CHAPTER 17

The day after my...*meeting* with the Crown Prince of Aistris, Healer Melania had come to my room with her pupils radiating intense magical energy. Whatever Dityss had supplied them with made their magic amplify. I could feel the combined tendrils of healing magic wind up and down my legs, the atrophied muscles swelling under the magic as they returned to their original state. It still took another hour or so of physical therapy as I tried to walk around my room with the support of the healers to remember the feeling of one leg in front of the other without explicitly thinking about it. By the time the evening sun had started its descent, I could walk, jog, and stretch as if I had never been poisoned within an inch of my life.

"Is there anything else I need to know about Dryaden before I go?"

I was in the process of getting ready for the task I had promised Dityss as thanks for getting me back on my feet so quickly, throwing on a nice long-sleeved shirt that nestled tightly against my body and buttoning it up to my breasts. It was a simple outfit I had chosen to wear from the selection Dityss brought that allowed me to stay comfortable yet agile, consisting of a shirt and a nice pair of pants with running shoes that looked like basic flats. Nothing outlandish or expensive that would get me noticed, but nice enough, I would not be kicked to the curb as common folk in such a fancy location.

"He is an ancient unicorn who likes to serve booze and stories, and he will do whatever he can to divert you from the subject of the lily. Once he is telling the story, be sure to listen to every word, as it will all be true. It takes him too much energy to lie while telling a story, and he gets too heated to try to form a false scenario." Dityss explained from outside of the washroom, where she leaned against the doorframe. "Appeal to his adventures and stories, and he will fall head over heels in your hands. Especially since you are a unicorn yourself."

I nodded as I brushed my hair loosely behind me, letting some strands form side-swept bangs over my face. "Appeal to his ego, and I'll get the answers. Understood." I repeated, leaving the washroom to stand beside the bed, checking over the items I had laid out for the excursion.

Dityss looked at me with a quick head-to-toe examination, nodding in approval of my outfit before reaching into the pouch I had set up on my bed and tossing me a metal object. I quickly caught it, confusion knitting my eyebrows as I turned it over in my hands. It was a simple silver chain with a sapphire intertwined with gold leaves as the hanging pendant, the light from the garden windows catching the gems as they glowed under the rays.

"Selli designed it and had it made for you," Dityss said with a bit of a huff, shaking her head. "She is not ready to see you, but she is happy you are back on your feet. She mentioned wanting to give you something you could keep that had not been ruined that night and to see it as the turning of a new leaf instead of focusing on the night's horrific turn."

My throat tightened at the kindness in the gift as I reached behind my neck to latch the beautiful trinket to its permanent home. "You'll have to tell her thank you for me. It's beautiful."

"You can tell her when she is ready to see you. I am not a messenger for the two of you." The princess snorted, crossing her arms as she looked past me to the setting sun. "Get to the pub before rush hour so that you can attain his undivided attention. Do you remember the way?"

"Out the castle gates, follow the river until it connects to several creeks and an abnormally large gazebo. It isn't terrain-magic." I stuck my tongue out slightly before throwing the satchel over my head, settling it comfortably over my shoulder. "You have me covered if your brother or anyone else comes looking for me?"

"It is an unnecessary concern, but yes. I will be back here first thing tomorrow morning to find out what you could get from him." She led the way to the door and opened it for me to exit first, giving me a slight smile as I walked past her. "Do not make me regret trusting you with this research."

"I may be a prisoner desperate to get home," A half-lie, I realized, "But I owe you for saving my life. I don't make promises I can't keep."

I could hear her steady laughter echo down the hall as we separated at the exit of Rendros' wing, "Have a good night, Willow."

I could not help the warm smile that passed over my lips as I exited the castle doors and into the bustling city of Abraxis, where everything felt a bit more like home.

CHAPTER 18

The city streets of Abraxis were filled with life and laughter, and I could not help the smile that sat comfortably on my face as I wandered down the cobbled streets. It had been nearly a month since I first set foot in this city, making this my first real chance to enjoy its splendor since arriving.

It is a fitting way to celebrate being able to walk again after almost dying.

Most of the houses that lined the city streets in this district were large cottage-style buildings built with elegance and wealth in mind, but I could still see the small village beginnings each of the buildings held onto. Most of the upper stories of the buildings were later additions to the original framework; many had replaced the original fixtures and doors to become more modernized, but some still had original pine plank doors that had held on for at least a few centuries.

The families that lived in these historical homes all seemed to be from some source of wealth, considering its proximity to the castle, but that did not stop the children that ran across the street and down the large hill to the lower districts. Some hope ran through my system at the idea that maybe one day, those children would see wild-born children and accept them as friends. They would run to smaller villages in the forests and plains nearby to play knights and princesses, chase, or any other game the kids came up with.

There was a bump at my side, bringing my attention from the scenery to the young girl from my first day in the capital city staring up at me wide-eyed. She was holding a tiny wooden unicorn in her hand alongside a stuffed teddy bear in her other, a spark of recognition in her eyes that reminded me of natural magic.

Humans could handle elemental spells and could light their homes with them, but they needed to have it written somewhere or taught to them to be able to use it. Natural magic was not ordinary among their kind—which I thought was a cruel rule given by a crueler god that had decided that would be the natural order of the world. It was hard enough that they could not shift and feel the call of a genuine part of themselves in the wild, but not even being able to handle the most basic of magic without a spell book sounded like a cage to me.

If I had made the choices all those centuries ago, everyone would at least be able to cast magic spells to their heart's content.

"Y-You're that pretty unicorn!" Her voice was so high-pitched with excitement that I could not help wincing as it tore past my ears, but I gave a warm smile as I crouched down to meet her eye level.

"And how do you know that little Miss?"

"Your eyes! They are the same, and so is your hair, though now it's grayer. How old *are* you?" Her excitement was pouring out of every inch of her beaming smile as she looked over me, curiosity blended with joy.

"I'm twenty-six, and the silver in my hair is something new I wanted to try. What do you think of it?" I smiled, running my hand through a strand as I asked.

"I think...I think it's really pretty!" She giggled, reaching out a small hand to gently touch the ends of the silver before her mouth opened in a vast gasping motion as she held up a tiny wooden unicorn in my face. "This is Gingersnap! She's a very beautiful unicorn princess who beats up all the nightmares and bad guys in the world with her sparkly magic. She's *really* strong."

"She sure is! I can feel her magic protecting you like a warm blanket," I encouraged with a warm smile before giving the little wooden toy a small pat as I stood once more. "I'm happy she's there to keep you and others safe."

The young girl looked all over herself as if she could see Gingersnap's magic around her, a small giggle escaping my throat as she spun around in a small circle. Her eyes were wide as she looked at the little wooden toy, then back to a nearby cottage, before taking off with squeals of excitement towards the home where a younger woman—her mother, I assumed—waved towards me in greeting.

I was sure the woman would not be happy if she realized who her daughter was talking to, but seeing her daughter and Gingersnap had made my evening. Even if the meeting with the owner of The Golden Garden did not go well, I would at least be able to say I had a good night.

I waved my hand in farewell before I continued down the pathway that followed the small river toward my intended destination.

The river was not naturally made as it was not connected to any significant lake or mountain source, but it would have looked like one to an untrained eye. The banks were carefully crafted to have smooth curves and turns, and rocks were haphazardly strewn about from the slow-moving waters. The housing and pathways were built over and around the lazy river, with some houses having direct access to the water below.

As I continued my way down the river, I took the time to breathe in the normalness of the city. Even though some of the smells were unpleasant, it was the closest to feeling like I was home. From the sounds of the children playing to the conversations of adults talking about the daily updates of the city, it was a place where the biggest worry was getting to the bakery early enough to snare a loaf of fresh bread before they sold out. It was a city of people living everyday lives and enjoying the company of their neighbors instead of the worries of war—a place where I would be happy to stay if this were another life.

The sounds of children and lines of homes on the cobbled street began to thin out as more trees and grass started to litter the area, the beginnings of music beginning to cut through the foliage from ahead of me. They were soft but upbeat registers accompanied by an enchanting voice joining the instrumental chorus when I finally came across the interlocking creeks leading toward an enormous gazebo in the distance.

The location of the pub was an ideal location for any business, but Mr. Dryaden knew how to take it to another level, letting the nature of the spot speak more than anything else. The entire pub was open to the elements except for the pavilion's ceiling, golden fabrics trailing from the higher rafters, and branches that caught the light in sparkling brilliance. The music bounced between the foliage like natural backup musicians, luring me in like a siren song as I entered the bar with an awe-struck smile.

The pavilion's interior was just as elegant as its exterior, and nearly every seat and table in the area was taken. People were standing all around as they enjoyed drinks and pleasant conversation, but I pointed my attention to the bar where an older man was mixing some drinks for a young couple. The wrinkles on his face were crinkled in a happy smile as he laughed, making it hard to believe that he was the one that gave Dityss so much trouble.

I made my way to the bar, took an empty seat to wait for the owner to finish his current obligation, and looked through the glass-encased shelves behind the bar. There were probably hundreds of trinkets in there, but my attention was drawn to the lily in a secondary case in the middle of the shelves. Dityss's drawing was a perfect rendition of the flower, but it gave off a different feeling seeing it in person. The purple and white were swirled together in a smoke-like veil across the petals, seeming to pull the light from the nearby firelight like a hungry child. A shiver ran down my spine as I examined the double-layered glass cage the flower was locked away in, where it felt like the world around me chilled.

"I wouldn't give it too much of your attention, miss. It is not a plant intended to bring life and joy, but death and sorrow."

The older man's voice pulled me out of my intense stare at the plant, my gaze quickly snapping to his with the acknowledgment of my interest. His face held the warmth of his previous engagement, but the green eyes had frozen into an icy glare that almost matched the sting of the death lily behind him. His white and grey beard passed his chest in a disorganized braid while his long hair fell in strands down his back, age and wisdom etching deep lines in his face that made me want to kneel in respect to the knowledge this unicorn held.

"What are you?" He murmured, taking a deep whiff of the air around me. "You are a unicorn, but you also reek of dragon. You cannot be both unless—" Recognition flickered in his eyes briefly before the icy glare returned. "I see."

"And what exactly do you see or smell, sir?" I asked, feigning that I knew what he had scented.

"It is not my job to reveal such things to you. The inquisitive nature of your spirit will find it eventually." He said as he picked up a glass and began to pour some golden whisky into it before pushing it towards me. "You are here about Vomuna's Lily."

"I know little about the plant beyond that it may have been used to make a poison, but there are no records of what it has done," I murmured, twirling the glass in my fingers before taking a sip. "I've been told you have a story of its power, though."

The warmth of his face entirely drained to the shade of a white sheet, his head shaking slowly back and forth. "It is not a story I like to retell, wild-born."

I nearly spit out my drink at the mention of my true origins found so easily by a bartender.

"How do you know that?" My voice was barely above a whisper as I gently placed the glass down, keeping my eyes level with his.

"It is written in your very essence, dear girl. Along with many other things that few can read and understand." His green eyes seared into my face as a deceiving smile crossed his lips. "I'd like to offer you a task, filly. I have a very demanding table that is nearly out of entertainment and drinks in the Silver Maples. I want you to serve them for the next fifteen minutes while my servers get a break from their...*enthusiasm*." The kindness I had seen when he spoke to the couple evaporated with his conniving grin. "Your outfit already fits the dress code for my employees, so you should be able to slip in the open window between entertainers with no issue."

"As much as I want the information, I will not whore myself out to get it," I growled, leaving the glass on the counter as I prepared to stand.

"I'm offended you think my establishment stoops to such levels." He brought a hand up to his chest in mock offense. "All I ask is that you bring them drinks and maybe give them a show that requires no removal of clothes, and everything is done how you'd like: if you wish to strip, strip, or if you wish to dance, dance. Anything you want, so long as my customers leave with a smile."

A serving platter of several drinks appeared on the counter before me, and he leaned back from the bar to look me up and down. "Fifteen minutes of being a conversation piece, and you will get all I know about the lily."

I stared at Dryaden for what seemed like an eternity as I weighed my options. I had promised Dityss I would get the information about the flower, but I did not think I would have to jump hurdles and hide secrets to get it.

If I went back to her now, I would know nothing more about the poison that nearly killed me, thus breaking the promise I had given her. If I stayed, it would likely take fifteen minutes of humiliation; then I would get the needed information.

I growled as I picked up the tray without breaking eye contact.

"In fifteen minutes, I expect an uninterrupted and detailed story, Mr. Dryaden." I gave the sweetest smile I could muster before I walked out of the main pavilion of The Golden Gardens and over small bridges to a collection of silver maples that surrounded a floating platform dotted with several private tables. The firelight in this section of the business had been given a blue glow, creating intimate spaces at every table while helping hide the appearances of those who sat here from prying eyes.

I realized I did not know where I was going when a young human male stopped me as I entered, holding an empty tray under his arm. "You're the temporary replacement, right?" His eyes were a shimmering yellow that matched well with his dark brown hair and tan skin, but his demeanor was shaky. "I don't know what you did to piss off Dryaden, but you better start praying to whatever god you are closest to. The duke and his friends are in some mood tonight, and it's *not* friendly." He swallowed, shaking his head before pointing to the table in the far-right corner of the space. "Good luck."

He was gone seconds after that, hurrying along the bridges back to the pavilion.

Those fifteen minutes began to sound like fifteen hours as I approached the table, its shaded cover not hiding the shouting happening behind it.

"You fucking bastard, that was a lie, and you know it!"

"Who gives a shit if it was? It was just a waiter boring us out of our minds anyway, and we won't see him again."

"I still have an image to protect, and if that boy decides to leak something preposterous—"

"Then Daddy and Mommy's protection squadron will take care of the problem, and you'll run some tours to boost your image."

"Like they already did with *this* trip that you two started."

I stepped into the shadowed firelight of the table and put on a pleasing smile as I placed the tray on the table. "I'm sorry to interrupt, but I've brought your next round."

There were four men gathered around the table. There was one that was flushed red with anger, his blonde hair messy from running his fingers through it in frustration. Another was a female quietly sipping on a barely touched glass of wine, with her red hair pulled back in a tight braid. The third's black hair was lying over his shoulders in gently curled mounds, with icy-white eyes pinning me to the spot.

The fourth seemed the most frustrated as he laid back in a soft blue lounge chair, a cigarette hanging loosely in his hand, and deep blue eyes wandered up and down my body before locking with mine. "Dryaden knows not to send unicorns to our table. Why are you here?" His muscles tensed as he leaned forward, the fancy blue suit he had put on crinkling from the movement.

Most girls would have been drooling over the strength and commandment that was held by the unicorn male in front of me, considering most unicorn males were more academic than sturdy. Still, I had no interest in the irritated being before me.

"There was a lapse in coverage this evening, so I'm here to serve your drinks and bring entertainment for the next," I looked up to the sky as if I could count the minutes by watching the moon, "Fifteen minutes or so. What are you boys interested in?"

"For you to leave." The one with the cigarette growled, waving me off like a pestering fly.

"Oh, come on, Z, let her stay and give us a show. It's only fifteen minutes, and I wouldn't mind getting a good look at this mare since you don't allow us to find *any*." The blonde one groaned, standing up to walk up to me and get a closer look. "You aren't from Ivimea, but it's rare for a unicorn to be born outside our borders. What's your name, sweetheart?"

"You can look and call me whatever you want, but do *not* touch me," I growled, stepping away from Blondie to hold my stare at the apparent lead of the group. He still looked at me with irritation in his eyes, but now curiosity sparked alongside it.

"Then I want you to answer questions while making it look like you are just doing what anyone else would be doing here." He commanded, pointing to the raised platform in the center of the chairs. "Get up there, stay clothed, and dance. The firelight will mostly cover our actions, but shadows will still be cast through them."

Blondie looked like he would argue more but fell back into his plush chair with a sigh.

I looked around the floating platform to see the other shrouded seating areas, watching the shadows that moved and danced beneath their shrouds while counting how many were in each. Z's plan was not a bad one and arguably the best way I could handle the next thirteen-ish minutes.

I was not looking forward to the sudden interrogation as I pulled myself up on the small circular stage.

"My name is Willow," I announced as I began to slowly twirl on the stage, quietly trying to recall what little ballet lessons I had taken when I was three or four while trying to fight the strain on new muscles that had only just barely remembered how to walk. "I don't know where I was born, but I was raised in the Untamed Wilds." I knew my best bet would be lying or telling half-truths, but something about the leader of this troop told me he could detect a lie.

It was the red-headed woman who spoke up next, her chocolate brown eyes examining me up and down in disinterest. "Why are you here working for Dryaden instead of going to Ivimea?" It was hard to miss that she took great care of her figure and was proud of it, considering the clothes she wore barely covered her breasts and upper waist.

"Any of the segments of the kingdom, Ivimea included, have never felt like home," I answered, finishing a spin before bowing over and stretching my other leg behind me. Despite having to dance, stretching my legs discreetly in this fashion was nice. "This was the first place I could reach."

Something like recognition flickered in Z's face, my eyes narrowing as his eyes widened.

"You were the unicorn that night that got pacted to the prince." He breathed.

The group's interest doubled with every pair of eyes suddenly examining me like an enemy. The black-haired male's hand went to rest on the handle of a sword beside his chair. I observed as I stood as if I had just finished a set and was preparing to continue, but I was ready to sprint away should things turn against me.

"Why are you here, Willow?" Blondie spoke again, the hair on my neck standing straight in awareness as the male with the sword stood.

"I'm here because I pissed off the bossman, and he saw your group as a fitting punishment for the job." I snarled back, beginning to head toward the edge of the platform to run. "I may be pacted, but I was given the night off."

All three of Z's henchmen turned back towards him as they waited for the order when his ocean-blue eyes locked with mine, freezing me mid-escape as I felt the cold sensation of golden fingers clawing at the sides of my thoughts.

Fuck.

This man in front of me was not any ordinary unicorn with elemental powers—he was part of their head family, blessed with the power of chronovision that allowed him to investigate the thoughts of others.

I tried to thrash and kick and bite at the mental intruders, slamming walls down on them where I could, but with every rebuff, he came from a different direction, causing my mental fortitude to diminish with every hit quickly. I had been halfway off the platform when his power froze me in my spot, forcing my legs to silently cry out in pain as one leg was painfully outstretched.

Just as I believed he was going to break the final ounce of strength that kept him out of my mind, his lackeys were quickly on their feet with weapons aimed behind me as more players in this absurd game entered the shadowed space, bringing an aura of war with it.

"Remove your prying bullshit from her before I remove your head, Midstead."

CHAPTER 19

"That is no way to greet one of the palace's guests, is it now Rendros?"

The prying golden hand trying to break into my head backed away when Z spoke, giving me a chance to exhale heavily as I finally put both feet on the ground with a desperate shake of my head.

"You have no right to use those powers on any member of my court, Duke Zane." Ren's voice loomed in the shadowed spot like an eager beast as he moved closer to me to extend a hand to help me down from the stand. I took it in earnest gratitude, mouthing a soft *'Thank you'* as I attempted to fix my clothes nervously. Rygur and Jaeden were with him in less formal clothes, though they had several unbuttoned pieces of clothing as if they had been interrupted.

"Oh, she's a member of your court now, hm? Not just your pretty prisoner?" The duke purred, leaning back against the chair while inhaling the cigarette deeply before exhaling it with a knowing smile. "I did hear that you lost poor Petey, my condolences. Though I am sure she is better than him in more ways than one. How does a mare feel compared to female dragons, hmm?"

Ren nudged me towards Jaeden and Rygur before closing the distance between him and Zane within seconds. There was no time for anyone to react as his hands wrapped around the unicorn's arms and squeezed tightly to the point that he dropped his cigarette. Zane's strained face was the only sign of pain, but his smile only broadened further.

"Please, crown prince, show me with your fists how wrong I am." Ren tightened his grip, causing the duke's eyebrows to knit as his teeth ground together, though he kept his smile wide. "That way, all of these lovely witnesses can go tell your father and have her ripped from your pact and killed in return?"

All I could do was blink, watching the interaction play out in front of me in confusion. Why would he care if I was taken and killed? It was a useless threat, one that the prince would happily take to be rid of me—

He let go of the duke's arms with a swift movement, "Don't you dare touch her again, Zane. Magically *or* physically." Ren growled, turning back towards me and his friends. "If you do, I'll know. And I'll make sure the Midstead line *ends* with you."

Then his arm was locked into mine, and I was led out of the shadowed space with only one last glance to the people inside. The duke did not seem upset or even in pain anymore, but pure malice had crossed into his features before the shadows swallowed his reaction whole.

"As for you," Ren said, leading me to another shadowed spot distinctly different from the dukes that smelled heavily of fresh rain and food, "You are going to explain *why* you are here and what the *fuck* you were doing dancing on that pedestal." Rage thundered through his eyes like thunderstorms while Rygur and Jaeden took seats on opposing ends of the center stage and welcomed some equally disheveled partners back to their sides.

Before I could give any reaction to the male's evening partners, Ren grabbed my waist as he fell into an oversized plush chair and placed my ass firmly in his lap, holding me there.

"Is this position necessary?" I asked, wiggling a bit to get comfortable, but his hands grabbed tighter to keep me in place. Heat shot through my system like a strike of lightning when I finally met his eyes from my seat, "I came out here to talk to Dryaden about that flower of his behind the counter," I could barely breathe as the temperature in my system shot up so quickly. I attempted to dissuade my thoughts from falling further into the gutter by instead leaning into my curiosity, "But I pissed him off by asking about it, and he punished me by sending me to that table. Who's Duke Zane?"

"You're not the one who gets to ask questions here." He growled. "Why do you want to know about that flower?"

His growl and commanding demeanor destroyed any attempts. I had started to take my mind off my position as my imagination played different ways we could make this entire night change. All I could think of was his lips crashing into mine, claws extended to tear through my clothes, slamming me into the couch with each thrust as he took me—

No, as he *claimed* me.

An electric shiver ran down my spine at the very idea, forcing me to close my eyes to try and avoid making those thoughts a reality, but the taut groin of his pants underneath me made it very difficult to escape from the starved thoughts. I barely moved to settle more comfortably on his lap when I felt his cock jump in eagerness to the movement, making me bite my lip to avoid making any noise as I tried to return to the conversation.

"Dityss thinks it might have something to do with...with what poisoned me," I breathed, holding my hands in a tight grip on my knees. I wanted to let them wander up to his chest and over his arms and chest, to let them explore places concealed by clothing. "But Dryaden wouldn't tell me unless I did something for him, which was tasked as serving that group of assholes as my half of the deal."

"I didn't know you could walk yet." He whispered low enough that I could hear the hurt in his voice, pulling me out of my lewd thoughts to open my eyes. His grip had loosened slightly as he ran a thumb over my thigh, his eyes downcast as he avoided my gaze. "After our conversation last night, I thought it would be soon, but I did not imagine it would be the next day."

"I figured you would have chastised me for wanting to go out or instantly brought me into training. Besides, Dityss thought it wouldn't be best for you to know until after I finished this conversation with Dryaden." I let one of my hands free to cup his chin gently, lifting his head slightly to bring his attention back to my face. I could see so many different emotions tearing through his face, but I did not want to think about the sorrow or worry that lined it. "I thought you would have put off several more days of coming to visit me anyways, *master*."

His entire body went taught as his eyes refocused on mine, sharp intent cutting into his voice when he spoke. "You only call me that during training." The heat that pooled in between my thighs was a deep burning furnace as his rough voice curled around my mind. His hips bucked upwards with considerable force when I tried to reposition to try to redistribute the discomfort, a moan escaping me before I could stop it.

The predatory intent in his eyes deepened as he held my gaze, the low growl in his throat causing his whole body to rumble in response. His hands slowly trailed my sides to my shoulders, causing whatever last semblance of self-control I had as the hand left on my knee joined the other on the opposite side of his face. He leaned into the touch as I ran my fingers down his jawline, lost in the warmth that had now overtaken both of our bodies as we looked at each other.

"This is a bad idea," Ren whispered, his eyes softening slightly.

"Does it matter if it is?" I countered.

"I don't want it to happen like this," He breathed, one of his hands moving through my hair before he picked me up and laid me on the chair, cursing under his breath as he readjusted his jeans in an attempt to escape from the discomfort of the considerable length of his manhood pressed against the zipper.

Everything in my body fell from its rushed high, a soft frown settling on my face as I watched him step away.

Was I unattractive to him? Every time we got close, he would push me away, carving a hole in my gut as potential reasons *why* ran through my head.

Why did I even have any hope that a prince like him would want to do anything with me anyway?

He cleared his throat, but I could not lift my gaze to meet him.

"From what I've heard of it from Argus, that flower is one of a kind. There's no way it could have been used, especially since he keeps it so well-protected." He thought aloud, sitting on the pedestal across from the chair I had been left in to try and reach my eye level. "Wildie?"

I took a deep breath, steeling myself to meet his eyes and the disinterest that welled in them. However, what I saw sitting there was a betrayal of his original dismissal. His muscles were straining to keep him sitting on the pedestal, and the hazel in his eyes was bright with that predatory hunger as he tried and failed not to examine every inch of my body from his distant perch.

A slow smile spread on my face as I realized that I could play a different sort of game. I could—and I *would*—make him regret his sudden turn to abstinence.

"Supposedly, but Dityss doesn't believe that's where the lily's potential in the attack ends." I shrugged lightly, leaning forward on my knees, closing the distance between us until I was a mere inch from his face. The storm of desire's conflict ravaged deep in his hazel eyes, making my confident smile grow all the wider.

"What are you thinking of, Wildie?" His voice was raspy, searching my eyes for their intent.

I slammed my lips into him with a sudden ferocity that he could not prepare himself for, bringing my hands to his face while his hands snapped into my hair. His tongue parted my lips as he forced himself closer, and I wiggled myself between his legs to press my waistline into his. Every taste I got of him had me craving more, and the way he pulled me tightly against his chest with every piece of clothing straining under the contact, I knew he wanted more.

He *needed* more.

His hand traveled down my lower back as I pressed my breasts against his chest, barely able to stop myself from taking everything then and there. It had been weeks of this ongoing tension, weeks of no contact, and all I wanted was this was him—

I pulled away from the kiss before I became lost in it, pressing my forehead against his in a close yet comforting manner. We were both panting heavily as we stared into each other's eyes, letting only our breathing and our looks do the talking for several heartbeats before he spoke.

"Wildie, I—"

"You said you wanted to wait so I will honor that," I whispered, "But I wanted you to regret it."

A mischievous grin broke onto his face as he reluctantly let me go, watching me stand and dust off invisible dirt from my clothes as I tried to clear my mind to walk away from this without becoming a slobbering mess. His hair quickly became disheveled as my hands ran through its short length, but the desire in his eyes had only doubled with new strength as I tried to hold my ground a step away from him.

"I have places to be and a flower to learn about. Enjoy your evening, your Highass." I purred, ruffling his hair once more before walking out of the magical shade.

If you think you are winning this battle of regrets, Wildie, you are sorely mistaken. The prince's gravelly voice entered my mind as I walked over the bridges leading back to the pavilion, goosebumps trailing down my body.

Then make me regret it, master.

His hardened laughter echoed in my mind as I stepped back onto the solid ground that was the main stage of the entertainment venue, re-acquainting myself with its layout as a distraction from the pulsing heat in my thighs.

It had become more packed in the little time I was gone as the moon hung higher overhead, but there was still an empty seat at the bar. Fae and Human were all around the bar in warm conversations, ignoring the empty chair as if it had been cursed or left alone by someone who had recently sat there. As I approached it with growing curiosity and a raised eyebrow, I noticed that there *had* been something left on the seat.

A lily petal.

My heart hitched as I stared at the seemingly innocent sign, looking towards the bar. A younger employee had replaced the older man, and by the quizzical looks and casual questions on those who came by to grab a drink, the man's disappearance from his place behind the bar was uncommon. My ears twitched as if trying to sense some unseen danger from the sudden change in barkeep before a light hand landed on my shoulder, causing me to spin on my heel to meet its owner.

A young woman wearing a simple t-shirt and jeans stood there, with light green eyes looking me over in a calculating fashion, not unlike Dityss would. "You are the mare asking about the lily?" Her question was soft, but something in her eyes became shadowed when she looked over my face like it was not who she was expecting—or wanting.

I gave a curt nod in response, watching the young woman cautiously when she waved her hands toward the back of the bar as magic sparked on her fingertips.

Bottles and trinkets began to shake gently as harsh lines were drawn between open spaces on the shelves in the shape of a door, though nothing moved from its perch as it inched open. I looked around at the guests surrounding the bar to see if they were witnessing the sudden appearance of a door, but no one seemed to pay attention or notice anything had changed. Conversations continued as the bartender kept serving drinks to those who asked for them, reaching for bottles all around the now-obvious door.

A very advanced veil, then.

"He is waiting downstairs to give you the information you asked for," The woman murmured, looking around the bar to find something that caught more of her interest. She settled on a group of young women beginning to sing along with the band in a drunk daze, leaving me standing in front of the now-revealed door.

Less than twelve hours of being able to walk again after nearly dying a week ago, and I was standing at the top of a staircase that descended into near pitch black and most certainly the unknown. My mare pranced idly in my mind, clearly uneased by the small confines of a place no one knew about and what awaited at the bottom of the stairs. It was like staring into an abyss that no one came out of, unlocked by a mysterious figure who very well could have been someone in on the plot to kill me. Was there a murderer waiting down its dark steps? Or was there something worse?

Horrible scenarios seemed to play faster and faster until one gripped my imagination into vivid focus.

I had made it to the bottom of the stairs, having finally gathered my confidence to face what was down there. I was greeted by a small living room with some incense burning on a coffee table, breathing the fresh scent of jasmine and lavender into the space.

It was not the horrifying murder room I was expecting, but as I crept closer into the open space, my breath became visible as the temperature plummeted.

The old unicorn I was supposed to have met was nowhere to be seen, but next to one of the sitting chairs was a soft glow of white emanating from Vomuna's Lily, removed from its case and standing alone on a table with no support.

Curiosity overwhelmed my fear as I stepped toward it, barely reaching my hand for its petals when a scream echoed down the stairs, and everything began to shake in its echo. The lily stood without moving as chaos wrecked the rest of the room, pictures, and paintings falling to the floor with the loud sounds of glass shattering.

Then, there was a single scream that echoed down the stairs and tore through my very core, shattering my soul as it clattered through the underground room.

I turned back towards the stairs before I could even think through what could potentially be happening on the surface, but the door was gone. Dissolved back into place like a door had never existed in the first place.

I screamed as I pounded on the surface of the door, coughing violently. I could not breathe; Ren was out there, very possibly dying, and I could not breathe or move or make a single inch closer to him. Blood burst from my mouth as another cough shook my body, a hand lifting to hold my chest to calm the fit, but there was nothing there. There was only a gaping hole where something unseen had punched through my chest cavity.

No, Ren's *chest.*

The pact was killing me just as he was being killed, but instead of reacting with fear of my impending death, all I wanted to do was be right there with him. To save him—but I was trapped.

The scene cut off as I slammed my fist into my chest to bring myself back to reality—to remind myself that it was nothing more than my imagination, even though I could still feel the blood dripping from my lips as I looked down the stairs again. Everything felt so undeniably wrong as I investigated the darkness before taking a deep breath. I looked back toward the Silver Maples in the distance as if I could still see the prince's smile and teasing laugh that I had left only moments ago.

I reached for the pact and the invisible rope between us, desperate to ensure it was still there.

Ren? I called softly, shoving down the fear that shook me from the remnants of the imaginary scene my brain had so kindly shared with me.

Yes, Wildie? His voice was calm, its soft tone running over my frayed system like a soothing caress.

I should not have felt this amount of relief hearing him alive and still calling me that stupid nickname, but the smile that instantly fell on my face was a visible representation of it.

Is everything all right? Where are you?

I'm at the bar, and I need you here. The words were out of my thoughts before I could catch them, and I quickly amended them. *I need your help, I mean. To get this information from Mr. Dryaden.*

A chuckle rippled across the pact, causing the icy claws that had gripped my lungs to release fully.

Only a minute passed before I saw him striding across the pavilion. Those hazel eyes lit up with amusement, and an award-winning smile spread across his face as far as it could go. Heat instantly warmed my cheeks as I quickly shifted my attention back to the staircase to break my stare.

"You need me, hmm?" He teased, leaning close to my ear to whisper, "I thought you made me want to regret my inaction?"

His warm breath against my ears was too much for what I had just seen, my hands quickly pushing his face away as I closed my eyes to try and repel the fear that still sat in the corner of my mind like a waiting predator. "I still intend to do that, but I need your help here." I grumbled, "I've got a bad feeling about what's down those stairs, and I don't want to be alone when I find out what it is."

The statement was mostly true, but if something was to happen up here while I was down there, I did *not* want to feel that pain again. A betraying part of my consciousness reminded me what else I honestly thought, but I did my best to ignore it. He was still someone I could not fully trust—how could I believe such things when we both held each other at a safe distance?

He was silent for a moment before he asked, "A staircase? Darling, there's nothing there."

Oh. The veil. Right.

I took his hand and followed the same movement the young woman had done to reveal the door, my hands automatically committing the action to memory after my imagination sent my senses into overdrive. His eyes widened when the door opened, and I could feel the ripple of discomfort run over his system from the pact as he stared down into its depths.

"Ah." He whispered, looking down at me with a smile that did not quite reach his eyes. "I see why you were so nervous, Wildie. I'll do you a favor and join you in this endeavor—so long as I get something in return later."

I snorted as his teasing nature dissolved the remaining hesitance in my heart but returned his smile with a genuine one. "I've already made one deal today; what's the harm in making another?"

Those hazel eyes sparked with acknowledgment as he took the first few steps down the stairs, carefully watching our surroundings and keeping me close as we descended into the underground space.

It was damp and musty in the narrow hallway as we continued for what felt like an hour until we finally reached a flat plateau, staring into a seemingly normal-looking living room with incense burning on side tables around the space.

My heart dropped in my chest at the familiarity before it completely plummeted when I saw the uncased flower on the side table. The same eerie glow emanated from it, calling me towards it, causing me to grip Ren's hand tighter until the white of my knuckles showed. He squeezed it in reassurance, but I could feel his stance become rigid as he looked around the room for whatever threat I had perceived.

"I did not realize you'd bring a guest, wild-born." Dryaden emerged from a darker corner of the room, his eyes looking over Ren in casual disinterest. "Let alone the crowned prince of Aistris."

"I didn't realize you lived under the bar, old man." My attention did not leave the bartender as Ren spoke to him, letting the familiarity I felt between the two of them as they stood across from each other instead start the conversation for me.

"Work is my life, Mr. Roamion. You know this better than most." The older male smiled, sitting in the chair beside Vomuna's Lily, before motioning toward the couch before us. "Take a seat, tamed and untamed. I believe there is a story to be told."

CHAPTER 20

Ren and I sat on the couch with little distance between us when Dryaden snapped his fingers, and two cups of tea appeared on the table. I watched the steam rise from the cup while the Golden Garden's owner got comfortable in his seat, a hand hovering near Vomuna's Lily.

"Who was poisoned to cause the crown to begin looking into this flower?" The unicorn's voice had returned to more of a steady shake from age, but firmness in his features showed no weakness. His eyes moved between Rendros and me, and I sat a little straighter in my seat as I made eye contact with him.

"I was," I began, feeling Rendros squeeze my hand in quiet warning before I continued. "In a matter of an hour, all my muscles had begun to wither away. I was minutes from losing my life."

"Yet you live and walk before me today." Dryaden absentmindedly circled a spoon in his cup, the clinking against the glass the only other noise in the room. "How long did it take you to recover?"

"A little over a week."

"Then it was not Vomuna's Lily that poisoned you, filly. If it were, you would have died as soon as the poison reached every vein, about a week into your recovery." His green eyes were as cold as ice as he looked at the flower at his side. "Though, that's not the only reason why the lily could not have been used."

Ren and I exchanged confused glances, not entirely convinced by the elder's answer. Flickers of the imaginary scenario I had made slithered into my head again, and I raised my hand to rub my forehead to get them to go away.

They seemed to only fight back with a burning resolve.

"What are those other reasons, Argus?" Ren's voice broke through my thoughts, which helped keep the memory away a little longer than rubbing my forehead did.

"For starters, your friend, there would be dead and dust in the wind." His finger pointed towards me lazily before he leaned back again to sip from his teacup as he watched us. "Secondly, the flower is cursed with a spell intent to kill, as the magic that swirls within it is made from death itself." His gaze drifted back to the flower as it seemed to hum in place, almost acknowledging it was being spoken about, "Even with those factors, there is only one Vomuna's Lily, and it has been dutifully under my guard for the last one hundred and fifty years."

I blinked in gentle surprise at how easily the time slipped from his tongue, though I kept myself composed to maintain a calm demeanor. I already feared the flower a healthy amount that seemed to grow with the passing minutes, but the age in Dryaden's eyes and their unnatural coldness stilled me in my tracks similarly. The hand that was not intertwined with the Ren's began to open and close as my anxiety increased.

"So, it's a plant that has consequences, and the very idea of using it is impossible," Ren's voice had taken on a more commanding royal tone, and I looked up at him as he stared down the unicorn on the opposing chair. His jawline had locked into place with an irritated tick, but his face radiated kingly authority. "Why does a bartender have such a weapon locked behind his bar like a trophy piece?"

Dryaden's eyes moved back towards the prince, the energy in the room going taut as two powerful forces collided. "I found the bloom long ago and believed it would be a unique gift for my mate." His eyes went dark with grief as he held Ren's gaze as if trying to brand his words into the prince's mind. "It was a unique gift, but the after-effects of the Lily took its toll on me. It went after her, and it took her from me. I saw what it could do, and I do not wish its effects even on my worst enemy. So, I found a way to contain it so no one could take it in foolish glory like I did."

Ren stiffened beside me at the mention of Dryaden's loss, my heart tightening with grief as I moved my attention from Dryaden and back to Rendros. Had he found his mate and was afraid of that happening to her? My gut soured at the thought. Why did I even care if he found his mate? Some dragoness was out there perfect for him—I was only a prisoner from an unimportant family who had somehow created feelings for a prince.

It was a mill fairytale for children, yet here I was, trying to live it and make that reality with each kiss and gentle touch I gave him.

My breath hitched at my internal confession, and I pulled my hand away from the prince with a quick yet gentle movement. He looked in my direction with a flash of concern, but I only rubbed my hands together as if they were cold as my silent excuse. There was nothing I could say to him as butterflies danced in my stomach at the worry shining brightly in those hazel eyes, but I tried to hold onto my broken emotions as I looked back to Dryaden.

"Our deal was for you to tell me the story of Vomuna's Lily, Dryaden. Even though you are adamant it wasn't used in the poison against me, I want to know the *whole* story." I reminded him, trying to keep my eyes from returning to the deep pools of hazel and blue that stared at his now empty palm.

The bartender watched us with a soft interest, his cold exterior softening as his eyes glazed over in memory. He sighed softly as he fixed himself in his chair, looking over the two of us with what looked like regret in his face.

"Vomuna's Lily has a tale far older than this kingdom, the Roamions, or even the tamed lifestyles most have become accustomed to." He began, and the flower seemed to glow brighter.

It felt like its story was being told.

"Long ago, the gods roamed these lands like we do now. They had friends, family, lovers, and even mates standing alongside them—immortal creatures with no qualms about the world they created or each other. They all loved and understood each other's positions in the realm, and it was not uncommon for some of them to find love within themselves and pursue it. Only two had found the true eternal mate bond: Vomuna and Sinos."

"The Goddess of Death and the God of the Moon," I barely whispered, though my observation was only noted by a nod.

"Their love was a whirlwind romance that made every other divine being jealous of what they had. They had all had romantic flings with one another, but none truly felt connected as Vomuna and Sinos had. Truly *loved*, as they did. That was when they then made the Fae, hoping to find their love stories written amongst their creations. To find their mate bond in a world where one had not existed yet, and Sinos and Vomuna were happy to lend their powers to their found family to help them try to find that bond." Sadness weighed the air like a damp blanket, and I wrapped my arms around myself in a gentle embrace to keep fro getting lost in it. "However, centuries passed, and the others never found their mates. A couple found optimism in believing it was not the century, that they just had to wait for that perfect bond to be born unto this world, but most were ripe with anger at the strings of fate believed that their mate's string or bond had been destroyed—never to appear."

"The angered gods took it out on Vomuna and Sinos, blaming them for fate's trickery and lack of eternal bonds. They tried to spread doubt or mistrust between the two, but the Moon and Death's song was a perfect melody that no clash could break." Dryaden's attention lingered on us as he spoke, "Athos, Sinos' brother and embodiment of the day and the sun, was the one who held the most resentment towards his brother and bond sister. He often ranted to his followers about how they had pleaded the fates to weave their strings together at the cost of every divine entity's chance of finding the same, and many listened. Some scholars even say that the fracture in the brothers caused some Fae to abandon the gods entirely, resigning to live as mortal humans. However, removing some of his brother's followers was not the only plan Athos had against the Sinos. The worst happened on what we now call Moondrop's Zenith."

"That holiday is likely the most joyous of the year." Ren interrupted this time, confusion evident on his face, "And where we celebrate Sinos for his gift of the stars in the night sky by exchanging gifts and happiness to those we love and appreciate." He leaned forward with his elbows on his knees, sucked into the story like a child.

"That is how we celebrate it, yes. Over millennia, the true tale has been almost entirely lost to time. In fact, it *would* have been if not for Vomuna's Lily and the tireless work of the unicorn scholars at the Ivory Atheneum. But we do not give gifts for the sake of following in Sinos's footsteps to bring joy and happiness to others by the comfort of his night. We do it to remind him of the joy and happiness that still exists in the realm he created, for that night was the worst night of his entire existence."

"What happened?" I asked quietly, my hand absentmindedly moving toward Ren's in search of comfort.

I stopped myself before I let it get too far.

"The Lily was a gift to Vomuna that Sinos had worked on for nearly half a century with Myspha and Etia to blend moonlight and death's whispers into a plant that Vomuna could hold for the rest of their immortal lives. It was a reminder of their bond and love for one another that Vomuna always kept tucked in her hair no matter what they were doing. The lily was everything to Vomuna, and she cherished it almost as much as she cherished her mate and their children." A sad smile flickered across Dryaden's face as I saw silver line his eyes, his voice thickening with emotion as he continued. "On Selis 21 st, the day we call Moondrop's Zenith, Athos had devised a plan. He would set up a private meeting with his brother at his home in the deserts of what we know as the Eugara Expanse, but he would leave his eldest son in his place while Athos traveled to his brother's home in the Sinos Cordillera."

"When Sinos reached his brother's desert home, he was struck with a sudden intense pain in his lower abdomen that continued to grow in agony and range as it traveled along his entire upper body. Nurses and aids at Athos' house instantly tried to help him, but there was nothing on his body that explained the cause of the pain. There was no clear indication that he was hurt, but the agony he suffered did not cease. It kept growing and growing until he realized what was happening—finally hearing Vomuna's cries across the bond." The unicorn's voice was thick with emotion as he continued, "He raced to fly back to her, but by the time he had arrived, his castle was completely silent—as if someone had taken all the air and life from home. He ran to their room, and the roar that emerged from that castle is still rumored to be heard to this day."

A tear ran down Argus's cheek as my heart broke for the God of the Moon. I had assumed there was no more tremendous pain than losing someone you loved, but to lose your mate, the other half that the fates created especially for you...Tears fell into my lap as I watched spots darken on the fabric, Vomuna's Lily seemingly letting the weight drown those in the room in sorrow.

Ren's hand had wrapped around mine tightly at some point during the story, but instead of fighting it, I clasped onto it as tight as I could, as if it were an anchor to reality, as my imagination crept forward once more.

It brought the image of blood dripping from my lips and soaking my clothing instead of tears.

"Sinos had found his beautiful Vomuna in tattered ribbons on their bed, her insides torn out for everyone to see and delicately placed as if on display. The room was destroyed; no piece of furniture went untouched, and white blood had splattered across every surface. This level of damage could have only been done by another god—one he knew all too well."

"But he did not confront his brother that night, grief too powerful of a force as he held his mate and cried sparkling drops of starlight. Sinos's tears from the loss of Vomuna filled our night sky with the thousands of millions of stars that now inhabit it, and the Fae of the time had felt the ripples of the loss of the goddess of death from the roar that had sounded across all Aistris. The ceremony of Moondrop's Zenith was first celebrated with millions of candles worldwide to mimic the stars that had appeared in the sky while everyone held their loved ones a little closer that day."

The room went quiet, Vomuna's Lily becoming the only source of any light or sound as its magic seemed to leave a constant thrum in the room. Ren's grip on my hand shook lightly from the force he grabbed it, and I pulled my free hand over to lay it on top of his. I lazily rubbed my thumb against it, seeing Ren's silver-lined gaze quietly move to our hands before I looked back to Argus.

"Did Sinos eventually get his revenge on his brother?" I asked quietly, my voice cutting through the silence like a knife. Argus fixed his attention on our hands, cleared his throat, and continued.

"It took about a century, but Sinos did. He used the lily that he had so painstakingly crafted for his mate, and he brought it to his brother's wedding. It was a beautiful event, perfectly crafted to the sun god's desires—and that of his mate's."

I took a sharp breath and felt something dark coil in my stomach when Argus confirmed my shock with a silent nod.

"Athos had found his mate about fifty years after the death of Vomuna, and he invited his brother to their ceremony. Sinos had never publicly announced who Vomuna's killer was, always playing that he was investigating to the best of his ability with every waking moment he had. But Sinos had always been the more patient brother, allowing his grief and pain to ripen until the perfect moment to get his revenge. In that time, he had learned something about the flower he now wore in his hair like his wife had, and he intended to show everyone its power as statement to the world." Argus cleared his throat as he continued, looking up at the ceiling like he could see the events play out across the painted wood. "As a gift to his brother, Sinos presented his love's greatest treasure, Vomuna's Lily. He promised it would bring great joy and spirit to their home as it once had for him. Athos took it in great haste and triumph, believing his brother had no idea that he was his bond sister's killer and had gotten away with murder."

"Only an hour passed after Athos had taken the flower when doubled over in pain at the bar. He had left his mate out in the courtyard to enjoy the party with her friends, but even from beyond the glass doors separating them, he could hear the screams and the terror that now filled his castle. But most of all, he could hear his mate's cries of agony ringing above every terrified shriek. He ran past demons and shadow creatures that were destroying everything in his castle with brutal efficiency, though he could not care about his worldly possessions as he raced to find the female he had waited so long to find. When he finally reached the courtyard, he was met with a colossal, shadowed unicorn standing with his mate impaled on its horn. She had been the picture of health before the attack, but now she was nothing but a shriveled husk on the end of a sharpened keratin spear." His voice slightly lowered, "Then there was a flash of black as a shadowed dragon the size of a mountain tore into his entire body, leaving Athos in ribbons."

Argus cleared his throat as he seemed to stretch in his seat, rolling his neck before he finished, "Rumors after that point are all over the place, but the only thing that is repeatedly said in agreement was that after the shadowed black dragon killed the God of the Sun, it said, 'The sun casts the largest shadows.'" He shrugged, "No one particularly seemed to know what it meant, but it was a clear end to Athos. Sinos was never seen again after that, and the other gods retreated to whatever personal realms they wander now."

Argus' demeanor changed back into a cool bartender front faster than I expected, shaking my head as I tried to process the story. "Did that shadow dragon or Sinos curse the flower then? Is that what brought the shadow unicorn and other beasts?"

"No one can agree where the curse came from, but since that first use of the flower was confirmed at Athos's wedding, it has been connected that the shadows and demons seem to be summoned by the curse when enacted."

"There are records of the flower being used after that point?" Ren's voice was dark when he spoke; the sheer ice that laced it sent shivers down my spine. "When was the last time it was used?"

Argus sighed, looking at the tea that had gone cold in his cup. "The last time the curse was activated was when it was handed to me by my elder brother. I wasn't supposed to take on the responsibility of its care, but my brother had contracted an incurable illness. Whenever it switches hands to a new holder, the curse goes after their mate by summoning demons and shadows that listen to only Vomuna's Lily. I tried to convince my brother to find someone else, but it had been transported to me before I could say no." His eyes shone with great pain, bringing a hand to his chest in a movement of attempted comfort. "I had already found my mate by the time I became its guardian, believing I would never have to worry about losing her. However, she withered away in about a week as the shadows stood and watched, sapping up her life force. I saw that terrifying unicorn of shadowed death stand at her side for the entirety of that painful death, and I spent hours pleading for her life with that unicorn. For me and our daughter, Alice." He shook his head, "But there is no bargaining with death's spirits."

Rage swelled in my gut, my gaze instinctively cutting to the flower as it let out another wave of grief into the room. "Why was it such an instant death for Athos and his mate when an innocent suffered an agonizing *week*?" I felt the tears fall on my face as I stood, looking at Ren, his hazel eyes hollow as he seemed pointed on the spot on the ground before I looked back to Argus. "You did nothing wrong but continue the duty of your line that has become as cursed as that flower and lost your *mate* to it. Why did it make you suffer?"

"I think the curse believes it does our line a kindness by letting us be around them longer before they die. To say goodbyes." Argus admitted, shifting in his seat. "But it is not a living organism that can understand pain and suffering, and after Sinos used it to kill Athos, I believe it went along on an order of its own that was given to it. It's not something that can be changed."

"Well, I think it should be destroyed once and for all." I snarled, something dark overtaking my movement as I pushed for the flow before I could think. All I wanted to do was destroy such a horrid plant that only brought grief and agony to the innocent, to remove whatever curse Dryaden and his family had endured, how many centuries it killed —

I was swiftly gripped by the waist and nearly thrown back onto the couch, Ren's gaze burning with vibrant anger and horror as it met mine, his voice dropping into a low growl.

"Don't you fucking *dare* touch that thing." He whispered, "As much as I want it gone, I don't want to lose my mate to destroy it, and I don't want you to lose yours." I could feel the tremor in his voice as he pulled me closer, my senses clearing from my dark descent into a sudden beam of light that cleared the way.

I was once a shooting star lost in space, unsure of her future. That was until I crashed into a strong planet enveloped by the smell of fresh rain and cedar, its warmth bringing me into a place I could call home. One I never thought I could find.

CHAPTER 21

"I'm not convinced that it wasn't what was used to poison you," Ren whispered as we walked through the now quiet streets of Agraxis.

Shortly after my attempted attack on Vomuna's Lily, we left t Golden Garden and Argus Dryaden behind us. The ancient unicorn had nothing more to explain or desire to say anything else, and we had no intentions of prying any further. It was evident that the memories of his mate had taken their mental toll on him and us, so we left with gentle farewells.

The bar was still filled with guests, but it had turned from party to softer conversations as the waxing moon hung high over the sky. Our shocked silence continued as we passed through the streets of Upper Agraxis that led back to the castle, listening only to the lazy movement of the river and the occasional greeting of a fellow night owl.

"Are you suggesting Argus was the one who did it to me? He seems to be the only one who knows the lily's true abilities." I murmured, looking at Ren as our feet created rough noises against the stone path while we walked. A grave expression had settled on his face since before we had left Argus, and the moonlight only cast more giant shadows on h creased features. "He already lost his mate from the curse; there'd be no reason to suddenly come after me or mine when I had only been here a few days. Not to mention the fact that I'm only a prisoner of the crown."

"You know you're not a prisoner, right?" Ren's hazel eyes drifted down to me, staring so deep into mine that I felt like I was going to drown in their beauty before I quickly shook off the feeling, instead choosing to look at the stars above us.

"Of course I am, or did you forget our first meeting when you wanted me thrown into the dungeons?" I rolled my eyes, "Besides, I'm pretty sure I must stay in some range of you for the pact to make sure I can fling myself in front of you like a unicorn shield should death come knocking. You get a little too far sometimes, and I get all...*itchy.*"

A small smile crept onto his face as he began to laugh ever so gently, the sound pulling my attention back to his face.

"You're right; how could I forget? Though you've reminded me, I'd like to speak with you about your 'cell,'" His gaze warmed my bones before his smile faltered, "I've been asked to move to the front lines for a couple of months to bring morale to my men and re-evaluate plans."

The warmth that had been filling my body froze entirely, and I knew I had sent a shock of that worry through the pact when he stopped walking to face me fully.

"I'm not leaving you here, Willow." His voice was so soft and filled with so much kindness that my heart swelled in response, as if his words were enough to promise me complete safety. "That itchiness you feel is because there is some distance tether on this pact, so we must stay in the range of one another. However, it's not for that reason alone that you will be coming along. I refuse to leave you somewhere that an assassin could come after you again."

Where I can't help you again. Was the silent addition he made through the pact bond.

Be careful there, Highass; you might make people believe you care about the untamed. I quipped back.

And what if I do?

Something short-circuited at that question, and I had to blink a few times to register it. Then, his laugh gently echoed against the walls of the surrounding homes, leaving our private conversation behind.

And what if I do? It replayed in my head like a singer trying to remember the following line in her lyrics.

"We will be leaving tomorrow, sometime in the afternoon. You can give your findings and farewells to Dityss, but then we will move." He explained, beginning the walk toward the Palace of Ascension once again. "It will be just you, Jaeden, Rygur, and I since all my forces are already there. We will do most of our traveling shifted, but we will take time to rest in the evenings. In the mornings, before we leave, we will be doing your training."

The castle walls loomed over us in the moonlight as we entered through a side gate. Though the castle looked regal and inspired from the outside during the day, at night, the entire building became a tomb. A mass of black shadows and horrifying whispers made me want to run in the other direction as fast as I could.

I tried to shake it off, but some odd feeling gnawed at the back of my neck like someone was watching me.

"I don't have much of a choice, but it sounds fine," I whispered, moving closer to Ren as we entered the castle. The haunting feeling only doubled inside its walls, with moonlight draping over paintings that caused shadows to darken their faces and the whites of their eyes gleamingly apparent in the darkness.

I wanted to be back in my room so badly that I was about to start running.

He seemed to understand that I was growing increasingly panicked at the darkening surroundings and picked up his pace ever so slightly that I would not have noticed if my legs were not so much shorter than his, and I almost *did* have to run to keep up with him.

We were in his wing within the next few minutes, the common room where I had first seen Ren's council empty. Despite being connected to the walls of portraits and being made of the same cold stone as the palace, it carried an aura of warmth and safety that the rest of the castle did not.

"Wildie?" Ren's voice was soft—a gentle question to try to pull my attention from whatever panicked hole it had crawled into. "I'd like you to stay with me tonight if you don't mind. After Argus, the poisoning, and the fact that you can move now, I'd feel much better if you were closer."

After everything I had witnessed that night and the sense of knowing that crept up my spine, I wanted to curl into my sheets and scream for the rest of the night. I wanted to curse gods and fates for their decisions of mates, to cry in the wake of the knowledge that I was *falling* for the prince beside me, or to sob in the panic that I had felt his death like it was my own. I wanted to scream into the garden of my conflicted agony that I would be leaving for the borders of my homeland tomorrow to fight the people I was supposed to be fighting *for*.

I also wanted to go into Ren's room with him and sleep in his arms, forgetting about the world and the worries that surrounded us.

"I suppose your big fearsome pact-tector can sleep on your floor tonight to make you feel safe," I turned to the one thing I felt I could play well in this situation—confident and playful. "Lead the way, your Highass."

"Pact-tector?" He chuffed, his hazel eyes filled with amusement.

"Pact and protector combined. I think it works rather well, don't you?" I smiled, his grin widening in response.

"Why yes, I do. You've got quite the imagination, Wildie."

"You truly don't know the half of it, prince." I snorted as I followed him down the hall, stopping outside the door closest to the dark atrium. I felt a spark of nervousness flash through my system alongside a dash of heat, and I shook my hands out as if that would make the conflicting emotions disappear as he opened the door.

The room was like the atrium: more extensive than any bedroom needed to be. It was the size of a large house, with the ceilings soaring into their supports nearly twenty feet in the air.

A line of bookshelves on one wall encased a small fireplace surrounded by two sitting lounges and books scattered across the floor. A small table sat between the two sitting places, covered in more books piled on each other alongside an empty cup. On the wall across from it was another doorway that I assumed led into private bathing chambers and an archway into what seemed to be another bookcase-lined room, but Ren's comfortable walk into the room brought my attention to the farthest wall.

The room's back wall was covered in stained glass windows, and the moonlight that filtered through them made the colors seem silver in the light. His bed was pressed against the bottom of the windows alongside several sitting spaces and carpets, and by the way he looked at the glass, it seemed this was where he spent most of his time.

The glass held a giant black dragon with its wings outstretched to encompass the entirety of the window as if cradling the glass sce beneath it. Rolling hills and a large mountain stood directly in the center, seemingly cutting the hills in half, but the dragon's eyes seemed pointed to that spot.

"My mother told me that he watches all the mountains and landscapes to protect them as best he can." Ren smiled, "She believes it was made for Akis, and Dityss is inclined to agree, so that's who I think it is."

"Did he have one mountain he loved above all else? Because the only mountains I can think of extend as far as the fields depicted below it, not just a single mountain top." I snorted, walking up to examine the glass from his side. "Or did he get rid of it too before he died when he decided to split territories and the families in it up?"

If there was any surprise or irritation at my question, he did not show it. "I don't believe he split the shifters or the tamed apart, only us from Velhea or some other continent we were once attached to."

His gaze remained on the glass, the silvery colors filtering through the glass, covering his body and highlighting his features. His face was creased in thought and some sadness while his muscles were softened in quiet comfort, the light catching every fold and crease in his clothing as he watched whatever silent memory was taking place in the glass as he watched it.

It took me a second too long to look back to the glass when hazel eyes met mine.

"How else would you explain why the tamed and untamed have been at each other's throats for centuries? At Velhea for harboring fugitives of the crown?" I sighed, shaking my head lightly as I tried to avoid staring.

"From the history I have learned, it seems that it all came to a head after Akis used his magic to manipulate the terrain to its current state."

His eyes softened slightly as he looked back to the stained glass, "I think it was after Akis died that war broke out, not when he changed the terrain, but I can't prove it. Any history books created before Akis became king were lost when the castle's library was destroyed in conflict with another province." He sighed, walking over to his bed to fall into it with a soft *thud*. "I've had too much confusing history tonight, and I'd rather not try to dig up more. For now, at least."

I walked over to the bed and slid down the side of it until I landed on the floor, beginning to play with a few strands of hair that fell from the ponytail. "I can agree with you on that, though taking me with you to the borders of my homeland will only garner more of these conversations—and likely arguments."

"Then let's not talk about gods or kings or war tonight." The mattress moved behind me as he sat up, pushing one of his legs over the top of my head to straddle my shoulders to sit behind me. His hands moved into the strands of hair in my ponytail, gently pulling his fingers through the strands in soft movements. "Let's talk about the untamed. I've never had a good chance to meet one that *didn't* want to kill me, so I'd like to learn."

My eyes were trained on a specific spot of embroidered silver leaves on the carpet before me as my heart threatened to beat out of my chest. I took in a deep breath of air as I tried to calm it, but his fingers running through my hair sent goosebumps down my arms. "Are you...brushing my hair?"

"And if I am?" I could hear the smile in his voice, sending butterflies soaring through my stomach.

"Then, let me take it out of my ponytail at least." I smiled back playfully, looking back at him from the corner of my eye. He summoned the hairbrush from my room into his hand while his combat-trained hands delicately took out the band that held my hair up with intense concentration. A giggle escaped my lips at the level of attention he was giving to the simple action before I reached my hands behind my head to pull the band out with a quick pull, shaking my hair out as it fell in waves to my shoulders. The smile on his face made his eyes sparkle as the moonlight blended into the blue ring, and I quickly pulled my attention back to the carpet before I could fall any further.

I had to keep my distance.

Or at least *try* to.

"What do you want to know?"

His hands softly ran through my hair to level it out before I felt the first pulls of the brush through the tangled strands.

"You mentioned in your letter that you were raised there as a mare by your mother when you were thirteen, and it had taken you ten years to free yourself from your herd and walk as Fae once again," His tone was not accusatory, but my breathing hitched. "Yet you were talking and walking with ease when you shifted in the throne room—as if you had been using the form for some time."

"Starting rather personal, huh?" I tried to laugh, though the sound that came out was drier than I intended.

"Argus called you wild-born." His voice was soft and hesitant but not accusatory.

I pulled my knees up to my chest and wrapped my arms around them slowly, trying to piece together how to respond. I should have known that the general of the Imperial Army would have picked that up and remembered it.

"What makes you think he wasn't lying?"

"Argus has never lied to me before, and he knows things far beyond me." A soft hand landed on my shoulder, his thumb rubbing into the muscles comfortingly. "And your nerves sky-rocketed when I asked."

Stupid pact bond.

I let out a sigh, keeping my attention on my knees. There was no point in lying when he knew the truth already, especially when he had not thrown me to the deepest pits of the dungeons upon confirmation. "Yeah, I'm wild-born. My mother and father ran to the Untamed Wilds border when she was close to having me, ensuring I was born freely on the other side." My mind wandered to the song that my father had sung to me every night all those years ago, but the melody sounded out of tune as I tried to remember my mother. "After she recovered from the birth, she left, leaving my father and I on our own. He was stuck as Fae, and me a newborn with the ability to shift outside of the magical limitations."

"Why lie about that in your letter?" Ren asked, the gentleness in his voice coaxing my nerves to calm.

"Wild-born are considered much higher threats to the kingdom than the wild-raised. I thought that if I had disclosed that, I would have been killed without a second thought, no matter the information." I sighed, running my thumb over my knee. "So, I just changed the story a bit."

"I'd like to say things wouldn't be so brutal, but a month ago, I likely would have removed the threat myself."

The admission made ice run down my spine at the idea of that reality, my imagination swiftly pulling together the image of his blade impaled in my chest.

"So now that you know, why don't you just do it? Doesn't that still make me a higher threat?" My voice was barely audible—unsure if I wanted to know the answer.

The brush ran through my hair gently, but silence filled the space between us as he continued the mundane motions through my hair. He seemed to be lost in thought or considering his options.

"No, I don't think you are. I think you care a lot for the people you left behind, but you've also started to care about the people in this castle. You never tried to harm Rygur, Jaeden, Dityss, or Sellias. You never tried to harm me, either. Your heart is strong and beats for the people you care about, even if it makes you weak in the eyes of an enemy."

"Thanks for the vote of confidence, your Highass," I grumbled, his gentle laugh echoing in the room in response.

"You want to protect your family and those you love, but you were never taught how to do so with actual warfare involved. Hence why, I will help train you in the more physical aspects."

"A part of me doesn't want to fight physically," I admitted. The memory of the sobbing mother covered in ash reappeared like a ghost in my vision, prompting me to close my eyes like it would make them disappear. "I wish I could do more with just words, but I need to know how to fight and physically protect those I love. Words don't work anymore."

Ren's agonizing roar of pain echoed in my head, and I buried it in my knees to try and silence the pain it brought with it. I begged my imagination to shut down as both memories played in unison, the combination threatening to push me past my breaking point.

"Wildie, hey," Ren's voice had moved in front of me, his hand brushing over the sides of my face and over the tips of my pointed ears as I tilted my head to look at him. He must have stopped brushing to kneel before me, lowering his head to reach eye level as our eyes met. "I'm right here."

All I could do was shake my head as the tears pressed past the broken barrier I had tried to build, falling down my cheeks. I did not want to cry in here—where my breakdown could be seen and acknowledged—but whatever willpower I had crumbled as my head pounded in the beginnings of a headache.

Every time I tried to suppress my imagination in the past, I always ended up with the worst headaches afterward. I could smother them to silence for a short period, but every time I did, I would experience a debilitating headache that would knock me out for the rest of the day.

Strong arms grabbed me and picked me up, pulling me out of my concentration as I realized I was being carried somewhere. I did not need to open my eyes to know that Ren was holding me. I pressed my head closer to his chest to try to stop the tears that ran down my face, the room warming around us as I heard water begin to run somewhere from behind.

He sat me down on a soft surface, only moving a step or two away until I heard him moving something. "I won't leave you, Wildie. It's been a long day." He was silent as I responded with only a dip of my head before he added, "A warm bath usually helps me clear my mind and helps me relax. I figured it might help you, too."

I finally opened my eyes to examine the firelit room, the magical flames scattering across the sealing to help spread the dim light they shed. The room was nearly as big as mine, though the bath was double the size of the one in my chambers. Black marble veined with gold coated the tiles of the room, with furniture made of light oak or birch to contrast the darkness of it. A line of thin windows ran across the upper wall, letting moonlight run across the cabinetry to give it a somewhat ethereal appearance.

I stepped out of my clothes, too tired to care about the male standing in the room. Earlier that evening, I might have tried to be more seductive with the movement, but my limbs felt like they were weighted with stone. The voices and images from my imagination had dulled, the sounds muddied like they had been submerged under the running bathwater.

I moved over to the bath once I was completely naked, standing before the white stone that held the steaming water in its place before I slowly moved my attention to where Ren was. He had made himself comfortable leaning against a pillar at the side of the bath, though he did not attempt to hide his examination of my bare body.

"I told you I looked better when I wasn't half dead." I smiled weakly, bringing Ren's attention slowly back to my face with a sultry smile settled on his features.

"You did, and it takes every inch of my willpower to stay standing here like a gentlemale." His voice was like a low purr now, the return of our little game helping to push away my imagination as I stepped into the bath and sunk into the water. "Though I found you beautiful then, too."

My face heated at the compliment, prompting me to swiftly wash my face to try to hide the reddening cheeks behind warm water.

"When did you start having those waking nightmares?" Ren asked, almost so quietly that I nearly missed the question. He moved over to the side of the tub to sit on its rim, one hand beginning to draw circles in the warm water lazily.

"This wanting to know more about the untamed is starting to sound more like personal question hour." I retorted, the steam clearing my thoughts as my muscles relaxed. "I'll answer it, so long as I get to answer a question about you after."

His jaw ticked once, but he gave a small smile with a nod. "I suppose it's only fair."

"I've had them since I was around five. I think, at least." I sat up to pull my head farther above the water to make speaking and watching him easier. He was staring into the water with his attention bouncing between my breasts and the apex of my thighs, hunger darkening his gorgeous hazel eyes as he tried to stay away. I pushed myself from the far side of the bath—and away from my imagination—to flip onto my stomach and idle in front of him, placing my wet hands on his thighs and giving a soft squeeze.

His attention instantly cut to my gaze, a coy smile appearing as the hand in the water moved to start running through the wet strands of my hair.

Careful, Wildie.

"Where'd you meet Jaeden and Rygur?" I continued the question game, paying no heed to his warning as I laid my head on his thigh to look up at him. He was so warm and so damn gentle, letting the little bit of my imagination dream of the idea of getting to stay like this with him forever. To enjoy these games, we continued to find ourselves playing, laughing, smiling, and bringing ourselves to points of joy that it seemed neither of us had enjoyed for a long time.

The joy continued for a heartbeat longer before it drifted aside, my mind reminding me that he would likely reject a future with me to choose some dragoness instead since the Roamion lines never crossed with a different breed of shifter.

The fates were wicked and cruel.

"Rygur's father is the captain of the royal guard here, so we've known each other since we were hatchlings. He was assigned as my personal guard in line for his father's position when he passes into Vomuna's judgment." He answered, his hand moving to hold the side of my face and softly petting over the tips of my ears. The action brought a shaky exhale from my lips as he continued, "Jaeden was one of the soldiers in the army who had started to gain a reputation for beating the hells out of his command when he disagreed with a plan, and no one could beat him into submission for his disobedience. They had plans to execute him had I not stepped in and given him a place in my council."

"What did he disagree with?" A soft pull of my hair interrupted my question, his hazel eyes sparkling with amusement.

"My turn, darling." He purred, his other hand moving to my back to rub and knead the muscles beneath the skin. "Have you been with a male before?" Something protective and proud had moved in his stature as he stared into my eyes, searching for the truth like it was plainly written beneath my gold and blue irises.

I hesitated, letting my eyes drop to my hands as I tried to avoid the embarrassing question. His hand moved from my ear to cup my chin, bringing my face closer to his while also holding my attention so I could not look away. The heat in my thighs grew in intensity, and with what little air I could suck in for a better breath, I answered.

"No."

His penetrating stare into my soul stopped as a grin grew on his face, which was wild and wicked.

If I did not know better, he almost looked like he had returned to the wilds and became untamed.

He softly pressed me back into the bath, spinning me around while leading my hands to push against the cold marble as he followed in after me, soaking his clothes as he crouched over me with his mouth near my neck. His other hand had moved to my breasts, the kneading motions from his back massage continuing around the peaks.

I should have been afraid, running in another direction, screaming for help. Crying for my freedom and pleading with him to allow me to live another day.

A predator had pinned me in a bath where I was exposed to whatever he wanted to do to his prey.

And I wanted him to devour me whole.

My back arched as he squeezed my breast in a hard grasp, his hips moving forward to grind against my ass, his cock straining against its fabric cage. His growl at the movement rumbled against my ear as he pressed his lips against the sensitive skin and gently tugged at it with his teeth, pulling a soft moan from my throat. Ren pulled me flush to his body with the sound, his hand moving from my breasts to the dip in my waist, rugged hands exploring the swollen flesh.

"Ren," I moaned, and his lips moved down to my neck to lick the skin gently. His hips moved up and down the curve of my ass, pressing himself against me with no actual skin contact as he slipped a finger inside of me.

I had fingered myself once before in an attempt to feel what others felt when they were with their partners. It was a futile and pitiful event when I could not even bring myself to finish what I had started, even when I could hear what *good* it could cause whenever Theo would bring someone home.

The warmth and the feeling that Ren's fingers and movements had on my body made me believe that it might be possible for me to know what release felt like.

"Say my name again, and I'll add another." He murmured against my neck, a second finger circling my entrance in teasing motions.

I whimpered in pure need as my moan echoed in the chamber when the second finger began its descent, stretching the soft folds of my core as he passed. "Ren, please, I—"

The hand holding my hands moved to cover my mouth, his smile brushing my neck.

"I know what you want, darling." His voice was a dark promise as he continued to run his fingers in and out of me, "But you asked me to make you regret your decision to tease me earlier."

Stupid, cocky, past me.

"So you'll feel what you could have gotten, and I'll finger fuck you into oblivion." He growled, biting my neck just hard enough to draw pleasure—not blood. His fingers continued plunging in and out of me, the water splashing as our movements rocked the world around us.

The movements were electrifying, each movement of his carefully planned, his hand pressing tightly against my mouth to help hide the sounds of pleasure that fell out of me like words on a drunken night. Whatever remaining horrors my imagination tried to give me whol dissipated with every thrust of his body against mine and every added finger, his growls and grunts of pleasure a distracting theme. I felt like my body was being ravaged in the center of a summer storm, ea movement drawing out several layers of heat and pleasure as I felt the tip of his shaft press past the waistline of his jeans.

The tension in my lower abdomen tightened to a new level at the closeness of that contact, combined with a deep thrust of four of his fingers. I cried out his name as my climax washed out the storm like a monsoon, a thousand different colors flashing behind my eyes as the world fell out from under me. His hands kept me from falling into the water in a spazzing heap, but his thrusts had become wilder as he thrust his waist up and down my backside.

"Fuck!" He growled as he grabbed my pussy like a handle to bring his cock closer to my ass, and the spasming of his release pulled another moan from me as he finished on my back. The room fell quiet except for the heaviness of our breaths, the final movements of the water settling with gentle splashes as we stilled.

He removed his hand from my mouth to turn my face to his, placing a gentle kiss on my lips. There was still hunger left in his eyes from the desire for more, but he kept the kiss gentle and filled with so much more than lust or passion.

Then he stopped, pressing my forehead against his while our eyes locked.

"You will not allow anyone else to touch you. You will only cry out *my* name." He whispered, and I could have melted at the possession in his gaze.

"I am only yours to touch and to crave," I whispered back, the pact mark on my back burning something primal inside me in response.

"Good girl." He smiled, kissing my forehead gently before pulling away and standing in the water. His muscles were so prominent under the soaked clothing, and I swear I had started drooling as I reached up towards his hips in an attempt to bring him back down to my level. His hand grabbed my outreached one swiftly, "Not tonight, Wildie. We need to get *some* sleep before we leave in..." He looked up toward the thin windows lining the room, "...a few hours."

Then he was gone from the chamber, leaving me in my thoughts and the aftermath of such an exhilarating moment. I was beyond ready for a second round, but it seemed he was keeping his promise to make me regret my attempt at making *him* regret, and I was pissed at my past self for pressing this game with him. I wanted him to fully claim me, to say fuck it to tradition and bonds, and I wanted the rest of the world to melt away.

He returned only a few moments later, holding a hand out to help me stand from the water like the gentlemale he had *tried* to be. He had changed into some loose black sleepwear that hung over his body comfortably, the baggy clothing making him look like anyone other than a crown prince. I took his hand and carefully stepped out of the bath after I finished washing myself off, grabbing one of his towels that hung near the basin's edge and breathing in his strong scent of fresh rain before drying myself off as he watched.

Once I finished, he handed me a light blue shirt that was definitely *not* mine, bringing me to raise an eyebrow as I looked over it.

"You didn't grab any sleepwear," He shrugged, but amusement was plain on his face as I slipped it over my head. He smiled with possessiveness that threatened to be my undoing when I pulled it down over my thighs.

He led me back to the bed under the stained-glass windows, sinking into it as he stretched out onto the surface. He groaned a little as he fixed his pants to be more comfortable over his still-hardened length, the sight bringing a teasing smile to my face as I moved toward the cushions.

"I'll sleep amongst the bed of cushions you've created here to help alleviate...*him*." I smiled before he quickly sat up and moved to the spot among several pillows that I had planned to settle in. He stopped me with a shake of his head, waving towards the bed with a gentlemale's bow.

"I would be a terrible host if I let such a beautiful female sleep on my floor, no matter the amount of cushion." His grin turned ravenous, "If you hadn't started this silly game of unicorn and dragon between us, I would have taken you on the bed before sleeping in you all night. But alas, we are both competitive fools who refuse to be the first to buckle, so I will take the cushions."

My face was as red as the brightest piece of glass on the wall as I turned to his bed and crawled under the covers. It smelled so richly of him, and every sense in my body was high on the smell as I pulled the blankets closer around me, taking one more glance at the male on the floor beside me.

"You could just sleep up here with me, you know. No sex necessary?" I offered, though the heat in my core rose in anticipation.

"I refuse to be the first to buckle, Willow. You may tempt me all you'd like, but I am stronger than you in my attempts at restraint." He smiled with a teasing chuckle, though it softly tapered off until he spoke again. "You're safe here, Wildie. Get some good rest tonight." His voice was gentle as he nestled into a pile of cushions, his hands behind his head with his eyes closed.

"I'm here too, Ren; I am safe." I smiled lightly, feeling sleep tugging at my very bones. His face had softened even more as if he could finally relax.

"Sleep well, my prince."

CHAPTER 22

By the time the sun rose in the morning and as I finally pulled myself out of my sleepy cocoon of blankets, Ren had already left the room. Two large bags were packed at the end of the bed, curiosity pulling me to them when I noticed folded clothes on top of one, pinned with a note.

My clothes won't do for you for extended travel, so I had Sellias design some new outfits for you. Be sure to say thank you to her in the atrium before we depart. – Your Highass

I shook my head as I pulled up the outfit to examine the clothing, which consisted of a pair of thick nylon pants bore a black that was scattered with little white dashes and dots that looked like stars in the night sky, along with a matching long-sleeve made from the same material. The upper half of the shirt was a mixture of soft blues that slowly blended into the same black as the pants in a smooth gradient cascading downward from the neckline. It was a set of gear that was perfect for versatile movement and comfort. One I would have looked for myself, though the thought of its creator made my heart ache as I remembered the last conversation I had with Sellias.

Gods, please let her forgive me.

It took only a few minutes to slip into the new outfit, the fabric bringing a smile to my face as I looked over myself in a mirror in Ren's bathing chambers. It did wonders for the curves and what little muscle I had survived the poison's effects, though I was more impressed that it had so many pockets and places for me to place weapons.

It was likely something Ren had ordered added to the outfit, but they were nonetheless comforting.

I walked back into the room to quickly rifle through what was already packed in the bag and was pleasantly surprised at how neatly it was packed. There were several more outfits for the travel and some books that Dityss had likely stashed aside for me, ranging from romance to history.

Another thing to thank the sisters for and another reminder that I was eternally in their debt.

I put away all of the things I had disrupted in the bag before I stepped out of the room, carefully shutting the door to help avoid any unwanted attention, but by the time I turned to walk into the atrium, Jaeden and Rygur were both standing in front of me.

They were both wearing darker-colored traveling gear adorned in chain metal and weapons with bags slung over their shoulders, their faces wearing matching evil grins as Jaeden unabashedly sniffed the air.

"He finally did it then?" Rygur asked the wolf Fae, his short hair combed back and the gold sparkling in his dark eyes as he looked me over. Jaeden seemed slightly more perplexed, then visibly frustrated, as his honeyed gold eyes rolled over to Rygur in exaggerated disappointment. His light brown hair had been tucked into its familiar bun, bouncing with the movement.

"No, he didn't. A taste, maybe, but nothing more. His scent on her smells distant." Jae groaned though he kept walking to the atrium with grumblings about Ren and his uptight ass.

Rygur held a low chuckle, his smile turning kinder as he met my gaze. I knew my cheeks were flushed from Jae's observation, but I did my best to hold my head high despite the embarrassment that rolled through my stomach. "How are you doing, Willow? I haven't had the chance to talk to you since before the Fall Feasts ball."

"Did none of you think it would have been kind to stop by? In case you forgot, we all live in the same wing of the castle." I grumbled, crossing my arms as soon as I finished tightening my ponytail, though a warm smile was on my face. "I'm doing good, however. I'm ready to stretch my legs and run for several days. What about you, Rygur?"

His free hand sheepishly rubbed the back of his head, "Let's just say we had orders that kept us very busy and entirely unable to visit." He laughed and then relaxed as he looked toward the atrium, where I could hear Jae yelling about something. "I'm doing well, despite the sudden change in station and Peter's…"

"I know." I smiled, putting a hand on his arm, squeezing it in understanding. "I'm sorry that I caused that to happen. It wasn't my intention to break up the boy band."

"You hold no fault for what happened that day, Willow. Peter made a poor decision, and he has paid for it." He shrugged, though I could see the sadness in his eyes.

"Since I've seemingly joined the council now, you can call me Lo if you want." I chuckled, turning to walk into the atrium.

He came up close behind me, placing a hand on my shoulder. "Welcome to the band, Lo."

The atrium was the same mess of plans and paper that it had been on the first day I saw it, but there were a few extra bags stuffed with supplies and maps in the room and a lot more noise as people ran about ensuring the prince had all his supplies.

Ren and Jae were arguing about something or another in the center of the room, though their conversation had hushed to a mixture of mumbles and hushed words that I could not discern from the entrance of the atrium. I had only been there a moment before Ren's eyes found me, the frustration in his eyes melting for a moment. Jaeden smacked his shoulder to bring his attention back to him, which was returned with a low growl as the argument continued.

A small chuckle escaped my lips, Rygur joining in with a soft chuckle before he sighed, "I better go intervene before they start fighting." He smiled as he bowed slightly and walked over to the two bickering males, hands up in surrender as he approached.

"I don't know how you will handle those three alone, Willow. Far too much testosterone for me." Dityss spoke by way of greeting as I spun around quickly to meet her with a warm smile. Her black hair was messily tied in a bun, glasses sitting on top of her head, and she was holding a book in one arm alongside a quill. Behind her, I could see Sellias in a simple purple gown, her pale violet eyes holding my gaze with forced confidence.

"Dityss, Sellias, I'm so glad you're here. I was afraid I wouldn't get to say goodbye," I smiled, though I could not take my gaze off the softer twin. It felt like it had been so long since I had seen her, though it was, at most, only a week or so ago.

Dityss seemed to notice my lost attention as she stepped away from Sellias so her sister could not hide behind her. She sighed with an irritated groan, turning her head to the side to look at something by her brother. "I will talk to Ren about his plans and what you learned about Vomuna's Lily last night. You two, figure this out."

Her boots clicked across the atrium floor towards Ren, leaving Sellias and me alone for the first time since the attack.

We stood quiet for several moments, but something had changed in the princess before me. Innocence and joyfulness had once sparked in her eyes, but now they seemed so...hollow.

"Selli, I'm so sorry for putting your brother in danger that night. I didn't know he would come for me—"

"I don't forgive you for it," Her voice was quiet and reserved, but those eyes had turned into a blaze I almost did not recognize from the soft princess. "You nearly got yourself killed, and then, on top of it all, you nearly killed my brother."

"Ren handled himself, and I didn't see any injury—"

"You know *damn* well he would have died if you had." Her presence had changed, and I barely held my ground as I brought my arms up to wrap them around my chest, my blood recoiling at the accusation. "You decided to run around as a mare on the day of Winulla within the kingdom's borders, and you seduced two men to come after you and succumb to the shift. One of which was my brother."

I had always seen Sellias as the quiet princess with big dreams for freedom and making dresses for the masses—the softer between the twins and the one who stood down at any significant confrontation. But the woman that stood before me was not the Sellias I had known, her frozen anger making my blood chill.

"Why would Ren have died if I had? The pact only goes one way: if he dies, I die. Not the other way around." I was feeling increasingly defensive as the princess pinned me with her stare.

The smile on her face was abnormally wicked as she responded, "As two of the strongest magical races in our world, do you not understand that the bonds between them are stronger? A way to keep them even, to balance out the strength that could come from them?" She stepped closer, the air seemingly disappearing around me as she leaned in to whisper, "Especially when it's a mate bond."

I could feel all the color drain from my face, my fingernails digging into my upper arms as I stammered back. The world seemed to spin, and I had to do all I could to keep myself from falling. "We don't have a mate bond."

'There is no use in lying to me, untamed traitor. I saw what happened that night." Her voice was low when she pulled away, comfortably putting her hands together in front of her. I could have sworn her eyes had darkened to an entirely different purple for a split second, but the softer violet returned before I could confirm it.

"There is no mate bond, Princess Sellias. Don't you think one of us would have noticed by now?" I tried to reposition myself to stand taller and with more confidence, even as my heart was torn apart at the words. Even though I dreamed of that reality, it was not possible. I could only pine for a future we would never have from a distance, keeping my hopes and desires quiet. We could continue our games and enjoy the time we had, but what Sellias accused was never going to happen.

Even if it were true, I would hide it to keep him safe. If we never claimed the bond—if it existed—his life would never be tied to mine in a way that could harm him.

Even if it would kill me to deny such a thing.

Sellias opened her mouth to respond, but boots clicking on the floor alerted both of us that Dityss was coming back. She shook her head and gave a warm smile as tears lined her eyes, pulling me into a hug and giggling like the conversation had never happened.

"I'm just so glad you're okay, Lo! I'm so sorry I was so distant; I was afraid you would never want to talk to me again." Her voice was back to its bubbly happiness, pulling herself back to run her hands up and down my arms.

My whole body was stiff as she smiled at Dityss, who looked pleased to see that the conversation had gone well and was looking at me for my response. I wanted to shake her shoulders and ask what had happened to her and what was going on, but I put on my best smile instead.

"I could never be upset with you, Selli. I'll keep Rendros safe while we are gone."

"I know you will," the princess smiled, grabbing Dityss and pulling her back towards the hallway. "Come on, Diti. I don't want to take up any more of their time. They have to make sure they are ready to go." Sellias sighed as she pulled Dityss toward the exit into the hallway. The older twin's eyes widened in surprise at the sudden tug but went along with barely a wave as the sisters disappeared into the hallway.

I felt like I was going to throw up as I finally took in a full breath of air, leaning against a nearby table and staring at the papers below me without actually looking at what was on them. The interaction played again in my mind, and I tried to focus on the dark purple I *knew* I had seen instead of Sellias's.

No play of my imagination, memory, or anything helped me place the behavior or the color.

"I hope you know I'm not looking forward to running alongside you for the beginning of this journey." A teasing sigh came from behind me, but I could not move to turn to Jae as he leaned against the table. "Ren has made it clear that you need to run and get your mare out for at least a couple of days, and I have been designated to stay on the ground with you. Usually, I'd just get carried by one of them since their flying is faster than any running speed, but we don't get air dragons one and two until you get all your energy out. So do me a favor and get that out quick, yeah?"

He turned to look at me, and I could feel the gaze turn from teasing to concerned when I did not respond. I was too busy holding onto the table, trying to rifle through everything in my brain to make sense of what had happened to Sellias, but I could not think of anything. Frustrated, I slammed my fist into the table, letting my head fall to my chest in defeat.

There was no way that was Sellias...right?

"Willow?" Jae's voice was a distant echo in my ears.

"I'm just worried. About seeing the wilds again." I lied, shrugging as I tried to recompose myself with a sigh, finally turning my head to meet the concerned honey gaze that watched my every movement. "About seeing people I knew and being on the opposing side of that war."

His concerned face seemed to relax as understanding took its place. "I have a hunch that Ren won't let you near the front lines or fights themselves, so I don't think you'll need to worry about seeing someone you recognize. Though I know how difficult it would be." He smiled lightly, and I remembered the conversation with Ren last night about Jae's past with previous captains and his units. If anyone did understand, it might just be the wolf beside me.

"Thank you, Jae." I smiled, "And for whatever it means, I'm looking forward to smoking you in a race again as soon as we get going." He bumped my shoulder in irritated jest, but a broad, contagious grin was on his face that brought one to mine.

Then, there was a hush that fell over the room, accompanied by two sets of footsteps.

"Mother, Father. Here to see us off, I presume?" Ren's princely voice cleared the silence, though no one else dared to speak.

I turned slowly to the center of the room, and I felt like all the wind was blasted out of my lungs as I met dark purple eyes that watched mine, their familiarity shooting directly through me like a spear.

There they were—the purple I saw for that split second in Sellias's usually gentle violet. I had not been able to get a good look at her in the throne room the day I arrived.

That dark, cold, and outright murderous purple belonged to the Queen.

CHAPTER 23

Since I was little, I have always had an overactive imagination. My father would find me playing with little toys and talking to imaginary friends rather than real ones, and though he had been concerned, he let me go about my days with no actual interference. When I could start to remember some of what I imagined, I remember feeling like they were always right in front of me and as accurate as reality itself.

Eventually, the imaginary friends I had made disappeared as I aged. After my father passed, my imagination stayed to show me different scenarios in excruciatingly painful detail. It turned my overthinking and worried thoughts into paralyzing reality. When my thoughts would start overpowering my mental state in tense situations, I would run to let them run the course through the worst potential scenarios.

I had expected them to start baring down on my brain as I saw the darkness of the Queen, but instead of horrifying scenarios, I spotted an old friend standing behind her.

She looked the same as when I last saw her in my imagination when I was eleven. She stood about as tall as I did now, with dark brown hair cascading down her shoulders and over her breasts in loose curls. Her eyes shined in pure gold, and she wore a black dress adorned with thousands of real stars sparkling in the dark fabric.

She always had an affinity for shadows and often put on shadow puppet shows for me when I was younger and needed a smile. Her shadows would bounce off the walls to play with me, almost feeling like tangible beings that sang and spent time with me like real friends.

I wished she was my mother.

Instead of shadow puppets and friends, the grim she commanded flowed like black waves in the room, though no one else could see them. The waves contorted and let out small strands of magic as they wound themselves around the ankles of each person in the atrium, becoming a snare in which everyone was trapped. My eyes narrowed on them as I tried to figure out what she was doing here *now*, fifteen years after her last appearance.

The ropes of shadow seemed to be completing some examination of the room before most retreated to their master as she held her hand up towards me in a silent invitation, even though I was too far to reach her hand.

What is it? I sent the question into the void, her gold eyes glimmering in silent recognition of the question. She never had to say anything for me to know she was listening, her gaze slowly moving to the Queen with a new emotion I had never seen her show.

Anger.

My attention joined hers as I looked over Queen Ezyla, who had started contributing to the conversation with her son and King Eilbeir. She wore a billowing purple dress drawn out into shades of grey and white, with far too many bunches of frills and jewelry for my taste. The crown on her head was entirely made of pure silver, representing her dragoness's horns, curling back with tiny curved barbs wrapped around amethyst jewels. It was far too much for a farewell to her son on a semi-regular move to the front.

A glance back to the shadow woman noted that she was not staring at the queen herself anymore—but instead at the long trail of black and grey that fell behind her.

The shadows were an extensive train that seemed to writhe in distress as they swallowed up the walls and the hallway behind her, all light disappearing and flickering out of existence in its path.

A single strand of the horrifying grim seemed to struggle to escape from the large mass, captivating my attention as it fought its shackles to break free. It writhed and twisted until it finally became a singular shadow in the atrium with no owner, seemingly lost in the sun, looking for its home.

The golden eyes of the shadow woman caught my attention as she conjured herself in front of me, her hand still held out like it was an invitation to dance. Questions rallied through my mind as the horror of the shadows that seemed to swallow all light stayed in the forefront of my mind.

The ghostly woman before me shook her head, then slowly turned her attention to the lone shadow that had followed its imaginary master. It did not immediately rejoin her, instead waiting for something else as it slowly slithered on the floor like a smoke-born snake.

The woman's hand turned over before me, pulling my attention to her again with worry heavy in my thoughts. It was a silent question and plea to know what was happening—to have my unasked questions answered—but to ask anymore was a risk in a room full of enemies.

Those golden eyes were soft with sorrow and kindness mixed into one as she grabbed my hand.

Everything exploded at once, my hands quickly grabbing onto the table behind me to keep from falling from the sudden force that pounded in my head. Memories, visions, and so many thoughts flickered through my head like thousands of paintings that I could not discern a single one. I could not breathe, could not *see*, but I felt something cold and dark slither up my thigh where the healed wounds of the attack still scarred my body. The mysterious presence settled above the wounds until I felt the trickle of dark energy seeping into it like ice melting on skin. My entire system froze at the sensation as something new emerged amidst the chaos that attacked my body.

A dark coil of power that had flickered through my system once before but felt locked off and unobtainable.

I inhaled deeply as I opened my eyes, readjusting to the room's brightness as I held my head with one hand. The shadowed woman was gone, along with the individual shadow that had separated from the trail that the queen had.

Still *has*, I realized, as I could still see the bleak trail that rolled out behind her.

I could hear it screaming—as if the mass of black was a living thing that was in pure agony.

"Is everything all right, my dear?" Queen Ezyla Roamion addressed me directly; her eyes narrowed in hostility. Everything in my body seemed to shrink away under her glare, but I had to keep standing to face her, even if it made my stomach churn with bile.

"Just a small headache, your Majesty." I bowed my head in a quick apology, "It often happens when I'm stressed or when my mare is impatient." I kept my voice level as I stared into those dark eyes, frustration bubbling in the back of my mind as I kept thinking about the trail of shadows and the lone strand that freed itself before disappearing.

She was hiding *something*, but whatever it was eluded my best ability to try and find it. The shadowed woman had wanted to show me, to give me a hint, but I could not interpret what it was.

"I see," She smiled with an attempt at kindness, but the venom that stung from her words washed away any belief that it was truthful. "It's a boon that you will be leaving to stretch your legs for several days then, I assume."

"Indeed. I am thankful for the opportunity to join Prince Rendros on this task."

The tension between us was as taught as a bowstring as the shadows behind her began to curl into her hand as it began to ball into a fist. The darkness in my gut coiled in response, like a viper ready to strike, when King Eilbeir cleared his throat with a slight nod to Ren.

"Be careful out there, son. I've heard the front has gotten quite volatile lately, and I do not wish to lose you to primitive rebels." The dismissive stab to what I called my family finally had me look away as the heads of the Roamion lineage exited the room, though I could still feel the queen's hatred-fueled stare until the hallway blocked me from view.

My knees buckled, forcing me to grab harder onto the table behind me to help me stay upright as I took in a shaky breath.

After a minute had passed, there was a long whistle that sounded from my left, where Jaeden had his arms crossed while he looked at Ren. "Have I ever told you how much your mother gives me the creeps?"

"Every time you are in the same room," Ren mumbled, his footsteps growing closer as he reached out a hand to help me stand from where my hands had a death grip on the table. I brought my gaze up to his, concern shining in his eyes. "Are you all right?"

Another waking nightmare? Was the silent question shot across the pact bond.

"You know, just seeing the king and queen on a casual visit to their son to take care of 'primitive rebels' might be a tad jarring." I smiled slightly, taking his hand to anchor myself back to reality. All signs of the grim and the power the imaginary shadowed woman radiated and that the queen harbored were gone from the room, which helped alleviate the headache that plagued my mind.

Yes. was my silent answer.

He gave a slight nod, looking at Rygur and Jae before his gaze drifted to the fields outside the atrium. The sun had risen above the tree line, his eyebrows knitting together in frustration that it had gotten so late. "We need to get moving to make it a decent distance tonight. I want to be in the lower plains before we make the first camp."

"Can I stretch out my mare first?" I asked, looking up at the prince as his attention returned to me. "It's been a while, and I'd prefer not to strain myself in the first hour after I kick Jae's ass in a race." I smiled playfully, watching Jae's jaw tick with irritation from the corner of my eye. He did not need to say anything for me to know that he was already rising to the challenge with a taunting response.

"Of course, Wildie. I'll even give you a head start." He winked, pinching my arm slightly before stepping back and swinging his arms wide in the space of the atrium. "Let's see that mare's return, shall we?"

"Hey, that's not fair, Ren!" I barely heard Jae's protest as I felt the warm sensation of my ability to shift rippling over my body. It shot through my nerves like lightning as I bounced in place, focusing on the mare galloping toward freedom from her mental stall.

There was the familiar blast of silver over my body as I focused on the balance of four legs instead of two, my hooves clicking on the stone beneath me as I shook myself out. It was like a good stretch after a long nap to be back in what I considered my most unrestricted form, even as I could still see the renewed pact over my dun and grey dappled coat, the black lines still tracing large wings from my sides onto my haunches.

I could not stop myself from trotting in a pleased circle, trying not to break into a sprint before everyone was ready.

Rygur and Jae had gone about packing their things into even larger leather bags—which I assumed were for Rygur and Ren to carry in dragon form—but Ren had not moved from his spot beside me.

Please don't tell me you're another awe-struck boy who's never seen a unicorn. I sent across the bond, though my nicker of amusement echoed in the atrium.

He refocused his hazel eyes with a few swift blinks, looking into my face as we finally reached eye level. "I've seen unicorns, but never so… uniquely beautiful." He murmured and lifted a hand towards my face.

In all past events of proximity, I would have flattened my ears and backed away with a stamp of a hoof. But as his hand reached my muzzle, I closed the distance by leaning forward and letting him run his hand over the soft fur.

Quite the flattery, your Highass.

"Most unicorns I've ever met have been solid colors. White most commonly, but sometimes black or dun. Never a mixture, and never a single pattern out of place." He smiled, gently running his thumb over the broken stripe down my face. Then his attention moved down my side to the injured thigh, where the scars stayed prominent through the fur, his smile faltering into something darker.

He's in the dungeons, and I'm about to run through the fields again, Ren. I pressed my nose against his shoulder, pushing it softly. *I'm right here.*

He laughed a bit as his smile returned, stretching his arms behind his head as he looked me over. "I suppose if a lady gets to show off, I should too, hmm? I don't think you've had the pleasure." Ren turned with a wink as he walked back to the center of the room where the table we usually discussed camps with was. He began to push it across the stone floor with little effort as he announced, "Ry, Jae, I'm going to shift. You know how this goes."

"I'm surprised we got a warning this time," Jae grumbled, jogging over to where I stood with Rygur close behind.

"Which usually means he's going to play up the shift and make a huge mess." Rygur sighed, standing beside Jae with his arms crossed.

There was a sudden change in the air as the smell of rain filled the atrium, a soft wind beginning to drift in from the archway to the fields to spin around the man standing in the middle of the room. Lightning began to spark the air around us, and I snorted in amusement at the irritation on both Rygur's and Jaeden's faces.

Rygur looked at me with a deadpan stare, "You get to clean up the mess when we get home since *you* are the reason for this show."

I bumped my shoulder into Jaeden with enough force to push him into Rygur, who both cut me harsh glances with a hint of amusement underneath as I whinnied in laughter.

My amusement was silenced as a flash of dark clouds filled the atrium, suddenly making it feel too small for anyone in the room as a giant beast now stood in the middle of it. Despite the expansive space of the room, Ren's dragon nearly took up the entire area. His wings were tucked neatly at his sides, having had to move into a low-laying position to fit the space better.

His scaled face turned towards the three of us with giant hazel and blue eyes narrowed in slight scolding.

His entire body was a deep black that reflected and absorbed the sunlight that touched it, while his scales had a gorgeous sheen of a deep blue that entranced me. I walked closer as he watched my movements, his pupils narrowing as I moved within his biting distance. His white and grey ashen horns had small streaks of lightning bouncing between the two zig-zag shapes, trailing down a line of similar spikes down his neck and between his wings.

The only thing breaking the black scales were long spiral scars that seemed to wind up his back legs and towards his back, but they were not like any scars I had seen. Instead of pale or flesh-colored, they were a stark white that cut through the black scales like razors, leaving deep wounds that I had not even realized existed.

As I got closer to look at the ribbons of silver, his wings shifted to cover them from my view as if he did not want me to see them. The large limbs were their own sheets of beauty, decorated with a familiar sheen of black dotted with white dots that seemed to resemble stars scattered across the wing's membrane.

Those stars were becoming an increasingly familiar pattern that I had seen on the shadowed woman, as well as on the clothes Sellias had designed for me.

I tried to step closer to rub my nose against a cluster of star-like markings, but his wing tucked closer to his body as soon as I tried to make contact.

Sensitive.

My attention finally turned back to the massive head that had followed me during my inspection, bringing me snout-to-snout with the deadliest predator I knew.

"Keep him distracted while we load up, yeah? He's helpful in his Fae form, but his dragon is ridiculously stubborn." Rygur called out, beginning to haul the large bags over with large grunts as he dragged them across the floor.

In response, I scratched at the ground while keeping a curious gaze on the dragon. I had seen dragon shifters before, but none of them had the size nor colorings of the prince before me. They were usually my size or smaller and used more as messengers than warriors.

Impressed, or just attempting to be a very enticing meal? Even across the bond, his voice was slightly rougher in this form, as if a permanent growl had been added to his tone.

I'll compliment you and say I'm impressed. Most dragon shifters are only the size of unicorns or wolves, and even fewer are built for combat.

Thank the Roamion line for that one. Potentially, the only thing good about it. He snorted, his warm breath blowing over me like a summer's breeze.

I tilted my head to the side curiously, flicking my tail behind me as my heart wrestled with the potential of that admission. *You don't like being a Roamion?*

Why is your heart rate stumbling? He asked, his eyes pinpointed on my chest. *Is something wrong?*

Ah, yes, predator senses. I nearly forgot about their accuracy, I thought aloud across the bond, rolling my eyes. *Nothing's wrong, no— except you deflecting my question.*

They are hard to ignore, especially when you are the subject. He resettled himself as Rygur climbed a wheeled ladder to throw some bags over Ren's shoulders, but his eyes were still focused on my chest. *I'm not the biggest fan of my position, no. Do you think I enjoy lording over people and being discussed like breeding stock to sell to the highest bidder?*

I blinked a few times in shock, my ears unintentionally pinning against my head as I examined the floor underneath us like it had become the most exciting thing in the world. *You are not some breeding stock to sell.*

A slight growl echoed through the atrium, causing both Jae and Rygur to freeze on either side of Ren's body. Tense silence ticked by before a deep exhale blew over my fur as he pressed his giant nose into my neck with his eyes closed. *Is that jealousy I smell, Wildie?*

I had frozen in my spot with the touch as my heart beat faster at his words, breaking me of my stupor. I turned my back to him and took off in a brisk trot to the green fields outside the atrium, continuing to move until I was far enough away from the atrium to not be directly in contact with Ren but close enough that I could still see his enormous form watching me from the atrium.

Do not go where I cannot see you. He growled loud enough that it almost covered Rygur and Jae's distant yells, telling Ren to keep still.

I am just eating dandelions, your Highass. I retorted—even though I *did* start eating some wildflowers by my hooves.

I had no right to be jealous, but I had to get out of the castle before I did something stupid and got myself either killed or heartbroken.

The latter seemed like the worst option out of the two.

At the same point, Ren did not *like* that part of being a Roamion. It seemed like he hated being a constant pawn to be played around with for the kingdom and hated the idea of the arranged marriages that were used regularly in the patriarchy. That tiny hope was enough to ease the worry eating at the edge of my mind, making it easier to breathe.

Maybe, in the end, I could be his choice over the crown.

Sellias's warning repeatedly played over in my mind, though I was quick to shove it away to the darkest recesses of my mind, even if it began to make my head pound. I did not want to think about potentially being the reason that Ren would die because of my foolishness.

I did not want to think about life without him, either.

CHAPTER 24

Are you still holding up down there?

Ren's voice suddenly jolted my thoughts as I weaved through the lower forests of Agraxis, carefully avoiding loose rocks and branches that were scattered under the fallen leaves. The expanse of trees had already started to go dormant as winter descended into the realm after her sister's visit left the leaves on the ground.

Jae was pacing steadily forward a few trees to my left with his dark chocolate coat puffed out against the cold, his breath puffing white with every exhale.

After I departed from the atrium to escape Ren and his prying gaze, the boys finished getting ready for the trip in less than thirty minutes. Ren had several straps and bags draped over him, and he had explained that he would likely stay shifted so they did not have to constantly pack and unpack every morning, which meant that my training would start in shift.

I would have preferred a sword, but it was apparent that Ren had already made the training decision.

Now, the sun was dipping low over the horizon, meaning we had already been on the road for several hours. I could see the lag in Jae's pace from the corner of my eye.

Are we planning to stop soon? Jae may collapse—I think I pushed him too hard earlier.

I could hear an audible grumble from above the tree line, making me give a light snicker of amusement that echoed against the hollow trees.

We haven't made it to the plains yet, and at this pace, we've still got a few hours before then. I could have sworn I heard the quill scratching paper in his brain as he thought through several plans. *Break to your left; there's a clearing there. Shift when you arrive.*

I rolled my eyes as I turned to the left, dipping into my magic to illuminate my white horn as a small light in the darkening forest to notify Jae that I was switching directions. The wolf instantly caught the signal and padded up to my side to trot alongside me; his head tilted as if to ask what was going on.

I shook my head in the direction of the clearing, attempting to point to it as an answer as we drew closer to it.

If there was one thing I was looking forward to, it was communicating with actual words.

Jae and I had figured out some signals and ways to communicate with no pact bond to create a bridge across our minds, and one of those signals was illuminating my horn to show a change of direction. Since I had direct contact with Ren, it was easier for him to follow my lead, though he initially seemed disgruntled at being put as a third instead of a second.

Once his honey eyes saw the clearing, they widened in excitement while his lips curled back in some attempt of a wolf's smile before taking off quickly for the opening.

I was not as enthusiastic, pinning my ears to my head as I watched him take off. Since the wordless conversation with the shadowed woman earlier that morning, I had been plagued with a constant headache and increasing paranoia at the way the shadows curled around me as we traveled. They seemed to whisper as I passed each tree, calling for me like haunted ghosts, and each brush against my pastern felt like a clawing hand. Before the interaction in the atrium, the grim had been a consistent comfort, but now they made me more skittish, as if one might pull me down into the monstrous mist of the queen's shadow.

Her eyes seemed like a constant imprint on my mind now, watching over my every move. I had to continue telling myself repeatedly that I was hours away from the castle and headed towards the forests I called home.

The sound of beating wings pulled me out of my thoughts as Ren and Rygur landed in the clearing, my attention caught by the flash of grey as Jaeden's familiar dark Fae returned with arms spread wide in greeting.

"Please tell me Lo complained finally, and we can fly the rest of the way," Jae smiled, looking at Ren with confident eyes that tried to hide the pleading that was in his voice.

"I didn't complain, but you were." I teased as I stepped out of the forest with a flash of silver, leaving my mare to slumber. "So, I called in the *men* of the group who can carry the baby boy." I stuck my tongue out towards the wolf shifter, who flashed me a vulgar gesture in response.

Ren's head swiveled towards me as he curled his neck to set his head higher to give me a once over to ensure I had not injured myself until he was satisfied.

"Maybe I should call you a baby, too, with those big hatchling eyes that can't seem to stay away."

His head—about five times my size—came barreling towards me at an alarming rate that I could not evade, pushing me over into the frigid grass that had already begun to frost in the twilight. I landed directly on my back; the droplets of freezing water seeping into the thin fabric of my clothes caused me to squeal at the frigidness.

I gave him a nasty glare that promised I would return the gesture at some point, but his hazel eyes were filled with amusement as I assumed the rumble in his chest was a dragon's version of laughter.

Rygur moved forward from behind Rendros, his form about half the size of the massive dragon. He was big enough to carry a rider so long as he was only carrying a few packs, his scales a metallic silver that seemed to be used as a signaling tool between Ren and him as they flew through the sky. His horns curled around small ears that twitched with every sound that came from the forest, though his attention stayed on our group.

His black and gold-flecked eyes moved from me to Jaeden, who moved over to pat the side of Rygur's neck. "I have cut back on the pastries, as you asked, so I should be much easier to carry now that Ren has better luggage." He snorted, though the metallic dragon snapped at his hand in warning.

Jae quickly held his hands up, "Got it, no petting."

Then Jae settled between Rygur's shoulder blades and wings, sitting comfortably like he had done this thousands of times before. Rygur seemed unimpressed at the supposed 'weight loss' that Jae had boasted about as he tried to reset his balance, though he did not seem to outwardly struggle as he flexed his claws into the dirt and stretched his wings with ease.

Your turn, Wildie.

I turned my attention back to the black dragon who had moved into a bowing position, his front leg extended towards me in an invitation to climb up.

His dragon was so immense that I did not have the luxury of throwing a leg over his neck and being done with it, as Jae had done. I would have to climb masses and muscles of scales to reach a relatively easy sitting position.

I stepped forward to place my hand on one of his claws to lift myself onto the human-sized keratin, but I hesitated.

Flying meant getting off of the ground and the earth.

Very, *very* high above solid ground.

"Are you sure I can't just keep running?" I whispered, although it was primarily to myself. I already knew the answer, but my heart was racing ahead of me in a rising panic.

Heights had never been my friend, and they were unlikely to become close companions in the next few minutes. I had always insisted that I stay on the ground floors and away from higher spaces where I could not quickly feel or touch the earth beneath my feet and take off if needed. If I needed to go onto any floor above that, I always stayed as close to the exit as possible, away from windows and balconies.

If I got too close to either, I was just as likely to freeze like prey as I was to vomit from fear,

While I know you can run exceptionally fast for a mare, you must still deal with obstacles that slow you down to avoid them. The sky does not carry such things. Ren's voice was gentle, his head hovering close beside me in silent comfort. Movement stirred from behind me as I assumed Rygur had taken off with Jae, my suspicion confirmed by the beating of leather wings filling the growing silence of the early night.

However, I could not move as if I was rooted to the spot as I focused on a particular scale on Ren's knuckle. At the least, it was the size of a tower shield and reflected a blurry version of me through the dark coloring.

Wildie, look at me.

The command seemed to break a bit of my paralyzed state as my head turned to look at him, the sparking lightning in his horns lighting the space between us.

His scaled head was tilted with a somewhat gentle expression, his lips fully covering his teeth, and his big eyes swirled between the clash of hazel and blue. The eye contact helped ground me away from the dangerously close precipice of panic as I brought my small hand to his muzzle.

He pressed gently into the movement, closing his eyes. *Flying for the first time is difficult and scary, I won't lie to you. But you were not afraid to get close to death's flower, you were not scared to walk into the den of your enemies, and you were not afraid to become my pacted.*

I sighed, shaking my head slowly. "I was deathly afraid of each of those moments."

Yet you persevered. A portion of his lip lifted in an attempt to smile, revealing the large teeth that, in most circumstances, would have caused me to faint from the panic that froze my lungs.

Instead, I returned a small chuckle as a smile appeared on my face. "Watching a dragon try to smile is a blend of terrifying and hilarious, and I don't know which way I sway towards."

I prefer the latter since it brings a smile to your face along with that beautiful laugh. His smile widened, and I smacked his nose like I was trying to push away the several-ton beast. The grumbling that swayed between loud and quiet in a terrible excuse for laughter surrounded the small clearing, his eyes sparkling as he watched my laughter subside. *Do you trust me?*

I held his hazel gaze, searching for any reason *not* to trust him. There had to be some reason not to, to keep him from taking me into the air where he could quickly get rid of me if he wanted. I ignored the gnawing thought that the time alone could be used to complete the task that brought me to the tamed provinces in the first place. I should be trying to find some minuscule reason to say no and slow this journey further for the sake of the untamed I left behind, even if it made him upset.

Yet I knew there was no argument to be had about not trusting him because I *did.*

There was only the kindness he had shown me since the night of Winulla's Feast, the sparks of light and happiness that had brightened the last few days in Agraxis—the kiss we shared at the Golden Garden, and how he held my hand when Dryaden told us the story of Vomuna's Lily.

The night in the bath where I submitted entirely to him.

Behind the prince's façade was a Fae filled with mysterious kindness and a story few knew. There was Ren, and there was Crown Prince Rendros.

I liked the Ren I had started to see.

"I do, so don't spoil it." I finally grumbled, turning back to his arm as it extended once more to help ease my ascent. I took a large inhale of air as I kicked at the dirt below me and reminded myself that I could close my eyes to imagine myself anywhere else but on the back of a dragon thousands of feet in the air.

I would see and feel the ground again.

My hands grabbed onto the edges of the scales as I climbed up the limb, using the breaks and spaces between the scales as footholds as I gradually ascended. He kept surprisingly still as I climbed over his shoulder and to the dip between the blades on his back, where I landed in a white divot that stretched farther between his wings.

One of the scars.

I placed my hand over the streak of flesh between the scales, gently rubbing the softer area of the armored beast as he moved to a full-standing position before I remembered what was happening.

I wouldn't dream of betraying such a precious thing. Was his only response as he extended his wings behind me, and I quickly found a scale above the scar that I could fix my gaze on for the journey. It moved slightly as the muscles underneath it flexed when he pushed his head, trying to peer back to check where I was sitting and that I was secure amongst the other cargo.

Are you ready?

Please don't let me fall, Ren.

Never in all of eternity, darling.

Then he crouched and pushed off the ground in an impressively powerful movement, his wings pushing the wind downward as we became airborne.

I squeezed my eyes shut and pushed myself as close as possible to the dragon, hating how my ears kept popping with the sudden rise into the sky.

The wind in the open sky caught my ponytail in a steady stream, making it flick back and forth over my shoulders like a whip, but I did not dare remove my hands from the scales to fix it for fear of falling. I felt so distanced from the rest of the world that my mind and my mare were causing the panic that edged my vision to swarm in faster, and I pressed myself closer to Ren's warm body as I tried to fight away the terror.

Tell me a story, Willow. Ren's voice was distant as it settled above the chaos that threatened to pull me back to the earth with a dive of death. *Please tell me a story, and I'll tell one in return.*

I shook my head against his skin and scales, trying to desperately find a story my father told me somewhere in the panic that was moments away from drowning me. No story instantly came to mind, but a memory did.

When I nearly died the night Peter attacked me, I was close to letting go. To go to the pastures that were so warm and filled with only sunshine instead of war. I started, the memory playing vividly as it started to shine above the terror. *But someone...some goddess, criticized me for my weakness to give up. She told me that I had fought before, and she didn't understand why I wasn't fighting now.*

I remembered the explanations of feeling alone, a failed martyr who could not kill a prince, though I refused to bring those words to light.

When my answers didn't suffice, she brought me back to the room in the castle where you and your sisters were waiting for me to wake up. I saw Dityss frustrated as she researched to no avail, Sellias broken on the floor, and you... My voice trailed off as his agonized face came into view from the memory.

Devastated, destroyed, and hollow. He filled in the blank, his voice sounding as broken as he described that evening's version of himself.

My heart broke at the confession, the confirmation of what I thought I had seen that night. The fear of flying subsided as I pressed my head to the exposed scar in a silent reminder that I was there—not dying in that bed.

Then you sang that song I played that night in that music room, and I think something clicked in me that I didn't realize was possible, even if I didn't want to admit it myself. The memories and feelings came out too fast, and I was unable to stop the words from spilling out into truth. *So, I told the goddess that she was right, and I came back.*

Only the sound of the wind blowing past us filled the night air, its silent comfort filling the spaces where my voice disappeared. A few more moments passed before I barely cracked an eye open to try and discern what caused the silence and to check that he was okay.

For the most part, I could only see Ren's black scales covering the edges of the scar I was sitting in, the world silent except for the occasional beat of his wings. My stomach rolled as I let my eyes travel further beyond the dragon beneath me, expecting to see pitch black, but instead, I was greeted with the brilliance of thousands of stars that shined brighter than I ever thought they could. They sparkled in hundreds of shades of white, silver, and blue that created an infinite tapestry of ageless stories and memories.

Millions of tears shed for a lost mate.

One might find it challenging to look up at the stars only to be reminded of tragedy after learning such a story, but all I could see was love. So much love was lost in the teardrops of grief, even though so few remembered the true meaning of these balls of lights hanging in the sky every night.

If I could touch one, would I see one of the moments that Sinos and Vomuna shared?

A tear threatened to fall at the thought when my eyes caught a glimpse of hazel shining amidst the starlight. Ren had turned his head ever so slightly to look at me, and even though I could only see a sliver, I could see my emotions reflected in his hazel eyes.

When you didn't wake up quickly after the healers visited, some part of me knew you were giving up. I knew nothing in the castle could bring you back to us, and you had left all that you knew. What did a gilded cage have for a lost dove?

He turned his head forward again, hiding his eyes from view.

Yet some other part of me, a more significant part, couldn't let you leave. Would not let you die when you had so much left to give to this world, not let you pass without—

There was a quick inhale that interrupted his words, shuttering through him like it was hard to breathe. *So, I told you everything I needed to say and sang that song, desperate to see you open your eyes again.*

The tears that had been a mere threat were now overpowering as they slid down my cheek without hesitation. *I didn't hear what you said, but I heard you sing. It was a beautiful rendition of a song without lyrics.* I smiled sadly, running my thumb over his skin. *What did you say?*

The sky went silent again as we turned to the side with a slight dip, his head focused on the world below us once again as we descended.

We've made it to the lower fields; Rygur and Jaeden seem to have already started a fire for the camp, but they need our supplies for the camp. We'll be on the ground again in a moment.

That was the end of the conversation and the flight as we soared for the earth without another word.

CHAPTER 25

After some time pulling supplies from Ren to set up the rest of the camp, we all settled in with the silence of the fields surrounding us. The camp itself was made into a small circle that Ren could wrap around, his nose nearly touching the tip of his half-spaded tail in a makeshift wall from intruders. A campfire had been built in the middle with three tents around it, where Rygur, Jaeden, and I all retreated into our own for the night.

The tent I had settled into was small: built only for one person and maybe a personal blanket if one was packed. It was made of thin fabric that barely kept the wind out of the tiny space, but thankfully, the cold was mitigated by the giant dragon barrier curled around the camp.

Ren avoided contact with me all night, and our pact bond went silent as the conversation lulled.

Curling into a blanket Sellias must have packed, I stared at the beige canvas of the tent's ceiling. Sellias had spent so much time making sure my bag was packed and had outfits for all types of weather, but the woman I spoke to before we departed would not have even left a string. My hands gripped onto the fabric of the blanket tighter as the queen's eyes flashed in place of Sellias's, and I cursed under my breath as I shook the image away.

I had not considered the encounter with the shadow woman and the queen since Ren took me into the air. I could not focus on it when I was more focused on not falling from the sky, but the mysterious, dark feeling in my core twisted again, causing me to sit up.

A shadow stood at the entrance to my tent, its dark form lingering upwards to the folded top as it seemed to be observing me. Any light from the firelight outside was no longer visible through the thin walls, my lungs not daring to breathe when its form became separate from the wall as a standalone form, stalking the small space like a waiting wolf.

It's just my imagination. I thought to myself, though everything in my body screamed otherwise, including that dark pit in my stomach that had welled up into my throat.

"I am no imagination, filly." It spoke, the shadows around where its mouth might have been moved with each word.

It was speaking to me like I had spoken to it—which was impossible.

"I would not be standing before you if it were impossible." Its voice spoke in whispers as if it could barely find sound; its voice strained as if the very ability to communicate now was causing pain. "We do not have much time before the shadows call me home."

"What—*who* are you?"

"Trivial matters, filly." I could not see its eyes, but I felt frustration pinned squarely on my chest.

"Answer my question, and I will listen to you," I said with a bit more force behind my words, though my heart was a hammer in my chest. "Otherwise, you can return before the call arrives."

The frustration was thick, but it did not argue further. "I am what one would call an Ethe, a lower shadow beast. My name has been lost to time, so you can call me by what I am." The shadow's pull was like a magnet to my magic as it moved back against the wall; its three-dimensional form dissipated.

"Are you that dark presence lingering at the edge of my mind?" I questioned, "What is a shadow beast?"

"That is much stronger than any Ethe or higher shadow beast, but that power is not an enemy. You will learn more about it soon enough." The shadow moved as it crept around the darkened canvas, four legs moving across the bottom of the walls. "A shadow beast is a creature conjured from deep conviction or intent. I was created out of harm and suffering, intended to become a mindless pawn in a much larger game. Higher forces saved me from such a fate to place me with you so that I might help you understand your future on its board."

My mind swirled with so many questions, but the edges of the once sharp-edged shadow began to blur. "Why am *I* being sent a messenger about this game?"

"This game was set up centuries ago by old rulers and old rivalries, but the players for it did not arrive until recently. You are one of the last players to join the board, and with that, the game is set to start any day now, which means *you* need to stop this petty war between tamed and untamed before it begins." The Ethe's voice had become hoarse with strain as shadows blurred further. "Accept the bond given to you and use it well to ensure victory. Learn about the gifts you are blessed with and gain allies in the coming conflicts, bring beasts and balance back to the continent."

"I am not blessed with any gifts, and I don't know of the bond you talk about. A pact bond? A mate bond? I only have one of those, and my heart falls for someone who is fated to another." My eyes narrowed on the thinning shadow as its eyeless head bore into me. "I am no hero, Ethe."

"You are no hero, Willow Saugrave. You are a queen."

The entity shrunk until it became part of my shadow, staining the back of the tent from the returned firelight that now flickered through the slits in the canvas. Light snoring accompanied the campfire's crackles, but they were distant mumbles against the thunder of my thoughts trying to process the words the Ethe had said.

I did not move for the rest of the night, and sleep never found me.

CHAPTER 26

I was the first out of my tent that morning, wrapping the blanket around me to help keep the worst of the morning chill from seeping into my muscles and threatening to stop any chance to train with Ren.

The night with the Ethe had resulted in zero sleep, planted stiffly in the back of my tent, racing over far too many thoughts I could not piece together. I needed the training to help me combat enemies and reorganize my thoughts into proper files that I could sift through one at a time.

Luckily for me, Ren's head was already up and scanning the plains around the camp.

"Good morning, your Highass," I said with a smile that disguised the lack of sleep I had received the night before. "How long have you been up?"

He cut his gaze to mine; a soft surprise settled on his features. *Only about a half hour or so—though I'm surprised to see you up this early. Did you sleep well?*

I sighed, my shoulders falling as I stepped out of the camp 'wall.' I passed over the tip of his tail to stand in front of him, away from the tents, so I would not wake the remaining members of our party. "I should have guessed you would have felt it."

His eyes narrowed on me as lightning sparked between his horns. *Should I have felt what?*

Or not.

"Oh, uh," I cleared my throat, trying to figure out a way to play the fact I spoke with a shadow that called me a queen and stole any chance of sleep I had, "I had another nightmare last night—a bad one. The fear from it lingered after I woke up, and I couldn't go back to sleep."

He growled as he leaned forward, pressing his giant nose into my chest and taking in a deep breath.

"Hey, I'm fine. There's no need to deep-smell me." I snorted but did not move to try to push him away.

I didn't know, I didn't feel anything. His voice grated in irritation. Why *did you hide it from me, Wildie?*

"I don't even know how to do that, so if I did, it was subconsciously," I grumbled, placing a hand on his nose to rub the scales, even though one was three times the size of my hand. "But I wouldn't want to wake you up anyways, so I'm somewhat glad I did."

Please wake me up whenever it happens. Don't bullshit me about not wanting to wake me up because I feel worse knowing you suffered with no sleep than I would have been if my sleep was slightly interrupted. He growled, but his eyes softened as he pressed into my hand. *What scared you from rest?*

"I..." My brain knew I could not tell him what the Ethe had told me, but my heart wanted me to. I wanted so badly to have someone to talk to and help me figure it out, and Ren was currently the only person I trusted to talk about it with.

Even if he had the other end of my chain, he was the primary force of the fight against the untamed and was the prince of the kingdom.

Against my better judgment, I told him what had happened.

I told him about the shadow that spoke to me, and I told him about what he said—the game set centuries ago, the shadow beasts, the Ethe. Before I could stop myself, I told him what I was tasked to do—the bond I was supposed to accept and the 'blessings' to learn about.

I stopped before the part about being called a queen.

At some point during my retelling, I leaned into his muzzle, pressing my head against the steady comfort that Ren had become. His eyes had closed, but I could tell he was still listening by the way he tried to soften his breathing to make sure he heard it all.

"This was the first time I'd seen a shadow like that since I was a little girl, and even then, that was an imaginary friend. This was different." I finished, sighing gently. "I feel like I'm going crazy."

Silence fell over us like a blanket as the lack of response felt like he was agreeing with me. The reality of the thought weighed heavily on my shoulders as I stared into a small ring of dandelions that were scattered just beyond where Ren was lying when a flash of thunder blasted across the fields.

Familiar muscular arms suddenly pulled me into a warm chest alongside the intoxicating smell of fresh rain and a hand cradling the back of my head.

"You could never be crazy," Ren whispered by ear as he pulled me closer, his voice surprisingly rough from the near day without use. "If you are crazy, then I should be locked away in an asylum." The grip on the back of my head slowly pulled me back until our eyes met.

I could not stop the smile that spread on my face from seeing his Fae form again, though I smacked his chest with a blanket-wrapped hand as best as I could in the embrace. "You weren't supposed to shift until we arrived, Rendros. How un-general like of you to delay the trip."

"There were more pressing matters that needed attending to." He smiled back, surprising me with a soft kiss that melted away any lasting barriers I had. It was so unlike any we had shared before, gentle but filled with a reminder that had become like a soft prayer to us.

I'm here. I'm safe.

Then he pulled his head away to look into my eyes as if searching for something. "Do you know what bond the Ethe was talking about?" I felt my breath hitch as my gaze dropped from his to avoid blurting out any theories I had.

I did not care if there was some game or an apparent necessity to accept any *bond*—mainly when the only one I knew existed was our pact bond. Was there a mate bond that was somewhere around us that I needed to connect to? Someone I had met?

The idea of my mate being anyone other than the male holding me now made me sick to my stomach, to the point that I could not voice the idea mentally or aloud. My heart could not take losing him because of an imaginary red string that led us both in different directions, though the knowledge of that future being inevitable made it feel like the next gust of wind would take me with it.

So, I tried to deflect the question.

"I'm sorry about last night, Ren. Truly. I don't know why that story came to mind, and I knew it was painful, but...I didn't realize how *much*." I whispered, squirming my arms free from the blanket and wrapping my arms around his neck.

His entire form went still under my touch, but his eyes were gentle. "I was distraught over your feelings on the situation, but you did not give up. The rest does not matter." He ran a finger over my face tenderly, "Now, what was the bond?"

I squirmed, but his grip tightened.

I had put myself on a pedestal that I could not lie my way out of. The small twine of truth and lie would have to be woven delicately to ensure he did not find my true feelings or the worry that mixed with them. I trusted him—ultimately, in fact—but to give him the truth that I had fallen in love with him? We'd only known each other a month, and only within the last forty-eight hours did either of us start tangling emotions in the relationship.

"A mate bond, I think," I murmured, cutting my gaze to the sky, unable to afford to look at him and take in any emotion on his face to see how he reacted to the statement. "I'm assuming, at least, since I've already accepted the pact bond. Maybe one I've already found but don't know about? The only unicorn we've been around was Dryaden and that group at his bar, so maybe one of them?" I shrugged, trying to put as much disinterest in my voice as possible.

"Mate...bond," Ren slowly repeated, though I refused to look to see more of a reaction despite how badly I wanted to. Instead, I focused on the rays of sunlight that bathed the sky and the few clouds covered it. "You genuinely believe it would be with one of those idiots from Ivimea?"

More clouds gathered as the sun began to dim behind them, my heart sinking as I realized what was happening.

"I'm assuming it would have to be a unicorn—as far as I'm aware, unicorn mate bonds can't happen between different shifter types. So, who else could it be?"

There was a deep roll of thunder in the distance, one that promised devastating damage.

"I will kill every single one of them should you approach them with such thoughts of that bond existing."

Lightning cracked as it hit the ground in the distance of the field, rain crashing down alongside it in a forceful downpour.

I snapped my eyes back to Ren at that exact moment, the flash of white crafting dark shadows on his face as he stared at me. His once comforting embrace turned more into a protective hold, his eyes trained on my face with lethal precision. Gone was the gentleness that filled them minutes ago, transformed into pure, unbridled rage.

"What?" I barely whispered.

"The Ethe must have already known that your bond exists, but I know it is not with those unicorns. Mates are not designated by breed or type but by the very souls they are tied to. They do not care if you are mortal or immortal, human or Fae, unicorn or dragon." Lightning flashed again, allowing me to see past the anger in his eyes for half a second to see the panic that flared behind the anger. "That bond does not adhere to the rules of society but to the very fates themselves. And if fate has deemed you special for this game, then your mate is equally important. Those unicorns from Ivimea have no place in your story."

I blinked, happy to have the rain that poured over us to hide the tears running down my face. "Then I hope I will find him soon, and he will accept me as I want to accept him."

The rain eased a bit, along with the anger that had bunched his shoulders. "If he listens to the fates as they intended, he will. He'd be a fool to deny it."

The rain eased into a steady drizzle, but I could see the reservation in Ren's eyes as he pulled away to scan the clearing. "Since you have somehow found a way to stop my ability to feel your heightened emotions subconsciously, we will be starting with sword work today as Fae. We will only train for an hour before we continue to Vriwood." He nodded, going over to the large packs that had fallen into the mud.

There was loud grumbling from the camp as Jaeden stepped out of his tent with a hand over his head to help shield him from the drizzle. "Really, Ren? You promised that there would be no rain on this journey!" The wolf growled, looking for the giant dragon before realizing the barrier he had gone to sleep seeing had disappeared. His head whipped around quickly in search of him before he stopped on Ren rifling through some bags and me standing like a startled deer not far from him. "Oh, by the gods—I don't know what I expected. I'm going back to bed; you can wake me up when you're done fucking and ready to go. You're lucky you're my brother, Ren. I would not be willing to help you repack otherwise."

My cheeks flushed, but Jae disappeared back into his tent before I could retort.

Ren seemed to ignore Jae's complaints with a flick of his wrist and a vulgar gesture before returning to me to place a well-crafted silver sword in my hands. I had expected to grab onto a much heavier weapon, but it was light and balanced in my grip as I twirled it around. The handle was wrapped with blue leather, and several vines of daffodils crowned with a single lily were etched into the hilt. I could not help but stare as I looked over the exquisite detail of such a brutal piece of metal, nearly missing Ren asking me a question.

"Hmm?" I hummed, running my thumb over the engravement.

"I'm assuming the silence means you like it."

I shook my head to clear the trance as I looked up at Ren, my mouth silently open in awe. "You had this made for me?"

He shrugged, though his smug smile dissolved any attempt at humility he tried to give. "When we got the mission to head south, I went into town and had the best blacksmith in Aistris craft it." He smiled, pulling out a similar greatsword that glistened under the fresh rain. "He crafted mine as well."

The sword was similar in shape to mine but doubled in length and weight. The hilt had something engraved in it with black leather wrapped around the base, but from the angle I was looking at it, I could not discern anything more about the detail on its surface.

"I don't have words to say, Ren. I've never...*never* been given something so beautiful." I smiled, twirling the sword again before reaching for the scabbard he extended toward me. I carefully placed the sword in it before slinging the blade and leather over my shoulder. "Thank you—from the bottom of my heart."

"You deserve the best and better, darling." He smiled though something mischievous took over his kind features. "Now, let's use it to teach you some new moves, shall we?"

We walked a little farther from the camp to find a level section of clearing backed against the forest we had flown over the day before. Ren brought his greatsword along with several other variations of weapons, setting them down once he deemed the location suitable for practice. His eyes scanned the area before he lifted his hands like he was conducting an invisible orchestra, moving it with several different flicks of his wrist.

The grass's green began to transform into an array of several distinct lines of flowers, drawing circles and squares amongst the green landscape to create a makeshift training ring. Even though the movement was simple, the distinctive, unknown aura of nature magic was awe-inspiring as it created new growth in something so beautifully plain.

"What is the most extensive magic use, you know?" Ren asked as he pulled on the shirt tucked into his jeans, utterly unphased by the beauty he had just created.

"As I told the Ethe, I have nothing special. Just the usual basic element manipulation and some basic inklings of the unicorn's abilities to detect and scan magic surrounding them." I shrugged, rolling my shoulders with the movement to stretch the muscles in the area, my eyes never leaving Ren as he fiddled with his clothing. "What are you doing?"

Ren removed his shirt, revealing layers of muscles that tensed and relaxed as he threw his shirt aside and began his stretch routine. It was as if a master stonesmith had sculpted him to recreate the divine images of gods, and quite honestly, I would not have believed the level of depth of his figure had it not been standing right in front of me. The curves and shapes that pointed my gaze downwards into the hypnotizing 'V' shape they created—

"My eyes are up here, Wildie." He purred, my attention quickly returning to his face as my cheeks heated with embarrassment. However, the look in his eyes was anything but displeased, sending a heated shiver down my spine. "During battles, you will often be distracted by things around or in front of you. But no matter the distraction, you must stay focused on the fight engaged unless you're looking to get yourself killed. Seeing as we are in an empty field without any *real* distractions, I figured this might be an easily made one."

My throat bobbed with a sudden nervousness building at the idea of fighting so close to that male before me.

I started to wish he had stayed a dragon to avoid this kind of torture.

"Judging by your response, it will," he said teasingly, stretching his legs as he leaned over into a forward lunge. "Since you still need to build your muscles, we will focus this first session on exercises and muscle building. Then, we will work with swords and magic to see what we can learn about the supposed abilities the Ethe spoke of."

I leaned down into a full-leg stretch to try to focus on the rows of dandelions and roses that patterned the ground into training rings. "A rather dainty choice for the hardened storm prince, hmm?"

"If you didn't know, I was raised by two older sisters who loved everything to do with the dainty, though I also prefer to refresh the scenery than kill grass to make dirt lines." He shrugged nonchalantly, and I realized my gaze had drifted back up from the flowers.

"For a general whose entire job is to kill, I'm surprised to see you care so much for living things—inanimate ones at that." My tone was harsher than I intended, though I did not apologize. I had fallen for the prince in front of me, but even if a future was possible for the two of us, I refused to let my reservations and distaste fall to the wayside for the perfect fairytale ending.

"I don't believe you know the title's true meaning, Wildie." Ren came up in front of me and extended his hand to help me up from the deep lunge, which I accepted quietly in response for him to continue. Once I was up, we did some partner stretches, putting our hands on each other's shoulders and turning for a whole twist, then pressing the toes of our shoes together to extend the heels and ligaments. "Yes, I've had to kill some people. I've ordered the deaths of hundreds, if not thousands, more. I plan and strategize for the war we face and send orders to lower ranks to carry out plans that often cost more than they are worth in the loss of life. However, I don't do it because I enjoy it. I do it because I have my people to save—if I were to stop now, to turn around and go home, do you think the general *you* used to work for would stop? Or would he push forward to make a statement and kill who knows how many for that plan?"

I opened my mouth to reply that I thought he would, but I realized that was not entirely true and shut my mouth slowly. Theo was one of—if not the—primary general of the Southern Rebellion's forces, and he *had* sent me on a plan to kill a prince to make a statement. Theo had also kept planning attacks to continue to show strength after the prince's death to ensure the message got across.

That dark feeling twisted in the pit of my stomach as the wolf mother clutched her dead pup again, though she was now joined by the human mother holding that little girl with the wooden unicorn in Agraxis.

My feet took me off in a light jog, Ren right on my heels as I tried to get away from the haunting image. "War is not fun for me, Willow. I told you already that I am not empowered by the role I was born into. It is a burden that weighs constantly on my shoulders, and though I take pride in the protection of my people, I do not like the deaths that are required for that to happen. I would end the war with no more bloodshed if I could."

"Then why haven't you listened to what their general has to say? Find out what the end of this war would entail?" I pushed, keeping my attention straight ahead of me.

"You don't think I haven't?" His tone was strong even though we were jogging steadily. Still, there was a tiny wave of hurt that laced it. "I've reached out several times to their generals, specifically Theodore Hayes, the one who we believe is the lead of the southern operation. But he has never shown interest in speaking face to face or trying to solve the conflict without the loss of life."

I felt like I was going to vomit.

"What do you mean he's never shown interest?" I asked tentatively, afraid to know the answer.

"All of the letters sent addressed to him on disarmed men resulted in only the return of the correspondence with a piece of that soldier. A tongue, an eye, a finger, even things from below the belt." He whispered, my pace slowing to a stop as I turned to him, noting the hollow horror that haunted his eyes—he was reliving a moment in which one of those letters was returned.

He was not lying.

I turned away as I hurled what little I had left in my stomach into the grass.

"I'm sorry, that was a bit too descriptive. I forget that not many people are used to seeing, or thinking of, such horrors—" He instantly stopped to grab my ponytail, but I held a hand up to stop him.

"I have seen worse," I whispered, though I only turned away from my discarded rations to fall to my knees in disbelief. There was no way it was possible, no way that Theo had done such horrible, horrible things to unarmed *innocents*—

Theo and I were playing cards in the front yard when a young Fae dressed in a simple tunic and pants approached, his brown eyes shaded with doubt and worry. Theo did not even look away from our game when he asked, "What is it?"

"News from the frontlines, sir. I've brought a letter—"

I glanced up to see it, barely noticing the black wax that sealed the parchment that marked it as an essential war document. I could only see Theo's name accompanying the black seal, and I was under the assumption that it was a death report.

Theo stood with an abrupt drop of his cards on the table, revealing a winning hand.

"I win, sister. Remember to keep your cards up from your opponent so they can't see what they have against you." He smiled, then turned back to the civilian with an uncharacteristically solemn look. "I'll be back after I deal with this; why don't you see if Mother needs some assistance with dinner?"

I flipped him a vulgar gesture as I stood before walking back into the cabin, where I then stayed for the next few hours helping Amelia with her stew.

Theo returned when the sun fell below the ocean's waves, blood staining the edges of his jacket, making worry curdle my stomach. "Are you okay?"

"I'm fine, Lo. It was just a training exercise that got a little too rough. Get me a bowl while I clean up?" He smiled, as normal as he always was, evaporating the worry until I mirrored his expression and did as he asked.

I heaved into the grass again, but nothing came up as I let my tears fall into the grass. The black seal of that letter became more precise in my mind as if it was on the ground in front of me, bearing a dragon standing in proud defiance with its mouth opened in a silent roar.

It was not a death report. It was a letter sent from the prince kneeling behind me.

The blood was not from a training exercise; it was from a messenger Theo *killed.*

"Willow?" Ren's voice had turned from informative to concerned, though I shook my head in dismissal of the worry and what I had thought had been my innocent reality. Theo was on the right side of this war—he always had been—but now...

I did not know who he was anymore.

I took a shaky breath, unable to move my eyes from their spot in the grass. "Why would he do that? Why..." I felt the sob as it shook my system, and I was getting tired of how easy it was to break down in front of Ren. He moved to help pull me up as I tried to stand, but I pushed him away as I got to my feet. The darkness coiling in my stomach was becoming a swirling storm of anger, reminding me that there was a reason we came out to this spot. "Sword practice starts now."

Ren's eyebrows knotted together in confusion, but he followed me in reserved silence.

The sword was in my hand before I could think more about Theo and that evening when what looked like an innocent civilian walked toward us. I rushed towards Ren the second he stepped into the ring, sword hanging at my side as my hand gripped the leather handle.

His sword was instantly up against mine, the sound of the steel echoing into the open area around us as I thought of that person's face. The wideness in his eyes, the slightest tremble in his voice, the things I had not recognized before. The *fear* radiated from the poor boy like a phantom scent when he was guided away from the house with Theo as his guide.

The dark twist in my gut swirled in response to the anger I pushed into my next strike, but Ren kept perfect time and balance to my swings. I would swing to the left, he would parry, then to the right, and he would dodge, my anger growing with every blocked opportunity. I knew I could not hurt Ren, but I was so fragile and played like a fiddle—by *someone* I loved—that I wanted to do something to show that I was not some damsel in distress.

Ren turned on the offensive, pushing to catch me off balance. I felt the overwhelming strength of his blade and stature as the metallic clang of our swords rang out again, his weight pressing harder onto his blade. His gaze was reinforced with confidence in his movement, his attention finding my call of anger that pulsed through every movement I made, through every opening of our bond that I knew was there.

His weight made it difficult to stay where I was without taking a step back for stability, but I refused to falter back when that was something I had been doing for so long with Theo. I would no longer step back to be a pawn in someone else's game. I was not going to let innocents die because of foolish pride and blind faith.

Power surged up from my core, cold and demanding.

I reached for it as my muscles screamed against the strength of the Fae male pressing closer, screaming to yield.

Streaks of black raced past my peripherals as they shot straight at Ren, slamming into his chest and throwing him out of the ring and into the line of trees behind him as if he were nothing but a leaf in the wind.

I breathed heavily as I stared at the swirls of shadows that returned to me, lacing up my legs until they disappeared once more in a cascade of black that fell behind me from the sunlight. Instinct took control as I sheathed the sword on my back and stalked over to Rendros, my shadow restless as thunder boomed overhead. He was already back on his feet to meet me when I approached, blue lightning sparking over hazel eyes as anger burned the colors.

Ren watched me for a few moments longer, calculating something in his mind as he swung his sword in his hand, absentmindedly trying to dismiss his own emotions through familiar motions.

"What did that bastard do to you?" He growled, and I realized the anger was not directed at me.

"That *bastard* was my brother, and he lied to me."

CHAPTER 27

We were back in the air within the next hour, and though my anger had simmered into a soft boil, I was still shaking.

Ren and I had quickly returned to the camp after the spar, speaking little of what had happened beyond that. I *did* have special magic—shadow magic, we both assumed, even though its gift was near-extinct—and that I needed to guide my anger better when I was in battle. That would be what we worked on when we made it to Vriwood, further pushing off shifted practice with something he deemed more important.

After hearing the little I had said about Theo, his anger boiled alongside mine, and we changed our plans from a slow, planned trip to the front to a fast-paced one. He wanted to be in the town by the next morning, which meant we would be flying the rest of the day and most of the night.

I was not fazed or upset by the change of plans—instead, I had been the first to agree.

The sky remained cloudy black, with thunder continuously booming over the rounded shapes as we descended. The lightning between the dragon's horns was alive and energized as it struck between them in unison with the thrum of sounds.

Theodore Hayes is lion Fae. How is it that you two are siblings? Ren's voice was taut with anger as it came across the bond.

Adopted. After my father passed, Theo and his mother, Amelia, raised me, and living with them is what got me into the rebellion. There was no point in lying about the truth of the past anymore. *We learned that Amelia and my father were forever stuck in their Fae and had forgotten their shifted halves, which, to both of us, was a travesty. We investigated it further to find out where such a curse had come from when we found a small rally for the rebellion in Ullaven. It told us about the rules of choosing to become untamed that were laid by the Roamion crown, making it so that any citizen that crossed the border instantly lost the ability to shift unless they returned. We thought we were righteous and doing well by our parents to rise against such a corrupt crown, and Theo quickly rose in the ranks, taking me along with him as a pawn disguised as a trusted soldier.*

I spit out the last words like they were poison on my tongue.

Wildie, I need you to be honest with me. Your letter spoke of wanting to find refuge in my kingdom by telling me about the rebel forces. After everything I've learned, I'm inclined to believe that it was a lie, that the pact was an unwelcome change of plans. His voice had gone into a dark rumble I had never heard from him before, his whole body rattling with anger as he made a significant push forward with his wings.

I took a deep breath as my heart slowed to a near stop, trying how best to word it. Theo had been lying to me for *years* about righteousness and innocence to save bloodshed, but was he ever innocent himself? He was my brother, whom I had trusted completely, but the more I thought about his disappearances or the blood on his clothes when he was supposed to only be in strategy meetings...

That letter was written and perfected by Theo and the other rebellion generals. Considering my minimal contact with your army, my chance of being discovered as someone so close to leadership was near zero. Theo's trust in my ability to complete a task was leagues above anyone else.

Lightning webbed across the sky, the purple and blue light bouncing off Ren's scales.

What was the task you were provided with? The words were clipped.

Before I tell you, I need you to understand that I have no reason nor desire to complete that task anymore. I want you to know that I'm thankful for the pact for allowing me to get to know Ren *and not the Crown Prince of Aulari.*

The task, Willow.

Do you believe me, Rendros?

There was another blast of thunder as lightning blasted overhead, illuminating the pinpointed dragon eyes that were watching me with such feral intensity that, for the first time, it had me slinking back in terror.

The generals of the Southern Rebellion assigned me the task of killing Prince Rendros Roamion and making a statement of the rebellion's strength by whatever means necessary. Which included my death, should the situation call for it, but I could not do it, Ren. The pact was a hiccup, yes, but even then, I could not...I couldn't.

The sky went silent.

Ren went silent.

A deafening roar of thunder and anger shattered the silence as it crashed across the sky in tandem with a bellow from the dragon below me, lightning shooting across the sky so clear it was as if it was a web of electricity.

A flash of silver caught the corner of my eye as it shimmered in the blasts, Rygur darting past us like a blade cutting through the night as he headed straight for Ren's head as it leveled from the roar. A torrential downpour dampened any sound that was not thunder as Jaeden tried to communicate with the beast from atop Rygur, and I was barely able to register the worry that shot across his face when Jae looked back at me.

I shrunk into my spot in his back, holding on tightly to his scales as I heard more roars accompanied by muffled yelling and the snap of jaws as teeth collided against one another. The argument continued for a minute or two more before only the sound of the storm fully engulfed the sky, though there was a smaller sound that was growing closer.

My eyes shot up from the white scarring when I felt movement from behind me, dread pulling at my gut as Jaeden dismounted a silver dragon, nearly stomping over to me with anger and—was that fear in his eyes?

"You need to go with Rygur, Willow. Now!" He yelled across another roll of thunder.

"Jae, I don't want to hurt him, please, I—"

"NOW, Willow!" He growled, reaching for the back of my shirt and throwing me backward toward Rygur. "It doesn't matter what your intentions are or what you've done now, but you can do nothing when Rendros is this angry. You seem to be the source—getting *you* away will help."

I barely held my balance as Rygur grabbed my arm with his teeth to help me stay upright, piercing my skin but not hard enough to cause lasting damage. His dark eyes were shadowed with thought, but there was no lingering anger I could place as I hauled myself onto his back as lightning struck above us.

"I'm sorry, Jae. I didn't mean—" I tried to plead, but Rygur had jumped into the air and extended his wings to catch the draft of wind that pulled us alarmingly fast backward, my arms tightly wrapped around his neck in a panic to not fall from the smaller beast.

I could only watch the silhouette of Ren as he took off farther into the storm, leaving Rygur and me behind in the rain, another roar sounding as he became fully engulfed with the clouds.

The next wave of webbed bolts of power shattered my heart with it, tears rolling down my face as I pressed into Rygur's silver scales.

What had I done?

—◆—

Ren did not answer anything I tried to say for the rest of the flight, making the unbearable silence deafening as Rygur navigated the undercurrents of the storm Ren had conjured. It was hard to balance on the smaller dragon, especially with the quick maneuvers he would do to keep out of the way of a bolt of lightning. With no bond to speak mind to mind and one of us being shifted, we had no way to communicate beyond the occasional glance he gave me to ensure I was still there, making the silence all the worse.

I did not realize how much time had passed or how long we had been in the freezing rain until I saw the floating firelight of buildings and street lanterns forming in the distance. Only a few lights were illuminating the windows of the closer buildings, with few people wandering the streets, meaning that we had flown long into the night, even though it only felt like a few hours.

Rygur banked away from the streets as he slowed himself to a landing in a clearing just outside of town. He did not need to lean over for me to dismount, my eyes watching the dwellings in the distance as there was a flash of shift light behind me.

"What in the depths of Vomuna's realms did you do to piss off Ren that badly?" He growled as he reached into a pack and pulled out a small bandage wrap.

"I..." My voice was a distant tether to find as I pulled it back into use, my head dropping in regret. "He found out that the leading general of the Southern Rebellion is my adopted brother, and I told him the truth of the original letter that sent me to him, you, and Jaeden."

He stared at me in disbelief before his eyes glazed with a cold sheen, his attention turning to my arm as he walked back over to me and began to wrap the scabbed wound from his bite earlier. "Did you tell him everything about it?"

I had forgotten about the wound entirely, the pain in my heart overtaking all rational thought. "I told him everything about the letter. How Theo created it with each of the rebellion's generals' input, what the real point of my travel was." My breath was shaky as I continued, "That the plan was for me to kill him to begin the rest of the rebellion's plots, to take out whoever I could—even if that meant killing myself in the process."

He nodded, tightening the bandage with a yank and clipping it in place with a small pin. "I don't think he is angry with you as much as he is with Theodore at the moment," He murmured, putting the supplies back into his bag without looking toward me. "But he is angry with himself for letting you get so close, not only to him but to his sisters and Jaeden and me. I doubt you would have been any real threat, but the idea that you *could* have been a wolf in sheep's clothing has likely sent his anger to a level I have not seen in years."

Though the truth stung, it was unlikely that I would have been able to do any real damage unless it was by taking advantage of their kindness. I had not realized how little I knew about the art of fighting until that night in the imaginary music room, where it had become all too obvious that I was sent underprepared.

Rygur picked up the bags from the grass as he led the way into the quiet town where most denizens had already been cradled to sleep by the storm. "Do you think he will forgive me?"

"I do not think he is going to kill you. Forgiving you, however, I could not say. His sisters mean everything to him, and though you all got along very well, I do not know if he'll forgive you or himself for how close the three of you got after learning what your position was."

I nodded, turning to silence as I examined the town of Vriwood to avoid dwelling on the idea that Ren and I were genuinely destined for heartbreak.

It was a smaller town that reminded me of Ullaven's closely built structures, rough cobble streets, and spaced firelight lantern rods. Some abandoned carts with various goods were hastily stuffed into baskets or under blankets to protect them from the rain, while their owners had likely retreated to the local tavern or their homes to rest.

Whereas Ullaven would have been dancing in the rain and thriving in the joy of the water even this late at night, Vriwood seemed to have been dulled by the storm. Most of the homes had closed their shutters to sleep through the stormy night. However, there were a few that were cracked open with a light still illuminating the rooms as hushed conversations were had or an occasional glance from a strolling passerby who would watch me with tentative distance. It was an odd and unnerving feeling, my arms withdrawing to wrap around my chest to comfort the eerie feeling that crept over my spine.

Rygur eventually stopped at a tavern, holding his hand up to me in a motion to stop. "Stay out here while I check the inside and assess the situation," he ordered, looking back at me with a small sigh. "I'll get us rooms for the night. We'll stay here until the first light, then meet up with Jaeden and Rendros at the forward camp. Okay?"

I nodded, though I could not bring myself to ask any questions or argue. As much as I wanted to be near Ren and talk to him, I knew I was likely the last person he wanted to see right now, nor did I know what more I could say to convince him that I was genuine.

He left me with a curt nod, leaving me to watch the storm continue to drizzle overhead. It was a night that I knew I would hold little sleep despite the comfort of the storm; my entire chest felt like a dragon had just sat on it and suffocated me. Then, as hushed whispers spread between them, I watched a few people hurry along the streets and past a line of dark houses toward some farm fields.

Hushed whispers pulled me out of my self-loathing as I watched a group of people hurry along the streets, but where I had expected them to dive into a house to escape the rain, they disappeared behind a row of darkened homes. My attention looked in their direction as I tried to discern another home they could be running to, but I only found rolling hills of farmer's fields.

If most of Vriwood was rushing to get out of the rain, what was a group of shady people doing running into an uncovered section of the town?

I could feel the darkness—the shadow magic, apparently—stir with the weird movements of the group as I watched some tall stalks of corn shake as I assumed they ran through it. Very little caused my magic to stir like a cold trace of a finger on my bare skin, yet somehow it knew when something was off.

My head turned back to the tavern to look toward the front door, hoping Rygur would step out so I could tell him of the odd group, but there was no sight of the male. Only the muffled conversations of guests seeping out from cracked windows, utterly oblivious to the activities outside the doors.

Investigate, Willow. The Ethe's voice crept into my mind, sending goosebumps down my arms as the unfamiliar voice startled my silence. Its voice was only there for a second before the shadows of the fields seemed to call out for me again, the group's suspicious presence seeming to lure me closer like a fish caught on a lure.

I ran after the group, pulling my sword from its sheath as I entered the crop fields of Vriwood.

With winter on the capital's doorstep, most fields were barren or dormant until spring would arrive a few months from now. The farther I ran, the fewer homes spread across the land until only the dormant cornstalks remained, making the rain sound like crackling embers as it landed on the dry leaves.

I barely avoided stepping on a family of small rabbits that had nestled in some fallen leaves when voices came from ahead of me.

"Will it still work in the rain?" a young woman's voice asked.

"It should. It's not made of fire or anything susceptible to water," Another woman answered, though her confidence wavered as she spoke.

"Hurry up and let the cursed thing out already. We must do this before the general prince and his lackeys arrive." A third voice chastised, his voice rougher with age.

Something dark settled in my bones with the last voice, the shadows pushing nerves aside to bring anger and suspicion to the forefront. My instinct, or the Ethe, had been correct—something was very wrong about this group and their moonlight meeting.

I used my blade to gently push cornstalks out of my way to get closer, using the echoes of thunder and drizzle of rain as cover for the sound the dry leaves created.

I approached what seemed to be a trampled circle in the middle of the field, reaching into my new magic and weaving it to block the line of sight to where I was standing by the three figures but still allowing me to see them.

There were three members of the mysterious group, all huddled around a small box on the ground, their attention fixed on its angled features, which gave me an excellent opportunity to examine each conspirator. Though each was cloaked in dark clothing to help slip through the night, I could identify a few details to bring back to Rygur if I could not get all three now.

The largest one was a male Fae who seemed to be the one in charge. His hood was pulled down to show greying hair with a dark beard braided with rings and charms. His light russet brown complexion was taut with anxiety and nerves as his yellow eyes darted nervously around the field, scanning for any unwanted onlookers.

The other two were more petite human women. They had not let their hoods down, so I could not see most of their faces, but one's long blonde hair escaped the dark fabric like ribbons of gold that shimmered in the gloom.

"We are going as fast as possible, but *you* still need to remove the containment magic before we can unlock the final latch." The middle-aged woman snapped back, her blue eyes shining bright with anger toward the male as he leaned down to the box and started whispering words in a language I could not understand.

The box started to glow in response as the edges of the lion Fae magic unraveled, and visible cracks appeared in the metal case as the man spoke. My shadows wanted to both recoil and explore the box as the containment magic evaporated with his final words. However, whatever it was brought a sickening feeling to my gut as the last bit of magical sheen disappeared.

A slight sniffle brought my attention away from the box as the blonde woman tried to stifle unwanted tears.

"There. Now unleash the Vethen, Tisa." The man ordered, pulling out a small object from his robe and handing it to the young woman.

The box rattled against the ground as if it were alive—as if it were in anticipation of what came next.

When the young blonde named Tisa did not immediately move for the object she was given, the older woman stood to grab it and placed a hand on her shoulder. "The sun burns through the darkest shadows."

My heart slowed as I watched, the words spoken hauntingly familiar —though I could not place why—even as the grim I commanded whisked back into my core in retreat.

"To save us from the moon's eternal night," The blonde whispered in response, completing the phrase like the two sides of a single prayer intertwined.

My heartbeat was a slow, steady beat of horror as the glint of a silver blade caught in the moonlight, slicing the blonde's throat from ear to ear.

The hood fell back as her body convulsed with the killing slash, revealing bright green eyes wide with fear as her blood sprayed the box and the trampled field below her in waves of bright red. More of her life trickled out of her lips and her eyes as she tried to speak—tried to look for anything comforting or familiar, though this field harbored none of that.

There was a flash of light to my left as a grey wolf stood where the man had last been standing, the older woman dropping the blood-soaked dagger to bring her hands to her mouth in horror, almost as if she was unaware of what carving a crescent into the throat of another would do.

The young woman's lifeless body fell to the ground next to the box; the blood that pooled around her mingled with the darkness of her shadow. With every drop that still flowed from the still-warm corpse, the blood and shadow mixed into a swirl of black and red, the combination seeping toward and into the rattling box that now trembled with intense magical energy. As the box hungrily devoured more of the gruesome tonic, the young woman—Tisa's—body began to lose all saturation of life from her form.

Those bright golden curls turned to nothing but a dull grey, its color now blurring with the darkened ground.

Before I could watch more of the girl's demise, a giant beast came to stand directly in front of my hiding spot, blocking any vision I would have had. His growl was low as he let out a commanding bark toward the still-living woman to break her out of her horrified stupor, the sound of crunching leaves sounding from the other side of the furred wall as she hustled over toward him.

I will not back down.

"What the fuck did you *do?*" I growled, anger lacing my voice as I pushed out of the shadowed hole I had been hiding in, bringing my sword forward to meet the face of the wolf.

He pinned his ears to his head as he quickly jumped back, baring his teeth in a challenge.

The woman screamed as she ran in the other direction.

I pushed forward with my blade, aiming to pierce his neck, when he jumped to the side and lunged at me from my left. I quickly shifted to my right to avoid what could have been a nasty blow, my eyes darting around his muscles to try to keep an eye on his movements. All four of his shoulders and haunch muscles tensed all at once before he charged forward, teeth clashing with metal as he met my raised sword.

His maw clamped around the silver as he thrashed his head, trying to dislodge it from my grip. With the keen sense of smell that all wolf Fae had, I was sure that he had already discerned that I was prey, meaning to remove any weapon to lower any defense I had.

However, I was no longer afraid of losing a sword.

I reached into my core to grab a tendril of shadow—intending to blast the wolf back like I had Ren in the training session earlier that morning—but it fought my summons. All the power of shadow had retreated into a locked room of my internal library, hiding within its shelves to avoid the conflict that awaited it on the surface. It was *afraid*, and no amount of coaxing or pulling that I tried could pull it out of its home.

The distraction of the struggle pulled my attention from the fight as large teeth slammed into my left shoulder, a cry of pain ripping from my throat as canines tore through flesh and muscle.

I will not back down.

I dropped my sword to catch it in my right hand, imbuing whatever magic I could into the strike to plunge the silver blade into his right eye. Blood sprayed from the wound as the weapon hit true, his roar echoing through the field as he yanked himself back. The strong movement pulled me forward with him as his teeth dislodged from my shoulder, my blood falling down my arm as I watched blood spill from his eye socket.

I had done the damage I needed to free myself, but it was not enough to kill him.

Anger flashed in the remaining yellow eye as he stepped toward me, but a rush of black from the center of the trampled circle pulled both of our attentions back to the forgotten metal box. Deep within my core, I felt my shadow magic coil farther behind rows of locks and imaginary doors as I watched the now-open box reveal its horrifying contents as darkness spilled into the space.

Any awareness of the wolf was lost as the shadows began to cover the entire field in a wave of dark clouds that chilled deep into my bones, the power and sheer amount of it blocking out any bit of moonlight that tried to shine through. More darkness filled the area to the point of suffocation, my feet stumbling backward as I tried to find a spot that I could pull breath from once more. Though I fumbled for vision and air, I held my blade at the ready as the box shattered, bringing the spreading grim in fast retreat to its origin as it began to form something worse than my imagination could ever conjure.

Two orbs of red flashed in its core as a large serpentine-like head emerged from the writhing mass of darkness. The black mist spiraled further and further into shape until it stood nearly thirty feet in the air, its long body coiling into a snake of shadow. As if it were alive, its tongue quickly shot into the air to scent it, the shadows of the form rippling through it like waves of breath as it scanned the area.

There was a chime of midnight bells in the distance that had its attention instantly snapping toward it.

Vriwood.

"Hey!" I screamed, trying desperately to get the beast to focus anywhere *but* the innocent city just beyond the fields. Someone had to have been watching to grant some blessing as it cast its gaze down toward me, its mouth opening wide to display elongated teeth that dripped with an acidic green liquid that instantly killed any living plant on the ground as it landed.

Ren, I don't care if you hate me right now. I kept my attention on the snake as I waved my arms around, trying to keep its interest as the bell struck again. *But I need you to listen to me and trust me just one more time.* I had to fight down the terror that threatened to shred what little confidence I had. *Get everyone the hells out of Vriwood.*

The snake struck as I shifted in a flash of silver before sprinting in the opposite direction of the town. I could barely see where I was going through the rough, but cornstalks crumpled under the giant beast's weight as it took the bait, slithering after me with an unnatural speed.

I did not get a response from Ren, but I could not focus on the fear that gnawed in my conscious that he would not have listened. I had to pray that he was yelling orders at Jaeden to get to Vriwood and then would be giving orders to evacuate the town.

Otherwise, the potential reality would paralyze me, and I would die in the maw of the monstrous snake that gained on me with every second.

It struck again, just barely missing me on my right, the grass rapidly withering in a large radius where the teeth sank into the dirt.

I ran toward the nearest forest to finally break free of the farm fields and hopefully gain an advantage in the maze of trees. I prayed to whatever god was listening to let the beast follow me as far as possible from the city until it was in a good spot where I could try to kill it.

A commotion started in the direction of Vriwood as children's screams echoed through the empty expanse, making my entire body go numb when the snake stopped its pursuit. Its head turned toward the sound, only hesitating momentarily before taking off at a terrifying speed toward the vulnerable town.

I let out a shrill cry of despair as I took off after it, summoning fire to my side as I launched it towards the beast that was somehow gaining more and more distance toward its new target. Every blast of flame made it hiss and recoil, but it did not stop its forward momentum to pay attention to me.

Vriwood was here before I could realize that the screams that now sounded through the streets were filled with terror as the shadow beast reared its ugly head over a line of houses as it looked over the town.

Another shift and I raced towards it with my sword, screaming with all my might to tell them all to run as I reached the core of my magic. I tore past any barricades and locks that the grim magic had tried to hide behind, but with every layer, I removed another reformed. The fire was harming the serpent, but any real damage was negatable as it seemed unphased beyond irritation. However, if I could control the shadows with the shadow magic that was hiding deep within me, force the beast into submission, maybe I could dissolve it completely—

A line of lightning severed the end of its tail as light spread through its body, cutting me off from my sprint as I skid to a stop, its mouth opening wide in a roar of pain that sounded like tortured screams. Its blood-red orbs seemed to bounce back and forth in its misted form as it searched for the source of the devastating magic.

Another blast of lightning cast light over a Fae silhouette hovering above the beast, the user's identity unmistakable.

Ren?

If he was in his Fae form, how could he have been flying?

Lightning wreathed around his forearms as he called forward another blast to strike into the serpent's chest, the sharpened light hitting true as the beast collapsed on a row of darkened homes near the center of town. Children and adults alike screamed as I sprinted past them, trying to make it to where the head had fallen, but my fears were soon realized.

Its teeth had sunk into a pair of fleeing Fae, their bodies becoming sunken, colorless husks as their very life force was drained from them. The more they withered, the more the shadows of the beast rippled in growing mass, its power resurfacing as it began to recover from the damage.

A group of children began screaming nearby, with one breaking free of the group to run toward the pair on the ground.

"No!" I cried out, running forward and yanking the child back before he could step into the decaying radius of the beast's strike while my left shoulder screamed in pain. "You can't get near them!"

His wide ivory eyes turned to me, his pale skin dotted with tiny freckles. Tears poured out of his eyes as hard as the rain as he cried, "You have to save them! Heal them!"

Two more children stepped forward, freckles dotting each of their faces, the eldest probably around her early teens. Both were stricken with horrified grief like what I assumed their little brother I was holding was, but too stunned with shock to react in the way the little boy had.

"I'm afraid it's too late for them, sweetheart," I whispered, pushing a strand of the boy's auburn hair back in as calming of a motion as I could —both for me and him. "But it is not too late for you and your siblings. Get out of Vriwood and head somewhere safe until Prince Rendros calls you home, all right?"

"Rendros is here?" The eldest asked, the shadow beast beginning to writhe behind me as I heard the cracking of shale and stone.

I needed to get them out of here quickly.

"He's right up there, wielding the lightning that damages the monster." I nodded, pointing to the sky where I had last seen him. "He will protect you and avenge your parents without holding back. But to do that, you need to leave now." I nodded, handing the young boy to the sister when I heard the satisfied hiss of the beast somewhere high above me.

"Willow!" Thunder boomed from the sky as Ren screamed toward me, giving me barely enough warning to spin around just in time to hold up my blade against venom-coated fangs.

"GO!" I gritted through my teeth at the children, who thankfully ran without another word.

Electricity charged the air around me as I was now face to face with the shadow serpent, the acid dripping onto the ground before me as I put all my energy into pushing back despite how much my shoulder screamed. I refused to be another death that would haunt the children who were already traumatized from the death this monster had just brought to their doorstep.

Out of the corner of my eye, I saw familiar star-coated black wings race toward me. However, I knew that right now, his presence on the ground would not save anything. It would put him at a risk that those children and this kingdom could not afford.

That *I* could not afford.

"Strike its head, Rendros!" I screamed, my arms shaking against the strength the beast was pushing into its attack, my legs trying to catch any bump or crack in the path's stones. "Before it moves again!"

I could feel his hesitation, and with what ability I could muster, I pulled my gaze to meet his where he hovered near the tops of the nearby buildings, his leathery wings spread out to curb his rapid descent. All my strength was focused on keeping the deadly serpent from swallowing me whole, so though I could not say anything, I poured whatever emotion— care, desperation, confidence, *love*—I could into the bond, into his eyes.

A silent confession of things I wanted to say alongside a wary promise that I would be all right.

Conflict lit his gaze, but he raised his hand to conjure the clouds together in a swirl of dangerous power.

I slammed my eyes shut as an enormous *boom* shook the entire town. One moment, I was holding the beast back with only a sword, and the next, I was thrown back into a building as it hit the ground. My muscles and spine ached in agony as I pulled myself from the stone and wood walls, pushing myself forward one last time to swing my blade through the red orbs, slashing them out of the pile of grim.

The gems dimmed as they fell to the ground at my feet before the shadows that comprised the beast into form scattered back to the recess of buildings and people.

I pressed my sword into the ground to steady myself as I swayed, but I refused to fall to the pain or exhaustion that pressed at the side of my mind.

"What in the living hell was *that?*" Jaeden jogged into view from the direction of the tavern, a brass sword at the ready as Rygur followed quickly behind him, both of their eyes fixated on me in a mixture of exasperation and confusion.

Before I could answer either of them, Ren landed in front of me with a loud *thud* as his wings splayed out in adrenaline from the fight, his chest heaving from the exertion of magic and energy. "Are you all right?"

he asked, his eyes darting to the scabbing bite wound on my shoulder and the dirty wrap on my forearm.

I opened my mouth to answer, but the only thing that fell out was, "When did you get wings?"

CHAPTER 28

We were all staring at each other in the middle of the street, but my attention was mainly focused on the wings that had sprouted on Ren's back.

"Just recently." He snorted, and just as suddenly they were there, they disappeared with a tiny spark of light. "But they aren't permanent. It's something we can investigate later after we discuss what the *hells* just happened."

I blinked several times before reaching behind me to put the silver sword in its sheath once I regained my balance, grimacing as I accidentally stretched the wounded shoulder in the process. "That *thing* was apparently a Vethen. And before you ask, no, I did not summon it. I was doing everything possible to stop it before it reached Vriwood." I grumbled, rolling my shoulder a few times as if that would ease the tears in the muscle instead of making it worse.

"What the hell is a Vethen?" Rygur chimed in, though all I could do was shake my head in response.

"I have suspicions, but I'm more concerned about *how* it arrived rather than *what* it was," I said, picking up the red gems from the ground before walking past Ren, aiming toward the trampled crop fields as Ren quickly pulled up along my right side, walking with me.

"You need to be healed."

"And you have people who believe in your strength and your title. They will be horrified and asking questions the second they deem it safe, which is quickly approaching now that it has essentially disappeared." I argued, looking at him just in time to see the worry lighting the blue in his eyes. "I saw the people who brought this destruction to the town, and I can lead you to its origin point and tell you what I saw so *you* can confidently answer your people. I'll be fine."

There was silence between us that lasted until we reached the edges of the cornfield, with Rygur and Jaeden trailing somewhere close behind.

"I could never hate you, you know," Ren whispered, "I *should*, considering the danger and death you could have brought to my home, but I can't. I think I know why, but—"

"We can discuss that after we get through tonight." I interrupted, giving him a weak smile. I did not know what he wanted to say, but whatever it was sent my heart tripping over itself despite the calamity of the evening's events.

"All right." He smiled as we trudged ahead through the destruction of crops until we reached the flattened ring that the beast emerged from.

"Holy shit," Jaeden exhaled as we approached the scene, though I knew he was not staring at the destruction or the box.

The corpse of Tisa was sucked dry of any sign of recent life; her skin was sucked onto her bones as if she had been mummified for years. Her mouth was stuck open in an empty scream, while her once vibrant green eyes had sunk entirely into the hollow ridges of her skull, now dull and unseeing.

Ren grabbed my right shoulder as if in reflex to the sight to make sure I was still there, to which I put my hand on his reassuringly.

I'm here.

"Her name was Tisa, I think," I said as I led the males closer to the scene, crouching down to examine the haunting shell. All of them refused to get any closer as I looked over every inch of her body, noting that any blood that had been on or in her body was now completely gone. "There were three people here when I followed them—two humans and one Fae —but the other two ran after she died. They slit her throat next to that box, reciting the most cryptic prayer."

All their attention turned to the remnants of the metal box, which were now nothing but gold and iron shards in the field.

"'The sun burns through the darkest shadows to save us from the moon's eternal night.'" I recanted, and Rygur's attention shot to me in near disbelief.

"That sounds like the last words of the shadowed dragon to Athos before he was killed in the story of Vomuna's Lily: 'The sun casts the largest shadows.'" Ren murmured, his voice distant as he became lost in thought. "Why would a variation of that line have been here, connected to the shadow serpent? The lily is in Agraxis, and its signature is to go after only the mate of those who touch it. This monstrosity went after a town of people."

"I don't think it came from the Lily." I chimed in, pulling out the two red gems that glimmered in the remnants of the moonlight. "These were in its head, and they had to have been in the box before Tisa was killed, along with the main collection of grim that made up the beast. This likely means these held the initial spell or magic charm for the ritual but needed a sacrifice to complete it."

I ran my hand near Tisa again, searching for magic on why she was the chosen sacrifice, but there was nothing there that I could sense. She was a human sacrifice, unremarkable in terms of magic, who had been killed for the birth of a town-destroying monster of nightmares.

What was the point of the sacrifice if it was not for her magic or blood? From what I could assume, the creature needed more than blood alone to fill the power, but...

"Move away from her," I whispered, stepping back without moving my gaze from the mummified woman in the dirt. A second passed as everyone moved farther away before that familiar freezing chill shot up and down my spine as my shadow magic ran through my body like it wanted to get as far away as possible.

I had thought it was the beast, but now I could see the true reason for its fear. Despite the moonlight granting ample light from above us, there was no shadow trailing from the corpse.

Maybe it was because of the magic that ran through my veins or the familiarity with the drained woman in front of me because of my attack, but I felt sick as I grabbed onto Ren to keep my balance. He quickly held me up, his hand cradling my lower back in reassurance and stability.

"They took her fucking shadow? That's *possible?*" Anger and disgust radiated from Jae as he looked at the corpse, Rygur quickly turning his gaze downcast to not look at the horrifying reality of Tisa's demise.

I instinctively looked around us to ensure the dark silhouette of shadows still draped behind each of us, the chill down my spine easing as my magic instinctively relaxed at seeing the familiar silhouette reflections. "It's unnatural and sickening to the point that even the shadow magic I have recoiled in its presence," I murmured as my gaze drifted back toward Vriwood, memories of the battle flashing in my mind as I looked at the couple that still lay in their streets.

"Do you think another shadow user might have caused all this?" Ren's voice was soft, but the question set off several more in my head as I tried to rationalize the situation.

I had never heard of shadow magic in the little lessons of magic I was given, and as far as I was aware, it had not been a possible force to control in the first place. It had belonged solely to Vomuna and Vomuna alone, though her children received echoes of her magic in different forms.

If I had been able to harness its power, would that mean someone else could also have shadow-born gifts? No Fae type could harness that magic naturally, but could the gods be meddling in mortal affairs for the first time in centuries?

"That depends on if and how grim magic like that has been given out to the Fae." I nodded, steadily pulling myself back together and away from the corpse of the woman. "All I know is that I've never heard of shadow-gifted Fae, but I know someone who might."

"We can't travel back to Agraxis to ask Argus," Rygur argued, though I only smirked as I closed my eyes to enter the magic library in my core, searching for the tome that had hidden deep within a new shelf. It had hidden itself behind several layers of books, but the fear that radiated from its pages was more potent than any other book that resided in my magic repertoire.

"There's no need to return to Agraxis when who I'm talking about is attached to me," I growled in explanation as the book fought my call, digging my mental nails into it until it finally came free.

I brought my hands forward to focus on an empty spot in the field, straining as I pulled on the strings of shadow as if I were painting on a canvas. Sweat began to bead on my forehead as I felt the magic pull on the deepest strings of my soul, playing a melancholy tune that danced between grief and terror.

They were fighting my summons with so much fear-fueled strength that it was draining me far faster than any other magic had before, but I held my ground as the shadows finally began to form into an equine-like shape that I had seen when I first met them.

All three males readied their weapons behind me as the creature finished its apparition, its hooves anxiously digging at the ground as I held my hand up.

"You are a *fool* to use your magic so close to this abomination!" The Ethe snapped, white orbs of light now sitting in the place eyes would have been, as I did not feel like conversing with something I could not make eye contact with. "You have worn yourself out to dangerous levels for a foolish task, Willow Saugrave."

"Ethe, this is Crown Prince Rendros Roamion, Jaeden Carver, and Rygur Dozemm. Boys, this is the Ethe." I smiled sarcastically as I hardened my gaze onto the creature, and its gaze did not leave my face. "You are all we have for answers on what the hells just happened, so I'm afraid I had no choice. What is a Vethen, how was that thing created, and where is the shadow of that woman?"

"You've learned not to waste time on stupid questions," The beast mused in irritation, ignoring the deadly Fae around me as they tensed every time the disembodied voice seemed to bounce between them. "There are three classifications of a shadow beast: the Ethe, the Vethen, and the Aethel. The Ethe are often conjured from weaker souls like prey creatures or humans and are mostly used for quick communication or running information from one commanding Fae to another. The Vethen usually come from the weaker predators or diluted Fae, but they are deadly shadows meant for quick presses of power and destruction." Their whispered voice tapered off as they looked at Tisa's husk behind us, and though I could not see the emotion in the glowing white orbs, I could feel the pain that recoiled at the sight.

"Pray that you never meet an Aethel, as they are created only from the strongest sources found on this planet, and a lucky stroke of lightning on its own won't kill them." Their voice was quieter now, the rasp overwhelmingly apparent as they looked over me in a critical examination. "You haven't even started working on the tasks I gave you."

"I've found the shadow magic that suggests otherwise." I countered, but they shook their ghostly head in disappointment.

"I don't know how this one came about, but I can imagine its purpose was precisely for this attack and slumbered within that metal contraption until that spell the wolf recanted and finalized by the sacrifice of that girl's shadow. Whoever created this one has found new ways to transport beasts far from their deadly origins using an additional sacrifice, which is deeply concerning." The Ethe thought aloud, seemingly curious about the box and the girl but refusing to take any steps closer. "They should be your next target before that information reaches people of higher status." There was unspoken clarification in the warning, but the answer flickered to me through the shadows.

Queen Ezyla.

"I didn't find any identifiable features of a faction influence on the figures that could have been the reason for the attack." I turned to Ren, who had kneeled beside Tisa to roll over her exposed wrist. He was quiet, but the thunder that rumbled in the sky exposed the anger he was suppressing.

Jaeden and Rygur took a few steps closer to examine what he was looking at before they both hushed curses.

"Southern Rebellion scouts," Rygur announced, using his sword to trace the shape of a black sun in the dirt to mimic the one branded onto the underside of her wrist. "They wanted to make a power play before we arrived then."

The shadows around the area darkened with the next roll of thunder, my anger rising that somehow, *he* could be involved.

The tether with the Ethe began to weaken, indicating that there wasn't much time before he slunk away again. I did not turn away from the crude drawing of the symbol that Ren made as I asked, "Who is blessed with shadow magic to create such beasts?"

The entity hesitated before his wheeze broke the silence of the field, "Only one is blessed with the shadows, but that gift is unnecessary to make these mindless beasts. All you need is darkness in your heart, a forsaken soul, and a ruthless mind."

The Ethe retreated into the recesses of my mind, hiding themselves once more in the shelving of magic unknown.

"I could do without the riddles," I grumbled, looking over the three males, who seemed to communicate silently through brooding stares. "I could also do without the brooding. We need a game plan before this happens again." Jaeden and Rygur turned to each other with worried glances before looking at Ren.

"Absolutely not." His answer to their silent question was quick and stern.

"Ren, it's the best option for getting in there and figuring out what is happening," Jae's voice was soft and understanding, but Ren's growl echoed in the cornstalks. "I'll go too, so that way there's extra protection *and* leverage—"

"As your general, I forbid the request and the mission," Ren ordered, the voice of a king shining through with the statement, setting my skin on fire with goosebumps. "We will find another way."

"Willow, would you go back into the Wilds to find Theo and find out where this came from?" A strike of lightning, along with a growled curse, came from just beyond where Rygur was standing before me, his gold-speckled eyes watching my reaction intently. "Would you get us this information at the risk of your life for the betterment of Aistris?"

Ren had moved in front of me as quick as a summer storm, electricity coming off him in defensive crackles as he broke the eye contact between Rygur and me.

The world around me slowed as I debated my answer, turning my attention to the mud at my feet. Theo had been in my life since I was a filly—I considered him my best friend and my big brother in one. The people of Ullaven and the rebellion had become a part of my family that I was desperate to protect.

The wolf-Fae female clutching her child snuck into my mind again as I put myself in that destroyed camp for the first time to place an invisible hand on her shoulder. Theo had promised that he would get all he could out of that outpost before the army's forces arrived, and once, I had thought that it had been only a stubborn few who had perished in the battle. However, as I looked out at the imaginary scene again, all I could see were more broken bodies and parents holding dead children.

The scene changed to the group of haunted children crying over the bodies of their parents who died at the acid fangs of a shadow beast and who would have joined them if the males around me had not intervened.

The shameless annihilation of innocents for the advancement of a war.

"I do it because I have my own people to save—if I were to stop now, to turn around and go home, do you think the general you used to work for would stop? Or would he push forward to make a statement and kill who knows how many for that plan?"

Ren had given Theo letters requesting a truce to try to negotiate some semblance of peace to end the slaughter, and Theo killed innocent messengers in response.

"This attack would have been in place of Ren's death. It would have had less of an impact but enough of one to get you to notice when you arrived that he was taking things to the next level." I finally spoke, not moving my stare from the ground to watch the shadows of the males blocking the moonlight around me. "He knows I'm not dead and didn't complete my mission, and he must know that I'm pacted to Ren. I don't know if he knows I came with you guys, though." I was thinking aloud, but Rygur and Jae had turned to me in eager interest. "He will not be happy to see me."

"But he *would* see you, face to face. Maybe try to reinstate a new plan with you if you show up?" Rygur questioned, his voice inflecting cautious curiosity.

"He would see me, but I doubt his new plan would involve me returning to Vriwood or your camps."

"Then you won't be going back, as simple as that. It's a fruitless mission with more to lose than to gain." Ren huffed, crossing his arms over his chest.

"No," I said definitively, Ren's attention turning to mine as I finally lifted my head to meet his conflicted gaze. "I will take on this mission for the betterment of *our* people, but we have to take care of a few loose ends before I do." I smiled with a gentle nod, feeling more confident than I had when I originally left Ullaven. Though Ren's gaze writhed in my denial, I turned to the wolf Fae I had come to depend on. "Jae, I need you to do something for me first."

The storm intensified as Ren's anger flared. I passed him with only a gentle squeeze of bicep as I stood in front of Jaeden.

Trust me.

"While I'm thrilled you are agreeing to a potentially dangerous yet rewarding plan, I *really* don't want Ren to kill me for putting you in danger," Jae admitted sheepishly, running his hand through his light brown hair as he avoided his general's stare.

"Then it's a good thing you'll be doing both of us a favor instead." I shrugged, pulling down my shirt to better show the bite wound that had scabbed over. "Find the wolf who decided he wanted to lead this plan to condemn an innocent town to death and defended that decision by fighting me."

Despite the anger that rolled off Ren in waves, there was something more primal underneath it as he gave Jae a tight nod of confirmation that this request was allowed.

There was a slow smile on Jae's face that filled with hunt-fueled hunger as he leaned forward to take in a deep inhale of the wound, slowly analyzing all the smells as they hit him. His eyebrows knitted together as he tried to piece together the one scent he needed, following it down my right arm where there was dried blood that was not mine.

"I was able to get a good stab into his right eye, though I did not realize any got on me. Hopefully, that helps you pin down what you need." I shrugged, though Rygur had let out a soft laugh from somewhere behind him.

"That does help significantly," Jae flashed his teeth in a wild grin before he shifted, covering my eyes from the bright shift. He was quick to trot near Ren; his ears angled up toward him as if wanting confirmation for a simple question as his nose worked to keep the scent trail fresh.

"Bring him back to my tent in the war camp, alive, please." Ren nodded to the wolf, who snapped his teeth in response before disappearing into the cornstalks.

"What do you need him for?" Rygur asked, watching the darkness that Jae had run off into. "He was likely just some dispensable soldier who could perform the magic to wake up the Vethen."

"I was told how Theo responded to your general's letters with presents," I flashed him a wicked smile, "So I thought it would be rude of me not to bring my brother one."

CHAPTER 29

Over the next hour, exhaustion pulled on my shoulders like a phantom weight as I finished a wreath of flowers to place on the newest graves in Vriwood's cemetery.

After seeing Jae off, Rygur went early to the war camp to inform the standing generals that Ren would return the next day, along with details about what had happened in Vriwood that sent him and Jae away nearly immediately after their arrival. Ren and I stayed behind to help the townspeople resettle, with our first task being to inform those who had evacuated that they could come home. Ren answered hundreds of questions about the incident.

He responded with such gentle confidence to every question and every person who spoke up and often held the hands of those still overwhelmed by the attack. He was the general of an Imperial Army, yes, but he was also the champion of his people—a hero who genuinely cared for the innocents who could not defend themselves. He did not stand out like a prince or a general, but instead, he was a kind friend who fought off the enemy that threatened his neighbors.

"Prince Ren!" A familiar child's cry pulled me out of my thoughts, my attention turning from the wreath in my hands to see the group of children whom I had defended from the serpent run to the front of the dwindling line to swarm him.

Most of the crowd turned from the scene as sadness lined their faces as they recognized the children as they approached, none upset by the disruption of the line.

"Did you do it? Did you kill it for what it did?" The middle child hiccuped, her pigtails bouncing as she rubbed her face to stop the tears.

Ren kneeled to the group with a sad smile, running one hand over her head and another over the youngest one's back. "We did; Miss Willow and I ensured it would never return."

I left the wreath over a patch of flowers on the grave with a soft smile as I crossed my hands in front of me with a smooth bow. "I'm sorry I couldn't get there sooner."

"You saved my baby brother." The oldest one nodded, tearstains blotching her cheeks and her nightgown where her siblings had likely wiped their faces. "You did what you could, and I owe you everything for that."

"You owe me nothing," I replied quickly with a shake of my head. "I only wish for you all to live long and happy lives, just as your parents would have wanted."

She nodded as if she wanted to say something else, but she was interrupted by the small boy who was now sitting on Ren's shoulders.

"Is she your girly-friend, Prince Ren?"

The middle girl with pigtails chimed in, "Does that make her a princess?"

I could not help but laugh as I looked at the children before I looked at Ren, whose eyes settled on my face with a softness that warmed every bit of my heart. "She's not a princess," He smiled, though he gave a wink to the little girl as he added, "Not yet, at least."

I tried to wave away the blush that coated my cheeks in a deep crimson as I turned to the oldest. "Ren has already put your parents to rest here if you want to say a prayer for them. I'm sure he can babysit the little ones while you have a moment alone?"

"Oh please, please, *please*, Eve?" The little boy pleaded, and the little girl quickly joined in the chorus.

Eve's eyes bounced between each of her siblings in gentle hesitance, but as the little girl grabbed onto Ren's leg as the boy played with his hair on his shoulders, the tension in her face seemed to ease as she nodded to him.

He gave a warm smile as he hobbled away with the children, leaving Eve and me to walk over to the grave in relative silence.

The moon hung high in the sky as it shone through the clearing storm clouds, illuminating every grave marker made of piled stones or wooden stick crowns. It was a small-town cemetery that was constantly visited and cared for by the markings of the well-worn paths and freshly placed flowers, the newest residents of the hallowed ground farther toward the back. The three recently dug eternal resting beds had been covered in a blanket of flowers that Ren had added with a flick of his wrist with his magic, adding a pair of intertwined rosebushes over two of them as their grave markers.

"They deserve beautiful flowers in their final resting place to hopefully serve as a better sight than those children had to witness," Ren had explained to me as he finished them.

Eve did not speak as she knelt in quiet prayer, and I left her to her grief while I wandered over to a patch of dandelions to weave the wreath to place on the last grave.

I stayed in the patch of dandelions for so long that, at some point, I sat in the center of the ring. I had become so enamored and focused on the work that I was only pulled out of the trance when I caught the whiff of cedar mingling with the smell of fresh rain that had become a sign and a comfort.

"You don't have to sit vigil out here. They walk with Vomuna now."

"I know I don't, but I wanted to make a final wreath for Tisa before I made my way back to town." I shrugged, "I just watched as she was sacrificed, so I feel I owe it to her, too."

I felt his legs on either side of me as he eased onto the ground. His arms wrapped around my waist as he rested his head on my unbandaged shoulder, watching me weave the flowers together.

"Not princess *yet*, hmm? What was that about?" I asked with a gentle tease, though I kept my focus on the stems so I would not lose progress.

"Well, you're not made a princess by just being my *girly-friend;* we have to go through a few ceremonies to get that title added on there," He teased back, kissing the side of my neck that sent goosebumps flying. I pressed farther into his touch, desperate to take in the relief that he was there.

"I didn't realize I had been upgraded to the prestigious title of girly-friend."

"You got that title when you made me that promise a couple of nights ago," He whispered, his teeth rubbing against my skin. "You haven't broken that promise, have you?"

"How could I dream of doing such a thing?" I chuckled, though I shook my head as I began to put together the final dandelions. "Besides, I'm pretty sure I've been under your watch since that night anyway."

"Fair enough." He whispered, but there was a raw edge in his voice that sent a possessive chill up my spine and goosebumps down each of my limbs.

I shook off the feeling as I stood, leaving his warm embrace for only a moment to kneel at Tisa's grave, sending a small prayer to Vomuna to take care of her soul and for Sinos to guide her to his mate, wherever they were now. I left the crown I had woven on the circle of wooden sticks and branches that marked her grave before I wandered toward the outskirts of the cemetery.

Ren was never far behind, stopping me by a large oak that marked a fence line to pull my back to his chest, leaving a small trail of kisses down my neck to keep a nightmare spiral at bay.

"You know, watching you order Jae earlier like *you* were his general made me want to do all sorts of things to put you back in your place...but it was also fucking hot to see your command." He whispered, pressing harder against my back so I could feel the evidence of my actions.

His hands roamed up my torso to barely caress my breasts, the touch alone breaking a clipped moan free from my throat. "I think I'd love to plead my case for stepping out of line if you have a place where I can properly submit the evidence."

Ren's growl rumbled my entire body as he pressed his hips deeper into my lower back, leaving me gasping at the impressive length that pulsed in eagerness. "I believe I have just the place, Wildie." He whispered as he swiftly picked me up from my feet, his arms placed at my upper back and under my knees.

I giggled as he smiled wickedly, a small streak of lightning sparking from his back in a bright flash as his wings flared in place of the electricity. I could not help but reach out towards them, though his shoulder was quick to block my hand's advances with a soft bump.

"Unless you intend to be fucked senseless in a graveyard, I wouldn't do that. Sensitivity rules are the same as when I'm shifted." He winked, sending the heat that pooled in my lower abdomen spiraling at the ravenous thought.

"Then you better take me to that place before I lose my control, your Highass." My tone was hushed with lust as I licked my lips, his eyes darkening as he fought his impulses before his wings lifted us into the open air.

We began soaring over the town, where a relieved hush had calmed the panic that had happened only a few hours ago. The sounds of children fighting sleep and quiet laughter seemed to rise from the homes as families relished the comfort and safety of their lives once more. The town itself seemed to calm with the quiet as well, the building's cold stone pathways now seemingly warm under the gentle firelight that had been doubled after tonight's attack.

The lights began to fade as we headed to a more secluded part of the town, where homes seemed to be few and far apart, though their sizes were more extensive than the townhomes that followed the main pathway of Vriwood. Each house was quiet with rest, likely unaware or already calmed from the shadow serpent's wrath, though the building we were headed toward had no firelight illuminating its entry. It seemed empty and alone compared to the others, though it had the most beautiful garden that lined it. Each wall had a line of vibrant flower bushes and vines, and the yard had several fruit trees that seemed unperturbed by the cold winter air that crept on the edges of their leaves.

"You really like your flora, don't you?" I teased as he landed on the stone in front of the building, his wings disappearing with another spark of light. "Some might think it too feminine."

"Do you?" Ren asked, raising his eyebrows as he magically unlocked the door before pushing us both inside.

"I find it quite charming, a colorful side to the cold general of the Imperial Army." I smiled, wiggling free from his grasp as we headed into the main room.

The house itself was empty beyond the essentials, firelight flickering to life on sconces on the walls, illuminating the beautiful craftsmanship put into the interior. The floor was made of dark cedar planks placed in arrowhead patterns up and down the entirety of the space, with light-plastered white walls to contrast the dark flooring. Floor-to-ceiling windows were placed all over the house, displaying the lovingly planted garden that surrounded the home like they were in a display case. In the main room, there was a couch centered in the room and a fireplace that came alive with a burst of flame with a rear archway that led into a short hallway and a rear bedroom.

Before I could investigate the back room, I was pressed into one of the walls by a demanding kiss, Ren's hands instantly pulling my hair out of its ponytail. His tongue pushed into my mouth to meet mine—just as eager to dance with his—as I brought my hands up to run a hand through his hair while the other cupped his cheek.

His hips pressed into mine, his length straining to stay within its confines as it rubbed directly against the second skin I called clothes.

I groaned in response as I pushed him back, our eyes locking. "I told you I had a case to plead." I panted, letting my hand travel from his head to his crotch to grasp his cock firmly through his pants, giving it a small pump as he growled in affirmation.

It seemed he was beyond words already, and I bit my lip as I pulled him over to the couch and sat him down.

"I'd like to present my first piece of evidence before I plead." I teased as my fingers curled under the bottom of my shirt to pull it up and off, slowly presenting the skin while his hands reached to touch my hips. My breasts fell into soft heaps as their bindings finally let them loose, a sigh of relief escaping my lips as I tossed the piece of clothing aside. I grabbed one of his roaming hands as I kneeled between his legs, leading it to one of my breasts. "Please examine it while I continue."

His eyes were completely dark with lust and focus, the predatory gleam in his eyes bright with hunger as I fumbled with his jeans, distracted by the teasing little circles his fingers drew over my breast.

His cock sprung free from its cage as I finally released the last clasp. It took both of my hands to grasp the entire length before I wrapped my lips over the head as I started to pump it.

"Oh, *fuck.*" He groaned, his hand tightening on my breast as he throbbed with need beneath my touch. I gave a soft growl in response as I slowly pushed my head down, removing one hand after another until I could fit as much as I could in my throat. I moved my head up and down in a combination of slow and fast movements, his free hand gripping the roots of my hair.

His fingers began to carefully squeeze the peaks of my breasts, kneading them as if they were dough, a moan escaping my throat over his cock as I slammed my head back down to envelop as much of him again.

His groan of pleasure answered in response as he pulsed in my throat before I pulled back to the tip to look up at him and witness the male that I had fallen so hard for.

Ren's eyes met mine as he watched me lick over him, a smile spreading on my face at the feral growl that reverberated throughout his entire body as I moved back to pumping him with both of my hands.

"Should I submit my next piece of evidence?" I whispered, kissing his length as I continued to work my hands around it.

"I'd like to submit a counter-argument to this one first." He whispered, gently pushing me back against the wooden floor before he quickly tore off the rest of his pants to easily straddle my waist. He pressed his hips between my breasts as he brought up my hands to hold the two mounds together before slowly moving his cock between them.

My lips had done enough to lubricate his member as it slowly pushed between my breasts, and the low growl that rumbled in his throat was intoxicating. He did not say anything else as he began to swing his hips back and forth faster and faster, leaving me moaning with every thrust as he placed his hands on the floor on either side of my head. "Plead, darling."

I could barely breathe when his eyes met mine, both of us nearly panting in unison as we stared into each other, my back arching at the heat that radiated throughout my entire body.

I was on fire; I was sure of it.

"I've wanted nothing but you since I first saw you, and I can think of no better master to tame me." I whispered, "You're all I can crave and want, and I want all of you."

He growled in response as he pushed forward with one powerful thrust, his climax sending ropes of his seed all over my neck and chest as he pulled back, kneeling just above my waist with a pleased huff. Ren's eyes traveled all over my upper body as he examined his work. The look was almost enough to send me over the edge, but I wanted *more*.

His grin turned wicked as that desire snuck across the bond, leaning down again to lick the side of my neck slowly. "I've reached a verdict of sinfully guilty." His voice was rough and soft at the same time, his hazel eyes flicking up to mine. "Would you like to know the punishment?"

"So long as it's as intense as the verdict," I whispered, running a finger over my chest to taste him as he watched, a low laugh escaping his throat.

He picked me up from the floor to press me against the mantle of the fireplace, the heat of the flames only intensifying the need that had only continued to grow. "Keep your hands on the mantle, darling." He whispered as he slowly traced his hands down my shoulders to my waist, his fingers playing with the clothing before he pulled them off with an effortless rip of the fabric. His hands cupped my ass as he pressed against the skin, "I've missed this view." He murmured, and I could hear him quickly discard his shirt as he flipped me around. One hand moved to the apex of my desire as he swiped a finger through the delicate folds devastatingly slowly.

"Please, Ren—" I panted as his hand moved to his mouth to suck all of my juices off of his finger slowly.

"Punishment, Wildie." He whispered as he pressed his lips to mine, making me taste every bit of heat that had slicked for him as his tongue battled mine for more of the taste. His hands twirled me around again until I was facing the mantle once the battle had been won, one hand pinching my breast, making me gasp in a mixture of pleasure and pain. "Don't move too much, darling. I don't want to hurt such a precious thing while it adjusts for the first time." He whispered in my ear as he bit the elongated lobe, his hand guiding himself between the slick folds of my pleasure.

He slowly pushed inside me, stretching every virgin inch of me to accommodate his intense size. I could hear the string of curses under his breath as he inched forward and back in slow, easing movements, the feeling so intensely filling and *right*. He pressed farther, a little harder this time, shattering whatever was left of my innocence with our combined moan that filled the entire space like a rumbling thundercloud. His name rolled off my tongue in a loud moan as he pressed the rest of himself in all the way to the hilt, panting over my shoulder as he stopped, his head pushing into mine.

I was on the tip of my toes as I was pressed against the mantle, no thoughts running through my mind except the desire for more as he held himself there, ensuring that I adjusted to the size that almost felt like it would split me in two. It was bliss; it was heaven, and it was far better than any field in any afterlife that waited for me.

"Don't stop—" I whined when he continued to stay still, my fingernails digging into the mantle as I felt the very words that I had been fearful of, the truth I had been hiding, spill out of my throat and into the open air.

"*Claim* me, Ren!"

Ren's breathing stopped when I spoke, but his hips were thrown back into motion before he could regain it. The gentleness of the first few strokes morphed into hard and powerful thrusts as he used one hand to massage a breast and the other to hold my hands against the fireplace. Our grunts and groans of pleasure silenced anything else that was said or thought as his thrusts turned into something different and primal.

He did not dare take more than an inch or two more out of me before he slammed to the hilt over and over again until one final thrust sent his teeth sinking deep into my right shoulder and into the throes of a combined release, our names cried out into the night by the other.

The feeling was unlike anything I had ever felt before, like a burning fire that exploded into a roaring inferno that consumed every nerve and feeling in my body and one that I wanted to experience again and again. It was a tsunami of pleasure and feeling that took out the strength in my knees, blotting my sight with stars as he pulsed deep inside me. We panted in tandem as he rested his head on the wound he had left, leaving gentle kisses on the marks where the pain should have been, but there was only comfort and relief.

After a few minutes of relishing our release, his arms moved under the crook of mine to keep me from falling to my knees. His kisses on my newly injured shoulder did not stop as he carried me from our discarded clothing to the bedroom I had been looking toward earlier, laying me out on the soft fabric before collapsing next to me.

"Is that how it is every time?" I asked between breaths, turning my head to look at him as he lay on his side to watch over me. His grin was sinful as he summoned a rag to his fingers, wiping all of the evidence of his first climax from my chest with slow precision.

"Only with you, Wildie." The rag was gone as quickly as it appeared as his hand reached up to my shoulder to run over the marks where his teeth had pierced my skin, quietly reveling in the mark as it scabbed over. "There is nothing and no one like you; you are the prize most males dream of." He met my eyes, "And you're mine."

Goosebumps ran over my body at the proclamation, returning the grin as I rolled over to face him fully. "Good, because I just might kill any female who touches you from now on." I teased, though a once quiet voice told me that the 'might' was a lie.

"I *will* kill any male who does, so be careful unless you want my hands to get bloodier."

"I'll keep that in mind, though I think you already have a target on your list."

His eyes darkened with a promise of death, though that was no longer a sight I was afraid of.

"That wolf that Jae is currently out hunting, consider that a *thank you* present." I grinned, my sharpened canines pressing into my lower lip.

"I cannot *wait* until that present arrives." His eyes traveled down again to the spot between my thighs, his hand drawing soft shapes over the curve. "We'll get plenty of silver rye tea before we leave town for camp in the morning."

"Silver rye tea?" I asked as I put my hand on his cheek, his attention flicking back to me at the confusion that lined my voice.

"It's a contraceptive tea for Fae to help avoid unplanned breeding." He smirked, though my face instantly flushed.

"I didn't think we *could* breed; I thought the magic between us was too strong to allow offspring."

"Perhaps, but I haven't heard of nor read what happens if a dragon and a unicorn were to try to breed, so we could also be the first to write that history." He smiled, "And while maybe one day I wouldn't mind seeing your beautiful eyes on a child of ours, I'd prefer it to be in a world where there is no difference between tamed and untamed."

I smacked his chest playfully before I nodded in quiet agreement, my gaze moving down his chest to pass the temptation of another round to catch on his legs, where the same swirls of silver scars that littered his dragon broke his skin. My hand gently ran over the lines of one, his muscles instantly tensing at the action before I pulled a breath away. "Does that hurt?"

He shook his head as he grabbed my wrist gently, pulling it away to place my hand on his chest. "Not physically, but the memories do. And I'd rather not revisit those memories right now. I'll tell you the story one day, but for now, rest. You're barely running on reserves, and we have plenty to do in the next few days to prepare for your reunion with your brother."

"I will, but you promised me we'd talk about your newly acquired wings." I smiled, a slight chuckle sounding from his chest as he rolled onto his back. I pulled myself from where I was on the bed to lay on his chest, "I didn't think that was something dragon Fae could do."

His hand moved to my back as he gently ran his fingers over the skin in comforting movements, his eyes locked onto the ceiling. "I didn't either. Another lapse in knowledge that isn't written in any history book; otherwise, I'm sure Dityss would have told me about it. Though I can't say I dislike it—it is rather freeing to be able to fly without needing to shift."

I nodded on his chest, my fingers absentmindedly running across the angles of his abdomen as I fought the sleep that tugged at the back of my mind. "If you didn't know, then how did you summon them in the first place?"

Ren hummed in thought as his other hand moved from behind his head to hold mine, "When you called out to me to tell me Vriwood was in danger, I knew I had to get there quickly. But there was..." He hesitated before continuing, "...*something* that told me you were in more danger, but I didn't know where you were. Shifting would get me there quickly, but something told me that the time it would take me to shift and get going, I would not make it in time. I tried to think of anything that would change such an outcome when my lightning crawled across my skin like a silent request. When I closed my eyes and focused on it, the wings appeared."

His hand on my back stopped, instead pulling me closer to him. "It sounds like the gods—Kanos, perhaps—blessed you with something rare and unheard of to aid you in your quest." I thought aloud, though a rumble of laughter pulled me from my theories and back to his upturned face.

"If that's true, then it makes us two of a 'rare and unheard of' kind." His smile was genuine as he looked down at me, his eyes softening as mine lulled behind heavy eyelids. "We can compare our gifts later on. Get some rest, darling."

I nodded with a perfectly timed yawn, curling farther into his chest.

The new wound on my shoulder was a dull throb as I laid on it, a gentle reminder that something far more profound than love had been cemented, even if I was scared to acknowledge it. My stomach threatened to drop at the truth, at the reminder of cruel Sellias's omen or the Ethe's prophecy, but Ren's comforting voice pulled me from the edge of a destructive spiral.

"I'm here, Willow."

"And I'm here, Ren. I'm not going anywhere."

CHAPTER 30

We had moved from the little house outside Vriwood a little over four days ago to the long stretch of tents that held this section of the Imperial Army, nearly ten thousand strong from what Ren had explained whenever I trotted along the lines of fabric tents. He would always walk next to me—a hand never far from the mark he left behind—even when I was shifted.

We still had not heard from Jae since he took off after the attack on my command, but Ren and Rygur constantly assured me that he was fine every time I asked and that I should focus on the training lessons that the two of them traded off between each other during the day. Ren had only reluctantly agreed to my plan to enter the Untamed Wilds with my 'present' for my brother if I spent every waking minute between now and then training my body for the encounter should things go south. Every night, I would sleep in the general's tent, where I would receive extra endurance 'lessons' and relaxing massages that lasted well into the night.

I barely pulled up my sword in time to stop the blade that was swinging towards my neck.

"Distracted this morning, Wildie?" Ren teased as he pulled his sword back to prowl around the arena's edge. No flowers marked the boundaries of this one, only the deep lines dug in the dirt from months of training by other soldiers.

"Not at all," I smiled, clearing my head as I ran forward, pulling shadows from a nearby patch of trees to swipe from the left toward Ren's legs. He quickly dodged the attack but fell directly into my next one, where the tip of my sword barely grazed his exposed side. "I have to play my opponent into false confidence, don't I?"

A laugh rumbled from deep in his chest—a sound that always made me want to kiss him and never let go—before putting his sword down to grip my hand with a soft shake. "Great work today."

"We're done already?" I grumbled, rolling my right shoulder a bit before I put my sword away to its place on my back. "We've only gone through a couple of the routines, and we haven't even touched aerial defense yet today." The wound where the wolf had bit into my shoulder had healed quickly without a scar thanks to one of the wolf-Fae medics in the camp, but the mark on my right itched as it took its time to heal naturally to scar.

"You've been doing well these last few days, and I feel pretty confident in your defense skills." Ren nodded, though his eyes betrayed a slight glint of anxiety I rarely saw from him. I bumped his hip with mine, giving him a smile that quietly portrayed that I saw through his bullshit.

"Rygur is busy today, then?"

"Yes," He smiled back, the worry in his eyes lessening as he bumped my hip back with so much force that I stumbled to the side with a giggle. "But what I said wasn't a lie either. You have grown significantly in your fighting abilities in just a few short days, and your control with your mysterious shadow magic is impressive."

"Compliments from a prince? I should be groveling at your feet." I snorted, walking back to his side as we began to weave back through the canvas tents and the soldiers running around. My humor dipped as I watched the stumbling chaos of soldiers around us as the general's tent became visible in the distance. "What's going on?"

Ren ran a hand through his hair, unfazed by the commotion. "There was a skirmish on the border in the middle of the night, which usually sets everyone on edge. But last night was...different." His sigh was heavy as he prepared himself to whisper, "They had placed some of our missing scouts and soldiers on spears in a kneeling position like they were begging. Most were intact, but several were...*not*."

I snuck my hand around his, squeezing it quietly while my heart squeezed as my imagination conjured up the scene in painful detail. "What are you going to do?"

"Soldiers are itching to fight, and I'm inclined to give it to them." He shrugged, interlacing his fingers through mine as we approached the camp's main tent. "Though I don't want to ruin the chances of your plan, so I'll hold off until Jae returns and we figure out our next steps. In the meantime, I have letters to write to the families of the soldiers we lost."

He pushed back the canvas flap to walk towards the desk in the middle of the canopied area while I sat on a leather chair opposite him, letting my eyes wander the mostly empty space that had become a sort of home.

The only furniture in the tent was the desk and a couple of leather chairs, but several rugs decorated the floor with weapons and armor placed on benches and weapon stands near each exit. On the northern wall, another doorway led into a similarly empty room where only a large cot and many blankets had been tossed in.

"I didn't realize you handwrote all of your notices to the families," I spoke as my attention returned to his quill gliding across a piece of paper. "Are they all made from a template?"

"I try to make them as unique as possible for every family, but they often have to follow a similar format since I can't get to know the soldiers as personally as I'd like to." He explained, finishing off the letter with a fancy signature. "But I still wish to honor them as my brothers and sisters and let their families know that while I can never repay the loss of a child, or a partner, or a parent, I will do everything in my power to ensure that their life was not given lightly."

I watched as he stamped the letter with the black wax seal I had seen during that game of cards with Theo, guilt twisting in my chest. "For someone who doesn't want to be a prince or a general, you excel at the positions."

"I like being able to be someone my people can look to in confidence and comfort, but I don't like the way I am expected to rule it by my predecessors."

"Then change it, Rendros," I murmured as I grabbed the following letter he finished, closing it with the wax seal. He stopped writing to listen, though he did not move his gaze from the next piece of paper as I placed the paper aside. "You have already been trying to stop this war between the untamed and tamed with as little bloodshed as possible, so why stop there? Use the crown to your advantage instead of dreading it."

"And what would that entail, Wildie?" Though I could not see his expression, the tension on his shoulders spoke volumes.

"Start with the end of this war against the Southern Rebellion how you are already going about it—with the intention of saving lives instead of taking them. Then, continue doing what you're doing: caring for your people. Seeing them *as* people instead of subjects is something you already do phenomenally. Make a stand against the stupid laws and scrolls that say you must marry and breed royalty and choose whom you want. Let your sisters make their own choices as well, letting them decide to run boutiques or travel the world in the pursuit of knowledge. Choose to distribute your wealth as you see fit rather than filling endless coffers."

His eyes slowly lifted to mine, storms of uncertainty apparent in the rings of hazel and blue. "You truly think it's possible?"

"You'll be King Rendros Roamion, the champion of his people." I smiled warmly, moving my hand forward to squeeze his while he gripped the quill tightly. "Make your name something you and your children will be proud of."

He nodded, resigning to silent thought as he wrote the rest of the letter he was working on, handing it to me for me to seal it. "And would you be beside me as the queen of those people?"

You are no hero, Willow Saugrave. You are a queen.

My heart pounded so loud I was sure he could hear it over the quiet ambiance of the room, but he said nothing as he left the unsealed parchment in my hand to start the following letter.

I was not a queen; I was an untamed mare whose strings had become intertwined with the crown princes by coincidence. I had never desired money or dresses. When I was a little girl, I would be dragged into princess games, and I frequently would pretend to be the valiant steed or one of the servants who helped the other princess get ready. I wanted to be anything *but* royalty, but here I was in the general prince's tent, being asked a question most girls dreamed of.

Despite every hesitance and memory, my heart knew the answer as I looked at the male seated across from me. If there were any crown I would stand beside and follow the children's stories for a royal happily ever after, it would be him. If not only to remind him of the people his choices affect but also to be there *with* him.

I opened my mouth to respond as I pressed the wax seal down on the letter when someone pushed through the tent's entrance, all inner conflicts gone as I spun around with a hand on my sword.

Jaeden was standing there with his arms crossed over his chest, his breath coming in big inhales from his rush. All the pressure that had sent my stress to a boiling point fell off my shoulders when I saw him standing there, unharmed. "I leave for a few days, and *that's* when you finally fucking grow the balls, Ren? If I had known that's all I needed to do, I would have left weeks ago." He snorted but flashed a grin my way. "I found your quarry, too. He tried to pull one over on me several times, but he did not realize who was on his tail."

"As annoying as you are, I'm glad to see you back in one piece, Jae." Ren smiled, walking over to the male and punching his shoulder before wrapping him in a firm hug. They clapped each other's backs with a warmth I only dreamed of having with siblings before Ren pulled back to ask, "Where did you put my present?"

"Your present?"

"The dumbass who decided it was smart to hurt my female."

The energy that rolled off Ren with the question was dark and filled with calm anger that I never wanted to be on the receiving end of, though it brought a different kind of heat to my core to know that it was because of me. I walked up to the reunion to give Jae a slight squeeze on his forearm, "Will you tie him to a post in the center of the training ring? I believe the soldiers would like to see the beginning of our new approach to the rebels."

Jae blinked a few times, his gaze bouncing between me and Ren. "Yeah, I saw that everyone was worked up. What did those bastards do while I was gone?"

"I'll explain along the way." Ren nodded, leading him out as I stayed behind in the tent a moment longer. I moved to his side of the desk, looking at the letters he had organized neatly into a pile that was left unsealed before sitting in his chair to finish sealing each, adding a small dandelion under the seal from the bag I kept on my hip. It was comforting and essential work to do, something a *queen* would do, and for once, I liked the ring of it.

As I continued through the stacked pile, there was a rustle of canvas from behind the desk, and my shadows went still as they encountered the unfamiliar source that had entered the space. I left my sword on my back as I reached for the letter knife that was propped on a stack of unopened letters to continue the illusion that I had no idea someone had entered the tent before I quickly turned around with the knife at the ready, my gaze scanning for the origin of the shuffling sound.

No one was in the main chamber, but I could hear glasses clinking from the space where Ren and I slept.

I stood quietly to creep over to the opening, using my shadows to help deafen the sound of my steps and my presence as I barely pushed back the fabric separating the rooms for a better view.

There was a figure huddled over the drinking glasses and pitcher that Ren and I always had filled with water, sprinkling some leaves and clear dust into the liquid, their fingers shaking as they made sure the substance was spread.

Something dark and deadly chilled every inch of my body as realization took hold.

I shot shadows towards it faster than ever before, shaping the black tendrils into fingers as they wrapped around their throat and squeezed. Their panic was quick as their hands clawed at the incorporeal force that pulled every breath out of their throat painfully, coughing and gurgling at the suddenness of the attack.

"What are you doing in the prince's private quarters?" My voice was terrifyingly steady as I approached, running the letter blade's flat side against my arm to clean off the blade before kneeling at her side, watching the tainted water return to the transparent color of fresh spring water.

The woman went entirely still, my attention finally turning back to look at her face. My breath stopped as I recognized the terror in her eyes —the woman who had slit Tisa's throat and ran before the shadow demon could kill her.

"*You.*" I snarled, slamming her to the ground with such a heavy force that I heard something *snap* in her arm, my shadows retreating as a blood-curdling scream ripped from her throat. "What did you put in there?"

She started crying as she tried to reposition herself away from me, but I brought myself closer with the knife gripped tightly in my hand, catching a glimmer of silver as she moved her uninjured arm.

The knife stopped at my throat as I sat back to catch it with my free hand, her eyes widening in surprise as I let the knife cross my throat, barely drawing blood. "I'm not afraid of a coward who hides behind others and *poison*. Do not make me repeat myself." Flames and shadows swirled from my hand that held her wrist, both writhing around the limb as she screamed again, dropping the silver dagger to her chest.

I could hear armor clanging as people rushed around the tent, following the source of the screams.

"Knade and hanging vine leaves! Please, *please* don't kill me!" My eyes narrowed as my magic dissipated from the burnt and suffocated skin as she confessed. "Knade is used to make you unbearably thirsty and fuzzy the mind into anger, and hanging vine—"

"I know damn well what that does," I growled, pressing my blade to her throat. "You killed a young girl, and you ran, and you participated in what could have been a massacre of innocents. Such things might have granted you a longer life for interrogation."

There was a rush of soldiers clamoring through the tent before stopping in the doorway, and I could hear Ren yelling orders as he rushed closer to the tent.

Her eyes widened as she recognized his voice and saw the soldiers standing at the entrance with their weapons ready, but my knife was too close to her throat for her to speak without slitting her own throat.

"However, you've decided to take a step further to try to kill someone I care about." I leaned closer to her ear as I put more weight on the knife, blood beginning to trickle from the wound, whispering only to her, "Actually, you tried to kill my *mate,* and that makes your life instantly forfeit." My voice felt like it was someone else's, but the freezing anger that chilled my blood fueled my next move. "May Vomuna send you to the torturous depths of her realms, *bitch*."

Armor shuffled once more as Ren pushed forward to the front of the crowd, though he was too late to stop the blade tearing messily through her throat while I shoved fire and shadow down the opening, her blood beginning to boil and pour out of the wound when I stood. The satisfaction of her death sent the flames leaping to a nearby blanket, quickly eating the flammable fabric.

I used the poisoned water to douse them before they grew out of control.

I flicked the blood off the blade as best as I could, though I was unable to clean the blood that had freshly stained the wrists of my shirt. I took a deep breath before I greeted the spectators, my anger finally simmering to a low rumble in the back of my mind as I handed him the letter opener. "Sorry, it was the closest thing I could find that wasn't a sword."

His eyes flicked over the small cut on my throat before meeting my eyes with a steeled quiet. "What did she do?"

"Attempted to poison our drinks with herbs that would make us go insane and try to kill each other while our bodies deteriorated. She won't be making such a foolish mistake again." My voice was uncharacteristically monotone, my hands shaking as I ran them down my thighs. "She was also the third person who orchestrated the attack on Vriwood."

His eyes slowly moved over to the corpse, staring at where her throat used to be, now replaced by a mixture of charred skin and dark black marks that stretched to her face. His arm reached out for me as I stepped into his chest, pulling me closer to him instinctively. "Clean up the room and throw away those glasses." He ordered the closest soldier. "Leave her on the border once you're done."

He led me out of the room into the sunlight, his hand protectively holding my shoulder as we walked to the arena. "I'm going to need extra time with this *example*, as you called it. His friend's visit has renewed my desire for information."

"Take your time, prince," I responded, looking past the lines of soldiers as they parted for us to pass, my attention squarely focused on the post. "I might have failed to pry anything from her, but luckily, you have more control." I glanced up at him as my blood began to settle, his hazel eyes meeting mine with bloodlust and promise.

"Not where you are involved, darling."

Soldiers had lined up around every inch of the training space, spitting curses and murmuring amongst themselves as Ren and I approached. Jae and Rygur were standing near the post erected in the dirt, and Rygur was cleaning blood from his hands.

Tied with his hands behind the post and his legs broken on the ground beneath him, the older Fae was still staring defiantly at Rygur. "You won't get nothing from me, whelp." His face was covered in bruises and scratches, and the lack of clothing on his body revealed countless other fresh wounds that likely came from the pair while Ren rushed back to the tent. The paleness of his skin only highlighted the bright color of blood and bruises that dotted his form.

"Then it's a good thing that's not my job. I just wanted to get a few hits in before you died." Rygur snorted, spitting on him before turning his gaze to Ren.

The old wolf followed his gaze and looked up at me with a flicker of recognition in the yellow eye that had not been sliced through. "Willow

Saugrave, Theodore's precious little sister." The words were laced with venom and disgust, "I knew you were useless."

"I'm afraid I can't replicate the same familiarity," I responded, moving my hands to ensure my ponytail was still secure to try to keep the recently calmed anger at bay as it rolled through my chest. "Who are you?"

Anger flashed in him as he pulled against the restraints, a deep laughter rumbling over the space. "You have grown some balls since you've left, I see. Though fucking a prince might have helped with that, hmm?"

Jae snarled as Rygur and Ren both tensed, the distant sound of lightning striking in the distance.

"Getting away from murderous butchers and liars might have helped me realize a few things, too." I shrugged, "Name and rank."

"Fourth General Malakai Burton, loyal to the Southern Rebellion and my superiors alone." He smiled, his canines glistening with fresh blood. "What changed your mission, Saugrave? You left us ready to die alongside the prince when you shoved a blade down his throat, but did that puny brand make you afraid? Or was the dicking so good—"

Ren's fist slammed so hard into the man's windpipe that it caused blood to splatter across the dirt as Malakai coughed violently in response, barely able to take in another wheeze of breath.

I had not even realized that Ren had left my side when he stood with blood trickling from the sharp scales that protruded from his fist, a dark warning encompassing the ring that made the entire crowd go silent.

This version of Ren was the general that I had once been horrified of.

He wore a black overcoat adorned with metals and a show of rank on the sleeves, the emblem of the crown emblazoned on each shoulder, with golden cufflinks that kept the shirt perfectly fitted to the length of his arms and the muscles even when fully extended. His dark pants were slightly dirty from our small training session this morning, but even the dirt barely stood out from the dark material.

As he turned around, I could see the grey contrast of his undershirt against the black. He adjusted its collar by pulling on its edges, not bothering to clean off the blood from his hand as it soaked into the fabric and stained it.

"Speak about her like that again, and you'll lose more than just your breath." His voice had dropped into that king-command octave, and I should not have been as attracted as I was.

"Well, I'll be damned, she's got you *whipped,* boy."

Jae walked around the post and cut the ropes that held Malakai's wrists. His ordinarily warm honey gold had iced into a cutting metallic color as he watched the wolf rub his wrists irritably. A small smile curved on the wolf's lips as he parted them to say something, but Jae moved faster than his words.

A hand fell into the dirt, still curled into a fist from where he was stretching it, dust curling around it.

Malakai's agonized scream bellowed throughout the entire camp, but no one in the crowd winced or gasped.

"You do not speak of my general or his female that way." Jae's voice cut through the silence, anger rolling through his voice that I had not yet heard from the usually relaxed wolf Fae.

"Don't test me or my men, Mr. Burton." Ren's voice was still calm as he crouched in front of the older Fae, who was grasping the stub where his hand was. Ice began to cover the wound to slow the bleeding, "How did you wrangle the Vethen?"

Despite the pain he was undoubtedly in, Malakai chuckled in between seething breaths of air. "You're going to kill me, so why should I share any information with you? Unfortunately, it's a lose-lose situation for me, and I'd rather die to maintain my loyalty."

"That would be my preferred choice as well. We can keep you alive longer and have some fun without listening to you try to plead." Ren grinned, showing off his canines as he turned to the crowd with his arms out like he was entertaining a show. "Early this morning, we lost a group of fine males and females to the butchers of the south. Many of you have been asking for a large-scale invasion to put their murderous hearts to rest for what they have done, and I don't blame you."

Malakai's eyes froze in fear as he realized what was happening, and a wave of agreement swam over the crowd.

"You all know me well enough by now that I would not let such heinous acts against my people go unanswered, and I promise you that the rebellion will pay." His gaze slid over to me, and I could see the steel resolve in his eyes. "It started with the death of the woman who had conducted the attack on Vriwood with him this morning. It continues now with the death of this bastard, and it ends with the death of *all* their generals."

There were shouts and cheers from the soldiers, though a few still murmured with mixed feelings of insecurity.

"Let us remind Fourth General Malakai Burton what it means to fuck with our kingdom, shall we?" He returned to the collapsed man on the ground, calling Jaeden over. "Heal his legs. I'd like to have a little fun with him before he enters the hands of Vomuna."

Jaeden smiled as he leaned over the wolf, holding his hands out toward the festering wounds. A soft white light began to emanate from them as the lines of power swirled and sunk into the injured flesh of the older Fae. From a close distance, I could hear his bones cracking and reforming, the sounds grinding against my ears in a sound I wished I would never hear again, no matter how much he deserved it.

The healing process took a minute at most—and Malakai was too busy writhing in pain and anger to stand immediately—so Ren grabbed him by the beard to stand him up, pushing him against the pole. Once he found his footing again and was stretching the wounds that had been inflicted, I could hear thunder tumbling in from the distance as lightning sparked from Ren's hands.

"Run like the *coward* you are."

Malakai's yellow eye showed little hesitation as he shifted and ran in the opposite direction of the training ring, Ren sauntering after him with little worry in his gaze as he turned to meet mine. His finger curled in a soft command to approach as the soldiers around us began to shift in flashes of magic.

"Will you hold onto this for me? It will take the poor laundress ages to get the blood out of the sleeve, and I don't want to burden her with more work." He smiled as he shrugged the overcoat off his shoulders to place it in my arms, kissing my forehead. "I'll be back within the hour to discuss how things will go tomorrow."

"Ren?"

"Yes Wildie?"

"Make him suffer, won't you?"

"I intend to do nothing less, darling."

I smiled as I pulled his collar down toward me for a better kiss, having to stand on the tips of my toes to reach him comfortably. "Then have fun hunting."

His grin was nothing less than wicked as he took off into a run in the direction of Malakai. He was shifted in a blast of thunder and storms, extending his star-speckled wings with a giant leap into the air and a triumphant roar. The shifted soldiers ran after him in a chorus of roars, howls, and whinnies that echoed his call in an impressive show of unity as ravaged beasts ran after a single target.

As they got farther and farther away, Ren suddenly rocketed high into the sky until he was hovering in front of the sun, his wings spreading out so wide that his shadow blocked out the sun and covered the army of Fae running after him. They all slowed to a trot beneath him as I watched their heads turn up while small dragon Fae flew closer toward him, all calling up in feral song.

His claws let go of something he had been holding, and the shape of a wolf fell from thousands of feet in the air.

Only to disappear into the waiting crowd.

Ren dived into the center of the mass, his large form easily overshadowing the chaos, though he was not pushing anyone away from the feast as the sun fell on the group of beasts.

I could not help the smile that pulled on my lips when I realized that the prince and his soldiers would never be part of the tamed.

CHAPTER 31

As soon as I entered the back space of the central tent, I fell into the pile of blankets, groaning dramatically as I rolled in the warmth of the small space.

Once the boys returned from their hunt, we spent the rest of the evening plotting out every detail of the plan for the next day, from the order of attack to the color of my hair. I was swapping from the assassin of the rebellion to an assassin for the crown, making everything feel so backward.

I continued to grumble as I got out of the stiff battle-ready clothes of the day and wrapped myself in the jacket Ren had given me to hold before he took care of Malakai Burton.

Took care of was the kind way to put it—the carnage that happened to his corpse was likely being eaten by the carrion and wildlife across the entire valley.

I took my hair out of my ponytail before running my hands in a cold-water basin to wash my face from the anger that threatened to resurface when I heard Ren enter the room.

"Can you hold off on making those kinds of noises while I'm working? They are outright maddening when I can't come in here to—" I turned to look at his smug smile when his eyes cut to my bare body, only partially covered by his military overcoat, and the playful smile disappeared. "You are playing a dangerous game wearing that, Saugrave."

"Mm, I thought I might be." I smiled, combing my hair with my fingers as I turned back to the water. "Jae and Rygur haven't left yet, so it's a game you can't win now."

His low growl was full of frustration and desire, but I ignored him by pouring water over my face and hair.

"It will be won shortly." He promised as he left. Though my desire was through the roof from the events of earlier that day and my confession to myself and the woman, my brain was still too focused on the battle that awaited me the next day.

I finished the small cleaning before moving to a corner of pillows I had put together in a much nicer and more comfortable fashion than the cot. On a flipped-over bucket that I had made into a bedside table, I conjured a small ball of firelight before grabbing the book that Dityss had packed me when we left a week ago. It was some old history book that described a forbidden love destined for ascension, but it was enough for me to stay interested in it when I had the rare moment to myself.

I had gotten to a part about the main character's beautiful marriage ceremony under the moon when Ren came back into the room an hour or so later, looking as tired as I felt. Whatever simmering tension between us had taken a backburner as he pulled off his shirt and shimmied off his pants, collapsing on his stomach next to me with an arm draped lazily over my waist.

"You couldn't figure out a good way to send any of you with me, I take it?" I sighed, closing the book and holding the page with a finger while I brought my other hand to rub his hair. It had become one of my favorite things to do because it was always so soft and just long enough that I could run my hands through it.

"No, we couldn't. All of us are too recognizable, and the plan you suggested *is* the best way to handle it." He turned his head to the side so he could look at me. "I really don't like that it has to be you alone, though." His eyes shone with quiet vulnerability, and I leaned over to kiss his forehead while I pushed his hair out of the way.

"I'm here now, Ren."

"But what if you're not this time tomorrow?" The worry in his voice was so intense that it caught me off guard. "If something happens—"

"*Nothing* will happen. I won't die tomorrow, and worrying about it helps no one." I grumbled, pulling his hair lightly to get him to look me in the eyes. "If something goes wrong, I've already promised you that I'd hightail it back to you with a failure than die for a success."

I did not mention that I refused to let myself die for the sake that would mean the end of him as well.

"Come here, Wildie." He smiled as he shifted to his back. I placed a hairband in place of my finger in the book before snuggling farther into the blankets and his chest. He traced gentle circles on my back as I listened to his heartbeat, a potent reminder that everything that happened was real and that *he* was real.

That he was here.

We sat comfortably in each other's company, listening to our breathing until I heard the faintest uptick in his heart rate. I turned my head upward on his chest to see what was going on. He watched me with quiet interest, but something conflicting was going on behind his hazel eyes. "What's wrong?"

He shook his head, giving a soft smile as he closed his eyes. "You are just the most beautiful thing I have ever seen, and I'm *so* damn lucky." His hand lazily played with my hair while he opened his eyes again, "I could have never even dreamed of someone like you, and yet here you are, in my arms, and mine."

There it was again, the conflict sparking behind the softness of his gaze. "You're not telling me something." I raised my head from his chest to lean on my arm, looking at him while my own heart started to race in panic. Was something wrong? Did he drink or touch some of that poisoned water earlier? Did Malakai do something—

"Easy, Wildie. Nothing's wrong; I just...don't know how to say it. Afraid to, I guess, is the better reasoning."

"That's not helping me settle, Rendros," I growled, though he only laughed softly as he sat forward. "You better tell me now, or I'm going to walk straight out of that tent and leave early for the mission—"

"I want to know the answer to the question I asked you earlier before I say anything," he said, his eyes rebuilding the steely gaze he had not given me for over a month. "If I were to be king tomorrow, would you stand beside me as my queen?"

I stopped fidgeting as my rapidly increasing heart rate stopped entirely as I looked at him. Though he had rebuilt a fraction of a steel wall around himself, I could see that he was the most vulnerable than he had likely been with anyone.

I could feel his terror spiking at the prolonged silence as his heart slowed, but I gave a gentle nod. "I can't say I'll be as proper as the ladies you've been introduced to, and I will fight you on things if I believe they are wrong, but...yes. I would, just so long as I get to stay beside you—"

He pulled me into such a tight hug that my sentence ended with a slight yelp that quickly turned into a giggle as he traced tiny kisses up and down my neck. "Then, you can finally make that little girl's dream come true and call yourself a princess. Unofficially by paper, but as true as the moon will rise tomorrow." He laughed, stopping his kisses as he reached my ears. "Everything stopped since I first saw you that day in the throne room. I didn't want you in the dungeon because I thought you were a threat to the kingdom—I wanted you there so that the bars may stop the storm that was rising in my soul. So that way, I knew, even in those conditions, that you could never leave me." He pressed his lips in a gentle kiss over the tip of my ear, "Then the pact was suggested, and I was both terrified and elated that you would be forever bound to me."

His hand idly swirled over the mark on my back, goosebumps rising in its wake. Something deep in my core burned as he pulled away to stare at the scarred flesh from his canines a few nights ago.

"Claim me with a mark to make me yours, Wildie, as I already claimed you."

A tear ran down my cheek as his hand quickly raised to wipe it away, concern now in the forefront of his gaze. "You knew?" My voice tremored in emotion, another tear joining the first. "I can't; there's no guarantee that your parents will allow it, that they'll force you away—" My thoughts began to tumble out of control as my imagination grappled with the worst ones, bringing them to the front until both of his hands were holding the side of my head instead of wiping away the torrent of tears that fell down my cheeks.

"I'm here, Willow. I will *always* be here." He whispered, pulling my head forward to kiss my forehead. "I have been here since that first night you stayed at the castle, and I have known it since the first moment I saw you. I didn't realize you had learned the bond either..." His voice trailed off, a soft frown settling on his face. "You knew that was what the Ethe was talking about, didn't you? Yet you still said those painful things about checking to see if it was one of those assholes from Ivimea?"

"I didn't say it to hurt you. I wasn't sure—afraid to admit even to myself that it could be you. I could set you free and save you from having to reject the mate bond and being miserable for the rest of your life." I whispered, bringing my hand up to his face. "I was afraid of the rejection or hurting you more if your parents forced you to marry someone else."

"I would rather leave that crown and everything behind than marry anyone other than you, Wildie. I'd choose you over the wildest riches or the greatest power, and I would choose you over my very life. I have dreamed of you since the day we met, but our nightmares—both waking and sleeping—kept us apart. I will never let that happen again, for the blood that runs through my veins and the heart that beats in my chest is yours as long as we live." His voice shook for the slightest moment as he took in a deep breath to ask, "Do you accept me as your mate, Crown Princess Willow Roamion?"

I felt like I had been transported to the highest heavens as I brought my fingers into his hair, repositioning to straddle his lap as I kissed him with all the force I could muster. The pointed canines I had spent years sharpening grazed over his bottom lip as I pulled back to look at him, a different emotion lining my eyes as I met his tantalizingly perfect hazel. "I accept you as my mate and my everything, Rendros Roamion. I am here."

"I am here." He repeated our prayer, our hope, our mantra. "Claim me, Wildie."

My whole body heated with suspense as I pressed my hips to his to feel the rugged ridge of his lust up against mine. He echoed it, not daring to take his eyes off me as I reached down to align him to my entrance, squeezing my fingers against his shaft until I replaced it with my slick core.

The entire world had gone silent for this moment as if it had been waiting with bated breath, the light of the moon the only thing barely present alongside our shadows in the pillows. Our breathing and voices were the only interruptions to the silent evening, and nothing could stop the wild buck of my senses now.

I was bouncing up and down as I pushed myself down to the hilt of his length, every nerve and every pore of my body wide awake with arousal and acceptance. Let me have him like he had me, to claim what was mine.

His hands were gripped hard onto my waist as he lifted me up and down with every movement, the apex of the moment growing with every pulse of our hearts that shot through the point of connection between us. There would be no holding it back as it grew farther and farther up my spine, the mark on my back and in my soul burning with anticipation.

With one last slam of my hips on his, every nerve in my body lit on fire, our names on each other's lips as we both reached our combined climax. My teeth pierced the skin on his right shoulder as his blood washed over my tongue, the taste like nothing I had ever had before. It was sweet yet savory, metallic yet smooth, as everything about the claiming felt like I had another brand burnt into my flesh, though it did not hurt.

His head pressed into my neck as he groaned, claws piercing my hips and teeth scraping his mark on me as his release gripped him even harder than mine had.

I barely recognized the space around us as I pulled away from the fresh bite on his shoulder to watch the blood rush to meet the open air. Something primal and possessive had me grinning at the mark as Ren did the same, his hand moving to rub the claiming mark on my shoulder.

We both leaned forward to press our foreheads together, smiling with panted breaths.

"I'm here." Our voices joined in unison, and the world completely faded away.

Everything was so, so dark.

Ren sat bloodied behind a wall, barely holding his arm as he floated in and out of consciousness.

"Brother, you must stay awake. Stay awake, damn it!" Rygur's voice cut through the dark, and somewhere, Jaeden was digging through the rubble. "If you die, she dies, Rendros! You have to stay alive!" His cries were getting more desperate, but Ren opened his eyes slowly with a pained groan.

"Where is she?"

"Somewhere up there fighting your mother, giving us time to escape," Rygur said, looking back at the rubble that blocked the exit. "When did the queen have this much time?" He cursed under his breath, and Ren stood, albeit wobbly.

"I don't know. But we can't stop it, not now." He growled, moving over to the rubble. "I have to go get her before it's too late."

"If you shift, you may be unable to shift back until your wounds are healed. Jae can only do so much; he's already depleted most of his stores." Rygur argued, standing beside the two males digging through the destroyed stone.

"Then I will head somewhere they can heal me faster and heal her too." He seemed to stumble as something invisible slammed into his chest, "The Cordillera."

Jae spoke next, his voice raised in alarm. "There is no guarantee that they will take you in, Ren. Yes, they are one of the closer regions to the crown, but if they learn of what your mother has done—"

"Then I will make it known that I am not aligned with her, and neither is she. Nor either of you."

"How do you intend to do that?"

There was silence except for the falling of rubble, where a stone finally began to show the beginnings of orange light seeping through the cracks.

"A new war has started, and alliances need to be drawn. I'll convince them that I intend to bring forward a crown that resembles the times of Akis rather than the abomination my bloodline has brought it to." His eyes locked on Jaeden, "Starting with the Sinos Cordillera."

Rygur stepped forward, putting a hand on Ren's shoulder.

Jaeden followed and did the same.

"You are our King and our general, Ren. Lead us against the corrupted, and we will fight until our last breath for a better kingdom."

I shot out of bed, my voice hoarse as if I had been screaming for hours, but the tired confusion and panic on Ren's face as he shot up beside me made it apparent that I had been silent.

"What's wrong? Are you hurt?" He whispered, quickly blinking the sleep out of his eyes to look me over and check for anything that caused me to wake so violently. When he found nothing, he pulled my hair out of my face and looked into my eyes. "A nightmare?"

"I—" My voice was so rough that I coughed and could barely breathe, bringing a hand up to my throat. "A terrible one. You were on the brink of death and *trapped*, and I wasn't there, and—" My breathing turned rapidly panicked, my hands gripping the blankets as I tried to bring myself back into reality. His arms wrapped around me and pulled me into his chest, running a hand over my head.

"I'm here, Wildie. I'm safe, and I'm fine." He whispered, the comforting movement barely able to slow the rushed breaths that escaped my chest. "What else was there?"

"Rygur and Jae were trapped with you, and I was...I think I was fighting your mother, and you wanted us to go to the Cordillera once you saved me from her." I murmured, my panic doubling as I grabbed at his arm. "You were so hurt that you needed their healing because Jae couldn't do it, but he wasn't sure that they would let you in after what she had done," I whispered, afraid that if I spoke too loudly, the nightmare would come true.

"Why would you be fighting my mother?" He asked, meeting my eyes curiously, though he had some guard up at the idea. "She's not very strong nor particularly interested in fighting herself."

"I...don't know," I answered, even as my imagination brought back that trail of endless shadow behind her from the day we had left. "Maybe my nightmare just remembered how intimidated I was of her and made her the enemy or something."

The shadows my imagination showed me that day terrified me, but I had not felt any presence beyond the one that had broken free—the Ethe, as I had understood it. If it spoke true and only one person could control the shadows, and that special blessing was given to me, then there was no way she could have been the enemy I was terrified of.

Right?

"I think it's nerves leading up to..." Ren squinted as he looked up at the tent's peak, where the light was beginning to pour in through the canvas. "Shit."

"At least we woke up on time." I sighed but was still so afraid that I could not move from his chest. "Can we stay here for a minute before we go? I don't want to see Ry and Jae while coming out of a nightmare."

"Of course, darling. You could change your mind too if you want to postpone, and we will spend more time figuring something out."

"I'm afraid not. It's step one in our grand scheme to make you the champion of the people and the best chance we've got." I tried to smile, but it came out as more of a barely lifted grimace.

A comfortable silence fell between us as I returned to reality, trying to prepare myself for the coming meeting with Theo instead of the nightmare my imagination had conjured up.

After a few minutes, the nightmare moved to the shadows of my mind as if trying to keep me from forgetting it.

As if my subconscious was trying to warn me.

CHAPTER 32

Muscle memory was all that I relied on as I wandered back within the forests of my birthland, maneuvering through old pathways that Theo and I had run along once long ago as children.

From what Rygur's intelligence could gather, the generals were supposed to meet somewhere near the old wolf camp they had cleared about a month ago—the one I had given information about. They wanted to discuss what had happened at Vriwood and get the story from Malakai but had been waiting to meet up until they deigned it safe to gather so close to the border.

I was not far from the rendezvous point now, but the sun was still too low in the sky for me to start my approach. The meeting was scheduled for midday when the sun was the highest in the sky, giving me about thirty minutes to hype myself up for the inevitable shit show.

I closed my eyes to take a deep breath as I leaned against the trunk of a nearby tree, running my fingers over the rough bark to ignore the bag that contained my delivery to the Southern Rebellion.

I only had to deliver the letter and the package, say whatever I wanted to Theo and the general, and give one last chance for a talk of peace. I would try to convince my brother that this entire war was pointless and that the prince was not the same underling of the crown as his parents. If anyone could persuade Theo to reconsider his actions and his view of the war, it was me.

I hoped.

I ran my fingers through the braid my hair was woven into, looking over the fields in a scan for any threat or early arrivals, but no one was there yet. Only the remnants and ghosts of a camp that had once stood in the field marked only with charred canvas and wood. Despite it being over a month since the attack, the smell of smoke and fire tainted the air alongside what I assumed was the lingering stench of burnt flesh. A glimmer of color in the center of the ash and charcoal attracted my attention: a patch of dandelions.

They seemed to be a relatively new growth as they weaved around the destruction, standing above the dark with a small pop of light. Maybe the optimist in me saw them as a sign of hope, of being able to grow in the most damaged conditions, but my heart swelled with a distant dream that this meeting would go well.

Footsteps sounded from somewhere to the east of the field, revealing a pride of lionesses following a Fae woman into the camp's remains, the sounds of their growls echoing through the field and into the trees.

Second General Esme Dixon was just as the reports described her—a strong woman that exuded the meaning of 'take no bullshit.' Her tan skin was taught against well-toned muscles as she crossed her arms over her tank top while tapping her foot impatiently. Her blonde hair was undercut with the symbol of a sun burned into the thinnest spot, and her emerald green eyes were bright with apprehension as she surveyed the area. A single command sent the lionesses sweeping the camp for any unwanted guests, and I pulled the shadows of the trees over me like a blanket to help obscure my view and scent.

"Lady Dixon, early as usual. How do things fare on the southern line?" A heavily Ivimean-accented male voice was carried across the wind, its owner cresting the other side of the hell from atop a white unicorn. Where Esme was a beacon of pure strength, Fifth General Jean-Luc Barthet epitomized wealth and financial power. He was wearing a luxurious white tuxedo that was professionally ironed and cleaned, with his silver hair meticulously groomed to the side. A gloved hand ran over his curled mustache while he watched the lionesses scope the grounds with a raised brow, "You believe something is amiss?"

"Quiet since the last breach from the tamed a month ago, though that's what has me on edge. It isn't often the opposing forces wait so long between probes." Esme responded, watching as one of the lionesses stalked the tree line I was cloaked in, "I don't like that Malakai hasn't returned news sooner. Not even a messenger to let us know if this meeting is even necessary."

"Sir Burton has always been...*inadequate* at relaying information between us," Jean-Luc mused, dismounting his steed in a single fluid motion to stand near the lioness matriarch. "We should recommend a new Alpha appointed once we get the results of Vriwood's experiment from Malakai."

The sun-gold lioness sniffing the trees around me stopped directly in front of my shield of shadows, sniffing the area curiously. I held my breath while she took a step closer, her mouth opening slightly to try and pick up the odd scent that existed just beyond the shadowed barrier.

I began to inch my hand to the sword strapped to my back, slowly wrapping my fingers around the grip in preparation to attack when her head whipped back towards her general.

A large group was coming from the west of the camp, comprised of at least thirty different shifters and Fae. The lioness instantly left in a soft lope and returned to her general alongside the others who had found the space sufficiently safe for the meeting.

Esme and Jean-Luc bowed as three group members approached the two generals, standing on opposite sides of the bright dandelions surrounded by ash.

I looked at the male and female, flanking the first general's side. Before the debrief of the mission, I had heard of the third and sixth generals thanks to their proximity to the Hayes house. The male to the left was Third General Julian Carvallo, a ferocious dragon that was the fastest in all of the Southern Rebellion and, despite the lower rank, was very rarely far from Theo. He was used for relaying messages to other generals and being a message carrier during the heat of battle that could alert an ally of an attack mere seconds before it happened.

Julian's tan complexion was beautifully contrasted by the light grey of his dress shirt and pants, and the pop of red in his pocket square elevated the unnatural red of his eyes as he darted his gaze across the second and fifth.

The female was the final piece of the Southern Rebellion hierarchy. She was dressed in a simple peasant's dress, with her dark brown hair loosely falling behind her. Sixth General Greta Olofsson was the silver tongue of the group, able to talk most anyone into joining their cause. Despite what most would consider rags as her outfit choice, no one dared call her anything less than the ruler of the humans she was.

"Malakai is dead."

I knew it was going to be difficult to hear his voice, but nothing quite prepared me for the ache that shot through me like I had lost a part of myself.

Theo's voice had not changed while I was gone, but his appearance had. He had grown out his hair even more, and it was tied loosely into a half bun-half down style that seemed to be brushed and groomed into a general's stance. His green eyes were dull, holding no emotion as he surveyed the responses of his lower generals, a hand raised to absentmindedly scratch at the short beard that was now on his face. He was Theo, but he was different. Any color or smile that had once danced across his features was gone entirely, and the cold statue of a ruthless general stood in its place.

He was what I had expected to see when I met Ren.

"Was he killed by the beast he was unleashing?" Jean-Luc questioned, though he seemed unperturbed by the announcement.

"No." A muscle ticked in Theo's jaw, "That was thanks to the Imperial Army that ripped him limb from limb after dropping him from several hundred feet in the sky."

Any coolness that the unicorn was trying to pass drained into quiet horror as silence crept through the grass on a phantom wind.

"By Athos' light." Esme cursed, "They've killed our people before, but never so brutally. Something's changed in the forces—have they learned of your upcoming business?"

"As far as I'm aware, they haven't. Which means that something, or *someone*, has." Theo growled, something dark burning away what was left of the brightness of his green eyes.

I could feel my heart in my throat, but my anger pushed it back down as Julian spoke. "You think your little sister has changed her allegiance?"

"Dick can change a great many minds, and I've heard several rumors about the crown prince." Esme snorted, rolling her eyes as she shifted the weight on her feet. "She doesn't seem the type to come to war, in any case. Relay information and help you here and there, but not one to encourage conflict."

"Hart raised her to be independent and avoid conflict where she could with a smile and a conversation. For her to be supporting such violence would be uncharacteristic of her." Theo sighed as he turned to Greta. "Since Malakai died, have any of your people in Vriwood reported back about the experiment?"

The human woman, standing maybe at five feet, nodded. "Its defeat only took about thirty minutes."

"What?" Jean-Luc gasped, his hand moving to his mouth. "Weapons and basic magics do not easily defeat the Vethen, and there's no way its weaknesses could have been found out by the forces so quickly—"

Greta lifted her hand, her light brown eyes lined with frustration as she turned to Theo. "Our reports were miscalculated. The general prince was there to combat it with his second and third, and the mare was there. She was the one who dealt the final blow through the gems."

"*Willow* was the end of the beast?" Theo cursed, running his hand through his hair. "Why the hell would she have even been in Vriwood? She wasn't supposed to be traveling with them, but beyond that...she's *prey*, for fucks sake. Why would she have fought?"

Any lingering hesitation about speaking to the lion I had once called brother evaporated with his exasperation. The man standing among people I had once considered strong forces fighting for a better world was nothing more than a stranger with familiar features.

Anger rolled through my body like its own storm as I stepped out of the shadows, holding my head high as I spun the letter in my hand to approach someone I no longer recognized.

"My dear brother, I'm hurt by your little faith in me." I mused as scores of growls and flashes of white and silver surrounded the five generals. Esme had reached for her sword while Jean-Luc seemed ready to run, but Greta and Julian stayed as still as stone.

Any color left in Theo's face drained as he watched me approach, though he took a step forward with astonishment plain on his face. "Lo, I —" He tried to pull some insincere smile of relief on his face as he moved for me, but I had learned in my months gone. My sword was pointed in front of me in seconds, stopping him from getting closer.

"Not another step, Theo," I growled, and it took every fiber of my being to keep myself from impaling him on my sword as cold anger pulsed through my veins. "Did you expect me to sit idle in some town while something attacked *innocents?*"

His hands were up as he smiled, stopping at the tip of my blade. "I figured you had leaned into instincts after what had happened in the throne room, once you became pacted to that monster—"

"You do not get to throw around a title that belongs to you, *brother.*" I spat out the last word like a curse and tossed the letter at his feet alongside the bag attached to my hip. "This is familiar, hm? Something I learned from you when you thought I was too busy picking flowers."

I did not let my sword leave his chest while he leaned down to the letter, breaking the seal to read its contents while Julian opened the bag.

"Gods—" The third general gagged, throwing the bag back to the ground. "It's Malakai's brand. Still burned into his wrist."

"One of the prince's letters of 'peace,'" Theo growled, throwing the letter into the circle of dandelions that I had not realized I had drifted toward. "So, the rumors are true. You've betrayed me and my mother for someone you've known only a few months. Do you not remember who bathed you, fed you, and took care of you after dear daddy died? Have you forgotten who *made* you?" His foot stomped into the mud and ash as he crushed the letter beneath his boot.

"I have not forgotten, but I seem to have lost that brother years ago. I was just too blind to realize what the rebellion was doing to you." I snarled in response, showing my teeth for the first time. Jean-Luc recoiled as he covered his mouth, the unicorn beside him shifting nervously at the sight of sharpened canines on one of their own. "I would have thought you would have emphasized my hesitance and fear to kill the prince once I had become a prisoner to his life, but no. It sounds like you would have rather me sacrifice myself to complete a mission."

"I would have!" He bristled, cutting his hand as he grabbed the end of my sword with a fist. "I would have gladly seen you dead if it meant that we would win this damn war! Hells, I would have done it *myself!*"

Any hard exterior of confidence I had shattered, but he pushed on as he watched my stance falter, even as blood ran down his palms.

"If I had to kill every town like Vriwood and sacrifice every citizen to bring freedom to the untamed and due karma to the tamed, I would do it. My resolve regarding my stance in this war is unbreakable, and I will not *falter.*" He growled, his overpowering frame towering over me as I stepped back. "I am a predator, and you are prey, Willow. You can sharpen your teeth and walk among them, but it does not change your nature."

As his hand reached for the handle of my blade, the world seemed to turn in slow motion. The stench of his blood was pulled to my nose as the wind shifted, and while I expected to recoil from the copper metallic scent, there was something dark and vile that changed its metallic scent that made me gag.

Flashes of long-standing nightmares of mothers holding children pounded against my skull, of corpses stretched beneath our very feet in a camp long since burned. Of children crying over their parents' corpses after a nightmare serpent drained them of everything they were.

Shadows coiled at my feet as anger pulsed through my veins with every beat of my heart. This man was no longer my brother—but the butcher who killed for the sake of power.

"You see prey as fearful puppets you can control," I snarled, reaching farther into the archive of magic and shadows that wreathed power around my core like I had not felt before, "But you forget the patience and the strength of prey willing to stand next to killers." Tendrils of shadow snuck along the ground, hiding beneath the ashes of senseless death. "The predator has become complacent in a world where the prey has learned to hunt."

The sound of bones snapping filled my ears, but this time, I did not recoil.

The sixth general and several of her soldiers fell in lifeless heaps on the ground while several more screamed in pain.

Theo snapped around, giving me the chance to pull my sword the rest of the way out of his grip, flicking his blood off the blade as I readied for the attack.

Lionesses charged my right, my attention quickly turning to meet them instead of my prime target. One leaped out of the way as I swung at their advance, while the other aimed for my back as I turned from them. A spear of shadow shot up from the ground, impaling them to their spot in the air before throwing it into the side of the one that dodged.

Both lionesses rolled away as I turned back to Theo, who had turned back to me with wild eyes full of anger. "You will regret this, you tamed *bitch*." He roared, but instead of charging towards me, he charged towards the group and what remained of his generals.

I could feel the surge of magic pulling my hair forward as he ran into the group, the familiar precursor to teleportation swirling ahead of me.

He was *running*.

"You *coward*!" I bellowed as I sprinted after him, but the scent of his conjuration magic was too strong. I pushed to reach him before he completed the pull, but they all disappeared when I finally reached one of the farther soldiers.

The wind stopped swirling as only the distant scent of the living generals of the Southern Rebellion remained in the fields of betrayal, leaving me alone with the corpses of those I had killed.

CHAPTER 33

The moon was already beginning its ascent in the sky when I returned to the border.

I had spent far too long burying corpses of enemies and marking their graves with wreaths of dandelions, but my job had been completed to the best of my ability. Theo did not give me or the letter a chance to change his mind, and instead, he left me with an empty heart and a mind plagued by nightmares I could no longer get to stop.

Ren had been trying to get my attention for the last hour or two through the bond, but I could not answer beyond a simple, 'I'm fine.' Our bond let him know all too well that it was not true, but I could not answer no matter how much he asked.

My feet carried me past the main road into the camp and towards a small lake used for clean water and bathing nearby.

The moonlight flickered off the water in soft dances of silver and starlight, causing the water to look like it was glowing in serenity. A mixture of pine and oak trees surrounded the lake that housed several critters settling into dens and homes for the night, and just beyond their shadows, I could see several deer migrating through the forest.

It was a place of silence and reflection, where the sounds of soldiers and war disappeared, and only nature flourished.

Or so I thought.

There was movement in the water as a familiar head of light brown hair shook off droplets from his face, honey-gold eyes catching me standing near the water's edge.

"Oh shit, you're back!" Jae smiled, swimming towards me. "Ren hadn't told us you had come back already."

"Ren doesn't know I'm back." I sighed, sliding to the ground as I kicked my shoes off and put my feet in the water, relishing the coolness of the lake. "Don't go run off and tell him either. I had hoped no one was here so I could wallow for a bit." I said, the cold edge of my voice a bit harsher than I had wanted it to be.

"I haven't been able to swim for days, and if that's what the lady wants, that's what the lady gets. But you'll have to deal with me, at least." He teased, settling into a comfortable float in the water with his gaze turned to the open sky. "Brother didn't take the gesture well?"

I removed my sword from its sheath and held it in front of me, looking at the dark red coloring that had stained the tip of the blade. The air had turned it into a dark crust already peeling from the silver surface, and all it would take was a swipe of a finger to fly away in the gentle wind. "No, he didn't."

"I'm sorry, for what it's worth." His voice carried over the wind, a soft comfort from a male who had come to remind me of the Theo I used to know. "Do you want to talk about it?"

I placed the blade in the grass and turned my attention to the stars. Millions of tears and raw emotion filled the sky with a beauty no one could ever understand, and I wanted to drown in the sparkling depths of that expanse. The waxing crescent moon was barely visible through thin clouds as they followed the wind, its light illuminating the space behind them.

Was Sinos up there now, watching the mortals who enjoyed the moon's light over that of the sun?

"The sun casts the largest shadows." I sighed, closing my eyes to enjoy the soft breeze that whisked over the lake. "A harrowing line from a tragic story, but the best fitting one to describe it all. He was always bright and confident, a beacon of home that would never grow cold, yet the man I saw today used that fire differently. He still radiated heat, but his shadows smothered everything comforting."

"Do you think he had something to do with the Vriwood beast? We know the rebellion sent it, but its actual creation..."

A silent nod was all I could muster, bringing my head back down to watch the water that rippled softly from Jae's idle movements. "He mentioned something about it being an experiment that the sixth general reported on, but they could not get good results because of how fast we dispatched it. Though nothing of its creation was mentioned, Barthet let it slip that the creature shouldn't have been able to be killed by weapons or simple magic alone."

I watched Jae's head bob in a curt nod, his eyes looking over some invisible sheet of information in the sky.

"He mentioned something about weaknesses, too, but was efficiently cut off before he could say more. If this was the first experiment, I'm worried about what the next might entail. I don't think he'll go for Vriwood again, but what if they choose something less defensible the next time they practice? What is it that they are trying to do with those demons?" I growled, curling my toes in the loose soil of the water's edge when bundling my fists was not enough. "Something is wrong, Jae. I just don't know *what*."

The ripples of the water grew more prominent as Jae swam closer, the almost glowing brightness of the water below him illuminating his honey gaze. I could not help but notice with a quick sweep of a glance over his muscles and the pleasing tone of his stature—everything lay bare for the world to see. He was attractive in a way males should not be able to be, but he could not hold a candle to Ren.

My Ren.

Guilt washed over my senses as I stared back into the water, but I could not bring myself to call for him across the pact or mate bond, whatever gave us the ability to speak through our minds. I feared his reaction to the utter failure of progress I had promised to find, even though I knew somewhere deep in my soul that he would not have the same look of disappointment that Theo had given me. He was too kind and understanding to stoop to such low levels, yet here I was, sitting on the bank of a river with one of his best friends, trying to avoid him.

"Did Ren ever tell you about how he and I came to work together?" Jae asked, turning to lean his back against the bank to look into the forest beyond.

My guilt dwindled as the conversation changed, my brain happily taking the distraction he was offering. "He told me that you used to get in fights with superiors because you didn't agree with their choices, so he took you in to avoid potentially...brutal consequences."

I could see the slight smirk on his face as he chuffed out a laugh, "The light version of it, then." His smile grew slightly as he became lost in good memories before it faltered as it found something not as pleasing. "He showed up to the war camp that had been settled in the Sinos Cordillera, just before the range that led into Velhea, on the day I was set to be executed for my insubordination."

From what I could recall, the Northern Rebellion was led by the King of Velhea, and they held a very similar stance to what the Southern Rebellion had regarding their thoughts on the Roamion Royals. They wanted freedom from the divide of the tamed and untamed and did not wish to be ruled over for no reason other than power. The crown of Aulari used the Untamed Wilds and the peninsula that Velhea sat on as prisons, where magic had faded, and shifting was impossible because of the lack of resources and curses on the lands.

However, the rebellion Velhea led had lasted for centuries, since before the time of Akis nearly six hundred years ago.

"My captain up north was a ruthless man who would take any length to secure victory in any given battle with the Velheans, even if it meant the butcher of children. He took pride and pleasure in the torture of every living soul he came across, and though I was a loyal soldier, I wasn't going to let it happen without some pushback of change." Jae continued, interrupting my attempt to recall all of the information regarding Velhea's history. "I had been sent under his command from several other captains who didn't like my tongue either, hoping that he would break me. Instead, it just made me angrier and bolder. Confidence is driven by pride, more often than night."

"A few days before Ren arrived, Captain Holland had decided to intercept a refugee group attempting to leave the Cordillera to enter Velhea. Our people who wanted to move somewhere else." His voice grew dangerously soft as he stared into the water, watching it move as he slowly opened and closed his fist. "He intended to string them up and pin them on the Velheans as another reason to keep the war going and a warning to whoever else wanted to run away. It didn't matter who or how many were in it, just that they needed to die to send a message."

"I started the confrontation with an argument, which led me nowhere. Then it came to punches, which left him with several new bruises and me with a black eye." He lifted his hand out of the water to show swirling scars leading up his left arm and onto his chest, "Then it came to weapons, where he left this lovely scar using that brutal bladed whip of his. His favorite tool, he had told me once."

His hand dropped back into the water as he turned his attention back to the stars. A gentle breeze blew through the trees, bringing pleasant scents of pine and cedar that seemed to calm him as he closed his eyes. "My punishment was to lead the front against the lone pack headed to Velhea, but I refused. I refused to use my blade nor my teeth against the lives of innocents who were searching for somewhere new that they deemed safer. So, he instead tied me to a heavy chain like nothing more than a common dog and made me watch as he tortured and skinned every single member of that party before stringing me up like one of the bodies in the trees." His breath turned shaky, "Mothers, daughters, fathers, and sons."

My hand slowly moved to my mouth in horror as Jae continued rubbing his face. "Ren showed up the following morning asking about his strongest warrior, and in his greed and pride, Captain Holland tried to say it was himself. His soldiers disagreed, and luckily, Ren was more inclined to listen to them. They led him over to me, hanging from my limbs in a tree like I was nothing but a corpse, and he brought me down with the quick shots of four arrows. Then he named me his second in command, with little information on me beyond my constant arguments and the wounds of a battered torture victim. He let me choose what to do with Holland before we left."

"Did you have him killed?" I finally spoke, my nails digging into my palms. "Brutalized for what he's done?"

"No, I didn't." He gave a sad smile, turning to look at me with sorrow and hatred I had not yet seen in the wolf Fae. "I let him live, and I appointed a close friend of mine, Juliette, as the captain of the squad. He was made one of the lowest ranks possible in the forces and is conscripted to do that until the day he dies."

"Why let him live after doing something so vile? Why did Ren let him live?"

"Ren had only recently been appointed the general, and he was still learning the ups and downs of the war, so he let me have full control over that choice. I didn't want to be like Holland, so instead of doing what I so desperately wanted to, I instead put him in what he would consider a fate worse than death. Running errands and cleaning shit, while a female leads his army to better futures." He snorted as he glanced back to the stars, "Though, I'm allowed to kill him whenever I deem fit. Maybe next time we visit, perhaps."

His perspective on the situation brought a small smile to my face despite the simmering anger that such a person was still breathing. "If I'm around, I'd like an invite to the party."

He turned his head to me with a gleaming grin, "Your reservation has been accepted, Lo."

"Are you finally planning Holland's death after fifty years of silence?" A new voice joined the conversation, laughter lacing its deeper tones. We quickly turned to see Ren and Rygur approaching with towels wrapped around their waists and smiles on their faces, though both still had weapons strapped across their backs—in case of an ambush, I assumed. "I'm hurt that you are planning it without me." Ren smiled, walking over to me and placing a soft kiss on the top of my head.

"I'm just taking reservations for the date, handsome." Jae teased, winking as he splashed water at us, splattering all over Ren and me. In a wasted attempt to defend myself from the water—raising my hands a second too late—I lost myself in laughter, smiling the most I had since the day before Vriwood.

All three boys stared at me in surprise and confusion at the noise as I tried to stop the hysteria by wiping away the tears. I gave them all a vulgar gesture, "You three are asking for a good dunk into the water if you keep staring at me!" I giggled while Jae's laughter howled from somewhere in the middle of the lake.

There was a splash of water as Rygur jumped in, landing right on top of Jae in a flurry of splashes and playful punches.

My laughter did not stop as the play fight started, Ren's deep chuckle joining mine as he sat beside me. "Hearing your laugh and seeing that smile is a drug I didn't realize could exist. My only wish was that I was the start of it." He purred, pulling me into his chest with an arm. "Since you have continued to ignore my silent questions, let me ask you where you can't run away: How are you doing?"

A couple of deep breaths finally got the relentless laughter to fade as I remembered the day's events, but my smile did not falter as I looked into those hazel eyes that just sang *home*. "I'm doing better now. But I don't know how long until I can say I'm okay." I answered honestly, looking at the two grown males reduced to schoolboys chasing each other in the water. "He admitted to being behind the Vethen in Vriwood, and he has plans for something else that he didn't divulge, but the biggest hit was that he was intentionally keeping me in an invisible cage to keep my prey instincts stronger than anything else." I sighed, my hand falling on his knee to ground me, even as his anger was turning into a storm threatening to cover the stars.

"I lost a brother today, but I gained two more." I giggled, closing my eyes as Jae and Rygur yelled at each other about some use of lakeweed being unfair. "On top of that, I've found something few people get to say they have in their lifetimes. My handsome, adoring, protective mate." I opened my eyes again with a soft giggle, watching as he examined every line and emotion on my face for any sign of a lie.

"Damn right, you did." He grinned, pulling me into a soft kiss of warmth and a reminder that he was here. "Please don't take as long as Jae did to finally start plotting the death of Holland because if I see Theodore, he *will* be meeting a fate worse than Burton's." He teased, though the threat was as real as the grass beneath us.

"If you see him before I do, you'll be doing him a favor by ending him however that mind of yours can imagine. Because if I am the one planning his death party, well, I will plan every little detail. He won't get the quick death that woman received in the tent."

His eyebrows raised in surprise, but the smile on his face was nothing less than predatory. "A part of me might prefer to wait for that party."

I gave a playful wink in response before leaning over to grab my sword, the moonlight glistening off the silver. I made to wipe off Theo's dried blood when I noticed that the red stain had been washed away by the splash of water that Jae had thrown at us, bringing a sad smile to my face as I looked closely at the sharp edge.

"Everything all right?" Ren asked, looking at the blade as I put it away in its sheath before throwing it back in the grass.

"I think I'd like to bathe before we head back into our war-torn reality," I responded, pulling on the bottom of my shirt and bringing it over my head with the memorized action. I stretched through sore muscles that had not quite relaxed from the day's ordeals before removing my pants, deliberately exaggerating some movements.

"You must be a goddess, truly." Ren breathed. Even though I had my back to him, I could feel the heat-filled gaze that took in every inch of my bare body.

I shrugged at the compliment as I flashed him a small smile before beginning my descent into the water. It was cold when I put my feet in, but I had forgotten we were in the winter months, so the freezing temperatures shot through my body like a sharp blade.

There was a stop in the splashing and laughter in the middle of the lake, my senses pulling my attention from the cold in sudden worry that something was wrong.

"Gods, Lo! A little warning next time?" Jae yelled, leaving me unable to stifle the giggle that rumbled in my chest as both males turned away like embarrassed teens.

Full-grown Fae, indeed.

"Oh, don't tell me you both have never seen a female naked before." I teased as I was finally able to wade in neck-deep water, surprise lighting my features as hands wrapped around me from behind.

"They turn because they know not to look at what is mine." Ren's voice growled in my ear, sending shivers down my spine that were not because of the cold water.

"Well, I should use that to my advantage." I grinned, pulling away from his hands to dive under the water and using him as a stop to propel me through the primarily clear depths.

Since my father taught me to swim, I have loved slipping under the water and hearing nothing but feeling weightless, diving into what felt like another reality. Even now, when my world seemed to fall apart, I could start to hear the melody of a gentle violin tune echoing in my head and drowning out the worries and fears that plagued me.

I pushed against the stillness of the water's surface until I came across the blurred image of four legs treading the water. I had memorized who was on the left and who was on the right before I disappeared under the water. Somewhere above me, I heard what sounded like a muffled question starting.

I grabbed the one to the right's legs, the surprise catching him off guard as I pulled Rygur under the water.

The dragon Fae flailed in surprise as I heard a muffled curse above the water, my laughter forcing me back to the surface before I drowned myself in hysterics.

The sounds of the forest greeted me alongside bellowing laughter; I shook out my hair quickly to take in the sight of Rygur popping out of the water; a flash of humorous anger was in his eyes as he pointed at me.

"You, my lady, are going to regret that." He snarled with a laugh, jumping towards me as he had Jae, and I could not steel myself against the mass of muscle that barreled us both back under the surface. I kept my eyes closed as we wrestled, pushing and throwing waves of water at each other with the slightest use of magic before we popped up again, laughing like we were nothing but children.

"Oh, you've done it now!" Jae laughed, beginning to swim away from the two of us in a laughing fit. Rygur and I looked at each other in confusion when we were suddenly slammed with a giant wave of water that sent us both spinning under the surface.

Rough hands grabbed my arms and pulled me up again to the surface, coughing laughter, trying to rid my lungs of the water I had accidentally swallowed. Ren's laugh had turned into a total fit as he helped me steady myself above the water, our gaze locking momentarily.

No world beyond this one mattered—where there was laughter and starlight, I was home.

"I love you, Ren," I murmured, and something in his gaze hesitated for barely a second before it warmed again.

He pressed his forehead against mine. "I love you more, Wildie."

"That's enough mate-crap, we are at war!" Jae's voice yelled alarmingly close, giving me barely enough time to push off Ren before he was tackled further into the water by his second and third.

Their silhouettes moved under the water until they resurfaced a few feet away, scattering waves of magic and punches of water toward each other in rapid succession, their laughter a song of happiness in the quiet dim of the night.

I trod the water as I looked up to the waning moon, which clouds had now entirely covered. Thunder sounded in the distance, but it differed from the ones Ren usually conjured—as if the deep rumbles were muted and filled with less energy than the ones he commanded.

I focused on the clouds again as something unsettled my thoughts, trying to send my magic into its depths to see if it was a natural or magical storm when thunder sounded again. No lightning or smell of rain followed its looming sound, and magic laced the clouds like a thin blanket of string.

Ren was still laughing and concentrated on Ry and Jae's combined efforts of attacks; the smile on his face was genuine. I had never seen him summon a storm out of anything but anger, and his storm magic was not what he was focusing on. Only the scent and strings of water magic surrounded him and his command, which meant that this storm was not of his design.

Hoofbeats sounded from the bank, quickly pulling my attention to a chestnut mare galloping at us at full speed, her horn sparkling with magic as she held some parchment in the air.

Any sound of the playful males stopped instantly, with Rygur being the first out of the water to approach the unicorn as she shifted in front of him. She was a younger soldier whose blue eyes were round with fear while the rest of us were holding our breath as Rygur spoke to her in hushed, quick sentences.

Jae and Ren trailed close behind as they approached the bank when a flash of blue illuminated the darkened space. The mare was off again, whinnying in a warning fashion.

The distant camp was suddenly booming with yelling and movement, flashes of shifters spotting around the massive station like exploding stars.

"We need to leave this instant," Rygur stated, his voice grave as he turned to his brothers standing beside him in the grass. Ren's face showed no emotion as he read over the letter. Jae and Rygur shifted in the quick sprint back to the camp, and the calm aura of the lake dissipated into tension.

"What's happened?" I asked, pulling myself out of the water to stand beside him. Now, I felt the pull of storm magic as his deep rumbles of thunder chased away the weaker one like it was nothing more than a pest.

"Agraxis is under siege."

CHAPTER 34

We flew without stopping for an entire day.

By the time we reached the city's outskirts, the smell of smoke had filled the air as we took our first glance at Agraxis, the once glorious capital of Aistris.

Now, it was nothing more than a living nightmare.

Even though we still had an hour or so of flight to reach the city, the ruin and destruction were beyond anything we could have dreamed about. The most defensible city in all of Aistris was a spotted field of fire, rubble, and grieving screams that sounded like they were straight out of the lowest pit of the hells. A darkness circled the city's perimeter and seeped into the farthest streets and alleys where light could not reach.

More screams sounded from the city's eastern side as we watched a mass of black emerging from the dark border, silencing them seconds later. Another from farther south as another crowd of people tried to push on the barrier.

Shadow beasts.

Ren had begun to pivot for the moving mass of shadows on the city's southern wall when a streak of metallic silver stopped him, with Jae frantically pointing towards the castle.

"There are bigger problems!" He yelled across the distance between us. The wind picked up as Ren pulled himself to a wide stop, looking at the standing pillar of the Roamion's rule.

The castle was coated in an unnatural darkness that blocked any reasonable view of its stone walls, though the longer we investigated, it began to move.

Giant blue eyes glinted through the dark as the mass morphed and contorted into a massive beast the size of the enormous castle. Shadowed claws dug into the stone as it lifted itself from the castle, large wings stretching to either side of the beast like a maw opening into the void. It began to move along the castle like a lizard on a wall while its tail dragged through homes and stones on the ground, silencing screams that had erupted in terror.

Then those haunting blue stared directly towards us while its mouth opened to bellow a roar that sounded more like a chorus of screams.

It was a warning and a promise.

I could feel Ren's chest beginning to rumble with the beginnings of a roar to return the threat, but I reached across the invisible bridge of the bond to stop him.

Do not taunt it. We need a plan, Rendros.

"We need to land and figure out a better way to do this, Ren!" Jae echoed the same sentiment as Rygur brought them closer to the sparking horns of lightning that sat on his head, "We go in there now, we die!"

My sisters are in there. Ren growled, his eyes narrowing at Jae as if he could hear him. *We do not have time to wait!*

Jae looked toward me, asking for a translation, but I shook my head. It was precisely what he had thought he said in the way grief sparked across his eyes. "Ren, I know that Sellias and Dityss are still in there, but if we have any chance of reaching them, we have to stop and regroup. We are no help to them dead!" His voice broke in his plea, Rygur barking a small chirp of agreement that carried the same weight of worry.

Ren's head swiveled toward the castle again, conflicted in his choices before he turned towards an empty road below us and dove for a spot of trees next to it.

I closed my eyes against the wind as we dove, reminding myself that Ren was conscious of his movements and would not send us straight into the ground like a cannonball aiming to explode. Still, even the comforting black of my thoughts was stalked by the blue eyes of the castle's beast.

Ren landed and instantly shifted, leaving me falling through thin air from the sudden disappearance of my ride. I panicked with a slight squeal before Ren caught me, holding me firmly to his chest. I opened my mouth to chastise him for such a foolish move, but his usual smug smile was nowhere in sight as he placed me on the grass, his eyes focused solely on Jae and Rygur, who had landed seconds after us.

Rygur spoke first as he readjusted to his feet, using Jae as a crutch to keep him upright. "We cannot go into Agraxis without forces, Ren. The forces we ordered to meet us here will not arrive for at least another twelve hours, and you saw the destruction. We go in there now, and those forces have no one left to command them when they arrive."

"They are using magic and things we don't understand. I want to go in there as bad as you do and save as many as possible, but the beast we fought in Vriwood was *half* the size of these, and only your lightning could do real damage." Jae added, "You could take on one or two, but there would be no hope to go against that demon surrounding the castle. You'd burn out and take the kingdom's future with you."

Thunder sounded through the sky, but no lightning followed.

"I can't just stand here waiting for an army that might not affect shadows. They could help with the foot soldiers that are more than likely crawling through the city like roaches, but the longer we wait, the more of our people die." Ren snarled, throwing his arms into the air as his eyes looked toward the castle like he could see it. "Our family is in there, and I'll be damned if I don't try to save them."

Rygur grabbed Ren's arm, the gold in his eyes glowing with defiance. "I will follow you into that dragon's maw, brother. But at least *think* about a plan that isn't an immediate death sentence."

I turned from the arguing to look back at the city, letting my imagination walk down the street filled with laughing children and a dream that I had hoped would be everywhere one day. It was likely nothing more than rubble now, but I stood in that street, watching that little girl play with her wooden unicorn.

Gingersnap, the beautiful unicorn princess that fought nightmares and bad guys.

I curled my hands into fists as I let my mind wander away from that street and into that magic library. My anger grew with every step as I turned down the newest aisle, focusing on the grim power that had become like a second consciousness in my mind until I found a gold and black book with an opal shimmering on its cover. "I've accepted the bond and practiced with the shadows, Ethe. Willingly pull yourself out of your book before I drag you out again, putting us both at risk before we enter somewhere I need every ounce."

The book stirred in my hands in silent answer as the opal lost its shimmer, pulling me back into reality as the shadowed beast stalked around the darkness of the night and trees around me.

"You've practiced, yes, but you have not mastered it. Nor the other blessing you still fail to see for what it is." Their raspy voice grated against my ears. "Regardless, we are too late. The gods' war has been reignited with more power than ever. Agraxis is lost."

"It cannot be lost; there must be *something* we can do. If we take out the leader, who's summoning all of these Vethen—"

"They are summoned, Willow. Even if you killed the monster behind their destruction, their terror would not end." The head of the shadow turned toward me, once again eyeless. "But their creation would cease, allowing the remaining beasts to be dealt with." Their silent steps pushed aside leaves as they circled me, watching me think.

"The heart of a hydra," I murmured, looking to the ground as I tried to sift through my memories. "Who would be the heart? Theo?" His blood had smelled wrong, and he had been behind the Vriwood attack—it would make sense, as much as it made my heart ache to think it.

"No. He has dabbled in the art of shadow beasts, but he doesn't have the power for this scale of control," The Ethe stated, coming to a stop in front of me, the air turning colder where they stood. "Look at me, Willow Saugrave, and put a hand to the shadow of my soul. See who made me the beast I am today."

I had nearly forgotten that the Ethe was considered one of these demons, even if only the lowest form of them.

I returned my gaze to where Rygur was quietly talking to Ren and Jae, who seemed to be on the verge of an argument turning physical.

Their backs were turned to me, but I caught Rygur glancing at me, watching as I spoke to the shadow who had become silent company over the last few weeks.

His attention did not last long before it cut back to Jae, who had begun yelling something that sent them all into raised voices.

I looked into the cold black of incorporeal mists ahead of me and placed a hand on their muzzle.

My mind darkened as the shadows curled around every facet of my thoughts, like a dark wind that only filled spaces with an empty void. As I moved to look around at the vision the Ethe was sharing with me, I felt the weight of something holding my hands behind me like metal shackles. Panic flared as I desperately searched for a way out or the cause of the imprisonment, but there was only bone-chilling laughter that echoed around the confines of my grim prison.

"My, my, my. You still fight, even with everything taken from you." The voice echoed, every vein in my body freezing. "Tell me, unicorn."

The dark mist in front of my face began to twist and contort, with thin strands of tendrilled shadow and a sliver of metal somewhere in the center, until pale skin appeared between the dark blinds.

Dark purple eyes and the grin of a psychopath flared in the thin mists, "How does your kind fare without their horn?"

I screamed as I fell out of that dark place and onto the ground of reality, holding my head as if it were being torn off my shoulders and staring at the feet—no, *hooves*—of the Ethe before me. I had conjured it in an equine shape before, but..."She—she didn't, did she?" I barely whispered, not daring to look up.

"That is a story for another time, filly." They whispered. Their voice was rougher than usual as I watched their hooves turn back toward the forest's shadows. "Do you remember how we parted the first time we spoke?"

The nightmare haunting my imagination for the last few days resurfaced again, listening as Ren and Jae argued in that imaginary scenario, much like they were now. It was a different time and place entirely, yet the hair on my arms rose at the similarity.

"You told me I was not a hero. That I was a queen." I responded, finally returning my gaze to the shadowed frame of a shattered beast—a unicorn without its horn.

They nodded, dissolving back into the shadows with a single parting sentence, "You'll do well to remember that."

My eyes did not leave the shadows they disappeared into, but my hearing focused on the world around me. The slight chirp of a cricket, the rustle of the leaves in the wind, the thunder rumbling in the distance. Here, at this moment, the world continued to thrive. The natural world that continued no matter the decision of crowns or people, an untamed spirit of life.

I turned my gaze in the direction of the city, my eyes narrowing as I imagined the people running from the beasts and the misted barrier that kept them from escaping to their natural homes. Back to lives where children played in the streets, and mothers gossiped about the latest family moving in down the road.

Unofficially, I had been named a princess. Hopefully, that was close enough to the meaning the Ethe seemed to cling to.

I stood from the dirt and the leaves, moving my hands up to my hair to fix it as best as I could to double-check that it was ready for whatever was next before my hands wandered over the knives and sword I had brought to check that they were adequately fixed into my clothes.

"Did they say anything useful?" Rygur called past Ren and Jae's irritated voices, breaking them from their argument as they realized that something else had been happening beyond their bubbles of anger.

"I'm afraid so," I said, holding my lips tight as I rejoined the group, looking at Rygur, Jae, and finally Ren. "Your brothers are right. We need a solid plan before we storm the castle, and you won't like it."

"Were you talking to the Ethe?" He asked, and I gave a slight nod in affirmation.

"I was hoping they'd have more information on how to beat their kind, but they instead told me who was behind their summoning." A deep frown formed on my lips, their tension spiking as I took in a deep breath. "Your sisters aren't safe in that castle, which should be our main target."

"Did you not see that demon curling around it like a dragon on a hoard? Of course, they aren't safe there." Lightning sparked across the sky from the pent-up anger swirling in Ren's system, but I shook my head as I held his hazel gaze.

"The visible threat, yes. But the one who has compiled and stored this level of beast and power, the heart of the hydra of shadow beasts, is in there too." I took a deep, shaky breath as I called upon whatever confidence I could. "Queen Ezyla."

Rygur and Jae cursed, but Ren stared at me with disbelief, then horror, shielded with distrust. "You expect me to believe that my mother could be the heart of death in the kingdom? In *her* kingdom?"

Jae stepped in, standing between me and Ren. "Haven't Ry and I mentioned how much we dislike being around her? Peter did, too, but you shoved it off because she's your mother. Now you've heard of nightmares from your *mate* about her, and you still can't even entertain the idea?" His voice had turned to a low growl, and Rygur walked up to put a hand on his shoulder.

"Rendros, do you remember what happened the night that Peter attacked Willow?" The black-haired male asked, his gold-speckled gaze not leaving the prince as Jae's attention fell to the ground. "Do you remember what Jae found after Peter was...*incarcerated*?" The final word was said with apprehension, as if Rygur knew there was more than just a prison sentence keeping their old friend.

Ren's eyebrows knitted in confusion as he tried to remember.

"No, you don't because you had a good reason to focus your attention elsewhere. And it bothers me that you didn't listen when we told you afterward, citing that Peter was taken care of and there was no reason to worry, even as you ensured Willow never left your sight for too long. I think your subconscious remembers, but you fight the truth of it." Rygur sighed, "What else did Jaeden smell that night alongside the poison in his claws?"

He was silent, but the shield of distrust shattered into regret and realization as he looked at his hands. "My mother's perfume."

"Your mother's perfume," Jae said, only a breath behind him, grief lining his voice as he looked at Ren.

The world spun around me like the ground had been removed from my feet, steadying myself with a swift replacement of my foot to remind myself I was on solid ground. Anger swelled in my chest as more thunder boomed through the sky, shaking my head as I looked back up at him.

"You knew or had a hint that my nightmare was well-placed, and yet you *still* argued it?" I snarled, putting my hand up to stop his advance when he tried to explain. "Right now, innocents are dying because of the actions of the woman you refused to see danger in." I snarled, turning back to Jae and Rygur with a sidestep past Rendros. "We head for the castle and try to save whoever we can from the beasts. But do not engage unless necessary—save your strength for whatever waits in the palace."

Both men nodded as Jae asked, "Should we shift?"

"Shifting is fine; I'll be doing such myself. As for you," I turned to Ren, narrowing my eyes at the hurt glistening in them, "I need you to be a general. I'm pissed at you, but I still love you, and I need the general willing to kill for the protection of his people. I need the dragon who dropped a man into the jaws of his army for revenge, not the one looking at me like nothing else but my approval matters. You have never been like that, and hells damn me if I let you start that shit now."

He blinked a few times at the frankness of my words, but the hurt cleared into a wall of steel as he gave a firm nod with the hint of a smile. "Jaeden, you may lose your title as second at the end of this."

"Brother, with all due respect, I wouldn't call that female a second. She's the one you stand beside at the front lines, not the one who stands behind you." The wolf Fae snorted, his voice returning to the chuff, relaxed tone it usually carried as the situation shifted into focus.

"Good point." Ren chuckled, though I could only return a tight smile as my frustration still held out. "Her plan is sound, but I can't go in shifted. My dragon is too large and too easy of a target to find, but I won't be able to keep up if everyone shifts."

"I'm carrying you in, as simple as that." I nodded, stretching out my arms as I jogged in place. "I beat Jae in every race we've participated in, and you can swing a sword a lot easier from the back of a unicorn than a wolf. He can keep any foot soldiers off of us and help where it becomes overwhelming." I nodded before Ren turned to Rygur.

"I need you to be a scout for this mission. Focus on finding us the clearest paths through the city to the castle gates," He ordered, looking between them. "When we reach the castle, we go in as Fae. I don't think the queen will order that demon to attack the castle directly with her still in it, so we don't need the additional strength. We need to be as quiet as possible, and our priority is getting Sellias and Dityss out of there."

"And the King?" I asked.

"He deserves whatever he gets," Jae whispered, and Ren gave a shallow nod.

A story for another time.

"After we get the princesses out, we confront Queen Ezyla. Try to get her to surrender and dismiss the beasts, or worst case, forcibly remove her from the throne." He finished, turning back to me as Jae and Rygur shifted in flashes of color.

"Are you ready?" I asked, finishing up a stretch of my lower legs as I met the hazel and blue eyes that clashed like supercell storms.

"I think so." He smiled, pulling me into a deep kiss that drowned out the horrors of war just beyond the ridge of trees ahead of us. It was full of grief, apology, love, and pride, my hands wrapping around his shoulders to hold his neck before he pulled back and put his forehead to mine.

"I'm here, Wildie."

"So am I, your Highass."

CHAPTER 35

The ring of shadows that kept citizens in Agraxis luckily was not a two-way barrier that kept others out, though entering the dark ring of death would have made me vomit had it not been for my inability to as a mare.

The shadowed smoke felt like nails dragging across my fur and down to my skin, but the worst part of it was the destruction that had left Agraxis in worse shape than we could have believed. Blood splattered every stone on the ground, with husked corpses scattered across the streets as we slowly entered the hellscape we had only seen from above. The screams around us echoed in the empty abyss of buildings and flames while the stomps of a creature far larger than I thought possible shook the loose rocks of the dirt beneath us.

We all stopped when the dirt roads turned into stone pathways, tossing my head in unease while scraping the ground with a hoof.

"I hate this," Jae grumbled in an echo of my sentiments, having shifted back to his Fae form to kneel beside a small body to cover it with a blanket. "These were all just people living their lives...children who played with toys and dreamed of their future."

Ren's hand ran down the side of my neck comfortingly, anger rolling off him like a wave as his thighs clenched around my sides in a gentle request to continue forward. "We will avenge them all, Jaeden. I will promise you that."

Jae did not respond with anything more than a nod, shifting to walk at my side as I moved forward into a trot, keeping my ears alert and swiveling to every tiny sound. Rygur moved onto the rooftops ahead of us, quietly scouting the areas and threats around us as a silver marker to guide us around the worst sections of the wreckage.

Ren's sword was drawn at my side, his attention divided amongst any potential threat and corner we passed.

A flash of silver appeared before us, and Rygur guided us down an alley to the left.

I did my best to avoid the splatters of blood and huddled groups of people as we passed through the dark path, but there was almost no piece of stone not stained by the massacre outside it. Some huddled groups were families desperately trying to stay quiet, while others were entirely still with death.

How will anyone see a better future after this?

Ren's fingers absentmindedly ran through my mane as a flash of lightning struck overhead, gentle rain following its frenzied strike.

Every storm runs out of rain, and the clear sky will bring better days. He sighed, watching a pair of children huddling close to one another to hide from the unknown travelers passing them by. The older boy looked defiant and ready to attack to protect his little sister, but she was watching with quiet wonder.

I bowed my head in a gentle sign of compassion, causing her eyes to light up with a big, toothy smile. Hope sparked in her eyes as I turned back to the alley, picking up into a trot as we broke onto a main street.

It was lined with mummified corpses and charred buildings as it led up toward the darkened gates of the castle, with rivers of red cascading down the stones like a bloody welcome mat. Some people were still moving and trying to free others from fallen beams and rubble, while others stood ready with stolen swords and wild eyes.

I kept my attention on Rygur, who had stopped at a nearby building. His attention was focused somewhere to our left.

"Prince Rendros? Is that you?" One of the men protecting a group of survivors trying to help a woman crushed under a pile of the remains of a building asked, the group quickly swinging their heads in our direction in disbelief. "Thank the gods, you came home! Have you brought the army?"

I turned my head from Rygur to look at Ren, who was watching the group with a gaze that was a mixture of regret and defiance. "I have, but they won't arrive for a few hours yet." His voice lowered into that of a king as he addressed the group, sending a simple signal for Jae to assist the struggling group with his wolf's gifted bonus of strength to help hold the heavy beam as others began to dig the woman out. "What is your name?"

"Um, my name is Iuver Atkins, sir." The young blonde nodded, quickly bowing his head.

"Iuver and all of you with him. I speak to you now as your crown prince and a citizen concerned for his brethren's safety." He dropped to the ground off my back, my anxiety spiking at the lack of weight and sudden detour from the plan. Rygur was still watching from the top of a nearby building, but his tail had stilled from its typical swiping motions of thought and calculations. "You need to evacuate and get as many people as you can out of this city until the threat has been neutralized and you hear from me again. These demons and the monster summoning them upon us hide in the palace, and I do not know how long their extermination will take. I refuse to lose more of our people and our families in an attempt to hold this city."

"But, your Highness, the barrier—" Another female tried to speak, but he held his hand up in a quiet command to listen.

"Is currently being held back by my magic just down this road. So long as I still stand, that will be an exit you and your people can use to escape and hide from the hell that has drowned our home." He clarified. The announcement made both Jae and I lock eyes in stunned silence as both of us realized how much power he had to exert for such a task. "Do you know any unicorn shifters?"

Iuver's attention glanced over a couple of the others in his group and gave a tight nod.

"Round up as many as you can, and use them as mounts to alert others and to carry the gravely wounded somewhere safe. If they try to refuse you, say that you bear the banner of Prince Rendros as his captain in this evacuation, and any further refusal will result in their punishment as soon as we can bring everyone home."

The small group's mouths opened in collective astonishment as they turned to Iuver as Rendros watched on.

His face mirrored much of his comrade's emotions, but his steel eyes locked with Ren's rigid determination as he returned to the group. "You heard the prince. Take her to safety, return, and help save however many you can."

Rygur's roar broke the confident resurgence as our attention all snapped in his direction, my heart sinking to my stomach when I finally saw what the dragon Fae had been watching.

A shadow beast, the size of the three-story townhomes that lined the streets, strolled in from the street to the left, large claws digging into the side of what used to be a bakery as it peered toward us with bright red eyes that shone straight through the magic dark that gave it form. Iuver quickly pulled up his sword in a defensive position with a few cut words of orders, and two flashes of light briefly illuminated the road before two stallions stood in its fade, dancing nervously in fear.

The nature of prey.

I had broken the mold of what the nature of my mare had wanted me to do. I was free from the bonds of nature and her commands to do the impossible and damn if I was going to watch these two stallions flee or die in their panic.

I turned my attention from the beast to stand in front of the equine dancing on their hooves, desperately searching for a way out and away in the quickest route possible, bringing myself onto my back legs in a rearing motion before stomping my hooves as hard as I could on the stone. Their attention focused on me with surprise and unease, their nostrils flaring in panic as they could not fully tear their attention from the grim demon approaching from behind me.

Shadows curled around their muzzles as I pulled their attention entirely to my eyes, my ears pinned flat to my head as I raised my lip to show the sharpened canines I had spent years working to get to this point. I had fought instinct and nature to pull off the unnatural incisors, making them a visible representation of the ability to break from prey instinct.

I snapped my teeth in their direction as they tried to pull back from my shadow ropes with their ears pointed towards me, but I could see recognition spark in the grey dapple as he stopped trying to flee.

We can fight.

My shadows loosened their grip on the grey stallion as he turned to his white-furred companion, making the same snapping motion with his teeth. The white equine flared his nostrils again in fear and shock, but a repeat of the snapping teeth towards him had the same effect as realization sparked in his brown eyes.

Ren was yelling somewhere behind me as the ground shook with an attack from the Vethen that sent stones flying past us, my shadows retreating to me as I held their gaze with a final parting thought—a burning gaze that spoke a thousand words and tried to show for a thousand more.

Fight for tomorrow.

I could no longer wait for their recognition as I spun around and launched towards Ren, who was standing his ground against the beast. His sword was pointed towards it, lightning speeding down the silver as he focused his magic into the mass of darkness. The electricity hit its mark as it traveled through the shadow with an electrifying amount of power, but the Vethen seemed unaffected even as a chunk of shadowed flush was carved from its side.

The serpent in Vriwood had suffered a similar effect but had at least stumbled from the damage it sustained. This grim bear seemed only irritated by it as it swung its arm to attack Ren and the few civilians who stood beside him.

The amount of magic he was diverting to leave a safe escape for his citizens left his magic as nothing more than an irritation against the shadow beasts.

Terror threatened to swallow my vision and send my hooves forward to defend him when a bark sounded from my right, pulling me from the rash panic. Jae was staring at me with determination and question as he quickly glanced toward the face of the shadow creature before looking back at me.

The rubies—he could not reach them from where we were, but if we combined our strength...

I turned my attention from Ren to charge straight for the face of the beast, racing alongside Jae as a wolfish grin spread across his face. Instinct had my heart rate spike as Jae leaped toward me, landing on my back and holding on with what he could of his paws as I pressed harder into my sprint.

"Willow!" Ren screamed, but I did not dare look behind as I tucked my head and slid myself to a complete stop, bucking my rear legs behind me while Jae launched himself with the momentum straight into the shadow's jaw. I watched as solid teeth met the edge of the right ruby, growls of demon and wolf echoing in the roadway as Jae tore at the solid object.

Shadows moved to my left as the bear's arm quickly swept up for its face, but I could do nothing to stop it but watch with a scream of warning.

A silver blade pierced through the paw as large black wings sprinkled with stars fought against the force of the swing's momentum, barely keeping the claws off of Jae as he wrestled the first gem free.

In a flash of magic, I was back on two legs, pulling out my blade as I ran to the other front limb that still held the beast steady in its fight with the wolf Fae. All of my focus centered on my magic and strength to keep my hands on the weapon as I speared the sword into the mist and dove into the depths of my power, desperate to provide a distraction so Jae could finish the job.

Whatever tendrils of shadows I sent down the sword were met with a dark, twisted version of the calming grim I commanded. I could hear screams of anguished and pained souls tied in with the suffocating mist that felt like it was grabbing and tearing at my arms as I pressed harder into its form with blade and magic.

The coils of magic colliding with one another felt like I was standing in the middle of a wave at sea, and the silver weapon in my hands was the stone to which I clung.

I do not know what I was searching for or what my plan was; all I knew was that Jae needed more time and more of a distraction to take out the other gem and end this battle swiftly. I had been unsuccessful in conjuring my shadows when it came to the serpent, but now I had the chance to try and take control of the rogue grim with a renewed confidence my shadows had not had before. I threw my magic against its seemingly never-ending pit of black again, grinding my teeth against the steel barrier it seemed to protect itself with. If I could keep its attention on me, Jae could finish it, and we would be fine.

Another slam of magic and something cracked.

My mind was suddenly swarmed with pain, blood, and a feeling of emptiness deep in my chest as I stared through half-blind eyes in a stone room. Blood, *my* blood, was splattered all over the place, and as I tried to clear my eyesight to evaluate my surroundings better, I could see the source of the blood coming from deep slashes in my belly. A deep, healthy red trickled down my clothes and skin, the blood loss throwing me in and out of consciousness. I tried to muster the strength to cover and apply pressure to the wounds, but my hands were chained above my head.

Shadows comfortingly crept against the flow of lifeblood leaving my body, and somewhere, I felt like I could hear a smooth, comforting voice. A gateway out of the pain, a way to let go—

"Willow!"

My eyes snapped open as I took in a deep gasp of breath, my free hands flying straight for my abdomen to stop the bleeding. Yet, as my attention cut to where I had been eviscerated, I was only greeted by an unscathed swath of chainmail and leather armor. I blinked again as I fell to the ground, glancing around at the buildings, fires, and pathway stones that littered the area. I stared at where my blade was fixed into the stone beneath it, with no sign of the demon anywhere.

That was not my memory.

"What happened? What did you do?" Ren's voice was tinged with anger as he grabbed my shoulders to steady me as I stood.

"I was...I don't know. I think I was in a memory, maybe?" I whispered, staring down at my hands as I grabbed the handle of the silver weapon and pulled it out of the road. "These beasts are made of shadow, so I tried to absorb it, to take control of it, but all I could see was...torture. Brutal, brutal torture." I whispered, recalling the last moments of the scene before I turned back toward him. His hazel eyes were laced with deep concern, but behind him, I could see Jae spitting out two rubies on the ground like they were poison. "You were able to take care of it?"

Ren nodded, turning his attention back toward Jaeden and Rygur, who were examining the stones with deep interest. "Whatever you did made it slow in its movements. It could still attack but moved as if time had affected it." He hummed in thought, turning his attention back to me. "In another time, I'd question you more, but we must keep moving."

I nodded, looking back towards the castle and the giant demon spiraling around it like a coiled spring. Luckily, we had not caught its attention in the fight, as its blue eyes were too busy scanning the sky for any potential threat.

We were only a tiny burst away from jumping the river into the castle, where who knew what was waiting beyond the near-black stone.

"Let's move!" Ren called, and Rygur swiftly pocketed the gems before circling back, Jae padding by his side. I gave them a determined nod before letting the shift's warmth surge through my nerves, traveling up my senses like diving into a hot spring.

As soon as the shift finished, Ren hopped on my back with an easy jump using his wings, tucking the leather limbs behind him comfortably as I took off at full gallop for the castle.

All around us, I could hear the agonizing screams of grief and anguish in a melody I would deem hell's chorus. Bodies were gored and beaten all over the main road, the amount compounding to more and more *piles* of lost innocents as we neared the lazy river that broke off the castle from the city. Ren's hand gripped my fur like it was a lifeline to this reality.

They went to the castle for sanctuary. His voice came in a hollowed tone across the bond, the steady drizzle of rain turning into a downpour as we grew closer.

I touched the invisible line of communication with a gentle feeling of magic, meaning to say something comforting and to remind him that he was not at fault for their death, but something heavy slammed into my side.

My body crumpled from the force as it passed over me, my eyes forced to shut in the suddenness of the attack as flesh hit stone. I could feel the sharp edges of the masoned rock tear into my skin and thick blood cake into my fur, but there was a sharper and deeper pain in my chest that screamed with so much agony that I unintentionally shifted back to my Fae form.

I barely held in a cry as I pulled myself up into a sitting position, holding my left arm to help cover a particularly nasty gash in my forearm. The sharp pain in my chest twisted again as I tried to gather my surroundings.

Everything in my body felt like it was on fire, but nothing was seriously injured beyond the gash that lacerated my forearm. Scratches and cuts covered every inch of my skin and burned with the smoke that plagued the air, but I was alive and relatively unscathed for such a devastating blow to my side.

Ren was not anywhere around me when I looked for him.

The pain in my chest flared again as panic flooded my system, spinning around in my spot to try to find the enemy or the male that had been on my back. My eyes bounced from every pile of rubble around me as I frantically searched the space outside the castle gates for Ren, Rygur, or Jae, but there was no sign of them.

I growled as I brought myself to stand, "Ren!"

No response.

"Rygur? Jaeden!" I called out again, spinning in a circle as I tried to spot any of their recognizable forms or features. Maybe a flash of silver, a mass of brown fur, black wings speckled in stardust—

My hopes were met with unfamiliar corpses and a circle of people I did not know pushing closer.

I pulled my sword out as I stared at them all, clad in matching iron armor with symbols of suns seared into the chest plates. All of them had swords at the ready, but from the direction of the castle, I could see two figures parting the circle as they stepped over and on the corpses of the deceased like they were nothing more than obstacles in their path.

The pain in my chest became more profound, causing me to stumble while trying to keep my sword pointed toward any soldier who got too close.

"I would stand down, little mare. Unless you wish to find yourself joining the collection of deceased around us." A voice laced with silk carried across the silence, snapping my attention to two golden armored males as they entered the ring I was trapped in.

My eyes narrowed as I tried to peek through the narrow slits on the golden helmets, but I was met with irregular magic and the scent of something familiar as they pulled closer.

"I would rather die than submit to followers of that *witch* you call a queen," I growled, trying to force down the pain that still pounded in my chest. "You are killing innocents for what? Power? Gold?"

I kept my stance ready as one of the golden-armored men stepped forward, a deep chuckle rumbling from behind the mask. "Power is a good guess, but what we aim for strives higher than what a mortal considers power." They growled, sending a shiver running down my spine at the hate that laced its tone.

"What does that *mean*?" I snarled, "Do you not see the damage and the horrors these shadow demons create? That she somehow brought to her kingdom and now holds like a dog on a leash? How is *anything* worth that kind of destruction!"

Gloved hands reached up to grab onto their golden helmet. Familiar fire blonde hair fell from its metal cage as it was removed, his simmering green eyes pinning me to the spot as my eyes crossed over new scars that slashed all over his head and neck like jewelry. "I have seen the damage and the truth of the heretics of this land, and I have greeted death because of their madness. These shadow demons, as you call them, are the mere hands of our liberator, weeding out those who stand against the truth."

He took a step closer, and whatever fight I had won against my prey drive that kept the flight response subdued completely dissolved as recognition took hold. Terror pulsed through my mind in such an overwhelming force that I could not stop myself from slamming straight into the arms of several soldiers, ripping and tearing at my limbs to hold me as I desperately tried to break free.

"As much as I want you to pay for what you caused me, little Willow, I'm afraid our Queen would like to take care of you herself." The smile on his face twisted with a scar that ran through it from above his left eye, "Isn't that right, brother of my blood?"

The hair on my neck stood up as I watched the second golden-plated soldier step forward, removing his helmet and shaking out the familiar long, golden-blonde strands of hair while meeting my gaze.

As I stared at the golden pair of lions staring me down, everything stopped moving.

Theo had teleported his band of generals to the capital, and Peter was no longer locked away in a dungeon.

CHAPTER 36

I was dragged through the castle with Peter and Theo holding me on either arm, my knees peeling against the hard stone flooring as we followed the same hallways that I had first seen only months ago.

Whatever unease I felt from the paintings that I had sworn watched my movements before Agraxis went to shit only doubled with the unnatural shadows that stained their frames. Not a single painting portrayed a happy person or moment; my heart sank with every canvas we passed as the doors to the throne room appeared down the hall.

The pain in my chest from the force of the hit outside of the castle gates had become a dull, unending ache. I could barely breathe despite seemingly no visual of physical damage, which only caused my fear to spike as I thought of what was going on internally. At the same time, another shaky breath rattled my system. I had been stripped of my sword and most of my knives, and my hair had been mercilessly torn out of its ponytail in what Peter had called a necessary 'search' to ensure no blades were hidden within the strands.

Despite the too-intimate lengths to find all of the weapons stashed on my body, I was lucky that the rigid bone of my spine and focused grim magic helped hide the thin knife that could help me get out of there.

Or, at the very least, let me die fighting.

"I hope that she lets me give you your punishment, sweetheart. I'd *love* to treat you to such delightful methods and the tools I've been so graciously blessed with to—"

"Enough, Peter," Theo growled, though whatever argument ensued was drowned out by the squealing of the doors opening to the throne room.

While the tile and limestone pillars had few changes beyond some additional dark smears and blood trails, the stained-glass windows—or the empty spaces they once occupied—left the court with no royal wonder. In each arch, where only shattered glass fell as a reminder of the gorgeous windows, were dark giants of shadow staring into the room. Their red gazes followed me as I was thrown to the ground in the middle of the room, but I was too busy staring at the thrones ahead.

They looked nearly identical to how they had before; however, the king's throne and the one I first saw Ren in front of were turned to nothing but ash.

The iced blue eyes of the dragon-like demon that had been wrapped around the castle stared from behind the queen's throne, a horrifying replacement of the glass rendition of the two Fae dancing. It was a dark and terrible attempt to replace something so beautiful and uplifting in a room that innately brought fear to the surface when the stained glass used to be the only thing that gave me peace of mind when I first arrived.

"The viper returns to the nest," The queen's voice did not echo through the room due to the lack of walls to trap the sound, but somehow, it still surrounded me when she spoke. "A miniscule part of me wished you stayed away in the wilds if only to save my daughter from having to watch you die. But a much larger part of me is grateful for your traitorous actions."

Queen Ezyla was dressed in a long black dress that trailed down the throne's staircase. Purple gems lined her waist and breasts while bands of gold wound around her arms. Her hair was tied into a braided crown above her head that laced behind a new tiara made of obsidian and gold, their dark metallics pushing away both natural and magical shadows from around her.

"Willow, I'm so sorry—" A familiar voice cried out from my left, pulling my attention to see Sellias standing in a thin violet gown that hooked on every curve and dip of her body. Her hair curled and settled behind her in flowing waves, though the regality her clothing beamed did not match the horror that widened her violet gaze.

"There will be no apologies to this whore, my love." Queen Ezyla snapped at her daughter, her voice a frigid calm as she eyed me up and down. "You were supposed to die weeks ago, yet you survived. You were supposed to die before reaching my doorstep, yet you still stand before me, sickeningly alive."

I barely paid attention to the black heart of the hydra as I scanned the room for the familiar stance of the studious Roamion sister, but she was nowhere to be seen. "Where is Dityss?"

I did not have to be looking at her to feel her irritation flicker across the room. "You do not interrupt me, child."

My chest rumbled with the beginnings of a growl to demand an answer when a fist slammed into my chest, sending me keeling over in sputtering coughs.

"Do. Not. Interrupt. Me." The queen snarled as the shadow beasts surrounding the broken archways echoed it in a sound that haunted nightmares. Ezyla's sheer skin was a beacon in the bleak room, pulling my attention to it when she repositioned herself to stare at her nails. "That spawn of mine no longer belongs to this court."

Horror sank deep into my stomach as I slowly turned to stare at Sellias, who had the beginnings of tears lining her eyes but gave a silent answer with only the movements of her mouth.

She left.

I knew it was supposed to be a comforting statement to tell me that she was not dead, but it only made that horror solidify into a heavy boulder in my stomach. I had never seen the sisters far from each other, but for Dityss to leave Sellias here after discovering something about her mother—

"She is no longer a worry nor a stain on our name and this keep." Ezyla reiterated, holding her gaze on me. "Just as you are about to become a worry no longer, though your blood will stain my beloved hall."

"Then why are you stalling, witch?" I snarled, "If you want me dead, then do it. Stop basking in the moment like you *mean* something." Shadows curled at my feet as I brought myself to stand, the magic helping alleviate some pain to give me a firm brace to hold myself with. "You may have found power. You may have found the ability to kill in ways cruel enough to make Vomuna herself wince, and you may have made an army. Yet you are a fool if you believe the crown born of blood on your head makes you memorable!" I yelled before another fist slammed into my chest, bringing with it the awful sound of snapping bones.

I did not allow myself to fall back from the blow, even as the pain in my chest became excruciating.

Ezyla stood from her chair, her shadow beasts darkening as anger fell throughout the room. Her heels clicked against the tile as she stormed with an elegant gait across the room, stopping a foot from me. "I was going to give you a chance to speak and have such a fun little game watching you realize my plans, bitch. Yet I no longer have such patience for a feral child."

Her eyes flickered towards one of the lions behind me even as I held her gaze.

"Truly a pinnacle of power, your Highness. You can't even kill me yourself." I smiled, spitting blood onto the trim of her dress as I bowed, my hand moving for the knife on my spine.

"Foolish girl. Your past lives would be so ashamed."

As I pulled the blade from its hidden sheath on my spine, dark claws moved to slash my throat as the queen lunged toward me with rage in her eyes.

I refused to fall to a demon when I could take her out with me. When I could save the people who still lived. When I could be the revenge the fallen needed—

A large formed bullet of metallic silver rushed in between us and interrupted my attack before the room erupted with roars and screams as chaos broke out in the throne room.

The shadows from the windows were lost in the battle as different forms and shapes swung around them, but I could recognize the mass of silver scales that carried a large male on his back, his mouth open in a scream drowned by the cacophony.

Rygur crashed in front of where Sellias was standing, the young princess's horrified screams joining in the chorus as she kneeled beside the metallic dragon as the sheen of his scales began to dull.

My attention snapped back to the queen, whose claws were dripping with that green acid substance used on me at the Fall Feasts, now infecting Rygur's shifted chest in deeply gouged wounds.

"RYGUR!" I bellowed, tears stinging as I dove for the queen.

Rage blinded my movements as I swung toward her, deafening every sound outside of my enemy's breaths before me. Ezyla's attention turned back to me once she recovered from the initial shock of the chaos, but it was not fast enough. My blade sliced through her cheek as flame and shadow seared down it, my screams of rage lost in the symphony.

Just as my blade came to slice through her throat, large claws dug into my shoulders, lifting me in the air and away from my target, my hands fumbling for purchase as the blade fell to the stones beside her. We began to speed away from the chaos of the scene as I spotted a gold and black dragon slightly smaller than Ren's speeding alongside us. On her back was the glowing blue of healing magic as Jaeden hovered over Rygur, who had lost far too much color.

"I was going to *kill* her, Rendros!" I screamed, tears streaming down my face as Sellias pulled ahead with Jaeden and Rygur, speeding toward the far mountain range. My breath was unsteady from hiccupping and coughing fits from the agony that tore through my system as Ren raised me from below him to carefully settle me just above his elbow, leveling the flight a bit to let me climb up and into a safer position. "Why didn't you let me kill her once and for all? *Why?"*

You were outnumbered, Wildie. She had her claws lined up for your chest just as you did her neck. Peter and Theo were ready to spear you—

"You should have let them!" I screamed, pulling on his scales as I found my way back to my spot between his shoulder blades while he continued to race away from the capital. My tears fell onto the softer flesh of his scar, my voice shaking with emotion, "At least she would have died for what she did, Ren. At least Rygur would have his revenge before he—"

We are heading for the Sinos Cordillera, where there are the best healers in all of Aistris. Jaeden can keep the illness at bay until we get there, and Sellias has always been the faster flier. His mental voice was rough with its own emotion as he turned to look at me, fear and grief mixing in the storm-filled hazel.

I shook my head as I turned to watch the city of Agraxis smolder in smoke and shadow as the first light of dawn began to break, barely choking back another sob. We were leaving so many innocent people behind, letting the vilest monsters of the planet continue to live and torment the survivors. We were *running*.

I will burn every soul that has wronged you in the universe, Willow. But I will not let you burn yourself.

10th of Vuht, 414 P.A.

Rendros' Account

Sellias, Jaeden, and Rygur had arrived several hours before we finally landed within the gates of Besmon, the only proper city within the Sinos Cordillera. Jaeden was there to greet us alongside a host of healers and servants—looking more tired than I had ever seen him—but instantly gave orders to the people around him as soon as we made footfall.

The orders were swiftly followed, and magic and topical medicinal ointments were applied to the worst of my wounds. Willow had slid off my back at some point in the commotion, not even sparing a second glance as she disappeared behind the chapel walls with Jaeden escorting her somewhere within.

The healing process with magic often felt like a gentle caress from a basking spot in the sun, but the extent of my wounds had been so damaging that the rush of power that was needed caused it to feel more like the wounds were being hastily stitched together with nails. Every part of me was struck rigid with the pain, but the healers around me continued their work efficiently to ensure the swiftness of the process was completed correctly.

Once I was healed enough to shift, Jaeden reappeared in the chapel doorway. The warm yellow eyes that usually sparked with humor and strength were dull with exhaustion, even as he put a slight smile on his face in an attempt to lighten the bleak mood of the situation.

"Has Rygur been tended to?" I asked as I stretched an arm out, earning a huff from a nearby healer who was still attempting to wrap the wounds that needed to heal on their own time past what they could do.

"He has, but it's not a good prognosis." Jae sighed, leaning against the doorframe of the chapel as his eyes traveled upward to examine the stone of the entry. "He can be healed like Lo was, but whatever the bitch used this time was stronger. Used more, too."

I ran a newly bandaged hand through my hair, trying to avoid the spiral of overthinking about my mother and her actions. She had been harsh throughout my entire life, sure, but to kill or even *attempt* to kill people I cared about...

It was far too confusing and too painful to think about.

"Any timeframe on its fix?"

"I'm afraid not. My mother and sister are using everything they have, but even as the top healers of the Crescent, it may take weeks or months to correct." His eyes lowered from their fixation on the stones to look at me again. "It's bad, Ren. They don't even know if it *can* be corrected."

The healers finally finished their wraps before they returned to their places within the chapel walls, and I took a few testing steps toward Jae. The wounds and scars still ached with the regular movement, but it was tolerable enough. "And Sellias?"

"Staying in a room here in the chapel, with full blessings for being able to lodge here." He pushed himself off the doorway to meet me at the bottom of the stairs. "Willow is staying at one of the visitor lodges within the Mirror of Stars, granted by Evan on behalf of your status."

The anger that sparked life back into his eyes was no surprise considering their history, though he was quick to shake his hand in dismissal of the feeling and thoughts that provoked it. "I will have to thank him personally in the morning for the extended kindness."

"Yeah, don't thank him yet. He doesn't know the full story of what happened in Agraxis, and his kindness to your title may be short-lived." Jae scoffed, sticking his hands in his pockets as he walked past me. "That will be tomorrow's problem. You have one more battle to make it through tonight, and Evan doesn't deserve your attention. Mom will handle him in the meantime."

I fell into a steady pace beside him, sighing as I examined the quiet tranquility of the forested home of the wolves. The flight had taken the entire day to arrive at the Besmon haven, and despite being the beginning of another night, all kinds of wolves and Fae scattered around us like it was nothing more than a busy day at the market. "I know," I whispered, watching a pair of pups run from some farther part of the chapel. "Did she say anything to you?"

The wolf Fae beside me watched as the pups wrestled in the dirt of a nearby flower patch, "She asked about Rygur, but otherwise, she kept quiet." A carer came running out of the far end of the chapel, barking orders and a line of reprimands at the pups for dirtying themselves. "She's a strong female, but I don't think she will recover from this fight as easily as we do. It's our job, and we've dealt with tragedy before, but she was hidden from the truth until that ass decided to let her go out on that fool's errand."

Another sigh escaped my lips again as I turned my attention to the sparsely scattered lodges that bordered the crescent-shaped lake the wolves called the Mirror of Stars, focusing on the one that seemed to be attempting to hide in the darkness of the night. "It's going to be another long night."

"Just give her time. Help here where you can, but this is something she will need time to digest herself. We can pick up plans when you feel comfortable enough leaving her, but for now, take care of yourself, brother. We'll talk soon." He smiled with a pat on my back before turning to the forest. He walked a few steps away before his Fae form disappeared in a flash of light, his brown wolf replacing his spot as he sprinted into the forest beyond the lake.

I continued toward the shadowed cabin, trying to steel myself for whatever awaited me.

The lodge was a work of exquisite craftsmanship, with its lower walls of river stone and the uppers made of full pine logs. Large windows looked over a portion of the lake that encased the chapel and the buildings around it, creating windows into a place that had become my favorite to visit whenever we had to travel the provinces, even if its leadership and I disagreed from time to time.

As I approached the wooden doors leading into the cabin, the familiarly intoxicating smell of sweet wildflowers assaulted my senses as the entrance opened without my intervention. Her sparkling blue and gold eyes looked over the swath of bandages and new scars that littered my skin with a combination of pain-filled emotions before she turned her back to me to walk back toward the main living space.

Moonlight poured into the cabin through the tall windows in the back of the building, lighting a room where no lights were illuminated and no candles were burning, creating long shadows that fell from each obstacle in the moon's path. Large couches lined the seating room with a carpet depicting a full moon surrounded by stars centered the space.

Alongside each wall were small tables that had differing decorations settled on each, and in the place of paintings, the wood logs themselves were burnt with images of happier times under scattered starlight.

Willow kept moving into the serene space, her hair pulled out of her ponytail, and her clothes changed to silk pajamas that perfectly enunciated her perfection. She pulled a blanket from its heap on the couch as she settled into the leather surface, not taking her eyes off the lake outside the window when she said, "I'll sleep out here. You can have the bedroom."

I closed the door before walking closer to where she sat, stopping a few feet from the couch. "Wildie, we don't have to sleep in separate rooms. We were given a cabin together by the alpha. As a mated couple that may as well just be married—"

"I'm aware of the reasoning behind our housing circumstances, Rendros." Her voice hit me like a freezing bucket of water poured over my head.

I hated it when she used my full name.

"Then why do you wish to sleep alone out here when there is a wonderful bed in the room over?" I argued gently, but her hands grabbed tighter onto her blanket as I saw the glimmer of tears lining her eyes. Any of the rising irritation that threatened to emerge was instantly dissipated at the sight.

"You healed well, yes? The Sinos Cordillera boasts its healing capabilities, and I imagine all you need is a good night's rest to help finalize it. So get some rest and wash up in the bath. I've already done so myself." Her voice was so unnaturally cold, causing something in my chest to crack at the icy tone.

"Willow, I'm sorry for what happened in the palace. If I could have done more—"

"If you had waited two seconds longer, the queen would be dead, and we'd be that much closer to taking back your throne." She snapped, "Yet fear ruled your actions, and we ran. We ran from your—*our*—people, Rendros. We saved your sister and your brothers, yes, but the innocents outside of that castle..."

I closed the distance between us, slowly kneeling beside the couch as I grabbed the hand that was gripping the blanket as tears fell down her cheeks. "If we had not moved when we did, we would be dead, and there would be no hope for our people." I urged, trying desperately to look into the eyes that were avoiding me. "I regret having to flee with nearly every fiber of my being, but I do not regret saving the future that we all want. I need you, Rygur, Jae, Sellias, and Dityss for that."

Silence was the only thing that filled the room after my words, but she did not move my hand from hers as her eyes flickered back to me. Old trails of tears stained her freckled face as I watched her look over my face, a small hand moving from the blanket as she cupped my cheek, pulling my face closer to hers until our foreheads rested together. I would trade the world and everything in it for these moments, for the caress of her hand, her skin on mine.

I moved to pull her into my arms and cradle her and her fears until she fell asleep, but her gentle whisper stopped me from sitting beside her.

"Go rest, Ren. We both need it."

My heart sank at the dismissal, my hand slowly pulling from hers as I stood, watching as the untamed female who had become my everything became a husk of the spunky mare I had first met. It reminded me of my first significant casualty event during an advance into Velhean territory a little over a decade ago, when a plan had gone so south that I lost nearly the entire squadron I had taken with me. I had not moved from my tent for days, spending all of the time I had writing my first personal messages to the dead's families and battling the nightmares of my decisions.

"I'm here, darling. If you need me." My voice was barely a whisper as I turned toward the bedroom, trying to ignore the guilt she shot across the bond like a wave of physical pain, even though I knew she wanted me to respect her request.

I was nearly through the bedroom door when I heard her quiet response.

"I'm here, and I'll be okay."

Despite the small ounce of comfort that surrounded the words and the knowledge that she was just in the other room, I did not sleep as the nightmares of the last forty-eight hours plagued my waking thoughts.

ACKNOWLEDGEMENTS

Ever since I was able to start writing and comprehending it, I have had a thousand worlds living in my imagination. From worlds containing modern mystery to ones that follow the dreams and escapes of the highest fantasies, they have plagued my thoughts, desperate to be put onto paper. Some have been in the form of personal writings or tabletop games with my friends, but most have stayed a distant dream that I occasionally write further notes for.

Untamed Pact and its world have always lived on the outskirts of my thoughts, waiting to be brought into reality one day. I have spent countless hours and days putting together its world and fantasy, pouring every inch of love I have for its wonderous forests and contrasting cities so that one day, I might finally be able to put it into a book.

Now, that dream has come to fruition, and a copy of that world is in the hands of my dearest readers.

While I have several people to thank for their part in my journey, the one I am the most thankful for is that of my husband. He has sat through my hours of writing and reading while I talked incessantly to him about different ideas or the plotlines of characters he knew nothing about yet, and he has always been the first in my corner to support me in whatever I wish to try. He has also tirelessly gone through my drafts as an additional editor, helping push my writing in a better direction and ensuring that what I'm trying to get across is appropriately understood, even after the long hours of his workdays. Without him, *Untamed Pact* and the rest of this series may have never left the sticky notes and journals that are saved all over our home.

With the lovely talent and unwavering support of my dear friend Amber Sanders, I found myself with the cover of my dreams. I would have never had a friend to constantly support and cheer me on even in my lowest moments, and without her work both as my daily chatter companion and the artist for the cover, I may have never had the confidence to publish this book. She is an invaluable friend and such a wildly talented artist, and I could not imagine a world without her and her friendship.

I must also thank all of my family from the bottom of my heart for supporting me and my dream of publishing a book like Untamed Pact. Many of them were surprised by the content it would have, and I was embarrassed about the initial pitch conversations when I told them about my desire to write an Adult Romantasy. Yet even with that initial hurdle, the support I have received from them is heart-warming, and I am forever thankful for it.

However, now I am most thankful to the readers who have made it through the first book of the series and have decided to support a new author trying to stake a place in this wild writing world. Whether you have found my book on purpose or by accident, I am thankful for your support and time in the world of *Untamed Pact*. I hope you have enjoyed reading about this silly little world of mine as much as I have enjoyed writing it, and I can't wait to see you in the next book of The Untamed Series.

Milton Keynes UK
Ingram Content Group UK Ltd.
UKHW030732210824
447167UK00016B/206/J

9 798991 300506